Al Turello is a lawyer w̶̶ with his wife and four children. Born in Trieste in 1952 he came to Australia with his parents when he was three years old. He grew up in Lithgow in New South Wales. Prior to becoming a lawyer he was a teacher of English and History.

WILD JUSTICE

AL TURELLO

ARROW

An Arrow Book
published by
Random House Australia Pty Ltd
20 Alfred Street, Milsons Point, NSW 2061

Sydney   New York   Toronto
London   Auckland   Johannesburg
and agencies throughout the world

First published in 1995

National Library of Australia
Cataloguing-in-Publication Data
Turello, Al, 1952–.
Wild justice.
ISBN 0 09 183138 5.
I. Title.
A823.3
Typeset by Midland Typesetters, Maryborough
Printed by Griffin Paperbacks, Adelaide
Production by Vantage Graphics, Sydney

For Bev, for our children, and for Elio and Alice.

My thanks to Helen Cunningham whose generous advice and assistance in getting this novel to publication was invaluable and will be forever appreciated.

PROLOGUE

Johnny Bora read the last sentence and below it the memo he'd written for himself at the end of the Pilbara file.

Satisfied, he hit the save button; then, for the first time in three hours, looked out of his twelfth-floor office window. It had grown dark without his noticing. Below, the street lights along London Circuit glowed yellow. There was hardly any traffic. Two days before Christmas and Canberra was a ghost town. A couple of cars went by, negotiating a bend in the road before pulling up at the lights on Northbourne Avenue. Pointless, he thought. No pedestrians, no other cars.

He turned back to the computer and punched a few buttons sending the Pilbara land claim file he'd been working on into the hidden file system. Nothing wrong with being cautious. He inserted a floppy, saved the files and ejected the disk.

His phone rang. It was his wife Ruth.

'I'm coming now,' he told her, cradling the phone in his neck as he slipped on his coat and pocketed the floppy.

1

She sounded annoyed. Too bad. He was accustomed to it these days.

'You'd better come soon, Johnny. Nick and Louisa have been very patient. You did say eight thirty you know. You are now an hour late.'

He heard Nick Milano say something in the background. Ruth relayed the comment.

'Nick said to ask you if you're writing a legal opinion or *War and Peace*.'

From Ruth, it sounded sarcastic. Johnny laughed. He knew his friend would have said it with easy familiarity. A mild reproach to him for Ruth's benefit. Not Johnny's.

'You just tell Nick not to start on the red until I get there.'

He hung up, switched off the computer, packed his briefcase and headed for the light switch.

He remembered old man Monyu. He'd be with family in Port Hedland now. One more call. Monyu's baritone was on the other end in seconds.

'I just wanted you to know that I think you've got a good case, old fella.'

Monyu didn't answer for a while. Then he asked, 'You talkin' as a lawyer or as a blackfella, Johnny?'

'I'm talking as a lawyer who happens to be a blackfella, Monyu. A bloody good lawyer and a bloody good blackfella.'

'And the other?' asked Monyu.

'The other's nearly there Monyu. We need a bit of patience, but we'll get there. I want it packaged so tight that it can't be got at before we get to a jury. Okay?'

'That's good Johnny Bora,' said Monyu.

Johnny put down the phone. He loved the sound of the old man's voice. It was timeless and reassuring. It resonated somewhere deep inside him, near his heart or

2

his soul, or wherever it was that his Aboriginality had its source.

It was his last good feeling before he turned and felt the hammering blow explode between his eyes. As he dropped to the carpet his final living sensation was a cracking pain to his right temple. He did not register the dozen or so blows that fragmented his skull and left the hair on his black head caked in blood.

*T*hrough the plane window McAngel peered out at
the encrustation of lights below him. He could see
where the lights mapped out a glittering coastal
contour and figured it was Sydney Harbour.

Momentarily he felt the flickering touch of some regret,
sadness, nostalgia. Something too evanescent to label.
Years ago he may have said it was homesickness. After
all, it was Christmas Eve and he was a long way from
home.

Home? Where exactly was home these days?

He pulled his eyes away from the abyss below as the
fair-haired woman sitting next to him stood to reach for
her hand luggage. She smiled at him when she sat down
again and McAngel's heart pumped just a little harder.
He wished it was just because of her. But he knew it
wasn't. Soon they'd be landing.

Earlier, during the long flight, he'd been sitting across
the aisle from her. Several times they had caught each
other's eye. She'd appeared to show some interest and he
reciprocated. You got to know looks after a while.
Sometimes, if it was an older and more wearied woman,

4

who had given up on expecting too much from men, a glance could promise sex on short acquaintance. This woman looked like she was in her late twenties. She was inquisitive. She was someone who was peering into a boxful of possibilities with the lid in one hand and the other hand behind her back. From his perspective it was tantalising. But it was clear the lid could drop at any time.

When the old guy sitting next to her had gone to the bathroom McAngel had made his way to the seat and started a conversation. At first she was a little embarrassed and for a while she did a lot of looking away as he spoke. But eventually she told him her name was Maggie Spires and she appeared to relax and began to smile easily. He explained to her that he was a writer doing a few pieces on Australia for an American travel magazine and eventually, when it was clear she liked him, he assured her he was single and had no transmittable diseases. He was relieved when she laughed.

In the meantime, the old guy, a polite Texan, returned from the bathroom and gladly agreed to swap seats with McAngel. As he left he whispered to McAngel that at his age access to bathrooms was more important than access to young women.

McAngel got around to asking her about herself and she told him she'd been to Washington on a short holiday. She had some family there, at the Australian Embassy. She'd intended to stay for Christmas. It hadn't worked out. She didn't elaborate and McAngel didn't press it.

Plans for Christmas Eve? No. Like him, no plans. Not now. She'd faltered only a little when he suggested they celebrate together.

It was still more than an hour to midnight when they found themselves in a cab heading for McAngel's hotel in the city. Maggie pointed out the things that he would see if it was daylight. Periodically they kissed long and hard

5

and caressed each other's tired bodies. Decorously they had agreed they would go their separate ways once in the city, McAngel to his hotel and Maggie to her friend's unit in Darlinghurst, and that they would meet again later. The plan was forgotten. McAngel checked into the Boulevard with Maggie. Soon afterwards, as Maggie's smooth thighs claimed his hips, McAngel heard from somewhere the sound of a familiar Christmas carol and momentarily longed for home.

Nick Milano pulled his car in beside Johnny's BMW in the loading zone outside the door of the AMP Building. There were no other cars about. He unfolded himself out of the seat and into the night air, which was soft and just starting to cool after a hot day. Nick breathed it in, stretched a little, easing away the tugging back pain that set in during the short drive to town. He would have to start exercising again, he told himself. Maybe some weight-lifting. Light stuff. Vince, his doctor, had been pushing him to do it.

'Man your bloody size can't give up exercise altogether and not expect back pain,' Vince had told him. 'Give up competitive weight-lifting when you're twenty-five, then lift nothing heavier than a pencil and the *Crimes Act* for the next fifteen years, and you're going to get back pain. Stands to reason.'

Yeah, he'd start the weights again. After Christmas. While the courts were quiet.

He looked up at the row of windows on the top floor of the building. Only one showed a light. Johnny's chambers. He looked at his watch. Ten thirty.

Nick hoped his relief hadn't been too obvious when his wife suggested he go and see what Johnny was doing. It had become tense over at his house. In between the unanswered phone calls to Johnny's chambers, he and

Louisa had tried to reassure Ruth that her embarrassment was unnecessary. They were all friends. It wasn't a problem that Johnny was late. After all, Johnny was Johnny.

But Ruth had her own agenda. One more grievance to add to an ever-growing pile. Bitter and tearful, she'd sat at the kitchen table, pulling at a box of tissues, airing other resentments. Johnny's non-appearances at dinner parties at her parents' home in Forrest. His rudeness to her old Ascham school friends. The way he was hardly ever at home these days.

Nick let himself in by inserting his mill key in the slot and ducking through the hair trigger sliding door. He'd figured that Johnny would still be at the office and not at a bar in Civic having a quick drink with some old acquaintance—Ruth's caustic speculation. Nick knew how sometimes, when you were working, an hour could shoot by like it was only five minutes. Still, there were the phone calls. Why hadn't Johnny answered?

He pressed the call button for the elevator. In the eerie emptiness of the big building, he was able to dwell on every nuance of protest made by the groaning machinery as the elevator descended to the ground floor.

It finally stopped with a clunk and he waited patiently for the doors to open. Inside, out of habit, he was about to press the button for the seventh floor, his own floor, the Offices of the Director of Public Prosecutions. He stopped himself and gave the twelfth-floor button a stab. There was a closing of doors and then the slow ascent, accompanied again by the metallic laments and groans from within the hollow of the elevator shaft.

On the twelfth, it was dark, except for a slab of light falling into the corridor from Johnny's room. Nick called out as he approached the room. There was no answer. Something about the stillness made him stop and listen

7

uneasily. Nothing. He called again, nervously, as he resumed his approach to the room. Again no answer.

When he reached the open door, he saw Johnny straightaway. Lying on the floor by his filing cabinet. His head appeared to be resting in a dark patch on the carpet. For a time Nick stood there, dumb, immobilised, not wanting to know what his senses were telling him. Then he was on one knee, cradling the battered head of his friend in both hands, unaware of what exactly it was that he was yelling into the darkness of the empty building.

A memorial service for Johnny was held at the
Aboriginal Tent Embassy. It had been a hot, dry
day. Now the lightest of breezes arrived and
appeared to set wavering the heat haze hanging in the
distance over the War Memorial across the lake. Men in
dark suits ran their fingers under hot collars. Other men,
black, tieless, suitless, in dusty T-shirts and jeans wiped
tears from their eyes. Several black women sobbed loudly.
Old man Monyu, great white bush of hair, skin black as
oil and kangaroo-hide tough, appeared in front of the fire
burning on the lawns of the tent embassy. He threw red
dirt from the Pilbara onto the fire, a tribute from his
people. He spoke of Johnny's achievements as an activist,
and leader and lawyer for Aborigines. Behind him on the
other side of the road, the old Parliament House, large,
white and empty, formed an incongruous backdrop for
each of the speakers who followed. After, there were the
painted men, who transformed into animals and ghosts as
they moved to the pulse of the didgeridoo and to song
which knew no time.

Nick Milano stood with Louisa and Ruth, amongst a

collection of lawyers. Some were Nick's fellow prosecutors, the rest solicitors and barristers from around town who had known Johnny or who were there in a formal show of comradeship.

As the crowd began to disperse from the tent embassy, Nick spotted Stratton and Lardner who still managed to look like cops. Fair enough. They weren't there to mourn. They were working. Lardner, the younger of the two, tall, brushed back hairdo, light grey double-breaster, looking slick and fit, stood impassively chewing gum. Stratton, much shorter, broad in the shoulders, paunch, flecks of grey in the hair, noticed Nick and moved towards him.

'Funny world Milano,' he said. 'Last time I was here I was arresting abos for trespassing in Parliament House. Your mate Johnny was one of them.'

Nick was glad his wife had taken Ruth away. Stratton was an insensitive bastard. He disliked Nick and made it obvious. Nick had declined to proceed on one of Stratton's briefs, an alleged armed robbery by Danny Lametta, a well-known local crim. Lametta had probably committed the robbery, Nick conceded that. But Stratton didn't bother to get a warrant when he searched Lametta's house for the stolen gear. Then there was the videotaped confession. Lametta had looked like an injured, frightened rabbit as he answered Stratton's questions for the record of interview. Explaining away that demeanour was not going to be easy for a prosecutor trying to prove that the confession was obtained without threat or inducement. So Nick dropped it. No malice, no personal agenda. A professional and objective decision. Stratton hadn't agreed. He said Nick was fucking spineless. That his heart wasn't in it because Lametta, like Nick, was a wog. Their subsequent meetings had been cold.

'Got anywhere on this?' Nick asked of Stratton.

10

He didn't expect to be told much. Stratton and Lardner had a reputation for getting the job done. They liked to say that they got it done quicker and better if no-one else knew what they were doing.

'We're still moving around it,' Stratton replied. He cocked his head and regarded Nick with a deliberately insincere show of sudden interest.

'I don't suppose Johnny told you what clients he was seeing did he? I mean, Johnny's clients used to be fairly serious crims at times.'

A genuine question or another barb to be deflected? Nick gave Stratton the benefit of the doubt. He'd try to be helpful.

'Johnny hasn't done any criminal work in ages. Anyway, all Johnny's clients liked him as far as I know.'

But Stratton couldn't help himself.

'Well so you say. But you know these people. A bit of piss in them and ...'

Nick Milano stiffened. It was always the same with this bastard.

'None of Johnny's clients would have killed him, Stratton. You might just have to look a bit wider than the Aboriginal Tent Embassy this time.'

A mistake. He'd displayed his resentment. Stratton looked pleased with himself. Nick thought how he'd love to slam him there and then. Bang. Right in the face. Stratton picked up the sentiment, dropped his smile, and without words momentarily dared him to try it. A stand-off long enough for them to realise where they were. Stratton relaxed into cynicism again, smiling as he said, 'Anyway as soon as we get this arsehole we'll let you know, Milano. Maybe you'll even let us prosecute him.'

With that he turned and moved off into the crowd with Lardner following him.

Nick looked around for his family. Louisa had her arm

11

about Ruth. Nick's thirteen-year-old daughter, Emily, nursed Johnny Bora's baby in her arms. She'd brought with her the prayer book she took to Mass on Sundays and while she held the baby the book dropped from her hands. As it hit the ground a small picture used as a bookmark fluttered out. When Nick picked it up for her he noticed the picture was of an angel, with a sword in its hand.

'You sound like a septic.'

'Pardon me?'

McAngel had been holding the Colt revolver with interest, feeling its weight, spinning the chamber. He had found the location easily—a short walk from his hotel. Bluey's Gun Shop, William Street. Dark inside, smelling of oiled wood and metal and leather. A long glass counter with hand guns on display, some hunting knives, rounds of ammunition. Rows of rifles on two walls, a small rack of semi-automatics on another.

McAngel regarded the nuggety red-haired man who appeared suddenly behind the counter with the distaste of someone unsure of whether or not he was being insulted.

'You're a septic,' the man repeated. 'You know? Septic tank for Yank. I heard you talkin' to yerself, about the gun.'

'Oh I see.'

The penny dropped for McAngel. He relaxed and looked at the man anew. It was a time for a quick assessment and a quick decision. If he got it wrong it could rebound on him badly later.

'Well mate, can I help you or you just happy to look around for a while?'

The enquiry was perfunctory. McAngel's expression of disapproval hadn't been lost on the man and he was

12

indicating that he couldn't care less if this particular Yank misunderstood him.

McAngel decided he was worth trusting.

'You're Bluey I take it?'

'That's right pal. My name over the door and all. You got anything particular in mind?'

Bluey's turn to give way a little. McAngel thrust onwards.

'Byron Williams. US 173rd Airborne Division? Bien Hoa, 1965?'

Bluey's face lightened up. Then he gave a short laugh.

'Well, I tell you what mate, no way you're Byron Williams. Unless you've been soaking in bleach for the last twenty years.'

He thrust out his hand. There was some fine work in the tattooed dragon on Bluey's thick forearm.

'Why didn't you tell me you knew Byron straight up, you silly bastard? I thought you was one of these Yank tourists who was gonna tell me all about the guns you can get back home. Here, come around the back. We can have a beer.'

McAngel followed him to a room containing a small table, a refrigerator, a sink, a small cupboard, a heavy safe in the corner and little else. Bluey pulled a couple of beer cans from the fridge and handed one to McAngel.

'Here. Get that into yer. How is that great big black bastard anyway? I suppose he told yer he saved me bloody life, did he?'

In fact, Byron had, but Bluey was going to tell the story anyway.

'I was with the First Battalion. At that stage we were still operating with you Yanks. Before Nui Dat. Before we realised the brains trust behind your mob didn't seem too fussed by high casualty rates.'

He said this reproachfully, like it had been McAngel

13

who'd personally handed out the commissions.

'Anyway, I'm in the jungle. Joint patrol with the Yanks. Hush-hush stuff. A branch pulled the pin on this grenade I had on me belt. I didn't hear it. Well Byron, he was about five yards away from me and saw this. He got to me, pulled the grenade out of me belt and chucked it just in time. *Boom!* You know there were others there that saw it as well. Aussie blokes. They just dived for the scrub. Saved their own skins. Anyway, that's why me and him's close now. That's when we got to know each other real well.'

Bluey sipped on his can and smiled as he warmed to his memories.

'You know that man had the biggest donger on him I've ever seen. He used to step out of the field shower naked as the day he was born and you'd swear he had a fuckin' python between his legs. Jesus Christ I laughed when I first saw that man. Couldn't believe it. I started yellin' to the other Aussie fellers, *Hey come and get a load of this bloke*, and old Byron he did the cruet. He fuckin' come at me like a demented rhino, big white eyes—and those hands! The guy could pick up watermelons in one hand, no joke. He had to chase me over a parked jeep and he slipped onto the gear handle and bruised his arse so badly he couldn't walk properly for a week. Jeez I was lucky he didn't get me that day. This was before he saved my life like. Funny old world isn't it. He was the only one willing to put his own safety on the line to help me. But you know what? I would've done the same thing for him. I know I would've.'

Bluey paused. It was a question he'd reflected on in the past. He now gave it some more thought before going on, with conviction.

'Yep. I would've. Maybe that's why we got on well. God knows, we had bugger all else in common.'

14

After a further pause, and with the air of a man greatly satisfied with the recollection, he asked McAngel, 'So how is he? You know he hasn't written for twelve months and it's his turn too. Generally we get off at least one letter each a year.'

McAngel reached into his coat pocket and handed him a thickly packed envelope. Bluey opened it and pulled out a long letter and a half-dozen photographs, mainly of young kids and a couple of the whole family. He held the letter at arm's length for a second or two, gave up and pulled on a pair of specs.

'Gettin' on a bit,' he said to McAngel gruffly and began reading.

'Well I'll be buggered,' he said, when he finished reading. 'He's got another nipper since the last letter. That makes five now. Fancy that. Well he's putting that big donger of his to good use anyway.'

He looked back up at McAngel.

'Well that's great. He's got a lovely family and he's doin' well. I'm really pleased for him. I should have looked to have a family meself, you know, instead of stuffin' around all these years, drinkin' piss and chasin' bloody tarts. A letter like that makes a bloke think. Wanna another beer?'

He got another couple of cans out before McAngel could reply. He picked up the letter again and read out aloud.

'Now he says here at the end of the letter—*Bluey, the man who gave you this letter is a good man and a close friend of mine. He's visiting your country for only a short time. He needs a gun. He needs to be able to get it without any questions asked and he needs to be able to trust someone. Believe me, it's for a good reason and I want you to help him if you can.*'

Bluey looked at McAngel shrewdly.

15

'No questions asked eh. You're not going to assassinate the prime minister are yer?'

McAngel shook his head.

'Pity,' sniffed Bluey.

He got up and went to the safe, fiddled with the combination, opened it and extracted a handgun. He threw it over to McAngel.

'Taurus fifteen-shot 9 mm semi-automatic. Brazilian,' he said. 'It'll do the job.'

McAngel examined it closely.

'Serial number's been filed down,' said Bluey. 'Untraceable.'

'Where'd you get it?' McAngel asked casually, feeling the gun's weight, feeling for the right answer from Bluey.

The right answer came. Delivered gruffly.

'I just said it was untraceable didn't I? No questions asked remember? Works both ways. I trust you, you trust me.'

McAngel smiled.

'Okay Bluey, okay,' he replied.

3

Nick Milano looked at his watch and saw it was five o'clock. Outside his office window it had begun to drizzle. He had a lecture in Evidence to deliver at six that evening, at the university. Another academic year, another new class. Usually he would feel some sense of enthusiasm at the prospect but today he felt dejected. It was now some two months since Johnny's murder and there'd been no progress on finding the killer. The leads on the nature of the murder weapon were ambiguous. Something heavy and blunt, possibly made of wood. Other than that, nothing. He called Stratton earlier, prepared to be conciliatory in the interests of getting at least some news on the investigation. But Stratton had resented it and interpreted Nick's call as pressure. He'd told Nick to let him get on with it.

Nick missed Johnny. Missed his laughter, his optimism, the occasions when they drank together after work. He had come to know the story of Johnny's life almost as well as he knew his own, extracting it from him piece by piece as Johnny grew to trust him. For Nick, Johnny's story was both inspiration in times of pessimism and a continual source of fascination. A mete against which he measured the circumstances of his own life and that of others.

He packed his things. There was more he could do at the office but he preferred to go. Maybe he could kill some time listening to music in the car until six o'clock. Outside he made his way through the drizzle to the carpark and his Falcon wagon. As he inserted the keys he noticed Louisa's cardigan, the one he'd bought her for her birthday, draped over the front seat. The area behind the back seat was a repository for tennis rackets, belly boards and beach towels. He got into the car. On the floor was the sand from Tathra Beach, picked up during the family holiday they'd taken before Christmas. These were things familiar and reassuring. Tangible reminders of love and family and life beyond work. A profound sadness embraced him, weighed him down so that he could barely move. Johnny Bora would never again feel warm reassurance from things familiar. He was dead. Nick leaned back in the bucket seat and thought about his friend.

Johnny Bora did most of his early growing up in a house in Garden Street in South Strathfield where he was known as Johnny Middleton, the Aboriginal son of Joe and Donna Middleton. Joe, a wiry, Ardath-smoking, fitter and turner at a clothing factory on Parramatta Road, liked to have a beer after work. The day his wife Donna, who was a lot younger than him, came up with the suggestion that they adopt the little kiddy, he'd reluctantly agreed, but only after she'd cried when he first said no. Donna was a small framed, big eyed, sensitive woman who worried a lot about Johnny and about what Father O'Mahony would say if the parish church wasn't got ready properly for the three Sunday services.

When Johnny was a teenager he wanted to find out

where he'd come from. They didn't know much more than what they'd already told him, Joe and Donna had said. That he was a State ward and that they'd got him from a home. When he'd pushed them for more, Donna would reply in a manner she thought was reassuring. She would say that he had no mother but Donna Middleton, no father but Joe Middleton. That for them he was born the day they brought him home to Garden Street where Father O'Mahony was waiting to baptise him into the Catholic Church. *Why do you need to know more?* they'd asked him. *You're cared for and you're loved Johnny*, they told him. Their home was his home. *Leave well enough alone Johnny*, Joe had advised.

But Johnny couldn't. School, which had always been difficult for him, now became impossible. He had spent so much of his young life biting, scratching, punching, kicking with other school kids, with nuns, brothers, lay teachers, welfare workers and even his own step-father.

'There came a time when I knew I just had to run,' Johnny had told Nick. 'I couldn't say why at the time. It wasn't that I didn't love Donna, and old Joe was okay as well. I want you to understand; it wouldn't be fair to them if I didn't explain that. But South Strathfield was suffocating me. I was black, my parents were white, I was black, my school friends were white, I was black, my teachers were white, I was black and the rest of the bloody world was white.'

And he did run. First to Redfern where some brothers helped him out with food and accommodation and a relaxed indifference to where he'd come from. He hitched rides to the north coast where for a couple of years he bummed around in Byron Bay, Ballina and Lismore. It wasn't an unhappy life. He slept on beaches and river banks, stole food, took the occasional car for a joy ride with other kids, had the odd street fight, drank coarse flagon wine, smoked grass grown on the banks of the Richmond River, learned how to make love to girls, and played Rugby League.

And Rugby League he was very good at. Johnny hadn't needed to tell Nick too much about that side of his life. Nick remembered seeing Johnny long before they'd met, when Johnny had made it as a professional in Sydney, out on the wing for Eastern Suburbs. He was the nineteeen-year-old Aboriginal kid from the bush. Along with thousands of others at the big games, Nick had seen Johnny step wraith-like through defences and accelerate away down the touchline. All speed and balance and grace. There was something child-like and gleeful about the way he took off that reminded Nick of a line from a Blake poem: *Piping down the Valleys Wild.* That was all he remembered of the poem. Even now as he recalled the line it stirred in him a nostalgic longing for something lost from his own youth.

Easts had picked Johnny up from a Lismore team where he'd been for a year or so as an eighteen-year-old. They offered him a contract. In return for playing he could work as a barman at their Leagues Club and have free accommodation, which meant sharing a flat in Bondi Junction with two older Aboriginal footballers already recruited by Easts from the bush. One of these was East's front-rower, Ernie Barnes, who Nick remembered as an amiable giant capable of casually throwing wondrous game-winning passes while carting along on his back two or three defenders. The other was Larry Simmons, an experienced and clever half-back who seemed to have been at Easts forever.

Johnny enjoyed being a footballer. Sports journalists wanted to interview him, fans wanted his autograph, girls, black and white, wanted to sleep with him.

'You don't have much judgment at nineteen,' he'd gone

on. 'I still thought it was a great life. That somehow I'd been privileged because I didn't have to live like a lot of other black people did. And of course it was true, I didn't have to live in a tin humpy somewhere. I had a bit of money and a good social life, and a lot of self-respect. And I actually felt *grateful* for all this. As if I'd won a lottery or something. I think I felt that because of my football ability white people looked on me as some sort of equal. Of course, the crippling of Ernie Barnes changed all that.'

They'd been friends for ... twelve, thirteen years? Johnny always passionate about one Aboriginal cause or another. Talking his head off, joking, provoking, cajoling one minute, fiery and aggressive the next. Nick was more subdued, reflective, phlegmatic almost. Generally he was happy to be along for the ride. Nick had occasionally wondered at Johnny's energy, envied it, drew from it.

Nick's thoughts turned to the lecture ahead of him. The first lecture of his course. He wondered about the class he would see in front of him. The usual collection probably, most looking as if they'd been especially bred by ambitious parents for the profession. Expensive clothes, expensive haircuts, the self-complacency of the pampered and pushed. Many, he knew, would be beckoned by the large city firms. They'd go there, their sights set on the big bucks. And they'd get them. They were born to it, a lot of them. It was an expectation satisfied by devotion to their parents' work ethic or their parents' contacts or both.

There'd be the sprinkling of older students. Mature, married, had kids, doing law degrees to get on in already established jobs. Mostly headed back to the public service and a life of vocational misery induced by petty jealousies and resentments with every missed office promotion.

He tried to imagine someone like Johnny in one of his classes. He couldn't. Where did Johnny fit? Or himself for that matter?

Nick's train of thought was momentarily arrested by a vivid mental picture of his father Ernesto, at the kitchen table, his sleeves rolled up, a copy of the *Daily Telegraph* in front of him, his lips moving as he resolutely tried to make sense of a language that was never to become his own. In Venice, Ernesto had been a stone mason and Nick remembered how the newspaper had looked so flimsy in his father's thick fingers which themselves looked as if they'd been fashioned from stone. Later in life, Ernesto had been baffled by the fact that his growing son was good at his studies and had actually won scholarships to selective state schools and eventually to the university. He'd shake his head, half with pride and half with regret that Nick had chosen to complicate his life by wanting to be something other than a good tradesman. Nick's mother Concetta didn't care what he was good at. She cared about his size. He was too thin. Even when he was a seventeen-stone university student grunting skyward bar-bending loads in intervarsity weight-lifting competitions, his mother thought he was thin.

Nick reflected on how he once wanted to leave the DDP and go to the private bar. He never got there. Never got past that barrier where the conditions of further progress were contacts and pedigree. He had neither, and he wasn't the type to overcome the disadvantage with gregariousness or deviousness or contrived visibility.

But then there was Johnny. All Johnny had shown at the barrier had been his black middle finger as he walked through. And it had worked. Nick smiled. Where had it come from, that audaciousness?

He remembered how Johnny had always resented any references to himself as an *Aboriginal lawyer*.

'There's no such creature, Nick,' he'd said, over a beer one afternoon. 'I can only be one or the other. I'm a lawyer only when I'm working. I can't be an Aborigine at the same time, it doesn't work. Each day my turning into a lawyer is an act of cynicism. A brazen exploitation of the system. Your system. The white European system. At bottom I feel nothing but contempt for it. White man's laws, white man's logic. With me there's my Aboriginal self and there's my lawyer self. The lawyer part's just a job Nick. The Aborigine part is me. I'm glad I don't have to be a fucking lawyer all the time.'

Johnny had laughed, remembering something that he'd been told as a student. He repeated it for Nick.

'The law sharpens the mind by narrowing it.'

It genuinely amused him.

'White man's law elevates a narrow mind into a virtue,' he said shaking his head. 'You have to be a lawyer to sell such an idea in the first place, eh Nick?'

Nick had asked Johnny why he'd become a lawyer and Johnny, after getting another couple of beers, had begun to tell him, his joviality gradually retreating as he got into the story of the crippling of Ernie Barnes.

Mid-August. Easts had won a big game at the Sydney Cricket Ground. The team had celebrated at the Leagues Club. Ernie Barnes had been named man of the match. Some money went with the award and Ernie had put it over the counter at the club for team drinks.

The big man was in an ebullient mood. On his way back to the table, nursing full schooner glasses in his broad hands, he'd had to tread carefully through the back slapping from the fans. Old girlfriends made a point of waving to him. At the table he was the centre of attention,

sitting with his friends and tolerating Larry Simmons'
stream of good natured ribbing about his numerous love
affairs, his horse racing tips, and his regrettable taste in
clothes. It had been a big night for Ernie. He was a
football star.

Not long after midnight, Larry and Johnny managed to
get Ernie away from the club. He was pretty drunk. They
were light headed and happy. They stopped in for a coffee
at Rinaldi's. The restaurant was just about empty except
for a dozen or so young men and women at a large table.
They had clearly finished eating and there were plenty of
empty bottles on the table. There was lots of laughter.
Johnny assumed they were pissed and having a good time.
He didn't take much notice of the group at first but then
he tuned in to what one of the men was saying.

'I thought we were in the middle of fucking Bondi
Junction not fucking Redfern.'

He heard one of the women shush the voice. Giggles
followed.

The same male voice said, 'Never mind going to fucking
Ayers Rock for your holidays, just come to Bondi
Junction.'

A pause, whispering, and then distinctly, 'Where's your
didgeridoo, Blue?'

The group erupted into laughter. Johnny saw in Larry's
face a mirror image of his own disappointment and
humiliation. You tried to stop it but it insinuated itself
into your very being when this sort of shit went on.

Again: 'Jeez it's suddenly got dark in here.' More
laughter.

By this time Ernie had turned around to look at the
group.

'What are they fuckin' on about,' he grumbled.

Larry had patted him on the forearm.

'Don't worry about them. They're fuckin' kids.

Nineteen, tops. C'mon, drink up and let's go home.'

Then the group started to rise and move out, some still suppressing giggles as they walked past Johnny and his friends. As the last couple moved past, Ernie happened to lean back on his chair and bump them. It was unintentional. The bloke was tall, well-built. He had short blond hair, and was wearing a white tracksuit top. He had his arm about his girlfriend's waist. She was brunette, attractive and wore a long white cheesecloth dress and very large silver earrings. Johnny had noted as they approached that they were both uncertain on their feet. The bump from Ernie had made them stumble.

The blond bloke, when he recovered his balance, was flushed with anger and pushed Ernie's shoulder. Ernie looked up at him indifferently.

'Why don't you watch what you're doing, you fat black prick.'

He stood glaring at Ernie.

Ernie had stood up slowly. The blond man was tall but suddenly seemed very slight next to Ernie's bulk. Johnny recognised the type. He was a hothead. He was full of booze, full of himself and he had a girlfriend to impress. Now he was squaring off at Ernie, playground style. Johnny remembered looking at Larry who looked back at him and shook his head wearily. The young bloke threw a punch. Had it landed Ernie may not have even noticed. Instead Ernie caught his arm, quickly wrapped it around the blond man's back as he pointed him toward the door and released it as he gave him a final push out onto the street. Then he stepped aside to politely usher the bloke's girlfriend out to the footpath where the rest of the group stood watching. A couple of the other men restrained the young bloke as he got up and made as if to return to the restaurant. Johnny remembered the guy's anger as they manoeuvered him off. It was a mix of the resentment of a

25

spoilt child and the indignant rage of someone unaccustomed to being treated off-handedly.

Ernie returned to his seat nonchalantly.

'What was all that shit about Ayers Rock?' he had asked Larry.

'Don't worry about it Ernie,' Larry had replied.

Rinaldi and his wife had seen them to the door. Relieved. Outside, the streets were almost empty. The theatre crowds and club crowds had long gone. It was winter and Johnny had described to Nick how, as they walked home, chilly gusts of wind scattered the newspapers in the gutters and sent castaway paper cups tumbling past. A few cabs and other cars droned past them as they crossed Bondi Road. While they were walking Johnny noticed that a grey Mercedes which glided past was being driven by the blond guy from the restaurant. He told the others. They both shrugged. The girl was still with him. He had recognised the white dress and the earrings. He had also been quietly intrigued by the coincidence of the number plate—ERN 111. Larry had never learned to read so Johnny had to explain the joke to him. Larry had laughed but the irony was lost on Ernie who had apparently already forgotten the blond-haired bloke and wanted only to find his bed.

In Mayo Street and nearly home, Johnny and Larry crossed the street. Ernie stopped for a piss in some bushes. They turned and waited for him to cross. It was then that they heard the quickly accelerating vehicle. Frozen in Johnny's memory had been the sight of Ernie leaning over the bonnet on the passenger side of a grey Mercedes with its headlights off, as it collected him waist high.

Ambulance, police, statements, casualty ward, doctors, operating theatre waiting rooms, club officials—all part of the chaos which followed that night. Then Ernie in a coma for three days and when he awoke the news that both his knees had been smashed. No more football for Ernie. He'd be lucky if he could walk again.

At the hospital Johnny and Larry had told the police about the fight at the restaurant and the number plate of the car that hit Ernie. The cops went off and traced the Mercedes the same night, finding it parked at the owner's address in Watsons Bay with damage to the passenger side headlights. They found the blond-haired man in bed, and arrested him.

The blond bloke had called his father from the lock-up and fifteen minutes later the father turned up with a solicitor. *Some solicitor!* Johnny had said. He found out the solicitor was Bernard Lane, the senior partner in Ermington, Lane and Gordon. Nick had raised his eyebrows. It was a big, big firm. Senior partners of such firms don't often go out in the middle of the night to visit the cells at Waverley. Lane had advised the kid to say nothing. The cops refused police bail and locked the kid up overnight. The next day Lane arrived at court with Gordon Leeson QC. The magistrate gave the kid bail.

'The heavyweight legal show was all explained when it turned out the kid was Scott Urquhart, the son of Sir Samuel Urquhart,' Johnny explained.

Everyone knew of Sir Samuel Urquhart. Big miner, fingers in corporate pies everywhere, bastion of the commercial world. *Time* magazine had called him an antipodean Croesus.

'Scott Urquhart was eventually committed for trial,' Johnny had said. 'He had to be. Even the most sycophantic magistrate couldn't ignore the prima facie evidence. But the trial ... '

Johnny had stopped. He seemed repelled, as if recollecting something so unpalatable and unhealthy that he could hardly bear to think about it. It seemed to

27

require a conscious effort for him to shake it off before he resumed.

'Normally you'd expect a topnotch prosecutor to be appointed for a trial like this. Right? You know the game. High profile defendant, serious charge, QC on the other side. You'd expect a QC to appear, wouldn't you?'

Nick agreed. The prosecution will usually get a silk if there's one on the other side.

'Instead the DPP allocated the case to Murray Ferguson. Old Murray had been at the DPP for about twenty years and I understand he was never much good. Yet he was appointed to run a trial against Leeson, one of the top half a dozen silks in the country.'

'Unusual,' Nick had said.

'Years later I managed to get hold of a transcript of the case and analyse what had happened. Ferguson gets up and addresses the jury with a bland account of the prosecution's case. Mind you, this is a jury which has been vetted by Leeson's challenges and is mainly composed of these fine, upstanding, middle class types who are going to be far more frightened of the witnesses for the prosecution than the accused. Anyway, then Ferguson takes us through our evidence in chief in a routine way. It was a bit scratchy but what needed to come out did come out. Leeson's cross-examination, however, is what is interesting. His tactics? Not very subtle but effective. Attack me and Larry and Ernie or at least our credibility as witnesses. He asked each of us about the strength of our relationship, tied it up to the fact that we were Kooris, that we lived in the same house, that we were footballers, that Rugby League is basically a game played by professional thugs, that we played in the same team, that we were drinking that night. Then he puts to each of us that we were going to back each other up no matter what. That in fact we hadn't seen a Mercedes at all, other than one parked near the restaurant which we knew belonged to Urquhart. That we'd concocted the story after a totally different car hit Ernie ... '

Johnny stopped briefly as if still exasperated.

'I mean the suggestions he was making were forensically ridiculous. We'd reported the whole thing within half an hour of it happening. But it didn't matter. His line was that we made up a story either because we wanted to get back at Urquhart or because we wanted to *believe* that it was him.'

Nick saw the point.

'Ferguson could have jumped in with a re-examination to show that your story had been consistent all the way through and that you didn't have time to concoct your early statements to police.'

'Exactly,' said Johnny. 'He could have used our prior consistent statements. The bastard didn't even re-examine. Then Leeson pulls out some criminal records relating to Ernie and Larry. Minor charges they'd been convicted of years ago. Offensive behaviour. Common assaults. That level of stuff. Ferguson, of course, should have been on his feet objecting to this. How was it relevant even to credit? He didn't object once. And the judge blithely lets it all in as well.'

'Pretty poor stuff,' Nick had agreed.

'So the end product of what should have been very strong prosecution evidence is an impression of three drunken abos making up stories to screw a poor, innocent white guy. Never mind that you have a vehicle with the reported number plate and a damaged front end sitting outside the house of an identified suspect.'

Johnny had stopped, again drawn by memory back into that courtroom. This time the pause was to allow a wave of anger to recede. That much had been apparent from Johnny's face. It was strange. Even during the course of his biggest and most demanding cases Johnny had always displayed a jauntiness and optimism which seemed at odds with the burden of responsibility most barristers carried with them into the courtroom. It was the same with private problems. Johnny had the capacity to dilute them with large doses of laughter or of frantic activity. Yet the Urquhart trial still got to him. When he resumed it was with the resentful air of a man resigned to telling a story with an irrevocably bad ending.

'It was time for the defence evidence. Leeson puts the girlfriend in the box. She says that she and Urquhart were together at all times after leaving the restaurant and that in fact they went parking for an hour or so. So Urquhart has his alibi. The prosecution had notice of the alibi but Ferguson didn't request the police to check it out. Why not? It is standard practice. They knew I'd seen she wasn't in the car with Urquhart when he hit Ernie. It may well have been possible to find someone who saw Urquhart drop her off. In any event, next to no cross-examination of her evidence from Ferguson. Then Sir Samuel Urquhart gives evidence. A lying old bastard. The boy didn't damage the car, he said. He did! The day before he had run into a tree in his drive. The damage was done before Scott Urquhart went to the restaurant that night. Corroborated completely by another kid from the restaurant who got in the box and said that he noticed the car was damaged when Scott Urquhart arrived at the restaurant. Mind you, no cross-examination by Ferguson on why the first anyone had heard of this explanation was at the trial and particularly why it hadn't been pointed out to police the night of the incident when Urquhart couldn't explain the damage.'

By this stage Nick, too, was shaking his head.

'Oh, there's more,' said Johnny, responding to Nick's body language. 'Scott Urquhart takes the stand. He, of course, tells a bullshit story confirming that the car was already damaged, that he went parking. The parking evidence remained unchallenged by Ferguson but really he should have cross-examined him strongly. Urquhart was arrested about two hours after he'd run over Ernie. He was asleep in his bed. In the box Urquhart said he was pretty sure he'd been parking for *two hours or maybe more*. He'd obviously got his lie wrong given what his girlfriend had said. But Leeson was stuck with the answer he gave. Ferguson, if he was serious, should have jumped at the opportunity and tested Urquhart's evidence against the time the police said they found him at his home. Urquhart couldn't have been with the girlfriend for two hours. But there was no cross-questioning on this point.'

Johnny had become increasingly vehement.

'And remember, by this stage Leeson has cross-examined us up hill and down dale on our characters. Opens Scott Urquhart up to cross-examination on *his* character, right? Ferguson stays silent. But he shouldn't have. The informant on this matter was a very good cop. Thorough. He did some background investigation on Scott Urquhart. He finds out that Urquhart was expelled from three very expensive schools for fighting. On two occasions he even punched his teachers. One of the kids Urquhart had fought with was interviewed by police. He'd had a disagreement with Urquhart in the playground after school. They were both seniors at the time, about seventeen years old. Urquhart gets flattened in the fight. Fifteen minutes later the kid's crossing the road near the school and Urquhart tries to run him over. In the same Mercedes he used to hit Ernie, a birthday present from Daddy. Ferguson had been given all this information. He didn't use it at all in court. For Christ's sake, he could have called the kid who'd fought with Urquhart and got it in as evidence in chief on the basis of similar fact evidence. Nothing. Ferguson was always hopeless but he couldn't have been *that* bad. I didn't know much about the law but I knew from the football field how to pick someone who wasn't having a go. Ferguson ran dead.'

Nick had agreed. Ferguson's performance had gone beyond incompetence.

'Then came the closing addresses.'

Johnny had mimicked Leeson's plum-mouthed delivery.

'*Ladies and gentleman, in the end this case is all about credibility. Sir Samuel, his son and a nice Eastern Suburbs girl or three drunken blacks who live a life of violence both professionally and domestically. Whom do you believe ladies and gentlemen?* He didn't use those exact words of course. It was a long address, the appeal to racism was dipped in honey. But in the end, it was what the jury heard. They were out for less than an hour. Urquhart was acquitted.'

Johnny had tossed down the rest of his drink as if washing away the bad taste of the acquittal. He'd then abruptly gone to the bar for another couple of beers. He resumed talking immediately on sitting down although now he was much calmer.

'The night of the acquittal I lay there thinking that I had just played in a totally rigged game. At that stage I didn't fully appreciate how bad Ferguson was. But other questions nagged at me. Why did the fact that we were black have anything at all to do with our credibility in the witness box? Why were Urquhart and his father and his friends believed instead of us? Why was strong evidence against him totally ignored? Questions, bloody questions. Problem was, I couldn't even begin to get a handle on the answers because I couldn't work out which were the legal questions and which weren't. And I found that frustrating. So I did something about it.'

Johnny had taken another long pull at his beer, draining the whole glass.

'Your shout I believe, my friend,' he said when he put the glass down.

Nick started the engine. It was time for his lecture.

4

'Theyʼve found the weapon that killed Johnny Bora.'

It was Peter Oliver. A barrister from the twelfth floor who was Nickʼs friend. Oliver was still excited. Nick gripped the phone hard. Heʼd been waiting for this moment.

'Go on.'

'Cops are up here on the twelfth floor now.'

'The twelfth floor!'

'Afraid so.'

Nick ran out of his office and into the reception area and pressed the button, cursing the slowness of the lift as he heard its familiar grind from seven floors below.

When he got there Stratton and Lardner and a couple of other detectives from Major Crime were huddled about the reception desk. Nick recognised the bulk of Fred Arthurton from the lab. Peter Oliver stood behind them along with a couple of the other barristers. Some were wigged and gowned ready for ten oʼclock appearances in court but were obviously in no hurry to go.

Oliver nodded toward the reception desk.

'The weapon's a little unusual,' he said.

Nick ignored the objections as he pushed his way through the group to a position behind Stratton. He was tall enough to see the object they were all staring at resting on a plastic groundsheet on the desk. It resembled a baseball bat but a fraction longer and was incised with designs, mainly of shuttle-type curves. It looked like an Aboriginal weapon, probably a club. Next to it was something that looked like two collections of feathers each held together by a congealed brownish substance and tangled up with netted twine. Nick suddenly felt hollow when he noticed the small but still grisly remains of blood and hair on the heavy end of the club. He turned away.

'Where'd they find it?' he asked of Oliver.

'It was here all the time Nick.'

'What?'

'They found it in Christian Pearl's room.'

Pearl was the President of the Bar Association. Nick couldn't believe what he was hearing.

'Pearl's room! Peter, they've been looking for a weapon for over two fucking months. And it's been in Pearl's room all the time!'

'Afraid so Nick. Come and have a look.'

Oliver led Nick up the corridor to Pearl's office and opened the door. On the far wall was a large Aboriginal painting. It was signed by Alice Kingawarreye. Several X-ray ochres on stringy bark hung beside it, above and below these an assortment of boomerangs and spear throwers, a spear shield surrounded by a decorative display of spears, and in each corner a display of wooden sculptures of human heads and totemic animals. Also in one of the corners a tall log coffin.

'They found the club inside that thing. Those feathers you saw fell out as well.' Oliver pointed to the log coffin, about two and a half metres tall and intricately decorated.

'Pearl's a collector of Aboriginal artefacts. He keeps them in his office—you know, good tax deduction, all that. The police had asked permission to do yet another search of the floor for the weapon this morning. And they found it.'

Nick shook his head.

'Why didn't they find it before?'

'Well, Pearl's been away since before the murder—tacked his holidays onto an International Advocates' Conference held in Paris two weeks ago. He only came back this morning. Poor chap ran into all of this. Anyway, because he was away, his office was locked when police first searched all our rooms. They asked to have it unlocked of course, and we obliged. I actually supervised and told them to take it easy because of all the valuable Aboriginal work. Obviously, at that stage they had no idea they were looking for an Aboriginal club. And we all thought the door had been locked at the time of the murder. They didn't search the coffin; too many other plausible priorities I suppose.'

'What was different today?'

'Well a different detective altogether was in charge of today's search. Grimshaw. He just had *everything* searched. Christian Pearl was back in his room and actually helped the police turn the coffin upside down. And there it all was. Poor bugger was very upset.'

Back out in the corridor Stratton and Lardner were approaching. Stratton looked mildly preoccupied. Unusual for him, thought Nick. He liked to look in control.

'Look, we'd like everyone to keep out of Pearl's office for a while if you wouldn't mind. If you walk all over the bloody place you could be walking all over evidence.'

Nick couldn't contain himself, 'Well done Stratton. Only took you two months to find a metre long Aboriginal fighting club within spitting distance of the murder scene.'

'Fuck you Milano.'

This defiantly from Lardner. Too young to know any better. Stratton betrayed no irritation.

'Better late than never, eh Milano?'

He brushed past Nick and Oliver with Lardner on his heels and disappeared into Pearl's room.

'Maggie it's for you.'

Stella Sanchez was disappointed. She'd been expecting a call from Alfie, her boyfriend. They'd had a fight the previous night. He always rang before work on the next day to apologise. But this was another man altogether. Wanted to talk to Stella's flatmate. Maggie Spires emerged from the bathroom, her hair wet, a towel about her, annoyed at having to field phone calls at eight thirty on work mornings.

Her mood changed on picking up the receiver. Stella recognised her friend's new expression and tone of voice—from irritable vixen to purring pussy cat. The guy on the other end was someone special.

Maggie put the phone down. 'That was him.'

'Who?'

'There's only one him, Stella. Damn. Is that the time?'

She hurriedly poured herself a coffee and popped a piece of bread in the toaster.

Stella affected a memory search.

'Oh you mean the French guy from Algiers, or is it that Melbourne surgeon? What was his name? Garry Kneebone was it? Or maybe it's the High Commissioner's son ... um ... let me see. Which *only one him* is it?'

'Very funny,' Maggie replied. 'Where's the Vegemite? No, none of those as a matter of fact. They are all ancient history Stella, as you very well know. This is the guy from the plane.'

'McAngel? I thought you'd given up hope on him.'

Stella was impressed. She'd known Maggie for many

years. She'd always attracted gorgeous men but Stella had never known her to be smitten in the way she was by McAngel.

'He's coming down tomorrow. He's still in Sydney. He's hiring a car.'

'Oh I see,' Stella nodded. 'And I suppose that he's invited to stay here and that yours truly should do the right thing and find alternative accommodation for a while.'

Maggie bit into her toast.

'You're a great chick Stella Sanchez.'

'Sure.'

McAngel finished off the last of his bacon and eggs and drained his coffee mug. He folded the map. It wasn't far to Canberra. Until this morning it was not on his itinerary. He looked out of his hotel window at Sydney Harbour. Sun, cloudless blue sky, morning water traffic trailing neat white lines, skyscrapers of bone and glass reflecting shards of light. He returned to the breakfast table and unfolded the *Canberra Times* he'd had sent up after he'd heard the radio report. He re-read the headline—*Barrister Bludgeoned by Aboriginal Club.*

His holiday was over.

McAngel found Byron Williams' number in New York and enjoyed the sound of his friend's voice on the other end.

'Byron you busy?'

'Hey no, I'm not busy man. Why would a man with five kids under ten be busy man?'

McAngel could hear TV noise and kid noise in the background, some crying, some laughing, some fighting. It must have been about 6 pm in New York.

'The lead was good, Byron,' said McAngel, pausing for a moment to let him take it in.

38

Then he said, 'Something for you to do.'

'Shoot man.'

The Great Wall Restaurant in Marcus Clarke Street at lunchtime was always busy. Nick spotted Fred Arthurton at a table behind one of the yum cha waitresses and joined him.

'Thanks for this Fred. You know I want to keep in touch with the investigation. No point my asking Stratton.'

Fred picked at a prawn roll. He was a big man who enjoyed his food.

'No worries, Nick. Stratton can be a bit of a prick when he wants to be. Good cop though. Mind you, he doesn't give away much to anyone—neither of them do. Stratton's got Lardner well trained.'

Nick agreed. He unfolded a napkin and put it on his knees.

'You know Nick,' said Fred pointing his fork at him, 'Stratton's a racist bastard.'

'Yeah?' Nick affected surprise. 'Can't say I ever noticed.'

Fred seemed to miss the sarcasm; he was a good natured guy.

'He's got this thing about the way Australia should be. No Asians, no Jews, no Southern Europeans. Just the good old Aussie digger and the occasional boatload of Irishmen and poms to remind us where we all came from. He's serious too. It's real Fifties stuff. Even people like yourself—doesn't matter that you've grown up here. As far as he's concerned you're still an eyetie. Part of the mob that was on the wrong side in the war, that sort of thing. In a way it's quaint I suppose.'

'Quaint?' said Nick, raising his eyebrows. It wasn't the first word that came to mind.

'Yeah,' said Fred. 'Like those old Arnott's tins, or FJ

Holdens. Part of old Australia. You know what I mean?'

'Fred, if you think racism's just part of old Australia, something that's dead or out of fashion, you must *live* in one of those old Arnott's tins.'

'Nah. You know what I mean, Nick. It's a particular sort of racism he's got. Like something another generation of Australians had in them just after the war. It's almost like he can't help himself. Like he's been so brainwashed, the racism's as much a part of him as his nose or ears. It's all explainable of course. It's his old man's fault. Stratton told me about him. He was a digger. He fought up in New Guinea during the war. Got shot by the Japanese. After the war he got tied up in a lot of real right-wing stuff. Wacky groups and associations that did things like petition governments to have all the postwar immigrants sent home or to have all the blacks rounded up and kept on reservations. Stratton told me his old man once had a visiting Ku Klux Klansman stop over. Stratton was just a kid but his old man let him stay up half the night listening to the stories of what the Klan did to American negroes back in good old Mississippi. No wonder he's the way he is.'

'Well let's excuse Stratton his racism Fred,' said Nick with mock generosity. 'But what's his excuse for taking two months to find a murder weapon that's planted within pissing distance of the murder scene. Pretty poor police work from a so-called good operator.'

'Oh, come on Nick,' objected Fred. 'Weapon like that could have been disposed of anywhere. All the likely rooms in the building were searched. There was no reason to suspect an Aboriginal club as a murder weapon, you know. So there was nothing significant about Pearl's office and its contents. Anyway, you know as well as I do it wasn't Stratton who personally did Pearl's room. Officer who did the room has had his arse kicked. Hard.'

40

Fred could see Nick was unconvinced. He went on. 'Look, they searched the fire stairs, the lift wells, the carpark under the building very thoroughly. All the exit areas from the lifts on each floor were gone over very closely. Then there was the immediate area of the building that had to be searched. A lot of resources went into those searches, Nick. You can't look everywhere with the same intensity.'

Nick left it alone. He'd challenged Fred's loyalties enough. Fred was no fan of Stratton's but he was still a cop. Raise the fallibility of one cop and you raise the fallibility of them all. There was no way Fred was going to damn Stratton on this one.

'Any explanation as to how the murderer walked though a locked door?'

'Not yet. Stratton's been chasing down all the keys we know about. Cleaners, caretaker, other building staff.'

He gave Nick a sly look as he added, 'You've probably heard that the barristers have also been questioned.'

Nick smiled. He certainly had. Everyone else had heard as well. Over at the courts there were brushfires of speculation and rumour. On the twelfth floor, the indignation was palpable, hanging in the air like smoke. Stratton had his faults but undue deference wasn't one of them.

'So what about this club Fred?' Nick asked. 'What do you know about it?'

Fred, who had forked a pork bun and then taken a bite, answered with his mouth full.

'Stratton's brought in this anthropology professor from the ANU—a Professor Maynard Welkin. I sat in on the interview in case they wanted more lab work done on the club. Welkin spent about three hours making sketches of the incisions and diagrams on the club then went off. Yesterday he gave us his statement. We'll get his findings

41

corroborated by another boffin from the University of Sydney but Welkin seems pretty certain about the origins of this club.'

Fred stopped a waitress and ordered a couple of coffees. Nick stirred impatiently in his chair.

'Well?' he prompted.

'Oh yeah, the club's Aboriginal of course. Made of hardwood mulga. Western Desert tree. *Acacia aneura.* Welkin says the club's from the Pilbara in Western Australia. The style of club and the incisions in it are consistent with artwork from that area. He's not quite sure whether he can attribute the club to a particular group but he's going to try for us.'

'Well you know Johnny was always up in those parts,' said Nick. 'Most of the land disputes he handled were either in the Northern Territory or in Western Australia.'

Fred nodded.

'What about the feathers?' asked Nick, remembering the congealed mess found with the club.

'More interesting still. You know what those little items were, don't you?'

Nick shook his head. A conversation with Fred could get frustrating. He liked to draw out explanations.

'*Wibia.*'

'Wibia?' Nick repeated. 'What's wibia?'

'Western Desert term for them. The Aranda call them *kurdaitcha.*'

'Still a mystery Fred. Just tell me what *you* call them will you.'

'Heard of featherfoot, Nick?'

'No, I fucking well haven't Fred.'

'Featherfoot wears *wibia*, Nick. *Wibia* are shoes. Special shoes. Worn by Aborigines who are out on a *wanmala*. A revenge expedition. The aim is to travel quietly, disguise your tracks, kill your enemy, usually someone held

42

responsible for the death of a member of your tribe, someone who's run away with a woman who belongs to a man from your tribe, that sort of thing. The shoes are made of emu feathers held together with congealed blood. That's the sole. The shoes' uppers are made of netted hair string. If you look at them closely you'll find that there's an opening at the little toe. The featherfoot killer has his small toe dislocated before setting out on the *wanmala*. The belief is that the toe contains an eye which helps featherfoot find his way.'

'This is crazy,' objected Nick. 'In Canberra?'

'Well let's go back to the club. Welkin says this type of club is still made and used by traditional Aborigines in the Western Desert. Now, there's a chance something like this had been picked up over the years and brought back to this area. By a tourist maybe. Or perhaps by a small museum, although most of the artefacts displayed in museums are usually regional stuff so it's unlikely that it would have come from a museum down here. Lardner's checking that out at the moment. If one of the local museums is missing something like that, then it's a start. But when you throw in the *wibia* it tends to suggest a different story. Three possibilities. One, we've got someone, white or black, who has been short changed upstairs and thinks he's a Western Desert Aborigine. Two, someone who's being a smart arse and strewing red herrings. Or three ... ?'

Making a generous gesture with his hands, Fred turned it over to Nick.

'A genuine tribal killing?'

Nick couldn't believe that. It was absurd.

'Welkin reckons the club's seen a lot of use apart from its use as the murder weapon and could be quite old, maybe fifty, sixty years. I agree with him. It's been used before for battering things. Animals probably. By the way,

43

if the Sydney boffin confirms Welkin's opinions, your friends Stratton and Lardner are off to the Pilbara Aboriginal communities to see if they can trace the club.'

Nick shook his head.

'Pilbara Aboriginal communities. Great destination for a neurotic racist like Stratton.'

The coffee arrived. Fred added three spoonfuls of sugar and took a slurp from his cup.

'Prints?'

Nick didn't expect there to be any. Fred's answer surprised him.

'All over the club Nick. Problem is we haven't anyone on record to match them.'

'Interstate?'

'All checked out. Nothing so far.'

'So where are you with the killer? You've got a club made three thousand kilometres away in the West along with something that looks like it's been found by the side of the road on a major highway. You're not much better off than before you found the thing really.'

Fred shrugged and forked another prawn.

5

'Why is this city so clean?'

McAngel was genuinely fascinated. He was on the bridge crossing the lake near Commonwealth Park in his hired car. He could see the buildings that the brochures, with typical insipidness, had described as either *stately* or *modern*—the High Court, the National Gallery, the National Library, and in the distance the priapic shape of the carillon. The lake was broad and clean, the traffic about him regular and obedient. There were paths for cyclists who pedalled by in helmets on shiny bicycles and for well-dressed pedestrians who strolled in the sunshine with serene self-complacency and, McAngel imagined, neatly cut sandwiches. He shook his head. You had to wonder about a city so seemingly pristine. Where did all the shit and garbage go?

Maggie sat next to him. She was thinking of asking him about the scarred hollow just below his left collarbone. She'd noticed it the first time they'd made love weeks ago in Sydney. And she'd seen it again that morning, out in the open, when they lay together in amongst the long grass and reeds by the lake. Startled sulphur-crested cockatoos had flown overhead and indignantly harangued them with squawks of outrage. Afterwards McAngel had taken a swim. His body had fascinated her. Not just because of the curious scar. It seemed the body of a younger man, an athlete, muscular and supple when he pulled through the water with long strong strokes, and rock hard and unyielding minutes earlier when they had climaxed on the shore of the lake.

Other ambiguities about the man intrigued her. In conversation he was relaxed, his manner was polite and cultured. When she asked him about himself he was vague rather than evasive. He carried himself with the sort of easy self-confidence she'd only found in the most accomplished of the men she'd known. And it was no affectation like it was with some. But at the same time she occasionally felt a thrill of fear being around him. It was as if he carried with him a barely suppressed impatience with the mundane, the average, the mediocre. Nothing appeared to preoccupy his mind unduly but at the same time there was nothing random about the way he moved, the things he did. There were no secret obsessions about this man nor any over-cautiousness. But he had a clear plan, something he certainly hadn't revealed to her, and she sensed a determination in him not to be caught out by any surprises. Maybe it was a good idea not to ask such a man about his scar.

Up near Civic McAngel pointed off to the left as they passed a squat white building.

'Courts,' she told him. 'This is the legal area of the town. A lot of the law firms have their offices around here. The barristers are up in that building.'

She pointed to a tall building behind the courts. He'd asked her earlier to show him where the barristers' chambers were. After all, he told her, he was here to do stories on Australian cities. He wanted to capture the essence of cities. Canberra was a public service town, populated by public servants and lawyers. He wanted to see where they worked, how they lived, maybe meet a few people.

He drove around London Circuit and eventually pulled in where she indicated—the steps of the tax department.

'Problem with being a working girl,' she said. 'Eventually you've got to go to work.'

She leaned over to kiss him on the cheek, gripping him high up on the inside thigh as she did so.

'Mind you, there's probably time for another close look at the lake,' she teased.

McAngel gave her a wide-eyed look of horror, pushed her out the door and drove off.

He returned to the building Maggie had pointed out to him, parked and took the lift to the twelfth floor. He introduced himself at the desk.

'My name is Martin Grant. I have an appointment with Mr Pearl.'

A short, dapper man, silver haired, dark striped suit, came out to greet him. McAngel shook his hand. It was soft and white and the grip was weak. McAngel took care not to betray his distaste.

Pearl led him down the corridor to his office. McAngel was taken with the Aboriginal work on the walls. Pearl poured him a drink and said, 'Well Mr Grant, it's a great pleasure to have you in this city. It's always nice to be able to reciprocate cordiality and courtesy amongst colleagues. Felix Attermeyer called me just yesterday afternoon to tell me that you were in town. I know of your firm by its reputation of course—the great Attermeyer and Lipstein. Now legendary since your firm successfully defended that action following the gas leak in Buenos

Aires. It's a great pity you can't have lunch with me Mr Grant. There's an excellent buffet at the Commonwealth Club.'

'Oh, I'm equally disappointed Mr Pearl. Unfortunately, as you know, I have a prior engagement at the embassy. But I am very pleased to be able to meet with you if only for a brief period. We make it our policy at Attermeyer and Lipstein, when our people are abroad, to maintain contact with our colleagues and, of course, we extend our warmest invitation to you to visit our offices in New York.'

McAngel didn't know Attermeyer and Lipstein from Laurel and Hardy. Byron Williams had picked a big firm in New York and rung Pearl posing as its main man. Byron expressed his great desire to promote fellowship and friendship between the Australian and New York bar and by way of encouraging such endeavours recommended a meeting between Pearl and Attermeyer's most promising criminal lawyer, Martin Lloyd Grant. Byron had given Maggie's number to Pearl, describing her as a niece with whom Mr Grant was staying whilst in Canberra as a matter of family courtesy. McAngel had fielded Pearl's call and accepted the invitation to visit Pearl at his office.

'You're a criminal lawyer, Mr Grant. I guess that would be very remunerative in a place like New York.'

'Well crime's much the same just about everywhere I guess, Mr Pearl.'

'Oh no. Absolutely nothing much in it for the advocate here I'm afraid. The criminal classes, being what they are, receive legal aid. Different story in the bigger cities of course. There you've a larger number of serious criminals, organised stuff, bigger bank balances. In Sydney and Melbourne the criminal bars can be quite lucrative if you've the stomach for it.'

McAngel shifted politely in his seat. A token demurrer to Pearl's tactlessness in the interests of authenticity.

48

'Oh, no offence intended Mr Grant. Personally I do admire the criminal lawyer. Not my cup of tea that's all.'

McAngel mounted and rode the opportunity.

'Not much serious crime in Canberra I take it then?'

'No, not much at all. Two, maybe three murders a year. Nothing like your neck of the woods. Unfortunately, and you may have heard of this, we in chambers have been touched by serious crime only recently.'

'I did read the newspapers Mr Pearl. The unfortunate victim was a colleague of yours I believe.'

'Yes. John Bora from these chambers. Aboriginal lad. Quite talented. Did a lot of land claims work. Achieved some eminence in the field actually. You know about the club?'

'Only what I've read in the papers. That it seems he was killed by an Aboriginal weapon—as you say, a club of some sort.'

'Yes and you've probably read that of all places, the killer hid the damn thing in my office. In my Goulburn Island log coffin over there. Along with some type of ritual Aboriginal shoe. Made of feathers. Quite remarkable and very mysterious. I was overseas of course, at the time he was killed. The strangest thing about that little surprise was that I was certain that I'd locked my door. There was no sign of a forced entry yet of all places the murder weapon turns up in my Goulburn Island coffin. And the door was locked when the police searched the premises the next morning.'

'Crazy happenings Mr Pearl. Have the police been able to trace the club?'

'Oh they've called in experts.'

'Oh?' McAngel didn't need to fake his interest in this.

'Yes. I don't suppose you're interested in Aborigines Mr Grant.'

'On the contrary Mr Pearl. I have had an amateur's

interest in anthropology since my student days. You were saying ... about the origins of the club.'

'Well, I understand that Maynard Welkin, probably the greatest living authority on Aboriginal anthropology, has told the police that the club is identifiable as having, at least some time in the last fifty years, belonged to an Aborigine from the Western Desert, probably from a clan now found in the Pilbara area of Western Australia. That, of course, is some 3000 kilometres from Canberra. It's an area which contains many of this nation's most productive mines, particularly iron ore. How on earth that club came to be in the possession of the murderer of Johnny Bora we don't know. Some Canberra detectives, I understand, have gone to the area to investigate the club's origins.'

McAngel gestured toward Pearl's exhibits.

'Appears to be a very fine collection you have, sir. Some beautiful native work.'

'Indeed. And appreciating in value like you wouldn't believe Mr Grant. Take my advice. If you're looking for something to take back to the States with you as well as something which will be a good investment, buy Aboriginal paintings. I can recommend you a dealer if you like.'

Pearl provided McAngel with a name.

As he left the building McAngel dropped the name into the nearest garbage bin. He stopped at a newsagency and purchased a large map of Australia.

Stratton and Lardner found Billy Jangala within 24 hours of arriving at Mt White.

They'd taken the Cessna flight into the iron ore town after a long flight to Perth. Stratton remained stoically composed as they flew over the thousands of square kilometres of scrub and desert way below them. Lardner tried to emulate Stratton's self-control but found himself squirming impatiently as they approached Mt White.

It was early afternoon when they landed. Stratton's first thought as he disembarked and encountered the wall of heat was that the aircraft was on fire. He immediately realised that the blast of heat at the aircraft door was the climate. He looked at Lardner who had put on his shades and was trying to ignore the trickle of sweat from his temples.

Constable Porter of the West Australian Police, a jovial, big gutted, florid man, met them with a handshake and a four-wheel drive. He threw their luggage into the vehicle and bid them hop in.

'A couple of beers in the esky there fellas.'

He pointed a thumb at the back seat. Stratton and Lardner pulled some cold beers from a six-pack buried in ice and gratefully downed them as Porter put the vehicle into gear and moved off. Some twenty kilometres later, he pulled off the main road, itself a narrow stretch of crumbling bitumen, and onto a much narrower red dirt track.

'You need one of these to get about on these roads.' Porter indicated the vehicle he was driving.

'Last year one silly bastard from Adelaide—up here on a holiday—went off the road for a bit of a look in a bloody sedan. Had his wife and three kids with him. He broke an axle. No radio, only a little water and food. No-one even knew he was missing. Light aircraft spotted the car two weeks later. All gone by then. It was the kids I felt sorry for.'

They had by now lost sight of the bitumen. The track in front of them made a crooked attempt at a straight line as it headed off through the heat and the red sand and the endless, joyless protrusions of mulga and tough spinifex. Occasionally as they drove, the monotony would be broken by outcrops of sandstone hills looking long

51

defeated by the elements and now littered with sun-beaten boulders.

'We're about half an hour from the settlement. The people you want to talk to are called the Wonyulgunna mob. After the area they live in. We ran the photos of the club around all the police stations in the area. Most of the blacks we spoke to who knew anything at all about this type of club could identify the incisions. We showed them photos of the *wibia* too. Didn't that fucking cause a commotion! *Featherfoot, featherfoot*, they said. No necessary connection between the shoe and the Wonyulgunna mind you. It's used throughout the Western Desert area. It just scares them to see the featherfoot shoe. They all know its significance.'

Porter grunted as they hit a deep rut. Lardner rearranged his shades which had shifted with the bump.

'Out here is part of the their old territory,' he went on. 'From the days when they roamed the desert. They went back to it about ten years ago after thirty years or so of living in Port Hedland and on the outskirts of some of the mining towns around here. Apparently a couple of the elders got sick of seeing their young kids get into the piss. And they were losing their language and everything. So they made a decision to move and to reassemble the people into this community out here.'

'Like a tribe or something?' asked Lardner.

'Not really,' replied Porter who'd been in these parts for a long time and was enjoying the opportunity to display some local knowledge. 'What you've got assembled at Wonyulgunna is a group of people who belong mainly to Western Desert language groups. A lot of them used to work in an asbestos mine here that closed down when they found out that asbestos caused cancer. Too late for some of the poor bastards who got asbestosis mind you. Anyway, they moved down here near the creek and others who liked the idea of going back to their roots did the same. As I said, a lot of abos who were living around Port Hedland came down. Then there's also a scattering from other Western Desert language groups who joined in as well.'

'And they all get painted up and play didgeridoos, hunt kangaroos and stuff do they?' scoffed Lardner, as naive as he was sceptical.

'Something like that,' said Porter amiably enough, sidestepping Lardner's invitation to mock.

'They don't wander continually like they used to. But they'll go out into the desert for periods of time and then come back. They've set up their own education system of sorts to teach the traditional culture. The older ones who've lived in towns come and go of course. Like Jackie Marikit. He's the head elder out here. But the younger ones are encouraged not to go into the towns too much. Most of the elders don't bother any more either.'

Stratton yawned.

'Very commendable,' he said. 'Personally, the less I see of blackfellas the better. We'll just talk to whoever there is to talk to about the *nulla-nulla* and piss off.'

They bumped along through the hot, red landscape without speaking for some time. The silence and his alien surroundings made Lardner edgy. His nervousness carried in his voice when he spoke again.

'Fuck me, what a godforsaken, useless piece of country this is. These blacks can have the bloody place as far as I'm concerned.'

Neither of the others answered him. He felt a little foolish and tried to recover some ground.

'Although I suppose if you give the boongs the country you give them the fucking minerals as well. Half a dozen blackfellas get to own the resources that can make this

53

country rich. They don't give a shit whether its mined or not half the time.'

Lardner saw Porter nod his head and took it as a sign of approval. He went on less hesitantly.

'Sometimes they're just as likely to say we don't want any mining on a certain spot because my fucking great Uncle Sambo and his whole tribe used to hold corroborrees here and it's a sacred site. Doesn't matter that millions of bloody white Australians are going to be worse off for it. You give them the land and they get to say whether you can mine it or not.'

'That's right mate,' said Porter patiently.

It was a token gesture of solidarity rather than of shared logic.

Stratton looked out of the window non-committedly. Lardner's usual simple view of the world. Still too fucking young to know any better. He had the right attitude anyway. Fucking blacks. Dirty, drunk and lazy. No good to themselves or to anyone else.

Signs of the community appeared in the distance. There was some smoke rising above some crude dwellings made of canvas or of scraps of timber and corrugated iron. As their car pulled up a small swarm of children, flies and underfed dogs collected to meet them. Behind them came the adults. A small boy tugged at Stratton's sleeve as he hopped out of the vehicle. Stratton pulled away quickly and tried to ignore him. Some older men arrived and stood with the children.

Porter approached a frail and stooped man who regarded them speculatively with his head cocked to one side.

'Jackie Marikit. Is Jackie Marikit here?' Porter asked.

Among the group of adults was a tall, full-bodied woman who looked like she was in her early thirties. Barefoot, she wore a now dusty and faded short black

54

dress made of a stretch material that clung voluptuously to her hips and bottom and which was held at the shoulders by thin straps so that her long brown arms and the tops of her breasts were also bare.

She stepped forward. Porter knew her.

'How are ya Sally?' he said. 'These men here are policemen. They want to talk to some elders. Where's Jackie Marikit?'

'He died.'

Her face remained as expressionless as her reply. Stratton, who had been looking at her intently since arriving, was struck by the incongruity of her appearance as she stood there against the background of swirling hot red dust, scattered thickets of mulga trees and the dilapidated shelters and huts. In the black dress the woman looked like some beauty out of a romance who had left the debutante ball and gone wild. She had brown eyes that pooled deep and defiant above high cheekbones and full sensual lips. She was now looking at him cautiously. What was she doing out here? With some distaste Stratton became aware of a creeping sexual desire and fought it off. She was a boong like the rest of them.

The old man stepped forward and said something.

'What'd he say Sally?' asked Porter.

'He wants to know what you want. He is the oldest man here. His name is Mamarika.'

'You say Jackie died?' said Porter.

'He was old,' Sally replied.

Lardner pulled the club from the bag in the back of the vehicle and handed it to Mamarika. The effect on the surrounding adults was immediate. There was much chattering. Mamarika spoke heatedly to Sally. The woman's head dropped as he continued to berate her. When he finished he handed her the club and moved away as if in disgust. The other adults followed him except

55

for one old man with a shock of white hair who stood by Sally without saying anything.

When Sally looked up again there were tears in her eyes.

'What was all that about?' Stratton asked Porter.

Sally answered the question

'He says it's my fault. That you're here. The police.'

'Your fault?' Stratton queried.

Sally looked over at the old man with white hair who continued to stand there. He nodded without looking at her. She turned back to Stratton.

'The name of the man you're looking for is Billy Jangala.'

Stratton hardly heard her. His eyes had followed Sally's and had met those of the old man standing next to her. Stratton now stood transfixed, caught for several seconds by the old man's compelling gaze. Then Monyu's eyes released him, allowing him to turn to Lardner.

'Billy Jangala,' Lardner was saying. 'Who's he?'

6

The news that Billy Jangala was in custody and being flown back from the West reached Nick from the car radio as he drove to work. When he got there he hit the phone and was on to Fred Arthurton in seconds.

'They got him straightaway Nick,' Fred Arthurton told him. 'This woman called Sally told Stratton and Lardner the whole story. They waited and got Jangala when he came in from the bush. Noble savage material apparently. Had a kangaroo over his shoulder and all. They took him into Port Hedland and printed him. The prints matched what they had on the club and so they arranged for the extradition warrants. In the meantime this Billy Jangala gives them the whole story—full confession. Including how he just walked into the nearest room and dropped the club into the coffin. Nothing to it. Looks like either Pearl was wrong about locking his room or someone else left it open and isn't saying. Stratton's over the moon. He's got a promotion to Commander in his sights and this won't do him any harm.'

Fred told him what he'd heard on the grapevine and

when he put the phone down Nick couldn't help feeling disappointed. An Aborigine from the desert killed Johnny. Poor, uneducated, acting under the dictates of some native law, the origins of which were remote in time and place from anything he knew or understood. It was pointless. Somehow he'd thought that there was more to Johnny's death. That his murder and the secret behind it had to be a matter of weight, of significance. The magnitude of the motive would have to equal the magnitude of the crime. It seemed it didn't. It left him feeling empty.

He rang Johnny's wife. The conversation was short. She'd heard all about it. The woman Sally? It was possible Johnny was involved with her, she said. He'd done it before, Nick knew that. The grief was the same anyway, whatever had happened. She had things to think about. He left her to it.

The sense of waste stayed with Nick the rest of the day. It was difficult for him to concentrate on his work. Thoughts of Johnny continually intruded. Johnny had gone into the law for idealistic reasons. He wanted to help his people and one of them had killed him. It was an unusual motive for a lawyer—idealism. You heard about it with priests and social workers, the occasional teacher, even doctors. Hardly ever with lawyers. But the Ernie Barnes affair had enlivened in Johnny some deeply held sense of justice. It wasn't as if he held any great faith in the capacity of the white legal system to provide that justice, but he'd figured that knowing something about it was a start.

'I went to the management committee of the football club,' Johnny once told Nick. 'My contract was up for renewal. I asked for new terms. More money and so on. I was playing well at the time so they agreed and then began to pack me off. I said *Hold on, I want something else*. Then I told them I wanted a scholarship to do some study.

'They all looked at me as if I was dreaming. They knew that my schooling didn't amount to much. But they didn't know that I spent most of my spare time buried in books. Good books. Classics. I read everything. Novels, history, philosophy, poetry. It used to drive old Ernie crazy when I'd tell him I couldn't go fishing or down the pub or for a drive because I was reading. And you know I didn't read because I was looking for an education or anything. I read because I bloody well enjoyed it.

'Anyway, they always had the club lawyer at these affairs. This was a guy called Zac Ruben the founding partner in Ruben and Fenton. Large firm. He was a big fan of the Roosters and patron and liked to come in on the contract negotiations himself just to see what his money was paying for. So then I turned to him and told him that there was no contract with me unless he promised to employ me when I graduated from law school. That was the first mention I made of being a lawyer. Rubens was a good guy. He was intelligent and he could see that I was serious and he made no attempt to be patronising. But he began to explain to me, quite rightly, that there was no way I could have a binding contract with him as the contract was between the club and myself not with him, and so on. I interrupted and told him I knew all about the law of privity because I'd researched my contract law before I came to the meeting. A simple handshake and his word would be enough for me. This impressed him no end and he agreed. In the end I walked out with a scholarship and a promise of a job.'

Not bad for someone who'd left school at fourteen. Johnny's magnificent self-confidence was already evident. A self-confidence which had been born where? It was a question Nick had always asked himself.

Johnny seemed to regard racial prejudice as a minor and temporary inconvenience. In fact, he regarded anything which stood in the way of his plans as an impediment barely worth his consideration. It had been like that when Johnny went to Ruben six years after his deal with club management. Zac Ruben kept his word, ignored the raised eyebrows and took Johnny onto the payroll. And there were plenty of raised eyebrows. Ruben and Fenton was predominantly a commercial law firm. Its clients included banks and other big corporations, including the miners.

The criticisms were all the more pointed because the firm was employing a person one of the Sydney newspapers, in an article on student politics, had floridly described as a *muscular and articulate Aboriginal urban hero and activist called Johnny Bora*. It was a description Johnny had gleefully repeated for Nick. Johnny explained that he had by then changed his name and had thrown himself into student politics and into the Aboriginal land rights movement. He had helped organise marches on campus protesting against mining of sacred sites in outback Australia. He became editor of an Aboriginal student journal called *Black as Black*. He was arrested at demonstrations, gaoled on one occasion, appeared on television interviews and debates, and was mentioned in patronising editorials of large dailies which counselled him to temper his fiery wit and rhetoric lest otherwise sympathetic whites be alienated by his radical proposals.

On his first day at Ruben and Fenton he wore, beneath an extravagant Afro hairdo, faded jeans and riding boots and a white T-shirt with the colours of the Aboriginal flag screen-printed on the front. The receptionist, a nervous matron from Milsons Point who worked one day a week, called the police rather than believe he was reporting for work. Johnny was delighted and waited happily in the foyer chatting to a roomful of the firm's clients till the cops arrived and things were sorted out. Thereafter, he said, he made a point of winking at her when he arrived for work in the mornings.

Ruben and Fenton occupied the four top floors in the Longmans Building overlooking Circular Quay. Nick recalled Johnny's account of the morning he took the lift to Ruben's office on the very top floor.

'When I walked in, Ruben had his back to this huge window overlooking the harbour. It made you dizzy if you got too close, you were that high. He turned around to me all businesslike and told me he was giving me the opportunity to start out in the criminal law section. It was a minor part of the firm's practice. I told him I didn't want to work in that area. I wanted to work for his mining clients. Well Ruben looked at me for a while and then he gave a bit of an uncertain smile like you give someone who's just told you a joke you don't really understand. I stood there. And then it dawned on him I wasn't joking.'

Johnny mimicked the warning tone of the answer he got.

'You're pushing your luck Johnny. I agreed to employ you. I didn't agree to let you come into the firm and frighten away millions of dollars a year in business. What do you think my fucking miners are going to do when I introduce you to them? Look at you. You're a miner's living nightmare. An Aborigine with a law degree and a land rights political agenda who, just for good measure, happened to play professional football. Jesus Christ, it's like someone from the KGB applying for a job with ASIO.'

'I don't have to meet your clients,' Johnny replied. 'I'm new, just learning the job. You don't have your junior solicitors in on the big stuff do you? All I want to be is a backroom boy. Let me do the research, prepare documents, that sort of stuff. I know the theory of the law in this area Mr Ruben, it's my passion. I want to see how it works in practice. I'm not going to use it to disadvantage your clients. I know my ethics and really, even if I wanted to, how can I screw your clients? You've got the law and some of the best legal brains in the country between me and them. My agenda is to get the law changed eventually and by political means. I'm not going to do it overnight and before I can do anything worthwhile I want to know how it all works. There, I'm being honest with you.'

Ruben seemed to relent immediately.

'I take it then Johnny, that your ambition isn't exactly a long-term relationship with Ruben and Fenton,' he had replied. 'Even if by some remote chance I should happen to want to keep you?'

'I think you knew that when you first promised to employ me Mr Ruben,' Johnny told him.

Ruben had then turned to the view. With his back still turned he said, 'You're not the only ones who know all about racial prejudice, Johnny. You realise that don't you?'

Johnny hadn't answered. Ruben had then suddenly hit his forehead with the palm of his hand and wheeled around and said, 'I'm an idiot. Always have been, always will. Johnny, tomorrow you start helping out Edgar Wright with the Neptune and Orion mining accounts. There are big leases at stake but don't get too excited. Land rights aren't involved and you'll be spending most of your time at the photocopier. Anything to do with Aborigines you play no active part in. You don't on any account meet the clients. Anything you issue to them goes out under Edgar's name. If I'm asked by anyone about your involvement I tell them you're just getting general legal experience and the mining clients are a small part of that. First murmur of discontent I get from a miner about your involvement in their affairs and you go straight into doing the criminal mentions in the magistrates court. Now piss off, I'm busy.'

There'd been demurrers amongst some of the other partners Johnny said, but Ruben sold it to them as a public relations move. Johnny's involvement with the miners presented Ruben and Fenton as a progressive law firm and a generous one, Ruben had said. A firm prepared to give intelligent and qualified young Aborigines opportunities to develop in the profession. Ruben and Fenton was willing to forgive a talented undergraduate his enthusiasm for student radicalism. After all, he argued, wasn't it true that in fact this was a means to make Aboriginal activism more conservative? And in any case, it wasn't as if Johnny didn't have the passes. He was an honours graduate for goodness' sake.

Within two years Edgar Wright was refusing to make a move on behalf of his mining clients without consulting Johnny Bora first.

McAngel had taken a cab from the aerodrome into Mt White and had booked into a pub called called The Iron Horse. It was a dump. The air-conditioning made a racket and there were flies buzzing about the dining room as he walked through it. He tried to ignore the heavy smell of some dubious stew dish which followed him from the dining area and up the stairs to his room. The room was small. There was a frail double bed, a yellowing ceramic sink with an old brass tap which dripped, a bar of Palmolive, a wooden wardrobe exuding its last musty breaths and an unshaded light bulb. An old black and white TV set with a broken antenna dozed in a dusty corner.

He was glad to come downstairs to the crowded bar. He found a gap and ordered a beer. He threw it down and ordered another. He was still a little tired from his flight. It was mid-afternoon, a Saturday. Men in blue singlets and shorts and big hats moved in and out of the bar area. Some still had on their work boots. Miners. Shiftworkers. He looked along the bar at the row of hands resting on the towelling covering it. They were workers' hands. Dirt under the nails, grease stained. Strong reliable hands. McAngel thought of his father. Coalminer, Pittsburgh, Pennsylvania. Tough man, union man, knew how to make a little boy feel proud and grown up. After his father died his mother had moved back to San Francisco. McAngel had preferred Pittsburgh. He ordered another beer.

There was a small beer garden outside, occupied mainly by mixed groups of men and women sitting at slatted tables which were sheltered from the sun by some perspex roofing. A couple of young kids ran about its confines. Further out the back on the red dirt, and in the sun, a group of Aboriginal men and women drunkenly passed around a flagon of sherry. A race caller on a radio somewhere competed with the strains of a jukebox playing country and western music and there was a pool table at which hard-looking men played for money.

McAngel bought a few beers and started some conversations with the owners of the hands at the bar. Most belonged to drivers of the giant Haul Paks that made their way up and down the mountain night and day, carting the ore from the open cut to the big crusher down below. Other hands operated the big stacker that patiently waited at the end of the conveyors while the belts spewed the ore onto existing mountains of ore. Below these stacks passed the three-kilometre long trains collecting the ore for transport to Port Hedland on the coast. McAngel kept drinking and enjoyed their company, their language, their laughter. He was a Yank tourist. He played it up and tolerated their good-natured baiting about American sport, politics and affluence.

A woman, tanned and with long dark hair, wearing tight jeans and a thin yellow singlet, brushed against him. He could see the shape of her nipples under the singlet. She smiled at him as she got her drinks and returned to a table outside. She was with some other women. He saw her say something to them and they looked toward where he was standing. He raised his glass to them and they laughed.

He'd noticed the pool table and asked about the two guys who seemed to be winning every game. He was told it was Tub Thompson and his mate Gunner Francisco. They'd paired up in the late morning and had held the table ever since. Tub's shirt pocket now bulged with the ten and twenty dollar notes they'd won. Gunner was very tall, lithe and muscular under a black T-shirt. He smoked Drum cigarettes, rolling them with one hand as he held his cue in the other. Tub Thompson was broad and big arsed, shorter than his mate with meaty, tattooed arms and a large stomach that hung over his shorts.

McAngel watched them for a while. Both of them had taken on a bit of an alcoholic sway when they stepped back from the table after a shot. But their accuracy on the table remained. As time passed, the two began to ogle the women who walked by. Tub would nudge Gunner, Gunner nudged Tub, they'd look, sometimes wolf whistle, occasionally pinch an arse, laugh aloud, push each other, swear, smoke, drink, fart.

McAngel continued to drink steadily. He was enjoying the hum of the pub, the music, the sight and smell of the women as they came to the bar for drinks and left again. The dark-haired woman with the singlet returned to the bar just as Tub and Gunner finished off of a pimply faced kid in cowboy gear and his friend.

'You play pool?' McAngel asked her.

She glanced at the table.

'Not with those two I don't.'

'Oh?'

She motioned for McAngel to bend over and whispered in his ear.

'They're arseholes.'

'I could do with a partner.' McAngel raised his eyebrows questioningly.

She eyed him off briefly then made up her mind.

'Okay partner. I'm Julie.'

McAngel pulled a twenty from his pocket and walked over and threw it onto the green felt. Tub was amused.

'You and the sheila, eh.'

Gunner didn't say anything. He was looking at the girl.

After the throw of the coin Julie bent over the table to break. Gunner was watching her arse instead of the ball. He brushed close to her as he took his position up for his own shot. She moved away in an obvious display of distaste. As she did so she bumped into Tub who bounced her away obscenely with a thrust of his belly. Gunner pocketed the four ball but missed a difficult angle on the two. McAngel bent over for his shot and saw that neither of the two men were watching. They'd both moved onto either side of Julie. McAngel pocketed the one, and followed with the five. The three and the seven were easy. He missed the next one as he saw Gunner grab a handful of Julie's backside and shout loudly, 'You beauty'. Julie reeled away. She thrust the cue at McAngel.

'Here. Play them yourself. They make me sick.'

McAngel took her hand instead to prevent her from moving.

'Of course you'll stay if this gentleman here apologises, won't you?'

66

Something about the certainty in this man's look stopped her from answering immediately.

'Won't you?' he repeated.

'Well, I guess I might,' she answered hesitantly. Gunner was now for the first time looking at McAngel intently. McAngel turned to face him.

'You apologise to that lady—now.'

There was no anger in McAngel's voice but the effect on the surroundings was like a sudden drop in temperature. In the brief pause that followed, the pub din all but ceased.

Then McAngel saw Gunner's knuckles whiten as his grip tightened on the pool cue. But it was Tub who moved first bringing the butt of the cue toward McAngel's head with a forearm push. McAngel barely moved as he deftly caught the blow on his own cue. Seeing Gunner lunge, he drove the thick end back sharply into his jaw. The tall man's mouth snapped shut on impact and he dropped to the ground without a sound. McAngel wheeled on Tub who was preparing a second swing and got him with short cracking blows to both his knuckles. The cue dropped to the floor with a rattle as Tub doubled over, aching hands under his armpits.

Gunner managed to raise himself on one elbow just before McAngel took a grip on the hair at the nape of his neck and forced him to his feet. He let Gunner go and stood beside him facing Julie.

'Apologise,' McAngel demanded.

Gunner, face distorted with discomfort, complied between clenched teeth. McAngel took Julie by the hand and left the bar.

There was a small crush around Court Five by the time Nick got there. A sign told people there was no seating left inside. Nick allowed the uniforms on duty to clear a path for him and he went in and took a seat at the bar table. Prosecutor's privilege. You could always get a seat in a criminal court. Ken Harrigan, the Assistant Director, had arrived already to appear for the prosecution. There wasn't much going to happen this morning. Billy Jangala would be charged before the court, his solicitor would ask for an adjournment and he'd be remanded in custody while his legal representatives decided what to do. Nick had asked to instruct Ken, which wasn't really necessary but it meant Nick was able to sit at the bar table from where he could take a close look at the action.

Ken Harrigan was a short, bald man with a flattened nose, a dour expression and a massive neck and torso. He looked like a retired wrestler who'd been stuffed into a grey suit for the day and told to be on his best behaviour. Now he nudged Nick and nodded his attention toward the guy appearing for Billy Jangala. It was Hayden Allcott from Aboriginal Legal Aid. He was bent over and squinting through thick spectacles into his bag. Hayden was an ex-academic only recently led into advocacy by altruism. He was learning that neither his background nor his motives were themselves of much use in the criminal courts.

Allcott looked up and squinted at them.

'Opposing bail?' he asked.

He was probably joking but with Allcott you could never tell.

'Good one Hayden,' said Harrigan.

'Can't say I didn't try, eh?'

He smiled. Evidently he *was* joking.

'We won't be asking for bail anyway,' said Allcott.

'What a relief,' mocked Harrigan. 'I was ready for a real tough fight on bail, Hayden.'

Everyone knew that if he was released it would be bye-bye Billy. No policeman would ever find him if he got back to the desert. There'd be no bail for Billy today.

Nick then listened to the knock he'd so often heard. It was the police guard from the cells below the court. He'd brought Billy Jangala up the steps and was now knocking from the other side of the door used as access to and from the cells. The duty officer inside the court opened the door. There was a murmur from the back of the court. Nick turned to look.

A frightened young Aboriginal man, no more than nineteen or twenty was led in, handcuffed. His eyes were wide with fear and confusion as he caught sight of all the faces at the back of the court. As he looked around, he met Nick's eyes briefly then continued gazing around the court, bewildered and lost. Billy was just under two metres tall and was wearing a yellow singlet and a pair of shorts. His feet were bare. He had the build of a middle distance runner and the skin glow and muscle tone of a man in peak condition.

'All stand please.'

It was Frank Chamberlain's monitor. The people stood and in came Chamberlain. He was silver haired, tall and stooped. Along with the plain black magistrate's gown he wore a look of accomplished world weariness that may have been mistaken for patience by some who didn't know better.

Harrigan and Allcott announced their appearances.

After years of appearing before him both Nick and Harrigan could predict Chamberlain's actions in a courtroom. They weren't surprised at what came next. As he sat, Chamberlain removed his glasses and pointed one of the stems to the back of the court where Billy Jangala was sitting.

'Why is that man cuffed?' he growled.

The guard, a young, powerfully built constable, stood up looking concerned.

'I was instructed to leave the defendant cuffed, your worship. By Detective Constable Lardner, your worship.'

'Well I'm *un*instructing you, constable. The man is now in my courtroom and I will not have defendants handcuffed in this courtroom. Understand?'

The young constable immediately took off the cuffs. Billy let his hands drop by his side. Again he looked around the room. There was a flicker of panic in his eyes when Allcott indicated to the constable that he wanted Billy to sit at the bar table. Billy came forward uncertainly. Allcott told him to sit. Billy stood and continued to survey the courtroom. Nick felt the tension. It came from Billy. Like a trapped animal he looked ready to dart in any direction that might afford him shelter and safety. He was responding to confinement, to danger. His main thought was of flight. That much was apparent to everyone. It made the cops on the doors nervous and they shifted from foot to foot.

There were three exits. One door led back down to the cells, one at the side which led into a corridor separating the courtrooms, and one at the back. Police were stationed at every door. Billy continued to look at each in turn. There was perspiration on his upper lip.

Then an old man appeared from the back of the courtroom. An old black man with a shock of white hair wearing a checked flannel shirt and dark trousers. Like Billy he was barefooted. He moved calmly to where Billy was standing and put his left hand on Billy's right shoulder and without saying anything stood there, not looking at Billy but rather at the magistrate, steadfastly. Billy saw it was the old man and appeared to relax. The old man tapped Billy's shoulder and he sat down. The tension abated.

Allcott was on his feet.

'Your worship, this is Mr Monyu. He is a Wonyulgunna

70

elder assisting my client. He is, of course, in a position to act as a translator at these proceedings. My client's English is imperfect, your worship.'

'Take a seat Mr Monyu,' said the magistrate.

Chamberlain liked the old guy, thought Nick. You could tell.

Allcott sat down and Harrigan stood up and read Billy the charge. The word murder seemed to hang in the air. It wasn't heard often in Canberra courts. With a voice low in pitch and strong, Monyu interpreted into a Western Desert dialect as Harrigan spoke. When Harrigan finished he sat and Allcott proceeded to explain that his client was not seeking bail, that he was to be represented by Aboriginal Legal Aid, and that he was seeking an adjournment. It was standard procedure. Monyu continued to interpret as Allcott spoke.

Harrigan was then asked if he had anything to say and he shook his head. Chamberlain set a date for a fortnight away and adjourned the court. Everyone was told to rise and Chamberlain left. The young constable came and took Billy by the arm and led him off back down the steps to the cells.

Old man Monyu watched him go before turning and heading for the back door, ignoring a couple of the journalists who tried to ask him questions.

7

Stella Sanchez pushed her boyfriend Alfie off her.
'There's someone out there,' she hissed and
pointed toward the kitchen.

Alfie was peeved. The times when Stella was wanting
it like she wanted it tonight were rare. Tonight she'd
hauled him off to the bedroom where she'd frantically
unzipped and released him and then wrapped her naked
legs about him and pulled him inside her so greedily he'd
struggled not to come immediately. And now she'd pushed
him out again. He lay back drawing breath, trying not to
express any irritation in case she got angry and didn't let
him back inside her.

'It may be Maggie,' he whispered back.

'No way. We had a deal. She's out with that lieutenant
from the Academy. She's not coming home until much
later.'

Alfie repressed his urge to grumble. It was no-one, he
knew it was no-one, but he'd still have to go and look just
so that she'd relax again, just so that she'd let him back
inside her warm pussy again. He swung his legs over the
side of the bed and pulled on his jocks. He looked at her.

She lay wide eyed and naked, small and firmly breasted, then she pulled a sheet over herself. Alfie moved silently out into the kitchen.

Stella waited. There was a short, fat, muffled sound like the slap of a wet rag then, except for a dog barking somewhere in the distant night, there was silence. Alfie was trying to scare her. The silence stretched on. Now she was frightened. Too frightened to move. A sound. A dragging sound. She'd stopped breathing. And then Alfie's shape against the half light at the bedroom doorway. Before she could speak Alfie took flight and landed on top of her, his head inches from her own. She saw his bloodied face at the same time as she saw the man who replaced him in the doorway, the man who'd flung Alfie's dead body onto the bed as if it were a broken puppet.

As he moved toward her, she opened her mouth to scream. Nothing came out but silent terror.

McAngel stretched. The bed next to him was empty. He drew the curtain and recoiled as the light instantly assailed his eyes. The heat in the room made his hangover worse. He ran his head under the tap, enjoying the cool on the back of his neck. As he dried himself he found the note from Julie written on a tissue. 'Gone to work,' it said, 'I enjoyed last night . . . and the night before . . . and the next morning and the afternoon. Good luck with your book.'

He smiled. He had to tell her he was there for something. Writing a book sounded plausible at the time.

He went downstairs. The pub was open for business but there were only a couple of customers. The publican, Hairy Harry Muldoon, dressed in khaki shorts and an old white singlet, stood over his beer taps holding a bucket under one of them. He nodded McAngel a greeting. Harry knew McAngel had been upstairs most of the previous day with Julie Brownlow. She was supposed to be separated from her husband but you never knew with the big fella. If Mac Brownlow knew his wife was with this bloke there'd be trouble. Mac could go a bit but this Yank looked as though he could hurt someone real bad if he had to. Anyway, word was he was out of town. You had to keep up with what was going on in a town like this. He wouldn't be telling Mac about the Yank—not while the Yank was there anyway.

McAngel approached him and ordered a Coke with plenty of ice.

'Quiet town, eh.'

'It's got its moments mate. You helped liven it up the other night—givin' it to Tub and Gunner the way you did. Not too many around here would have tried that you know.'

McAngel smiled and paid for his drink.

'Well we ended up friends didn't we?'

Hairy Harry opened his eyes wide.

'Glad you think so,' he said.

He finished pulling beer into the bucket with McAngel watching him in silence. Then Harry said, 'I'd say you'd better be careful that's all. People around here hold grudges. You bein' a Yank wouldn't help either.'

'Oh. What's wrong with Yanks Harry?'

Harry didn't answer.

McAngel pulled a photograph from his shirt pocket and showed it to Harry.

'Seen him?'

Hairy Harry took a look. It was a head and chest colour photograph of a blond man, neatly styled hair, serious. Looked European he thought, wearing a suit.

'Does he wear the bag of fruit all the time?'

McAngel shrugged.

Hairy Harry considered the photo for a while longer.

'Nah. Don't think so. Certainly no-one dressed like that around here lately. Sometimes you get a few people in

74

suits drop in if they're on their way to a mining conference somewhere. You know, businessmen who arrange to hold meets here, that sort of thing. Sometimes they'll dress up.'

McAngel was interested.

'When was the last time you saw people like that in town?'

'Just before Christmas last. There was a few blokes from the city here, dressed up, wanted special food and drinks, that sort of stuff. Can't recall your bloke though, but then again they all look the same to me.'

Hairy Harry developed a smirk.

'Tell you who'd know though. Those two boys you straightened out the other night. Both of them know the bush around here really well. They're not miners—they're kangaroo shooters. Bounty hunters. They've got the vehicles and they spent a lot of time driving this group around the bush. They talked about it for ages afterwards because these blokes paid so well.'

McAngel got directions, a case of beer as well as some gratuitous advice from Hairy Harry about upsetting the locals, and then went outside into the heat to find a cab.

At the DPP, Nick had already heard about the double murder by the time it hit the afternoon radio bulletins. It was pretty horrific stuff by any standards. By Canberra standards it was way out there. Twenty-eight year-old guy called Alfie shot between the eyes with probably a silenced thirty-eight and his girlfriend Stella Sanchez choked to death by someone's bare hands. The lab found traces of what appeared to be Alfie's sperm inside the dead girl but also quantities of someone else's, confirming the police suspicion that the couple had been interrupted by the murderer when they were making love. Looked like he'd shot Alfie then raped the girl. Apart from the bruising around her neck there were plenty of other marks to find elsewhere. The girl's terror had started long before she died.

The bodies had been found in the early hours of the morning by Stella's flatmate—a Maggie Spires— who'd come home earlier than expected after arguing with her date. She was still too frazzled by the whole thing to be of much use. Refused to even go back into the house.

From his window Nick could see across the road to the police station where news cars had come and gone all day. Reporters stood around with their heavily-equipped camera crews. Nick had heard that Stratton was running the investigation. It had only been a day since he'd got back into town with Billy Jangala. Billy had been charged in the morning. Stella Sanchez and her boyfriend were murdered that night. *Commander* Stratton. Nick shuddered at the thought.

He tried to concentrate on his work. He had a trial coming up: a big amphetamines bust. But he couldn't work up an appetite for the case. Johnny Bora was on his mind. He pulled out, once again, the statement of facts from the police brief. What nagged at him was the feeling that Johnny wasn't meant to die this way. It didn't fit. And there was something else. The locked door. Okay, it may have been open, allowing Billy to plant the club in Pearl's room. But it was the sort of door that had to be locked with a key. Morning after the murder, Pearl's door had to be unlocked by Oliver for the police search. So who was it came along and locked it after Billy dumped the club? No-one knew. And with Billy's candid confession safely on video tape, no-one really cared.

Ken Harrigan was on the intercom.

'Maynard Welkin is out at reception. He'll be our expert if this gets to trial. We're just touching base this morning. Come round if you like.'

Harrigan was looking out of the window when Nick came in.

'Busy time for the boys across the road,' he said.

'Yeah,' said Nick. 'But no featherfeet this time I hear.'

'No. Just your plain old psychopathic rapist-cum-murderer. Very humdrum.'

Nick smiled.

There was a knock and a small, neat man dressed in a blue suit and carrying a briefcase appeared at the door. His greying hair was neatly parted at the side and held together Fifties style with hair oil. He had bright, clear blue eyes and a firm handshake. He smelt of Palmolive soap. Nick was surprised by his appearance, for some reason he had expected someone quite different. Someone rugged and dressed in riding boots and khaki shorts. Looking at Welkin, Nick was reminded of a lay preacher, a missionary; a person destined to carry in their looks that certain wholesome youthfulness and innocence that often become the source of sardonic amusement among males of more varied experience.

Harrigan began by asking Welkin if he'd ever appeared in a criminal trial. He hadn't.

'Well, this matter may not go to trial,' Harrigan told him. 'Billy Jangala has made a full confession. He told us the lot. How Jackie Marikit ordered him to kill Johnny because of Sally's affair with Johnny Bora, how he used the buses to get all the way here from the Pilbara. Where he stopped, where he ate, where he used the toilet. Descriptions of this building we're in now, the twelfth floor, the disposal of the club and shoes in the hollow coffin. He's told us the works. It's on video tape, an interpreter was present, legal representative was present, his prints were on the murder weapon and so on. He may well plead guilty.'

Nick had wondered about that. This Billy was a young

man doing the bidding of an older man in the tribe. Someone more influential and powerful than he. Duress. Compulsion. They were legitimate issues for the defence to raise. The whole business *could* go to trial. He didn't agree with Harrigan. Much depended on the relationship between Billy and Jackie Marikit. And something else was troubling him. Something he remembered Johnny telling him about Aboriginal custom.

'This Jackie Marikit. He was an old man, right?' he asked Harrigan.

'About seventy it seems. No one really knows his exact age.'

'My understanding is that Aborigines living a traditional lifestyle weren't usually that fussed about extra-marital sex. Jackie was an old guy. He probably had a few other wives as well, did he?'

Harrigan shrugged. He didn't know. They both looked at Welkin.

'Actually I'd be very surprised if he didn't,' said Welkin. 'My understanding is that Jackie Marikit was one of the elders of the Wonyulgunna community but that expression doesn't really do justice to his position. As I understand it he was also the *mabanba*, the doctor or sorcerer of the community. It's a very powerful position. A position in traditional Aboriginal society of great standing and respect. Often the *mabanba*, depending on his personality, can also be a person who inspires considerable fear in other members of the group. Great powers of sorcery are attributed to him. He can order another's death by a *wanmala*, for example, or he can in fact curse the person from afar. You've both heard of the ritual of pointing a bone in the direction of someone, someone from another group who is thought to have caused the death of a member of the clan. It is not uncommon for the target of such revenge rituals to die from heart failure. Whether the cause is a supernatural power or self-induced illness arising from an overwhelming fear of the sorcerer's power is altogether a different question. But I think that a man of that standing and power in the group would almost certainly have more than one wife.'

'Are *you* surprised that he ordered this revenge expedition?' Nick asked.

Welkin thought for a moment before answering.

'The *wanmala* is certainly his responsibility. I've no doubt that it's true, given the use of the shoes and the determination to carry out the order, that the order must have emanated from the *mabanba*. As for his motive, that is more difficult. It is not unusual in traditional Aboriginal culture for there to be little fuss made of extra-marital affairs. It was common, for example, for a man to lend his wife to other men as a sign of courtesy. And as you say, there was little fuss made if there were temporary sexual relationships with people other than the spouse. We mustn't think of traditional Aboriginal marriages as being, in this respect, in any way governed by the same moral imperatives of white western society.'

Out of politeness both Harrigan and Nick tried to look grateful for the direction. In truth, assessing behaviour against moral imperatives wasn't a particularly time-consuming preoccupation among prosecutors. Welkin went on.

'Now in this case it's my guess that the woman, Sally, may have been promised from birth to this man. A newborn girl may be promised in marriage to the mother's grandmother's brother's son or one of them if there is more than one. If that was the case, Jackie Marikit would have married this girl when she reached puberty. Apparently she is now thirty years old or thereabouts. He was seventy or so. This would make him about forty years old at the

79

time of her birth. Fifty something when she reached puberty and he married her. I would say that a fifty-year-old *mabanba* would certainly have had other wives. Now, your question. Would a seventy-year-old *mabanba* with other wives be so jealous of a sexual liaison of his wife with another man that he would order a *wanmala*?'

Welkin sighed and thought with pursed lips for some time, as if the question had emanated from someone other than himself. Eventually he found an answer.

'I doubt it. He's an old man. Sometimes you might expect, despite customary acceptance of extra-marital affairs, that personal feelings become involved and there may be trouble if either of the married partners feel jealousy when there is someone else attracting the other partner's affection. But you would expect a jealous response more typically from someone younger than Jackie Marikit. Different, of course, if there was any suggestion that Sally had eloped with another or intended to. If that were the case then there would be sufficient insult for a *wanmala* to be ordered. That situation is not uncommon and both the eloping male and female have been slaughtered by *wanmala* parties. But barring that situation, it would be my guess that Jackie Marikit may have had some undisclosed reason for ordering Mr Bora's death. Doesn't make any difference, of course, to the power of the command to carry out the sentence of death. The young man, this Billy, has, I understand, spent most of his young life raised according to the dictates of traditional custom and ritual. He would have had no choice but to do as Jackie ordered. In fact, successful completion of the order would have been a source of great kudos for him.'

'He's still guilty of murder,' said Harrigan.

'Not for me to say I'm afraid,' said Welkin. 'I can appreciate however, that it poses a very difficult question.

80

What Billy did was certainly not illegal in traditional Aboriginal culture. It may have provoked retaliation of some type from Johnny's relatives, but it wasn't illegal in the sense that we understand that term.'

Nick wondered. Obedience to traditional law was not of itself a specific defence. It was something that could be raised in mitigation during sentencing. But *duress was a defence*. For anybody. It depended on the young man's state of mind. Was Jackie's influence so powerful that Billy's will was overborne by it? This was possible. Somehow he doubted that Johnny himself would have been looking at the young man as the culpable one in all of this.

They thanked Welkin and the little man left.

Nick returned to his office wondering for a while about Jackie Marikit's possible motives. Eventually he shook his head and tried once again to focus on the amphetamines brief, reading again Detective Constable Kyrios' earnest account of how the apprehended fets dealer had insisted on head-butting the window in the police vehicle several times. It was this self-abuse, Constable Kyrios pointed out in his statement, which accounted for the head injuries the fets dealer sustained during the arrest. The allegation by the dealer that the injuries had been caused by Constable Kyrios' size twelves was just not true. Nick shook his head and smiled. Was he supposed to believe that? Would the jury believe it?

The receptionist buzzed him. Ruth Bora was on the phone. She sounded tired. Geoffrey Rafferty, a Perth solicitor from a firm called Rafferty and Thompson, who'd briefed Johnny on his latest Aboriginal land claim matter, had called her she said. He'd put it off for some time because he knew she'd be grieving. But he was wondering if she wouldn't mind checking Johnny's papers to see if he'd finished an opinion he'd been working on at the time of his death. It was a matter of urgent interest to his clients who wanted to know whether or not to proceed with the claim. Ruth now had Johnny's computer at home. She had no idea how to access anything on it. Maybe Nick could help. He agreed to come.

8

*T*he cab, a decrepit Holden ute, dropped McAngel at the gate about twenty kilometres out of town. There was a red dirt path which led to a tin-roofed weatherboard baking in the heat about two hundred metres away. McAngel hoisted the beer on his shoulder and made his way toward the shack.

He was fifty metres down the track when he heard the crack and felt the box on his shoulder explode into foam. He stood motionless. One of the two was showing off. Probably Gunner who had the keener eye on the pool table. There was silence. He stood for what appeared to him to be a long time feeling the intensity of the heat about him, smelling the beer on his clothing begin to dry. Then he bent over and examined the beer carton. Two six-packs remained intact. He picked them up, held them up high then moved on.

There was another crack and dirt kicked up about five metres in front of him. It was good shooting. If they'd wanted to hit him he'd be dead by now. It was a game. He hoped. Two further cracks in quick succession brought branches down from nuggety eucalypts on either side of the path he was following. By now he was fifty metres from the door. He sighted the rifle barrel and the telescopic sights jutting out of one of the windows. He held the beer up again. Then from his pocket he pulled out a wad of twenty dollar notes which he waved above his head.

Silence again, then Gunner came to the front door.

'You're game,' he called to McAngel.

'A beer, a talk and an opportunity for you and your friend to make a few dollars,' McAngel called back.

He saw Tub fill the door space next to Gunner. Gunner motioned him to come on.

Inside the hut it stunk. There was the rancid smell of sweat from the two men. But then there was also the stench of shit from the dunny out the back which mingled with the smell of festering garbage and stale beer somewhere near the sink. Flies were circling over and settling on an old table sprinkled with crumbs and spilt sugar and breakfast cereal. In a corner a pile of beer cartons spilled over with empty beer cans and bottles and some chop bones. Through the open back door McAngel caught sight of the front end of an old Toyota four-wheel drive. A couple of rifles with telescopic sights were resting barrel-up against it.

Gunner kept the rifle in his hand and used his foot to push a chair over to McAngel. Tub took the six-packs off McAngel who noticed that several of Tub's fingers on both hands were still blue and swollen. He kept his eyes on McAngel as he gingerly peeled off the plastic packing and distributed a beer each to McAngel and Gunner. McAngel sensed Tub's caution.

McAngel showed them the photo he'd shown to Hairy Harry back at The Iron Horse. When he saw that they recognised the face McAngel felt the quickening of his heartbeat. He restrained himself from his impulse to beat out of them what he wanted to know. It would be so easy. Gunner had the rifle on his lap. He could have his fingers in his eyes before he had any chance of getting the rifle above table height. Tub with his dirty singlet, big gut and fat arms, several days stubble on his double chin, puffed eyes, living on a local reputation as a tough guy, would go down easily. Attack his kidneys and balls. But no. Let them think they were in control. He'd already whet their appetites for the money he'd shown them. If they went for the cash there'd be less trouble in the long run.

'Well?' he said.

'What if we do know him? What's it to do with you? Who the fuck are you anyway?' said Tub.

McAngel stared at him hard before chucking the money onto the table.

'Some or all of that is yours depending on what you can tell me.'

Gunner took the wad and counted it out.

'Three hundred. Got any more?'

'Not so far,' said McAngel.

Gunner lifted the rifle.

'Of course we could just take it all off you and not tell you nothin', couldn't we?'

Tub reached over and pushed the rifle back into Gunner's lap. He was older than Gunner and a little bit smarter. He knew better. He took a pull from the stubbie of Swan, looked at the money on the table and then at McAngel before deciding to talk.

'The bloke in the photograph called himself Keppler. He spoke funny, with a bit of an accent. Not that he spoke much. There were three others with him. Bloke in his forties. Tall, arrogant bastard he was. Gave the other two orders to do this and that. *Phone George*, he'd say and then get up them if George wasn't there for some reason. Or *Go and fax Melbourne and tell them to do this and that*, he'd say to one of them. And then he'd abuse the shit out of them if they didn't do it right. You could tell he was their boss and they had to kiss his arse all day long. They just called him Sir or Mr Arkett or something like that. They were called Gregory and Applecart. They were a couple of poofs we reckoned, didn't we Gunner?'

'Fuckin' doughnut punchers for sure mate,' Gunner agreed.

'What about Keppler?' McAngel asked. 'Was he taking orders from this Arkett?'

Tub shook his head.

'No way mate. I tell you what, this bloke was fuckin' scary. He dressed up every day. Suit and tie somedays. Sunglasses. Carried around this mouth spray and gave himself a squirt every now and then. Hardly said nothin'. But in control. All the time. This Arkett would bark and shout at the two horses' hoofs but then he'd be super polite with Keppler. One day we went over to the motel where they were stayin' to pick them up and this Keppler was out on the lawn in his pyjama pants and no top on doin' these exercises, like karate or something like that, only slower, and Gunner here said, *C'mon let's go mate, we haven't got all day*, and he just ignored Gunner, like he was concentratin' so hard on what he was doin'. Anyway, Gunner was a bit impatient to get away and so he went over and tapped him on the shoulder. Next minute he had Gunner on his back on the lawn with one hand around his throat and the other pulled back in a fist like he was gunna drive it through his head. Not angry, like out of control or anything, but just like really cold. He sort of realised it was only Gunner and went off to his room without sayin' anything and then came straight out ready to go. Head case if you ask me.'

'So what did they hire you for?'

'They wanted to have a look around the area, do a bit

of shooting, see some of the local abo settlements, get a taste of life up here I suppose. We never approached them or anything. They just asked around at the motel for someone who knew the country to drive them around and show them the sights. That was another thing about Keppler. When we got the rifles out to have a go at a roo or a pig or a buffalo or something he usually didn't bother. The others would have a shot and were pretty hopeless. One day we saw these roos over a hundred yards away moving real fast—a bit of a challenge for Gunner here. He shoots at them and manages to drop one. Next minute—bang, bang, bang—three more drop down. I looks around and here's bloody Keppler with a gun. No trouble for him at all. Gave Gunner the shits too, didn't it? You was bloody jealous as hell, you were.'

Tub gave a pleghmy laugh.

'You say you took them to see Aborigines?' McAngel asked.

'Yeah. This Arkett bloke was real interested he said. He told us he wanted to see the Wonyulgunna people for some reason so two times we took them over there. Although, it was funny. This Arkett guy never came with us, it was just Keppler and the two poofs.'

'Keppler was with you?' McAngel asked.

'Yeah, he came along. Although you couldn't really say he seemed to enjoy it much. You know, we introduced them to a couple of the abos we knew there, like old Mamarika and Jackie Marikit. Like, the other two at least shook their hands but Keppler wouldn't touch them. He didn't like abos that's for sure. He had this expression on his face—hard to describe—but like he just trod in a dog turd or somethin'. I dunno what they talked about. I was looking to ask Sally but she was off somewhere out of the area with that abo barrister like she mostly was in those times.'

'Sally?' McAngel enquired.

'How we doin' with the bank roll there,' Gunner nodded to the money.

'You've earned a good bit of it so far. What about Sally?'

Gunner took over.

'Sally's well-known around here. She speaks about five of the abo languages around these areas plus English. Really good lookin' abo, Sally. Old Tub tried to knock her off one night and Bill Porter chucked him in the lock up. Told him he was lucky she was a coon or he'd have charged him with attempted rape.'

Gunner thought this was funny.

'Is Sally about these days?' McAngel asked him.

'Should be. You heard about all the fuss I suppose?'

McAngel shook his head.

'About the abo from the Wonyulgunna that was supposed to have murdered the lawyer in Canberra. The one I just told you about who was knockin' off Sally when he was up here. Young abo—Billy Jangala did it. Cops from Canberra picked him up a few days ago.'

'What?'

McAngel had heard nothing about this. He'd been in bed with Julie. He hadn't expected events to have moved so fast. He'd intended to ask around, take his time. He thought at best it was a long shot coming up here anyway. This was too much too soon.

Tub and Gunner had seen his reaction and were looking at one another. Gunner showed some mossy teeth.

'Got any more of that stuff?'

He was nodding at the wad of money.

Nick hadn't seen Ruth for a couple of weeks. She had always been an elegant woman who'd watched her figure and kept an eye on the fashion pages. Now that she'd lost weight she didn't look well. Her eyes were puffy. She wore a cardigan which was too big for her. She fumbled nervously for cigarettes. She frequently checked the baby who lay asleep in the nearby bassinet.

They had some coffee and made some small talk about Nick's work, his kids, their holiday. Then she began to cry. Nick sat silently for a while before passing her some tissues. It was awkward and he knew what was coming.

'I thought with this baby there'd be no other women Nick. It was our last chance. Earlier on he'd always wanted a child. I thought the baby would help us stay together.'

Nick didn't reply. The baby hadn't been Johnny's idea. Before she'd become pregnant Johnny had been planning to leave his wife. There had been periods of separation and infidelities, his transitory, hers a more lasting relationship with another lawyer from Johnny's chambers. Then a reconciliation and the baby, Ruth's act of desperation. Johnny had been hurt. He'd grown up without his real father, with an insecure and fretful adoptive mother. He was not going to abandon his child to the same fate. But he didn't love his wife and he'd told Nick that he felt manipulated.

'There have been others since haven't there? Since this Aboriginal woman I mean. There have, haven't there?'

'I don't know,' he lied.

It was a weak lie and they both knew it. Nick thought of the time not too long ago he and Johnny had been having a drink after work in a bar in Civic. They'd stayed on till late and a couple of women joined them at their table. One of them, a dark-haired woman called Anita, had large and lively breasts and smooth nyloned thighs which showed when her mini rode up as she sat down and crossed her legs. Nick had had too much to drink and when she smiled at him and brushed her knees against his under the table he encouraged her by pressing back. At some point, Johnny said goodnight, and disappeared out the door with the other woman, an attractive legal secretary from a firm which occasionally briefed him.

Left alone with Anita, a half finished beer, an overflowing ash tray and a bar deserted by everyone except themselves and the bar tender, Nick suddenly could think only of Louisa and his kids and he stumbled out of the bar alone, embarrassed by the suddenness of his departure and the humiliation he saw in the eyes of the woman he left behind at the table.

Now he felt irritation along with the other discomforts of Ruth's presence. He remembered when Ruth and Johnny had first got together. It was not long after Johnny had gone to the bar in Canberra. His application to join the chambers upstairs had been accompanied by a polite letter explaining how he already had several Aboriginal land claims in the pipeline waiting to be fought out in the courts and about to be pressed by clients who would not hear of any other individual representing them. In the same letter he then canvassed the dollar benefits likely to be shared by other barristers in the chambers through spin-off work for a whole new client base, that is, Aborigines, created by his presence. For good measure he indicated that if he missed out on a room in these chambers he intended to pursue the matter in the national press as an example of open discrimination against Aborigines in the profession.

Johnny was given a room. Shortly after, Nick and Johnny met and became good friends. As Johnny went on to develop a reputation as a fine barrister, the local social set latched onto him. He became a minor celebrity in the city. He was an ex-professional footballer and a former prominent Aboriginal student activist whose name people remembered. He became the slightly risqué invitee to parties held by Canberra matrons with powerful husbands in the public service or in politics.

Ruth was the daughter of a former Canberra department head later kicked upstairs to diplomatic postings when the government changed. She'd seen herself as a radical when an arts student and had supported Aboriginal land rights. She had a quick and unsuccessful marriage to a local obstetrician before she met Johnny at one of these parties and they began seeing one another.

Nick met her on occasions and realised that she enjoyed the notoriety and the gossip her relationship with Johnny created. Much later in an intimate conversation, when Johnny was starting to have his doubts about the marriage, he told Nick that there was a particular time early in his relationship with Ruth when he suddenly realised that there was an expectation that he'd be attending parties and functions with Ruth by his side. Then suddenly there was the expectation that he was going to marry her. He was swept along by this. He was meeting important people all the time. His career at the bar was prospering. He was now appearing in general commercial litigation matters as well as Aboriginal land claims and was being described as brilliant in some circles.

Ruth was gregarious and charming and she complemented Johnny's witty self-confidence. Johnny made speeches about land rights to lawyers and he wrote articles for law journals about land rights and he spoke eloquently to law society conferences about the problems with Aborigines and the criminal law. He married Ruth on a windy day in spring. Ruth looked after the invitations. Apart from a handful of Johnny's closest friends, the guests were all white.

One day, some time later, Johnny visited the Aboriginal

Tent Embassy. Nick had gone with him. Johnny had an old friend who spent a lot of time there, James Waddy, the Aboriginal activist and poet. He hadn't seen him for about a year. James made them welcome with a cup of sweet tea. Johnny hadn't looked so happy in a long time. They talked mainly football and the name of Ernie Barnes came up. James told them Ernie had been killed in a bar room brawl in Tennant Creek some months ago. Johnny looked stunned.

'Thought you knew,' said James.

'Someone could have bloody told me,' Johnny complained.

He looked hurt and bewildered.

James remained calm.

'None of these people round here want to bother you Johnny. You're an important blackfella now,' he said.

The reproach was gentle but Nick could see Johnny's eyes blaze then water. James pushed on.

'Papers say you're a respected Aboriginal spokeman Johnny.'

James was calm but the look in his eyes was something powerful, demanding, and he stared back at Johnny unwaveringly for a long time. Then he said, 'Who respects you Johnny and why?'

James Waddy had been probing for Johnny's soul. He found it at that moment and pulled it shuddering and fearful into the tent at the Aboriginal Embassy where they sat at a rude wooden table on a dirt floor.

Johnny's head had dropped and he was crying.

'Johnny,' James had said and touched him lightly on the hand. 'Find out who you are. Forget the rest of the stuff for now. Find out who you are, then come back to us.'

And he did. Johnny disappeared for nine months. He used his legal skills to get access to bureaucratic and hospital records. When he came back he told Nick that he had found his real mother. In a grave at Grafton. He had some brothers and sisters spread along the north coast. They had told him about his mother. How nearly every day she'd talked about the baby boy the authorities had taken from her shortly after his birth at Ballina hospital when she was fifteen. How each of her next four children had been born out of hospital, in the bush or at a home, delivered by an Aboriginal midwife, for fear that the same thing would happen again. One of his brothers, Thomas, gave him a letter that she'd written some weeks before the cancer claimed her life.

My dear son who was taken from me,

Forgive me for the pain that I know this letter will cause you when it finds you. You may think that I never knew you. But I did. I looked into your eyes the day you were born. And when they told me you were gone your eyes were all I had left. So I stored them in my heart and every day since, I have seen your eyes again and again. And because of that I do know you. Each day as I looked into your eyes I learned something new about you and I know that you are now a fine and kind man. But I also know from your eyes that you hurt. You hurt for me, for yourself and for your people. And I can only cry for you from a distance. And love you, also from a distance. They took you from me my sweet boy but your eyes are in my heart and stay with me forever more. Continue to be brave my sweet.

Mum

He showed Nick the letter one day. He'd shown it no-one else since returning from Grafton. His trust was a privilege Nick cherished.

Ruth was now wiping at her eyes.

'He didn't love me. Not any more.'

She stared at Nick.

'You don't like me much either, do you Nick?'

It was true. He didn't.

'You'd better show me Johnny's computer, Ruth,' was all he said.

She led him to Johnny's study. The room showed little sign of use. There was a big Aboriginal flag on the wall, a few framed photographs of football teams, and some pennants and trophies. Nick had seen them all before, a long time ago. He knew that it was a room which had been used less and less by Johnny who had preferred to work from the office, away from home and away from Ruth.

As if to emphasise the point there was a calendar on the wall stuck at August of the previous year. It was one of those theme calendars with each month illustrated by a photographic print of an Aboriginal painting. August was illustrated with a print of a painting by Albert Nagonara called *Sacred Rocks and Caves in Artist's Father's Country*. Johnny's writing was on it. Ruth noticed Nick looking at it and read his mind.

'Time stops and no-one notices,' she said.

She took the calendar down and dropped it into a wastepaper basket.

Nick spotted Johnny's laptop IBM compatible on the desk. He knew his way around the software packages Johnny used so he turned on the computer and searched all the most recent files. There was a directory called Claims. It contained two sub-directories, one called Gove and one called Cape York. They were opinions on the viability of land claims in those areas. But neither was Rafferty's matter. He searched back through the older files. Again nothing. It was strange. Johnny did all his work on this computer. There were opinions, notes for trials and hearing matters, notes on important cases he needed for court. All these were clearly identified at the beginning of the file along with the name of instructing solicitors. Rafferty's did not appear. Nick was about to abandon the search when he recalled the hidden files facility. When you wanted to protect information from snooping it was possible to hide a file name. Its existence was known only to its author. Retrieving the file was a relatively simple matter if you knew how. He punched in the command to show hidden files and a previously hidden sub-directory popped into the screen under the Claims directory. It was called Pilbara. Johnny clicked it open and read. The name Rafferty and Thompson, Rafferty's firm, appeared as the instructing solicitor. Bingo. Nick shut the laptop. He'd take it with him, make a copy of the contents onto a floppy disc, print it out and send it off to Rafferty. Save Ruth any more bother.

Ruth had gone downstairs. On his way out when he explained his intentions, she didn't look very grateful, standing there with a cigarette in one hand and a drink in the other, a gaunt, dark eyed and very sad woman. Nick knew he should have felt some sympathy for her. He paused for a moment before going out the door, searching for something to say. There was nothing. She didn't say goodbye as he left.

McAngel threw the last of his belongings into the soft leather suitcase and zipped it up. Outside, night was falling. It was still hot but the fire of the day was now defeated and the air was velvety. He had an hour before his flight back to Perth, then onto Canberra. He sat on the bed with his back straight, his hands on his knees and his eyes closed. He began breathing slowly and deeply, expending all his breath as he did so and began to mentally repeat his mantra—*maranatha, maranatha, maranatha.*

Relaxation would come soon, his mind would still, grow blank, sweet nothingness. In the meantime he allowed his thoughts to play with the puzzle for a while. Keppler in Mt White, Aboriginal barrister in Canberra murdered by an Aborigine from the Mt White area. Barrister's background? It fitted. History of activism, land rights, respected in the Aboriginal and white communities, leadership, skilful advocate, popular, worked against the miners. Keppler. Where was he now?

In the room next door, occupied by a fat insurance salesman who'd tried to talk to him at the bar earlier, the television was on. McAngel could hear it. He concentrated on his mantra—*maranatha, maranatha, maranatha*. And then he couldn't but help hear the words—*Police in the nation's capital are tonight pondering possible motives for the killing of twenty-seven year-old Stella Sanchez and her boyfriend Alfred Petrillo in an effort to find some lead on the murder of the young couple.*

McAngel burst into the room and ignored the fat salesman's indignant objection. He saw the tail end of the story. A shot of Maggie Spires in sunglasses exiting from the Canberra police station flanked by what appeared to be two plain clothes detectives. *A woman who shared the house with Stella Sanchez is believed to be assisting police with their enquiries*, the voice-over said.

The fat salesman was on his feet saying something to McAngel. McAngel was looking at him but heard nothing except the name Stella Sanchez. Abruptly, he wheeled and returned to his own room.

He sat down on the bed once again, closed his eyes and concentrated—*maranatha, maranatha, maranatha, maranatha*. Keppler, Johnny Bora, Billy Jangala, Stella Sanchez and poor Alfie, Maggie. Put them aside for now. *Maranatha*. Empty the mind. *Maranatha*. Total annihilation of thought and feeling. *Maranatha*. The tightness in his chest began to dissolve. *Maranatha*. The rapid ascent to panic began to slow and then recede. *Maranatha*. The mind began to empty. *Maranatha*. It would be okay. *Maranatha*.

9

Nick was in his office. He loaded his work computer with the floppy on which he'd copied Johnny's opinion for Rafferty. Bit of a cheek about Rafferty he thought to himself. After all, one of the people Johnny was out to help with this opinion had killed him. Still, the rest of the clan weren't responsible for Johnny's murder. At least someone might benefit in the end from Johnny's work if it meant passing it on to another barrister.

Just as he pressed the print command the receptionist buzzed him. It was Rafferty on the other end, calling from Perth. Rafferty introduced himself and then after some phony sounding pleasantries came to the point of his call.

'Mrs Bora tells me you've managed to retrieve the opinion the late Mr Bora completed for us. As solicitors for the Wonyulgunna we'd certainly appreciate receiving the opinion as soon as possible. Naturally we would pay Mr Bora's fee into his estate.'

'You've been billed?' Nick asked. He may as well tie up all the loose ends for Ruth. A forty-page opinion from a barrister of Johnny's standing was worth a lot of money.

'Actually, no,' replied Rafferty. 'I was intending to proceed on the basis of the typical fee for an opinion of this type from Mr Bora. You know. Get the matter disposed of quickly.'

Nick was about to agree when he had an idea. Johnny had been using the same word processing program as he used himself. For each document created there was a summary facility which provided certain statistics including the word total of the document and the total amount of time spent working on it.

He explained this to Rafferty and asked him to hold while he checked the summary information. It would help Rafferty estimate the bill. Nick called up the information on the computer and began to jot it down. The total time spent editing the document was 2030 minutes. It consisted of 18,468 words, had first been opened on the August 3 at 11.30 am and had last been saved on the 23 December at ... 10.15 pm! Nick dropped the phone. The realisation of what he had just read had hit him like a punch to his stomach. He re-read the screen over and over. In the background he could hear Rafferty asking for him—'Mr Milano, Mr Milano ... '

It was late afternoon, warm, the lake as still as the National Gallery and the High Court building that sat on its edges. Some cyclists enjoying the late afternoon sunshine rode by on the stone path as they walked. She talked.

The house she'd shared with Stella was empty. Cops were still all over the place. She hadn't even returned to get her things. Couldn't bear to. She was living with a workmate's family. She was still shaken up, couldn't sleep, had nightmares. Time and time again she re-lived the moment she'd arrived home and discovered first the trail of blood from the kitchen to Stella's room and then their bodies. Alfie crumpled in a corner, the top half of his head blown away, and poor Stella on the bed, a twist of pain in her small, naked, damaged body as it lay on the sheet. Frozen into her face was a look of bewilderment as if in her last moments she had been appalled so far beyond pain and horror that normal human comprehension ceased to exist.

McAngel picked up a rock and sent it skipping across the water. Now was not the time to tell her why Stella Sanchez and her boyfriend were murdered. Right now was not the time to do anything impulsively. Right now he had to treat everyone with caution, even Maggie.

He let her talk.

She told him how she'd agreed to go on the date with the lieutenant the night of the murder. An old boyfriend from the Defence Academy. It had been an impulsive thing. McAngel had gone off on business suddenly when she'd expected him to stay longer. After all, there were no commitments on either side. Yes, she understood that. And yes, McAngel's sudden change of plans had irritated her. So she went out with the lieutenant. It was an old relationship. She'd told Stella and Alfie that she wouldn't be home till late. Give them a chance to be together for the night alone. The lieutenant was in a romantic mood. Maggie, it turned out, wasn't. They fought. She came home and found the bodies.

On the grassy hill at Regatta Point some kids were flying kites. Maggie and McAngel stopped and looked skyward in silence. A white cockatoo, flapping past, filled the sky with garrulous complaint. Maggie was reminded of the morning out in the open, by the lake, when they'd made love. She remembered the scar below McAngel's collarbone. Who was he?

Carefully, with an expression which was at once curious

and tender, but distant, like she was in an abstracted state and barely conscious of what she was doing, she now took McAngel's face into her hands, peering into his eyes.

The familiarity of the gesture unsettled McAngel. He resisted the temptation to recoil but he knew his eyes had given him away.

'Who are you McAngel?' she asked him, in a perplexed way, as if the answer to that question would explain everything.

Maggie waited. McAngel wasn't moving, but she had the sensation that he was withdrawing, distancing himself. Protecting himself. Who was he? Still holding his face, she drew her own towards it and clamped her mouth on his. McAngel stiffened and resisted momentarily, then let himself go, absorbed by the warmth and softness and security of her femininity. But then he stopped her.

This was not what he wanted. This was a dangerous time. What did she want from him? He couldn't give her the reassurance she was after. Violence and unpredictability were the way of the world. It wasn't something he could do anything about. She needed to learn for herself what he had learned through raw experience. That in the end it was best to take the most that was on offer. A couple of nights with Julie Brownlow, or someone else, where leaving in the morning was easy.

He saw anger and confusion on her face. She was affronted. He searched for something to say, his mind processing, and as quickly dismissing, a series of inadequate banalities. He needn't have bothered.

'Get stuffed McAngel,' she said, suddenly, as if she'd been reading his thoughts. And she wheeled and walked rapidly away from him.

McAngel waited for a while, resigned to watching her walk out of sight, forever. Then he heard himself call out.

'Maggie. Let's try again.'

101

She didn't stop. He ran after her, grabbed her arm and turned her around. He thought she might have been crying. She wasn't. She was defiantly calm. No trace of the vulnerability she'd exposed back on the hill when she kissed him. Instead, there was a fierce dignity in the way she met his eyes with a cool stare, her chin tilted upward, her shoulders drawn back a little as if to make herself seem taller. There would be no second humiliation.

'I just want to know who you are McAngel,' she said, as if he'd misunderstood everything.

His hands dropped away from her and for a time they stood looking at one another, she silently insistent, while McAngel wondered how much he could tell her.

Nick's office wasn't big so there was no choice but to endure the proximity of Stratton and Lardner who'd come over to look at Nick's computer screen. For the time being hostilities were suspended.

'Last saved 23 December 10.15 pm,' Lardner read aloud.

'I was in Johnny's office just after 10.30 pm,' said Nick. 'Johnny had been dead for an hour by then according to the lab. Someone else was into his computer at 10.15 p.m.'

'Hardly could have been Billy Jangala,' said Stratton. 'According to his confession he was well out of the place by then. We confirmed that with the bus people. He was on the ten o'clock bus to Adelaide. Shit, Billy wouldn't know anything about computers anyway.'

He looked at Nick with some doubt.

'I suppose you've checked to see that the computer clock's not an hour fast?'

Nick flipped open Johnny's laptop and punched a command into it. A digital clock and date appeared on the screen. It was the right time and the right date. He'd already rung and quizzed Ruth about it. She'd been there the day it had been delivered along with the rest of Johnny's belongings from his office. She'd put it in his study and forgotten about it until Rafferty's request. The computer's long-life battery had kept the clock and date running. Nick was convinced that someone other than Billy Jangala had visited Johnny's office that night and had done so after Johnny was dead. Not only that. Whoever it was had known how to search for hidden files, had opened the Rafferty file, had possibly done something to the text and then saved it.

'Problem is, what, if anything, has been done to the text?' said Nick. 'I've read through it and there are no gaps and nothing that smacks of a later insertion. In fact, there's nothing at all that affects the integrity of the argument.'

'Shit!'

It was Lardner, irritated.

'We've got the murderer in the cells at the remand centre. Confession, prints, corroboration. No suggestion from anyone that another party was involved in the murder. Case is dead, finished. There's got to be another explanation for this. Something technical, surely?'

Nick looked at Stratton who was rubbing at some late afternoon stubble on his chin. He'd expected Stratton to react in the same way as Lardner. Case was solved. Why speculate about other possibilities? But Stratton was troubled. Maybe this wasn't the first doubt he had about the case.

Nick put it to him bluntly.

'You know that Billy Jangala isn't the full story here, don't you Stratton? What about the door? Who locked it after Billy planted the club?'

Stratton just looked at him, a little vacantly. Then he

became brusque, putting his relationship with Nick back where it belonged.

'There's nothing I can do about this now, Milano. I've got Johnny Bora's murderer locked up awaiting sentence. I've got the Stella and Alfie double to work on.'

Stratton reached for his coat and Lardner stood up.

'You know where I am if any explanation occurs to you,' he said shortly on his way out.

Nick looked at the screen again, chewed at by doubt. He ran some possible reasons through his mind but nothing made sense. It was time to go home. He reached for his coat and put it on. Before turning off his own computer he slipped a floppy disk into the A drive and saved a document he'd been working on for the fets dealer's trial. He slipped the floppy into his suit pocket.

It was only when he reached the elevator that the thought occurred to him. It was worth trying. Johnny had been wearing a dark blue suit when he found him. The shoulders and back had been covered in Johnny's blood. Maybe he had backed up the Rafferty opinion. Maybe the disc had been in the suit pocket. If it was, then whatever Johnny saved on the floppy could be compared to what was left on the hard disk.

He ran back into his office and called Fred Arthurton. He was still at the lab. Nick told him he wanted a favour. Fred had been on his way out the door.

'Nick, my friend, look at your watch. What does it say?'

'I know it's after five thirty, Fred. You're not going to turn into a pumpkin if you spend an extra five minutes there.'

'Okay Nick. A lesser man than me would insist that you ring back tomorrow you know. Lucky for you I have a selfless devotion to duty that makes it impossible for me to tell you to piss off.'

'This is serious Fred. Do you have a list of what was

found on Johnny when they took his body in?'

'I do indeed old son. Just a second.'

Nick rapped out a rhythm on his desk with his fingertips while he waited. Then Fred was back on.

'Right. Johnny Bora. Items found on or in clothing. One wallet containing three hundred and fifty-five dollars in notes, various cards, etc.—stop me when you get interested Nick—one handkerchief, one set of car keys and house keys on the same ring, one small diary, a fountain pen, a computer disk, fifty-five cents ... '

Nick stopped him.

'The computer disk Fred. Where is it?'

'Should be back with Johnny's wife, Nick—with all the other things we returned to her.'

Fred heard the click of the phone and Nick was gone.

McAngel's hotel room was downmarket. Clean but simple, and small. He'd booked in earlier in the day, after he'd taken a cab past Maggie's house. It was still surrounded by police cordons. The hire-car he'd driven from Sydney was in the driveway. The cops would be interested in talking to him. He knew that. But he wasn't ready.

McAngel had agreed to tell Maggie more about himself and she, though disconsolate and somewhat wary, had returned to his hotel room. Now, as they drank some coffee, they avoided talking about McAngel, or about Stella and Alfie. Instead they made desultory attempts to chat. The conversation turned to their time together in Sydney when they'd first met. Tentatively, they reminisced, reminding each other about restaurants where they'd dined, brief acquaintances they'd met, music they listened to, films they'd seen. Each seemed to be hoping to find something recognisable, something capable of reviving the pleasures of that time. The hand-in-hand walks in parks and on beaches. The long afternoons and nights spent naked and sweaty in each other's embrace. But it became an uncertain search, like feeling around in a dark room for something they had both valued, but never bothered to look at in the light. The conversation laboured again. She was raw, touchy, occasionally teary as she thought of Stella. She still felt violence and death as if they were on her skin. Something that wouldn't wash away. McAngel was preoccupied, tense. A man on the edge of action. And for a while and for all these reasons, the mechanism of their previous attraction didn't work.

But then Maggie, after one of the many long pauses, had gone to the bathroom and then emerged naked, her golden hair loose and brushing her shoulders. She stopped, still sad faced, and let him look at her.

'I need to stop my mind dwelling on it, McAngel. If only for a while. I want to make love.'

With his eyes McAngel slowly took in her body. The elegant neck, the breasts gently rising, the long slow curve of her hips, legs of alabaster, long and unflawed, the heavenly opening just visible below the light pubic hair.

She moved toward him and she allowed him to take her down onto the bed with him. After a while, when they could wait no longer, he entered her and they both groaned with relief as well as pleasure and then continued to make love slowly, for a long time, until they were both finally spent.

'So McAngel,' she said after they'd lain together a while. 'You're not a writer are you? I mean even if you are, it's not what you've been doing here is it?'

McAngel sat up and began to dress.

'Sure. You're right,' he replied, not looking at her. 'I'm not here to write for any magazine. I'm here for reasons you may not want to know.'

Maggie regarded him suspiciously. She didn't like the

way he seemed to be preparing a sidestep.

'Don't be coy on my account McAngel,' she said.

There was something of a warning in her voice. McAngel hesitated, still indecisive.

'Let's go for a walk,' he said. 'Some of it I can tell you.'

'Some of it?' she objected, eyebrows arched. 'Why not tell me right here?'

'Most of it I can tell you,' he offered. 'But not here. I feel like I need to be out in the open.'

Maggie cocked her head sceptically.

'Please.' He smiled encouragingly. He knew he couldn't talk to her here. There were things he wanted to tell her and other things he needed to keep to himself. He wanted to remove himself from the intimacy they had just shared. It clouded his judgment.

'Please,' he repeated, when she didn't move.

Maggie shook her head in quiet exasperation and began dressing.

10

Nick Milano pulled into Ruth's drive. He'd rung and told her briefly that he needed to look at the disk that had been delivered to her along with the other stuff from the lab. She didn't specifically recall the disk but she remembered things arriving—Johnny's wallet, his pen and other items that had been in his pocket. At the time she'd still been too sensitive to deal with them. She'd placed them in a wardrobe somewhere. She'd look for them while Nick was getting there. Nick stopped her when she began to apologise for the coolness of their previous meeting. They'd both been in strange moods, he told her. It was to be expected.

He went to the front door and rang the bell. There was no answer. He rang again. Some house lights were on but there was no sound. It occurred to him that Ruth may have gone out briefly, but her Fiat was parked in the drive in front of his own car. He went to the back door. It was open but the screen door was locked. Again he listened carefully. No sound. He was about to leave when he heard the baby begin to cry. He was right outside his window. He waited. The baby continued to cry. Perhaps Ruth was in the toilet or bathroom. He'd return to the front and wait for her.

He found that the front door was now open but there was still no sign of Ruth. Perhaps she'd opened the door and gone to tend to the baby. He knocked tentatively at the open door and called out to Ruth. The baby was now screaming. He went in, calling Ruth's name as he did so.

Then there was a gun at his head. To the side near his right temple.

The realisation that he had a gun pointed at him and his totally involuntary reaction were virtually simultaneous. In a gesture which was purely reflex, and which, he later presumed, had caught the holder of the gun by surprise, Nick had jerked his head to the right and knocked the tip of the barrel sufficiently for the silenced bullet to miss his head and lodge into the brickwork behind him.

Fear did not paralyse Nick, instead it awakened in him every instinct for survival he possessed. Suddenly he knew he had hold of the man's gun hand with his own right hand and he forced it away from his body. The other hand was holding a plastic bag and he was trying to bring that elbow into Nick's face.

Their heads were now close. Instinctively Nick crashed his forehead into the other man's face. He heard the grunt and saw the blood from the nose. He clung to the gun hand and once again drove his forehead into the other man. This time he felt the strength of the other man slacken momentarily. Nick pushed hard with his body until he had him pinned against the wall. He had no doubt as to what he wanted to do next. He bent toward the gun hand and clamped into the thumb knuckle very hard with his teeth tasting the blood almost immediately and feeling first the gristle and then the bone in the joint give way. The man was screaming and writhing but Nick, who still

109

had his shoulder pinning him into the wall, clung to the hand with his teeth.

Inevitably the grip released and the gun fell to the ground. Then Nick felt the clubbing to the side of his head. The bloke had dropped the plastic bag and was now beating at Nick's head with his left fist, hard and accurately. The punches that found their mark crashed against Nick's face and stunned him. He had to let go with his teeth. As he did so the bloke gave a growl of relief and then managed to turn Nick around, wrapping his forearm around his throat. It was then that Nick realised the strength of the other man. He could not move and he could not breathe; he was sure he was going to die. The pressure did not abate. His head was going to explode. His arms flailed uselessly in front of him. Then he saw it. Directly above his head was the light fitting, a bulb encased in a tube of decorative glass suspended from the ceiling and within reach. Nick stretched and grasped the cord up above the tube and wrenched downward. It came away from the ceiling and Nick drove the lot into the top of the head behind him, feeling the pain as the splintering glass cut his hand. There was an aggrieved cry and the grip on his neck relaxed.

Nick fell to the ground, saw the gun, reached for it, gripped and rolled with it so that he had it pointed at the intruder. For the first time he got a good look a him. He saw a tall and wild eyed man, early thirties, broad in the shoulders. A blood-stained dark suit. Glass and blood in his blond hair, nursing his right hand with his left. He stood looking at Nick defiantly, but apprehensive. He expected to die.

Then, his face changed. Probably because it occurred to him that Nick was not going to kill him. It was a sneer, qualified by relief. He turned and ran out of the door leaving Nick collapsed on the floor. Only after several

110

seconds had passed did his mind begin to register the cries of Ruth's baby in the background and the pain he was feeling in his head. And Ruth, where was Ruth?

They sat at one of the Italian restaurant's outdoor tables in Garema Place. The air was redolent with a mix of coffee, good bread and pasta sauces. McAngel had ordered a short black and she a cappuccino.

It was a mild evening and there were a lot of people about. Maggie looked as if she belonged to this place, McAngel thought. Tastefully casual in her blue jeans and white blouse. Just a few bits of unostentatious but expensive jewellery. Mainly gold. Styled blonde hair. From a distance, there was nothing much to distinguish her from dozens of other attractive Canberra women. Women accustomed to the easy affluence of regular public service incomes. The sort of women in whom McAngel would have normally found a bland and sometimes offensive self-complacency. With Maggie, you could catch something different in those limpid green eyes. A searching intelligence and often a suggestion of secret ironic amusement. He found this sexy, and he liked how, behind it all, there was warmth and an ultimate kindness. Today he'd seen flashes of her anger. And a ferocious dignity. He wasn't quite sure, but he also suspected that she had courage. Real courage. She might need it.

Their drinks were soon delivered by a white-aproned waiter and Maggie sipped patiently at her cappuccino, not saying anything, giving him time. McAngel finally began.

'You follow world affairs?'

'My dear father's a diplomat, remember?'

McAngel recalled meeting her on the plane. How she'd intended to be in Washington for Christmas. With her family. She'd changed her plans. Never explained why.

111

'It's in your blood then? An interest in what's happening in the world?' he asked her.

'Not really,' she replied shortly.

She was about to elaborate, then appeared to stop herself.

'You were going to tell me about yourself,' she reminded him.

McAngel looked away. Nearby a guy was drawing Felix the Cat on the pavement in coloured chalk. His hat was upturned in front of him waiting for coins of appreciation.

'Political assassinations. The most recent you remember?' McAngel asked her.

'Political assassinations?' she repeated. McAngel turned back to her and nodded.

She looked at him dubiously but gave it some thought before replying.

'The guy in South Africa. Pre-independence. The black guy from the ANC. Communist. Chris Hani.'

'Gunned down in his driveway by pro-apartheid conservatives,' added McAngel. 'Immediate international outrage and growth in international sympathy for the ANC. All types of pressures to meet ANC demands and white government forced into concessions it could have otherwise withheld. Name me another. Any time, any place.'

Maggie made a quizzical gesture with her hands.

'I don't know. The Kennedys, Martin Luther King, Malcolm X. All from the history books I'm afraid. How am I doing?'

'Good. King's killing and that of Malcom X gives black America a couple of martyrs and lot of sympathy. Kennedy's killing, supposedly by a lunatic with no realistic motive of any importance, does nothing except create a saint. No great political ambitions are ostensibly furthered or stymied. Give me some more names.'

112

Maggie searched the air about her for inspiration. She found some.

'Let me see—in Italy, the Italian magistrate appointed to chase the mafia. Blown up.'

'Counterproductive. Brought immediate reaction, martyrdom and greater feeling against the mafia than ever before. Heard of Pope John Paul I?' McAngel was leaning forward.

'Of course I have! Died after a short term as Pope. I was only a kid but I'm aware of conspiracy theories about his death—the Bank of Rome and all that sort of stuff. What is this? "Mastermind"?'

'Assume that he was murdered. No responsibility claimed for his death, right? No Red Brigades or IRA or CIA or PLO. Nothing. Mystery. Yet word is that had he not died we're told he would have undertaken some of the most fundamental Church reforms since the whole thing started. Lots of vested interests at stake. But no-one claims responsibility. Some suspicions of foul play but unsubstantiated. His ideas die with him. His successor props up the status quo. Assume that he was killed to prevent the reforms and the killing has been very successful.'

'Okay,' she agreed. 'So most of these assassinations end up being counterproductive. What are you getting at?'

'Let's now try some less newsworthy demises. Simon Greatertree, Canadian, Cree Indian lawyer, activist, great popular following, had political aspirations. Heard of him?'

'A Canadian?'

Maggie gave it some thought then shook her head.

'Killed by a knife. In Montreal, two years ago. Mugging they said. Arnold Creevey, a fifty-eight-year-old park bench bum with hardly enough co-ordination or strength to lift the bottle to his lips confessed to the murder.

113

Greatertree was in his mid-thirties, an ex pro-footballer, tall and heavy and fit. He'd been stabbed from front on, neatly between the ribs. Police were sceptical. But Creevey showed the police the knife he supposedly used, and Greatertree's wallet. Police charged him. He pleaded guilty but died before he could be sentenced. Advanced cancer of the liver. The radiotherapy department at the Mater Hospital where he was going for treatment knew all about it. A week earlier he'd been told there wasn't long to go and to get his things in order. The day he died, his daughter, who was married and living in Toronto, received a cheque in the mail for twenty thousand dollars, signed by her father.'

'Lottery win?' Maggie asked, deadpan. Where was all this going?

McAngel ignored the interruption.

'With Greatertree dead, the political movement he represented ran out of steam. It was a movement that had successfully melded environmentalism and land rights for Indians as major policy platforms so it had attracted a lot of interest among young Canadians. Plenty of mining and business interests were nervous at the prospect of having a politically powerful conservationist lobby affecting their decisions. They weren't unhappy about his death.'

McAngel paused as the waiter approached. He ordered more coffee.

'Why are you telling me all this?' Maggie asked McAngel.

'Another one,' McAngel indicated with his index finger. 'There are others, but just one more to tell you about.'

'I'm still listening,' Maggie said.

'Mehmet Dincer, a young Turkish immigrant in Germany. His whole family—mother, father and four sisters—were burnt to death in their small unit. Neo-Nazis claimed responsibility.'

114

'I remember reading about it,' said Maggie helpfully.

'Yes. The arson made the international news,' McAngel went on. 'At the time Dincer was a nineteen-year-old night shift worker in a spare parts factory in Munich. He was at work when it happened. The incident turned Dincer into a politician. Within twelve months he had organised the European Turk Association. Over the next few years it lobbied politicians, created support networks for Turkish immigrants in Germany, set up newspapers, bonded the Turkish community both in Germany and later in Europe generally. It also did something else. It set up its own version of the Israeli Wiesenthal Centre, simply called Ankara. Much cruder than Wiesenthal and without the same expertise of course, but for all that reasonably successful. Any atrocity against Turks by European Nazis was as far as possible investigated by Ankara and the evidence given to the police.

'They presented the police with evidence of dozens of crimes. But only three major prosecutions resulted. Verdicts of not guilty in all cases. After this some of the Ankara investigators took a detour to justice by summarily executing Nazis. When Ankara actually found the Nazis that torched Dincer's family Mehmet was contacted. When he arrived they gave him a gun, expecting that he would want to kill them himself. He got pissed off at this suggestion and insisted that Ankara turn them over to the State for prosecution. They agreed. But the arsonists got off. Eyewitnesses changed their stories at the hearings. Dincer, it was said, got very depressed about it. So depressed apparently that he went for a swim in the river at midnight in the middle of November and drowned. The authorities found it to be suicide or an accident. There was nothing suspicious, they said. The heroin they found in his veins was self-administered apparently.

'Turkish people who had known Dincer like a brother

can't seem to ever recall Mehmet having anything to do with drugs. The neo-Nazis consistently denied being involved with his death. Not surprising of course, except Ankara investigated his death for two years and actually believed them. Although they did not accept the suicide finding. The connections they found weren't with the Nazis but with the visit to a Salzburg address by a prominent German industrialist whose garment manufacturing factories were predominantly staffed by Turkish labour. You see, Dincer's major preoccupation at the time of his death wasn't the neo-Nazis but a proposed national strike by all Turkish labour in Germany in support of better wages and conditions. Who killed him? Ankara never found out exactly but they found out about the Salzburg Club.'

McAngel stopped abruptly. The fresh coffees had arrived. He looked faintly relieved. 'Well, there you have it.'

'Have what?' Maggie queried. Why had he suddenly ceased talking? 'This Salzburg Club. What is it?'

McAngel looked at her but didn't answer. Secretly he remonstrated with himself. He shouldn't have mentioned it.

'McAngel,' she called, as if trying to wake him up. 'The Salzburg Club. What is it?'

He was looking at her oddly; his conversation had involuntarily stalled. Maggie shook her head, irritated, frustrated with his sudden silence. She tried again, same destination, different number.

'Are you saying there's some connection between these people you told me about and you?'

McAngel was now looking about him in a manner just a trifle too methodical to be called nonchalant. It occurred to her that he wasn't quite as self-possessed a creature as she'd thought. It wasn't fear she sensed, but expectation, some nervousness, though well disguised, almost as if he were a competitor awaiting the beginning of some sporting contest and playing psychological games with the opposition.

Abruptly, he took her hand and held it tight and spoke as if he were intent on telling her something urgently that he may have no chance to tell her at a later time.

'What I'm about to tell you is the truth. It's not some speculative third-hand fantasy, it's not a conspiracy theory, it's not an urban myth. It's true. It's happening. It's not in the newspapers and it's not on television and it's not being told from the political podiums. Nevertheless, it's the truth and the rest is a lie.'

Maggie pulled her hand away from him. This was a side of him she hadn't seen. Something feverish, obsessive.

McAngel dug into his pocket and extracted a photograph from his wallet.

'This man is called Keppler,' he said, 'and he is behind the death of Stella and Alfie.'

He waited for the blunt statement to have its effect on Maggie. She shook her head as if clearing it so as to hear better.

'What?'

'It's true. That man is behind their killing.'

Maggie didn't look at the photograph. Instead she regarded McAngel warily, examining his face, looking for signs of some sort of sick tease going on here. Perhaps he was mad. That was the problem. She didn't know who the hell he was. But his look was intent, determined, sincere. And she sensed the danger emanating from this man, like a smell. She felt a chill. She wanted to run.

McAngel was still holding the photograph. She took it from him slowly and then stared at it. Some blond man she'd never seen. Dressed in a suit.

'What are you talking about?' she demanded now of

McAngel. 'You say you're going to tell me about yourself. You bring me here. You ask me a lot of stupid questions about assassinations, tell me weird stories from a world an eternity away about Canadian Indians and Turkish vigilantes. Now you show me a photograph of this Keppler man and you tell me he murdered Stella.'

'No,' McAngel corrected her. 'I didn't say he murdered her. I said he was behind the murders.'

McAngel leant very close to her.

'You see, raping women, Maggie, is not Keppler's style. Not at all. Keppler would not have approved of that little bit of improvisation on the part of whoever it was that he got to do the job on Stella and Alfie.'

He could see Maggie was about to interrupt him. He spoke more rapidly to cut her off.

'Don't misunderstand, Maggie. Keppler's objections to that sort of thing aren't born of squeamishness. Not at all. Keppler would think that to rape a woman when you were sent out simply to kill her was an unnecessary and dangerous self-indulgence—a diversion, a frolic, a surrender to levity.'

Maggie's eyes had widened.

'Are you seriously suggesting that you know who killed Stella or who was behind it? Why aren't you going to the police, McAngel?'

He laughed and Maggie found the touch of hysteria in it unsettling.

'You can't prove things against people like Keppler in a court of law. Keppler's whole life is devoted to stuff like this. It's his profession. More. It's his calling, a vocation, a destiny, a fucking lifelong study of the art of eliminating people they say should cease to exist. The police and the courts and the whole justice system is an irrelevancy to Keppler, a minor irritant that has to be taken into account in planning the elimination.'

Maggie was becoming very agitated. It was as if McAngel had become somebody else. Somebody who now ceased to make any sense, who had pulled her into a weird world where she had no place and no familiar touchstones of rationality.

'Look,' she said. 'What are you saying? Are you saying that you know somebody who had something to do with Stella and Alfie's murder?'

'Yes,' said McAngel emphatically and loudly enough for people at other tables to turn around.

McAngel noticed their reaction but it left him unconcerned. He—and he admitted to himself it was perverse—was enjoying himself. It was bizarre. The prospect of unloading some of what he knew onto someone else suddenly thrilled him. He began to see how the necessity to keep it all so secret for so long had created in him a type of neurosis. Talking to Maggie was starting to become a purgative for him.

'Okay,' Maggie began.

McAngel felt curiously stimulated. He could see she was about to cajole him along cautiously, perhaps even a trifle patronisingly. She was starting to think he was crazy. But the joke was— it was all true! And he would have to convince her it was all true. Of course he *would* convince her. By the time he'd finished, the cogency of the story couldn't but fail to convince her. For the time being however, like Edgar on the heath when he was playing at being poor Tom, he would enjoy this moment, this small luxury of being regarded as a little crazy. Because for the most part, the reality of it all was his most onerous burden.

'Okay,' she repeated, 'Okay. Tell me why you think this man would hire someone to kill Alfie and Stella.'

'I didn't say that. I didn't say that Keppler hired anyone to kill Stella and Alfie. Sure, he hired the killer. But Stella and Alfie were killed by mistake.'

Maggie looked as if she was trying very hard to stay patient. She spoke slowly.

'Who did this man, this Keppler, intend to be killed?'

McAngel smiled a deliberately lunatic smile.

'Me.'

'You,' said Maggie dubiously. 'I see. And he mistook Stella for you?'

'No. He mistook Alfie for me. He mistook Stella for you.'

Maggie suddenly had had enough. She rose, pushed in her chair and strode away from the restaurant. McAngel threw some money on the table and walked after her quickly.

'I'm sorry,' he said when he was by her side.

Some young people on rollerblades whizzed by past McAngel's left shoulder, startling them both. She recovered first and began to walk faster. He stopped her and spun her around so she was facing him.

'I'm sorry, but it's too late. You can't walk away from all this now. You have to hear the lot. And if it makes you as crazy as I am, and it will, that's just too bad. There's no escaping it Maggie. It's bitter fruit you've tasted but you've started and now you have to finish it.'

She was scared. He could see she was scared and that she didn't know whether it was of him or of what he was about to tell her. He led her by the arm to a table and bench seats and sat across from her.

'I'm the one Keppler wanted dead, Maggie. And anyone else who happened to be with me at the time. But it all went wrong. I wasn't at your house and neither were you. But we were meant to be. And Stella and Alfie were there instead. Someone got it wrong in a big way. For now Maggie, that someone, whoever it is, has his own problems. You can bet on that.'

11

*O*llie Olafson, naked, peered into the bathroom mirror and winced as he pulled another piece of glass from his scalp with his left hand. His right was crudely bandaged with a singlet and he held it gingerly against his side. It fucking hurt alright. He'd settle with that prosecutor. Bit my fucking hand half off. You wait you shithead prosecutor. You wait.

He hadn't counted on that fucker being so strong. When they'd come together he felt the hard bulk of him under the clothes. Shithead had to be a weight-lifter with that bulk. Ollie knew weight-lifters. Everyone in jail lifted weights. Anyway, now he'd lost the gun and he'd screwed up again.

Not that the company people knew about the wrong hit on that Stella and Alfie pair. *Separate business*, Keppler had said. Nothing to do with company business. Don't tell them. You'll be in Canberra anyway. Arsehole that Keppler. Hadn't seen him since the fuck up. Ollie didn't want to see him. He'd get the job done first. Then he'd see him. Fuck him. Arrogant shithead.

Then this afternoon the little cat who worked for

Urquhart called him. Appleyard. Little fucker. Cat like that Ollie would have fucked in prison. Not now. Not on the outside with all this pussy around.

Another piece of glass came away bringing with it a small piece of his scalp and some strands of fine blond hair. His face creased with the pain.

He'd fucked her good the little bitch. Took him a long time to come. He smiled. The memory made him horny all over again. Banging her standing up at one stage, against the wall, his hand on her mouth to stop the bitch screaming. He looked at his bandaged hand which throbbed with pain. Pain and pleasure. Pleasure and fucking pain. He plucked at another piece of glass.

Bitch had gone quiet on him all of a sudden. Got this dumb sightless look on her face and went dead quiet as if she didn't give a shit any more. It was then that he got his hand around her neck, small fucking neck like a schoolkid's, and he pressed until she stopped breathing. Bitch.

Did Keppler want the bitch dead as well? He'd asked him that question. Fucker had shrugged. He didn't care. But he wanted the Yank. What a wad of notes he'd shown him! Twenty grand for the hit. But he'd blown it. Wrong guy, wrong girl. He hadn't seen Keppler since. He'd been hanging around waiting for another go at the Yank when Appleyard called. Get over quickly to that address. The place where the company people were tapping the phone. He had to get there before the shithead prosecutor got there. He had to retrieve the listening device planted in the phone and he had to get the computer disk before the prosecutor did.

He'd got the button-sized bug out of the phone, no worries. After he'd tied the bitch up. Flushed it away like they wanted. And he had the computer disc in the plastic bag with that other crap. Why'd they want it? He didn't know and didn't give a shit. With the type of money these pricks were paying he didn't ask no questions. He'd told them that back in WA. If you're prepared to pay, Ollie Olafson will do it for you. He told them that.

Funny business though. This time the company people didn't want Keppler to know what Ollie Olafson's doing. Separate business they said. Not like back in Mt White where Keppler and the poofs and their boss are all in it together. Now it's different. *Separate business*. Fuck them all. What did he care? As long as they paid. Bloody gold mine. He had the golden goose by the balls. Not that a fucking goose had any balls. No fucking worries.

Although that Keppler shithead was a worry. He didn't say much. He looked like he didn't like Ollie Olafson, that bastard. *Feeling's mutual*, he should have said. When this was all over and he got his money he might say that to him anyway. *I don't like you either, you fucking baby-faced cunt. Look at me like that again and I'll ram your head up your arse*. That's what he'd say to him, if he got the chance.

Holy shit!

It was Keppler's cold face there in the mirror in front of him, right there along with the white tiles and glass. Ollie Olafson was so startled, he let out a quick cry. He wheeled around. It was a small bathroom in a cheap Canberra hotel. Keppler was a metre from him. The chill Ollie suddenly felt had less to do with his nakedness than with the disdain in Keppler's eyes. Keppler had nothing in his hands, but Ollie knew at that moment that he was going to die. He did not even see the blow that crushed his trachea, and was only dimly aware of the swift twist and crack that broke his neck and ended his life.

Nick felt drained of energy, of will, of any initiative. He sat slumped in Johnny's study. How long had he been

123

there? It had to be hours—five maybe even six. His nervous system seemed to have lost its charge. Lifting his arm to feel at the lumps on his head was an effort. His right eye was closed behind a large purple egg. Some teeth were loose, but he wouldn't lose them the ambulance guy had said. The worst pain was in his neck which he could barely move, and he could only swallow with the greatest difficulty.

They'd taken Ruth and the baby away to the hospital. Lardner and Stratton came in and out periodically to ask him questions, ignoring Nick's complaint that his neck was hurting.

Earlier he'd rung Louisa and told her there had been a minor drama at Ruth's. He'd interrupted a burglar, he told her. There'd been a brief struggle and the burglar had got away. He was giving the police a statement. He minimised the details he gave to her. Even what she was told was enough to sicken her with worry, he knew that.

There were a couple of other detectives examining the scene. The gun had gone to the lab. The bullet had been dug out of the brickwork and had gone as well.

Stratton came in again.

'Let's try the simple and unlikely first Milano, and tell me what's wrong with it. The guy's a burglar, a desperate.' He searched for and found a type.

'Let's say a druggie, a shitbag. He sees a woman alone in a house. He enters. All he's after is a quick few bucks so he can score. He finds her putting a wallet, a valuable pen, some other stuff in a plastic bag. Takes it, ties her up, is about to go and you show up. He panics, waits for you to come in, maybe wants to blow you away but more likely wants to scare you. You bump the gun away with your big head making it fire. He grapples with you. You do a Rin Tin Tin on his hand, you bury some glass in his skull, you get the gun off him and point it at him and he

124

runs away. Why didn't it happen that way?'

Nick shook his head.

'That's a load of shit Stratton, and you know it. This guy had an expensive suit. He was no desperate. Even the suit aside, you can tell these things. And the gun—a Glock 17. No Saturday night special. And another thing. The guy was going to blow my head away. For a pen and a wallet? Come on. It was no accident that the gun went off. Like I told you before, he was there for something in the plastic bag. It was the last thing he dropped.'

'And you say he wanted the computer disk?'

'Yes I do.'

'And that somehow he knew that you were coming for the disk so he had to get here first?'

'That's right.'

'So you think we better look at that disk when we get a chance?'

'Or even sooner,' Nick suggested sardonically.

Stratton scratched away at the same stubble that had itched him earlier in Nick's office. The doubts again? Then Lardner appeared at the door. It was urgent.

'Fred Arthurton rang from the lab,' he said as he hurried in.

'And?' Stratton asked.

'Same gun was used to knock off Alfie Petrillo.'

'Jesus Christ!'

Nick too was stunned.

'There's more,' said Lardner. 'There were prints, good ones. They ran them on the computer database. Checked all the rapists first and hit the jackpot straightaway. Guy called Olaf Olafson. Did six years at Grafton for the rape of a sixteen-year-old when he was nineteen. Lots of juvenile priors, thefts, assaults, burgs. Picked up where he left off when he got out of Grafton. Went to Western Australia and he's done more time there in Fremantle.

Got eight to do three for a grievous bodily harm in Kalgoorlie. Only got out August last year.'

Stratton looked at Nick, both were thinking of Ruth. She'd been tied up, nothing else. Then Nick was thinking forensics.

'The guy had in his possession the same gun used to kill Alfie. And he happens to be a rapist. So far pretty good, but still circumstantial. Doesn't automatically get us over the line in court just yet if we're saying he killed Stella and Alfie.'

Lardner hadn't finished. He gave a self-satisfied grin.

'Not a problem Milano. Seeing as the blood group of Stella's rapist and the dead guy was identical.'

'Dead guy?' asked Stratton and Nick together.

'A couple of hours ago City Station got an anonymous call to go to Room 18 at the Constitution Motel at Fyshwick. It was a bloke on the other end. Not an Australian accent—the uniform who took the call couldn't pick its origins. Caller said there was a dead man there. Then he said—listen to this.'

Lardner consulted a piece of paper.

'Caller then said, *His name is Olaf Olafson. He was a piece of garbage. He murdered the boy and the girl.* Then he hung up. Some uniforms got there in no time and it was true. Olafson was in his bathroom, dead. Bandaged hand, holes in his scalp made by pieces of glass. He had a broken neck although he was probably either choked or hit in the throat with something first. No signs of a struggle in the bathroom. Anyway, because of the call the lab had the dead guy's name even before they identified the prints on the gun. No-one over there can believe the speed of what's going on here.'

'You better come over to the morgue and confirm it's the same person, Milano,' said Stratton.

Nick got up from his chair.

126

'No worries Stratton. And then you might like to have a look at the contents of that disk,' Nick said.

McAngel had worked hard to convince her to stay with him. He now steered her toward Glebe Park. Somewhere to talk. Maybe a park bench. It was dark. A tender night, late summer. The work day for most was now spent and the pace of the city had relaxed. People strolled rather than hurried. In the park there were children following their parents, or riding in strollers. Some young men and women, cheerful, attractive, laughing, dressed formally, probably heading for the casino, went by Maggie and McAngel leaving them in their wake, as if they didn't exist.

Maggie watched after them. At another time, before McAngel, it could have been her in such a group. At another time she would have delighted in being part of the human traffic of this gentle evening. Part of something civilised and safe. But now she felt at odds with it all. She felt washed out, brittle. And resentful. She was appalled that she had allowed McAngel into her life. Into the lives of Stella and Alfie. It seemed that because of him—because of her—they were now dead. She kept seeing Stella's death mask. The aggrieved, astonished face. Now McAngel was saying that it could happen to her as well. And McAngel was still with her, walking next to her, prepared to tell her more. He'd been right. She didn't want to know the rest of the story. But she also suspected, even though McAngel hadn't spelt it out, that her own survival was tied to his and that she had no choice but to know.

She stopped and turned toward him.

'So who is this Keppler?' she asked. 'And all that stuff you told me about the Canadian and the Turk. I don't understand. What have they got to do with Keppler, or with you for that matter?'

McAngel paused. It wasn't easy. What to tell her? In her own interests? In his own?

Maggie erupted, 'For God's sake McAngel! Will you stop all this procrastinating bullshit! You've just told me someone wanted to kill me. I'm entitled to know what's going on! Fuck your secrets!'

'Okay, okay,' agreed McAngel. She was right. He had to tell her. 'You ask questions. I'll answer if I can. If I can't, I'll tell you.'

Maggie collected herself. It was something.

'Keppler,' she said firmly. 'Why did he want to kill me?'

'Keppler probably wanted me dead. The orders would have been that if I was with anyone, they were to be killed as well. You undertand. It was nothing personal. But now he knows that it wasn't me who was killed. He'll be wondering what you know, what I've told you.'

Something tightened in her chest then welled toward her throat. Maggie controlled it. Resolutely, she went on.

'And why does he want to kill you?'

'Because I'm after him,' he said matter-of-factly. 'And before you ask, I can't tell you why. Not yet.'

She pursed her lips then continued with measured questions and determined restraint.

'Has it to do with those people you told me about?'

'In a way. Yes.'

'Did Keppler have something to do with their deaths?'

'Yes.'

'Why did he want them dead?'

'Because he was asked to kill them by people who hated what they stood for and who had a lot to lose if they stayed alive.'

'Which people?'

'I can't tell you yet.'

She breathed in hard. *Don't get angry*, she was telling herself. Think. It was important to think.

128

'A Canadian Indian, a Turk in Europe,' she resumed eventually. 'Is Keppler part of some sort of racist organisation?'

'You could say that.'

'Ku Klux Klan. A neo-Nazi?'

'Hell no!' McAngel replied, with amused vehemence. 'You know, Keppler would kill you on the spot just for suggesting as much. No way.'

Again Maggie was taken aback by McAngel's reaction. It was almost febrile, revealing in McAngel an unexpected fragility and volatility. She remembered his reaction at Regatta Point when she'd gone to him, kissed him. A momentary, fruitless search for warmth or safety. For life. For some understanding of this man. She learned that in the end she'd be on her own. Not that McAngel wouldn't try. Wouldn't, if called on, be brave, be prepared to play the part of some heroic, romantic, white knight. But he had his own grand plan. His own obsessions. He wouldn't be around for long. She had to think. Stay strong. For her own sake.

McAngel went on, waving his arms about as if addressing a crowd.

'Nazis? Jesus Christ! He regards these types as as an unintelligent and poorly educated sub-species of racist. Crude thugs. Tutti fruttis and nuts of all varieties. Keppler, on the other hand, represents the elite of racism. He is the annointed of the Salzburg Club. He is none other than Beowulf himself, the selected one, the epic warrior, the executioner. You'll find your average Klansman or neo-Nazi in various guises anywhere you care to look in this world, black or white. But your Kepplers don't grow on trees. He's special. And he kills. Not just for a living but as a matter of dogma.'

McAngel stopped. He had suddenly realised that he was talking very loudly and that already he'd told her more than he intended. He looked at her face carefully trying to make out her reaction in the half-hearted light of a nearby lamp post.

'Beowulf? The Salzburg Club?' Maggie asked, cautiously, as if the moment might slip away. 'You mentioned it before, at the restaurant. Something about the European Turks finding out about it. What is the Salzburg Club?'

McAngel hesitated. Not yet, he decided. He couldn't tell her yet.

'You'll have to be patient. It's a dangerous time,' he said to her taking her hand.

She pulled her hand away from him, suddenly horrified again at the stark realisation that it was all true.

'You're bloody serious about all this!' she said loudly. A woman strolling through the park with her husband looked back toward her.

McAngel nodded and Maggie turned from him, disgusted now. She didn't need all this in her life. Then suddenly she found herself screaming at him.

'I don't believe any of this shit. You're crazy McAngel!'

He remained silent. Up the path a bit the man and the woman stopped and looked back at them before resuming their walk.

The outburst helped to clear Maggie's head. For a long time she paced the path, for a regular distance, backwards and forwards, arms folded, thinking things through, stopping occasionally to look at McAngel who stood quietly, patiently, in the weak light, barely moving. It occurred to her that she was now living in an altered world. A world where things once familiar—a car, a dark room, a telephone call, a man in a suit—could now be mysteries, portents, things unknown and dangerous. It was a world roamed by this Keppler, and by the man she was looking at now. McAngel.

She'd already realised she needed him to show her how to survive. She had resisted the conclusion, preferring to dwell on a sense of grievance, rueing fate, blaming McAngel. Now she had this peculiar sense of rapidly adjusting; of suddenly *wanting* to know more. Not just for her own protection. No. It was a more dispassionate need now. Curiousity. More. A bizarre need to welcome, and even embrace, the uncertainty and the danger. Ugly visitors they might be. But they were exciting. It was weird. But it was happening.

'Tell me about this Keppler,' she said to McAngel, sitting down.

McAngel noticed the change. She was interested now. More than interested. Still wary, but interested for reasons other than her own safety. He recognised it all. She was a fellow traveller.

12

*I*t was after midnight and they were back in Nick's office. He'd been to the morgue and identified Olafson's body on the slab. It only took a minute. He was surprised at the effect the sight of the dead body had on him. There was no horror. He was neither repelled nor appalled. He felt no sense of providence that it was Olafson rather than himself there on the slab. Instead he found himself peculiarly intrigued by the whole business. It was as if in looking at Olafson's body he was standing at the gates of hell and that he was less interested in Olafson than in seeing what lay beyond. It was a grotesque thought but his day had turned grotesque much earlier. The familiar and monotonous rhythm and pattern of his life had this day already been so distorted that he no longer had any expectation of resuming them. In fact he didn't want to. He was possessed by a deadly fascination with the ugliness, the evil and the danger that had touched him.

Now he had gone past tiredness and his body had stopped hurting. It occurred to him that normally at this time he'd have been asleep or at least restlessly trying to go to sleep, perhaps turning over in his mind some legal problem the following day's prosecution held in store for him. Or he'd be worrying about his bills. Or some promotional opportunity lost. Or remonstrating with himself in the silence of the night over some unfair remark he'd made to his wife or to his kids.

But right now, as he inserted Johnny's disk into the computer, he felt tense and alert, and was conscious of a peculiar sensation that his eyes were dilated well beyond their normal capacity. He knew he stood at the edge of something dangerous and this gave him a peculiar thrill. A consciousness of self and of his capacities for action that he had never previously experienced.

He was certain that whatever evil was behind the death of Johnny was also behind the actions of the intruder at Ruth's and the killing of the young couple. Olafson's death wasn't going to be the end of it. Somehow he experienced a peculiar sensation of selection, as if fate had deemed him a player in this deadly game. And he didn't mind. Didn't mind at all. That was the strange bit.

Stratton and Lardner watched him. Nick no longer resented their presence.

He clicked onto the A drive and saw the menu from Johnny's floppy disk come up on the screen. It contained the Claims directory. There were only the two sub-directories, Gove and Cape York. No Pilbara. Nick was unperturbed. Pilbara had been hidden on the hard disk. It would have been copied onto the floppy as a hidden file. He punched in some more commands and Pilbara popped onto the screen. He explained for the benefit of Stratton and Lardner.

'The main directory is called Claims. Under that directory you see each of the sub-directories named after areas of Australia—Gove, Cape York and Pilbara. Johnny was briefed to assess the validity of land claims by

Aborigines in each of those areas. So each of those sub-directories contains Johnny's opinion on a claim in that area by a traditional Aboriginal group.'

'Are these *Mabo*-type land claims the blackfellas are making?' asked Stratton in a manner suggesting he had little time for them.

'That's right,' replied Nick. 'Since the High Court decision in *Mabo*, Aborigines can claim unalienated land if they can prove some type of continuous traditional connection to that land. Before *Mabo* this type of land was regarded as Crown land. But since the decision this land is regarded as still belonging to Aborigines if they can prove that they've been on it or connected to it since the time of white settlement. It's all new stuff in litigation. Johnny was the most experienced and most respected lawyer in the country on Aboriginal land issues. Whatever he achieved in court with these matters was going to determine the destiny of a lot of future land claims. It was sensitive stuff. That's probably why he hid these files on the hard disk.'

'Hid them?' asked Lardner.

'Yeah. Watch. This was the way the files on Johnny's hard disk looked when I first searched for the Pilbara file.'

Nick clicked onto the hard disk and brought up the files menu. There was no Pilbara sub-directory showing.

'Someone getting into Johnny's computer looking for what he was working on would see this—nothing here about Johnny's work on the Pilbara land claim.'

Nick punched some further commands in. Now the Pilbara sub-directory showed.

'Whoever got into Johnny's computer after he was murdered saved the contents of this sub-directory at 10.15.'

Nick indicated the Pilbara file. He then clicked back onto the A drive and brought up the contents of the floppy

Johnny had used to copy from the hard disk.

'What we do now is see what time *this* file was last saved by Johnny.'

He punched up the summary facility.

'Last saved 9.29 pm. 23 December.'

He'd been right. He didn't bother to boast to Stratton and Lardner who still were not quite sure what was happening. He explained.

'Johnny copied this file onto his floppy possibly minutes or even seconds before he was killed. Now we compare this with what's on the hard disk which was saved at 10.15 pm. Johnny's been dead for at least thirty minutes remember. Whatever's different between them is the work of someone other than Johnny.'

He was now moving quickly, intent on his task. Lardner and Stratton stood behind him equally intent. Nick split the computer screen in half. On the top half he clicked open the Pilbara file that was on the hard disk. On the bottom half he clicked open the same file that was on the floppy. He could now read and compare the contents of the A drive with those of the hard disk. He began to scroll through both screens. Nick read aloud from the top screen, Stratton read aloud from the bottom hoping in this way to pick up even the most minor diskrepancy. Page after page was read by them aloud and in unison. On and on they read, a dull drone in vibrato, and the documents remained identical. Except when they reached the end of the document. And there it was.

Stratton read it aloud:

Memo: December 23
Re: Crowbar
Called S 9.25 pm—L will talk but not in court—
Confirmed U, made manager 1973.

The three of them looked at the screen in silence until Lardner spoke.

'Means nothing to me.'

'Well it meant a lot to someone,' said Nick.

They both now felt that some new equilibrium had entered their relationship. Maggie sat at the table in McAngel's room, stirring her coffee, regarding him thoughtfully, reflecting on how the landscape in which she'd pictured this man had changed. She'd believed him to be a writer, comfortable with his own company except perhaps for a passing relationship or two with worldly and refined women he'd met here and there. She had pictured him working at a typewriter or enjoying the sun in exotic places; looking intelligent while he calmly observed people and scenery, processing it all so that he could put it on paper at some future stage, perhaps jotting stuff into a small notebook with a lead pencil.

Foolish and childish imaginings. She had yet to fill in the new landscape but McAngel was still there in the foreground, alert and expectant rather than calm and composed; part of the action, not a mere observer. The shape of the rest was not clear, but there was a promise of evil and of danger and even of death.

'Keppler's a killer. A very sophisticated killer.' McAngel said.

He was standing, hands in pockets. He liked the way she was looking now. Harder, more thoughtful. It happened to everyone eventually. Had to.

'Rarely is it hands-on stuff. Instead he mostly *arranges* for the elimination of people. People whose existence other people find inconvenient.'

'Which other people?' Maggie asked him, knowing it to be the question he was not going to answer. His look confirmed it so she gave in.

'Okay. Keppler arranges people's deaths. How?'

'Ideally, in a manner which leaves an explanation for

the death which in no way can be traced to the people who want the victim dead. You see, you have to understand Maggie that this Keppler's no ordinary person. He can impersonate people, he can manipulate, charm, convince, frighten and kill with his own hands if he thinks it necessary. He does all this stuff as his trade, his profession, his art. There's no-one like him.'

The trace of scepticism in Maggie's face was met with proportional irritation by McAngel.

'Maggie. Don't let yourself be killed through an incapacity to believe in the potential of a human being for action ... even if for evil action.'

'Go on,' was all she said. She was reserving final judgment.

'Leonard Jackson,' McAngel said bluntly.

Maggie knew about this one.

'Black activist in the States,' she filled in. 'Killed in bizarre circumstances about eighteeen months ago. My father was talking about him when I was in Washington.'

'And?' said McAngel, interested in what she knew.

'Reformist agenda. Plans for getting poor black people off the streets and into houses. Gun law reform. Taxation reforms. Social welfare reforms. Plans to organise black labour. He was becoming a big name in the States at the time of his death.'

'Correct,' said McAngel. 'And a lot of people, politicians, business people, establishment people, were getting nervous about Jackson. A whole new wave of black activism was building up around him. Particularly amongst poor blacks who were starting to go to meetings and to get organised. Like I said, some people were beginning to get nervous about their employees, their tenants, the safety of their property, the increasing prevalence of uppity niggers talking about social justice. It's one thing to be mugged by a single black man with a gun. All you lose is your wallet. It's altogether different to face an organised movement pressuring government with a reform agenda. The losses are potentially a lot higher.'

'He was killed by a prisoner while visiting a penitentiary wasn't he?' Maggie asked, remembering.

'Yes. Killed in a manner that was certain not to create any troublesome martyrdom after he was gone. He was killed by a fellow black man. A black man whose life he was trying to save.'

He began to pace again.

'Leonard Jackson was against the death sentence. He argued that death row was one of the most racially homogenous places on earth. Its residents are almost exclusively black. Jackson saw the abolition of the death sentence as a racial issue. He decided to raise public consciousness by touring the country with a film crew and visiting death row in various penitentiaries. One day he was visiting a black prisoner in Georgia. A murderer called Emmett Wilkins. Wilkins had killed two men, each of whom he suspected of sleeping with his wife. Knifed them both the same night. The defence pleaded insanity at the trial, arguing that Wilkins suffered from a so-called Othello Syndrome, a psychiatric condition characterised by a belief in the sufferer that the spouse or partner is being systematically unfaithful. The jury didn't buy it but they should have; Wilkins was as cuckoo as they come.

'Jackson had sought and was granted permission to film an interview with Wilkins in a designated room at the prison. Despite the presence of prison guards and a camera crew, Wilkins within seconds had leapt on Jackson and killed him. Bit out his throat. Why? Wilkins simply said, *The motherfucker's screwing my wife.* Jackson had never met Wilkins' wife, lived hundreds of miles away from her, had never been touched by the slightest hint of scandal, was widely known as an exemplary family man and so on. You get the picture. Wilkins pleaded guilty, got another death sentence and was executed. Black people mourned the loss of a potential leader.'

'Seems peculiar that Jackson would have taken that kind of risk,' Maggie observed.

'Not when you know the full story. For some weeks prior to the killing, Emmett Wilkins, who was a Catholic, had a number of visits from a fair-headed priest called Father Mortimer North. Wilkins had a sister who had met North at a church fete. He said he was the parish priest from somewhere or other, visiting relatives in her area. She told him all about her brother on death row and North encouraged her to take him along to talk to Wilkins. Mortimer North then visited alone a couple of times, and somehow talked the governor of the prison into letting Wilkins have some quiet time alone with him. To pray together he said. To allow Wilkins to examine his conscience, to reflect on some bad life choices, to repent. All that sort of stuff. So for a while, North and Wilkins met regularly and alone.

'In the meantime, Mortimer North wrote Leonard Jackson supporting Jackson's campaign and suggesting that a face-to-face interview with a black man on death row would do much to bring home to television viewers the predicament of those sentenced to death for violent crime. He suggested Emmett Wilkins as a suitable subject to interview because, in North's opinion, Wilkins had shown every sign of having repented for his crime. Wilkins had found God and was a person who he was sure would be unlikely to reoffend. An interview with Emmett Wilkins would illustrate that capital punishment was barbaric and unchristian. Wilkins was no longer dangerous the letter said. As quiet and affectionate as a puppy dog. Jackson thought it was an excellent idea and got his people to arrange the interview. You know the ending.'

'Anyone talk to this Father North?' Maggie asked.

'Disappeared. At his sentencing for the murder of Jackson, Emmett Wilkins was asked why he'd thought Jackson was cuckolding him and he replied that the priest who came to the prison had been keeping an eye on Wilkins' wife for him. It was the priest Wilkins said, who'd told him that not only had he seen Jackson visit his wife's home but that with his own eyes he had watched their lovemaking. Father North described it all for Wilkins in sordid imaginative detail. You can imagine what this did to someone with Wilkins' psychiatric condition. There was no way Jackson was going to come out of that interview alive.'

'North was Keppler?'

McAngel nodded.

After a pause she asked him, 'So why is Keppler in Australia?'

McAngel went to his bag and extracted the story from the *Canberra Times* which had first reported Johnny Bora's slaying, and showed it to her. She took it, scanned it, then asked, 'You see Keppler's hand in this? Why?'

'Johnny Bora was an Aboriginal activist, a high-profile lawyer, involved in land rights, an Aboriginal leader with respect and standing in the white community. There are a lot of people whose interests can be threatened by a person like that. A lot of mines in this country are on traditional lands, for example. Why Johnny Bora? Cut off the head and the rest of the body follows. But like I said, you don't want any martyrs. It's counterproductive to leave a suspicious trail to vested interests who get to benefit from the death of someone like Johnny. So you bring in a professional; the ultimate professional. One with a track record in this sort of thing. One who is not only good at having people eliminated but also one who manages to do it in a way which puts as much distance as possible between executioner and initiator. And there's a bonus. Keppler isn't just a killer with no conscience, some type of brutal thug who kills for money or the pleasure of it. No way. He's a visionary, an idealist, a theorist of racist politics. He believes in a world order in which there are superior and inferior species of people. When he kills some black person in America who is getting out of hand or some Turk in Germany who is making waves or some Indian in Canada threatening land interests, he regards it as an exercise in restoring order. His own contribution to a world garbage reduction program. Johnny Bora threatened someone's interests in this country. That someone called in Keppler. Keppler arranged to have Johnny Bora killed.'

Maggie was shaking her head.

'But how can he have got a tribal Aborigine from thousands of kilometres away to come to Canberra to execute a high-profile lawyer in his own office?' she objected. 'It's outrageous. No-one would believe it. I'm not sure I do.'

McAngel turned away from her and went to the drapes of the hotel room and pulled them aside slightly, looking out without speaking for a time. What he'd told her was true. Only the Salzburg Club was missing. When he answered her he could have been talking to himself.

'Whether you or anyone else believes it doesn't matter. Doesn't matter a damn.'

13

Nick was at his kitchen table. His children were still in bed. Louisa was in her dressing gown ignoring the now cold coffee in front of her and looking at her husband as he stared at a piece of paper on the table. She'd cried when she first saw him when he arrived home. His face was a mess of cuts and bruises. His clothes were bloodstained and damaged.

When he'd spoken to her on the phone the previous evening he'd been at Ruth's and he'd told her that he'd interrupted a burglar, that everything was okay. She hadn't believed him. She knew him well enough to know that he was concealing the information she may have found most worrying and that she would get the full story when he got home. But there was something more. Something operating at the level of instinct had told her that a time for caution was approaching. So she'd found a pretext to round the kids up into one room, checked all doors and windows, and she'd slept with the phone and her son's cricket bat near her head.

Nick had told her everything when he came in. He always did. It was a lot for her to digest at five in the morning but she'd listened to him carefully, and as the story became more horrendous she had controlled the panic and listened and understood. And the thoughts that had occurred to Nick only as he pulled into his drive that morning had occurred to her almost immediately.

Someone had wanted the computer disk very badly. Almost certainly it was someone other than this Olafson. Was his death anything to do with the disk? Whoever was out there would be wondering how much Nick Milano knew. Nick Milano had a family—a wife and three children. He was vulnerable.

At first she'd felt the enormous fear for the safety of her kids. The degree of fear that was called panic and that began at a full, terrifying gallop and had to be reined in, controlled, tamed, so that it was only level one fear, rational and therefore manageable. Then there was a sense of resentment. Resentment that all this was happening to her and her family, and she blamed Nick. It was as if he'd carried it all with him, like dog shit, when he stepped inside the house. This latter feeling was short lived and she felt ashamed. She felt she'd betrayed Nick by blaming him even if only mentally and temporarily. For better or for worse. She took that bit seriously. In repenting her lapse she was hit with the realisation that the sort of commitment that was born of years of sharing the same life was love in its most profound and satisfying form. She looked at his battered face and allowed that love to wash over her, and to absolve her lapse and to give her strength for what was ahead.

Now as she sat across from her husband she still feared but she was calm. There was something out there that was a threat to her family. What had been the previous night the product of instinct, something that had the immateriality of the merely possible, was now something on her doorstep, something quite palpably insidious and

143

evil. It was a time to take care and it was time to be strong.

Nick now raised his head. He passed her the piece of paper on which he'd written the memo from Johnny.

Louisa looked at it. It had made no sense to her when she saw it earlier. Nothing had changed. She pushed it back.

Nick continued to struggle with its meaning. Something in the message was distantly familiar. It had been bothering him.

'I've been through the stuff on Johnny's computer—all the files—and there's nothing which sheds light on any of this.'

Louisa reached over and took his hand.

'You could just forget about it and leave it to the police. It's their job, not yours. You can take some leave. We can both say goodbye to Canberra for a while and go to the house at Coogee. The police may clear everything up and then we can come back.'

Nick shook his head just as she'd expected. He articulated what she knew to be true.

'Someone was trying to stop me from getting the disk. I'm sure that it wasn't Olafson's idea. Whoever it is knows that I've probably examined the disk. That I've shown it to the police. They don't know how much I know or how much the police know. But they'd be anxious to find out. Running away won't solve the problem. The police aren't going to follow this up. Think about what's happened logically. The police have got Johnny's self-confessed killer at the remand centre. And they're certain Olafson killed Alfie and Stella. The only murder on their books left unsolved is Olafson's. Who killed Olaf Olafson? The police answer: Who cares? Olafson was a shitbag. A vicious criminal who'd done time and who was bound to have heaps of enemies who had the same disposition as himself. They'll assume one of those killed him. There will be a token effort to find his killer but it won't be a priority.'

Nick stood up and put the kettle on again.

'In the circumstances, everything to do with the disk involves speculation, mere possibilities, flitting shadows.'

'But you've diskussed the material on the disk with Stratton. Won't he follow it up?'

'I don't think so. Even if he wanted to he still has to justify putting resources into investigating a cryptic message on a computer disk which may not have anything to do with either Johnny's death or that of Olafson. When he left me this morning he spoke to Ruth at the hospital. It seems that after I called she searched her wardrobes and found the disk in a plastic bag along with Johnny's wallet and some other stuff the lab delivered to her. She took the whole bag out and placed it on the kitchen table. Then someone knocked at her door. She answered, thinking it would be me. Instead, Olafson pushed his way in. He had a gun and forced her into her bedroom and made her lie face down on the floor. All the time she pleaded with him not to harm her or the baby. He said nothing. Then he tied her hands and her feet and he gagged her and then went out again. She heard him opening wardrobes and things and then he went back out toward the kitchen. Then she heard me calling out and eventually she heard me fighting with Olafson.

'Those are the facts the police have to work on. How do they interpret those facts? A known rapist enters a house occupied by an attractive woman living with a small baby but otherwise on her own. He binds and gags her with the intention of raping her at some point later on and in the meantime looks for valuables to take with him after he's finished. He finds a plastic bag on the kitchen table that Ruth's got out of a wardrobe for me to pick up. In it there's a wallet and some other junk. He's examining the

145

bag when I pull into the drive. He waits to see if I'm going to come in. When I do he puts a gun to my head perhaps just to scare me and it goes off when I move my head. Then there's the struggle, he loses the gun and eventually he takes off and Ruth is saved from being raped. It makes sense. But it's not what happened. I know that.'

Louisa stood up. She knew her husband well. She knew that Nick had by logic arrived at the same conclusion she had reached intuitively. There was something dangerous and unwholesome out there, something that could threaten his family. They lived a quiet life. But she knew him well. Better than anyone. He wasn't the type to wait for it to find him.

'I'll get the kids up. We have to get ready,' she said.

There was a house that belonged to her parents, when they were alive, in Sydney, at Coogee. It was now used by the family for holidays. She could go there whenever she liked. Nick nodded. They both knew it was for the best. For a while.

Nick made a fresh coffee and sat down. Olafson's most recent haunts had been in Western Australia. Information about him had been coming in to Stratton and Lardner all night. He'd most recently done three years in Western Australia for taking off the ear of a reluctant bookie's debtor with a pair of scissors. He'd been released in August of last year. In his room at the Constitution Motel they found his airline ticket. He'd flown in from Perth on the thirteenth of March, the day before Stella and Alfie were killed.

Why on earth had Olafson come to Canberra? It couldn't have been anything to with Stella and Alfie. They were a quiet, typical young couple, no criminal record, stable local families. Nick was convinced the cryptic message on the disk provided the connection between Olafson and Johnny's death. But Stella and Alfie? Where did they fit in? Olafson was in town one day and had killed them the next. Why?

Earlier Nick had asked Stratton about Stella's friend who'd shared the house with her. She knew nothing according to Stratton. Perhaps she just thought she knew nothing. He'd try and talk to her. And then there was Rafferty, Johnny's instructing solicitor for the Pilbara matters. What did he know? Johnny's memo had been written at the end of the Pilbara file. There was no apparent connection. Was it an unrelated matter? Just a memo conveniently located when he resumed work on the Pilbara file? Or did it have to do with the Pilbara or the Pilbara land claim? Could he quote the memo to Rafferty? Maybe Rafferty couldn't be trusted either. Johnny had been in the Pilbara in August of last year. Olafson had been released from Fremantle in August. It was a big state. Big enough to call it a coincidence?

He heard Emily knocking on the bathroom door, demanding that Faith hurry up. Ben, his little boy, was calling out to Louisa. He wanted to get out of bed. The dog barked outside the back door wanting to get in. The Milano household was awake. Yesterday morning all this would have been normal and unremarkable. This morning he smiled and enjoyed the sounds because tomorrow the house would be silent and he would be missing it all. He rose from the table and went off to help with the packing.

McAngel was showering and Maggie had turned on the television, less in anticipation of watching anything in particular than as a means of using a familiar pastime to resume contact with a saner, safer world. She sat watching the screen for several minutes, without comprehension, her mind still preoccupied with McAngel's revelations. The morning news bulletin suddenly attracted her

147

attention. It was a picture of her house, the one she'd shared with Stella. She called loudly and urgently for McAngel who quickly joined her, still dripping wet, as the commentary continued.

'Today, unconfirmed reports are that police have solved what have become known as the Stella and Alfie killings. Recovered from a room at the Constitution Motel last night was the body of the man believed responsible for the killing. Police have not at this stage revealed the man's name but it appears that the dead man was earlier disturbed during a burglary at a house in the Canberra suburb of Deakin. A gun recovered at the scene of the burglary in Deakin is believed to have been the weapon used to kill Alfie Petrillo.'

McAngel was naked and dripping water onto the worn hotel room carpet. He stared at the television set for some time after the story had finished. Then he wheeled, without saying anything, and quickly returned to the shower. Maggie followed him standing at the shower cubicle as McAngel stood amidst the steam and shooting water of the shower.

'What's going on?' she demanded to know.

He didn't answer. He had his eyes tightly closed and his face facing upward into the shower stream.

Maggie persevered.

'You *know* what's going on don't you? Who is this man they've found? They are saying he killed Stella and Alfie. Is it Keppler? What is happening? Tell me McAngel.'

McAngel stopped the shower and began to dry himself, at first ignoring her.

'He's here' he said without looking at her. 'Here in Canberra.'

'*Who* is here?'

Again no response. It was maddening for her. It was as if for him she'd ceased to exist. Again he was withdrawing

148

from her. Shutting her out. No way, she thought to herself. She repeated the question, more loudly.

'Keppler,' McAngel replied fiercely, again without looking at her and now dressing quickly.

'And?' she persisted.

She'd moved in front of him insistently so that he *had* to look at her.

Still he didn't answer. Her resentment increased.

'I'm to be a good girl and just let you look after it all. I'm just to trust you, right? Is that the grand plan, McAngel?'

'I'm sorry,' said McAngel, his features softening. 'I really am. I didn't anticipate that you would become involved. I didn't know Keppler was already here, in person. It changes everything. Perhaps if you leave ...'

She knew what was coming.

'Bullshit McAngel,' she spat out. 'I live here remember. I lived here before you came into my life and before I ever heard of this Keppler. I'm not leaving.'

McAngel was looking at her uncertainly.

'I'm not leaving,' she repeated.

Nick was shown to Ruth Bora's bed at Calvary Hospital. She was awake and sitting up. She hadn't slept at all she told him.

'Me neither,' said Nick.

They went out into the grounds together so she could have a cigarette. Nick carried Johnny's baby out for her.

'I saw it on the news. Not long after, Stratton came here,' she said. 'He told me about finding this man Olafson. How it was him who murdered the young couple. And how he'd raped the girl. He said I was very lucky that you turned up.'

Ruth spoke slowly and seemed curiously distant in her conversation. In talking about herself she could have been

149

talking about another person all together, someone about whom it was possible to speak with the greatest objectivity.

'What do you think about that Ruth?' asked Nick. 'Do you think he was going to turn on you after he'd tied you up?'

She shook her head and dragged on her cigarette.

'I told Stratton that I didn't think the guy was going to rape me.'

She gave a shudder and she ran a hand over her breasts as she went on, not looking at Nick but at some point out beyond the hospital grounds.

'While he was tying me up he was feeling me. Sleazy. But then his mind was on something else. After he tied me up all I could think of was that he was there to harm the baby. To take him away. Then I realised he was looking for something. At first I thought he just wanted something valuable. Anything. But then he just kept looking. I could hear him going from room to room. As if he had something in mind.'

'You told this to Stratton?' Nick asked.

She nodded.

Ruth stubbed out her cigarette. She tried to extricate a fresh cigarette from the pack but her fingers shook and she couldn't quite manage so that the cigarette broke in half. She looked at it as if dumbfounded. Then quite suddenly she started to sob. Deep, pain-laden sobs, her head bowed, her arms folded across her chest, the broken cigarette dangling wretchedly from her fingers. Nick hesitated but then put an arm around her shoulders and turned her in towards him and he let her sob into his chest.

Later, from his office at the DPP, he gave Henry Fritz a call at the Parole Board.

'Henry, what are your contacts like with WA's parole system?'

Henry knew a bloke in Perth who worked there.

Nick spelt out Olafson's name, 'He was released in August of last year. Paroled. I want to know his movements before he came to Canberra. Can you do that for me?'

Henry was back to him within the hour.

'Released August 19, Nick. Spent two weeks in Fremantle then informed his parole officer that he'd been promised some labouring work in the iron ore fields. He got permission to report to the police station at Mt White.'

Nick's geography wasn't great but when he asked the whereabouts of Mt White he wasn't surprised at the answer.

'Big open-cut iron ore operation Nick. In the Hammersley Ranges. You know—the Pilbara area.'

It figured.

'How long was he there for?'

'Well it seems that in December he arranged with his parole officer to move again. To Perth. His reasons were that he had family there—an aunt. He wanted to spend Christmas with her. He had to report to the city police station Mondays and Fridays. He reported as required for about three weeks right up to the New Year and then he disappeared. No sign of him. Although I suppose everyone'll know where he is now won't they?'

Nick thanked Henry.

So Olafson was reporting to a police station in Perth every week up until the New Year. That meant he couldn't have been in Canberra on the day Johnny was killed. But he was in the Pilbara at the same time as Johnny. Coincidence? He doubted it.

14

*F*rom the car McAngel saw a young man and his
friend each make a simian gesture of lip pouting
approval and nudge each other as Maggie walked
past them and into the newsagent at the Deakin shops.
He waited until she had begun a conversation with the
woman behind the counter and then steered the
nondescript, late model Magna he'd hired in the name of
Martin Lloyd Grant back out onto Adelaide Avenue. She'd
be okay. Tapping into the gossip at the Deakin shops had
been her idea. Then she wanted to go to the church—for
Stella's funeral.

Just before he reached the Hyatt, McAngel took a left
past the Chinese Embassy. Soon, the lake appeared on
his right. He counted three entrances to lakeside picnic
areas and then took the fourth and parked. It was
deserted. Sunny. So quiet. The lake barely moved.
Occasionally, behind him on the main road, a car drove
past and way out on the lake a small colourful catamaran
sailed into view. McAngel watched for a while. He saw
four white cockatoos settle in a pine tree and begin
feeding and he was grateful for the distraction.

152

Eventually he emerged from the car affecting a casualness he did not feel. Still, he could see no-one. He headed for the large pine tree he'd been watching. It was isolated, standing at the extreme edge of the bounds of the picnic area. As he walked he could see out to the lake and he could see clearly behind him for some distance. There was open space all around; he'd picked this spot carefully. Little chance of an ambush by anyone waiting for him to retrieve it. Unless they were in the tree itself. Which they weren't or the cockatoos would would have been spooked.

When he reached the tree he nimbly pulled himself into the first layer of branches, setting off a commotion as the white cockatoos irritably flapped away from the higher branches. Then he reached up into a hollow and extracted the tightly bound parcel containing Bluey's Taurus. He was grateful he'd taken the precaution to conceal it properly when he flew to Mt White, rather than leaving it somewhere at Maggie's and Stella's house. Explaining its presence in a house where there'd been a double murder may have taxed his imagination. He jumped to the ground and returned to the vehicle.

Back at the Deakin shops Maggie was out and waiting for him.

'Dead man was disturbed in a house in Stenburn Place yesterday afternoon,' she said flatly as she put on her seat belt. 'Johnny Bora's house.'

Johnny Bora. McAngel started the car. Not something he had anticipated but he wasn't surprised. But why was this guy sniffing around the widow's house?

'Get a name?' he asked her.

'The chemist lives next door to a detective,' she replied, satisfied with her success, but subdued, sombre even, preparing mentally for Stella's funeral. 'He told me the dead man's name was something Scandinavian. He couldn't remember except that it sounded like Sven or Olaf or something like that. Ring a bell for you?'

McAngel shook his head.

'Tell me something,' Maggie said as they drove off. 'Johnny Bora was killed almost three months ago. Why is Keppler still around?'

The name Keppler was burned into her imagination now. Along with the image from the photo. A killer. Her enemy. Originally she'd thought of him as a poisonous snake. The more McAngel revealed, the more that image receded. Something larger, less reducible to simile was emerging. More a presence, a force. Far more frightening ... and intriguing for her.

'He usually hangs around for a while,' McAngel told her with an air of familiarity, as if Keppler was a next-door neighbour. 'Mops up residual problems, ties up loose ends, makes sure the customer's satisfied. That type of thing. Sort of like a personal warranty from a professional.'

'And this Scandinavian,' she went on. 'You say Keppler's gone and killed him. Why?'

McAngel shrugged speculatively.

'He must have screwed up.'

'So Keppler killed him to *punish* him?'

It wasn't part of Maggie's picture. She was sceptical.

'No,' replied McAngel. 'I'd say he attracted attention to himself. He may have been a lead to Keppler in some way—a danger for him. I don't know.'

'What about the police?' she asked. 'They'll be investigating this Sven or Olaf's murder won't they? There won't be any tribal Aborigines to blame, will there?'

'Keppler won't care,' McAngel answered confidently. 'He'll have left the police nothing. And when you think about it, this Scandinavian sounds like he was the worst type of criminal. The type whose demise no-one regrets.

The police won't be in any hurry to find his murderer. Keppler would have factored that in.'

'Okay,' reasoned Maggie. 'The Scandinavian is at Johnny Bora's house. Why? Is there something there that needs cleaning up.'

'Probably. But your guess is as good as mine. What else did you learn at the shops?'

Maggie recited it for him matter-of-factly. It hadn't been difficult. A polite enquiry with a smile for the newsagent—a fat bellied, heavy jowled fellow who'd been talking about it to his customers all morning and who'd known both Johnny and Ruth Bora to drop into his shop regularly—yielded a lot. Then the chemist, a young man, good looking in an appropriately antiseptic way, getting his morning paper, had chipped in with the stuff about the Scandinavian. A couple of women who had been listening threw in what they had heard as well.

'He tied up the woman, Johnny's widow,' she said. 'There's some debate about whether she was raped or not. Depends on who you talk to apparently. She was seen being taken away in an ambulance. There was a young baby in the house who is okay. They weren't quite sure who it was that interrupted this Olaf or Sven in the house but the woman at the cash register said she was told it was a man who was a friend of Johnny's. A prosecutor. At some stage he was shot at. He's not dead but he could have been wounded. But who knows what embellishment that little detail has had in the retelling. What now?'

'This friend got a name?' McAngel asked.

'A Mr Nick Milano.'

Maggie looked at her watch and felt the pain once again.

'Now you'd better take me to the church,' she told McAngel.

Nick parked outside Johnny's house and made his way

to the front door. He felt a residual uneasiness at being back there after the drama of his last visit and was watchful.

'Johnny's things from his office are all there in the one place in his study,' Ruth had told him when she gave him the keys. She wasn't going back. Ever. Peter Oliver and his wife had offered to put her up.

'I doubt you'll find anything of help anywhere else,' she'd said. 'He never worked at home. He kept next to nothing there. Except me.'

Now he let himself in. He entered the hallway where he'd struggled with Olafson. Glass still littered the tiled floor and there was some blood. He shuddered.

The hallway faced west and it was warm and stuffy at this time of the afternoon. Nick slid open a window to let in some air. As he did so he saw a red Toyota utility circle the cul-de-sac in front of the house and return down toward the main road. The driver looked straight ahead and appeared to be dressed in white overalls. Tradesman? Maybe. Nick took out a pen and scribbled down the registration number. It was probably nothing, just his own nervousness. But the vehicle had been pulling out of Johnny's street as he arrived. It was now making a second circuit. Johnny's house was at the top of the cul-de-sac. If you were driving around up there you were either visiting the house or you were lost. A third alternative might be that you were keeping an eye on the house to see who came and went.

Nick watched the vehicle pull into the main road at the bottom of the street and then stuffed the paper on which he'd written the number into his pocket.

What was he looking for? He wasn't even sure. All he knew was that somehow the memo that Johnny had left himself on the computer was important. He'd searched the computer files and found nothing that helped. Maybe there was something among Johnny's books and notes. He began shuffling around.

Johnny's diary was there amongst the things from his office. He made his way through the entries. Johnny was a busy barrister. The entries covered a lot of ground. But nothing in the diary spoke of Crowbar or shed any light on the remainder of the computer message. He felt despondent as he read the last entry. It appeared hopeless. Nothing in the diary explained the memo. And even if it did there was no way he would necessarily know.

He began sorting through Johnny's other papers. There were a lot of them. Defunct briefs tied with ribbons, a filing cabinet full of copies of cases, papers, extracts, books. More papers and more books bundled a metre high in places. Where to start? And would it be worthwhile? He had an uneasy feeling that if someone had gone to the trouble to delete a very short memo from a computer disk that same person would have been anxious to get rid of any more substantial references to whatever it was that he or she wanted to be kept secret. Nick could be days looking through all this and find nothing because it would have all been removed.

Again he was troubled by a faint recollection of something familiar about the memo. He looked about him and noticed the space where Johnny's calendar with the prints of indigenous paintings had been. The word *Crowbar.* He'd seen the name somewhere, and recently. Where?

Then he remembered. The calendar! Would it still be there? He looked in the wastepaper basket. It was. The calendar from the previous year. He pulled it out and hung it on the wall where it had been before. There it was, written in a space below Albert Nagonara's print. It was a small neat diagram in Johnny's handwriting depicting what looked like a family tree of companies. At the top of the tree was a company called Wessex Holdings. From Wessex there branched a number of subsidiaries. The one that caught his eye was a company called *Abacus Australia* and underneath it written in Johnny's hand was the word *Crowbar*.

Why write it all on the calendar? Then he saw the phone on Johnny's desk. He picked it up with his left hand and made as if to write on the calendar with his right. He could reach. It made sense. It was a fair bet that Johnny had scribbled down the information from a phone conversation.

Nick was back in his car in moments heading for the city and the business office of the Australian Securities Commission.

The Constitution Motel was on the road to Queanbeyan. McAngel pulled into its drive, which was just before the sign announcing that you'd left the Australian Capital Territory and were now in New South Wales. Not that you needed any signs, Maggie had said when he'd dropped her off at the church for Stella's funeral service. As soon as you noticed the texture of the road change beneath you from smooth to rough and you hit the first pothole you knew you'd left the ACT and were in New South Wales.

A couple of small, ill-tended and struggling trees lined a broken concrete entrance to the motel grounds. The building was a long, oblong block containing rooms on two tiers. Paint flaked from the walls and a couple of rusted downpipes from the roof weren't quite secured to the brickwork. The property was dilapidated and its condition was testimony to a poor business decision by the original owners to build the motel in that location.

McAngel pulled into the small bay in front of the motel reception office. He felt for the Taurus tucked

158

into his belt under his coat. He was nervous. Of the many places Keppler might expect him to come this would be one. This was now cat and mouse. McAngel found it unnerving not knowing whether he was rodent or feline. The only solution for him was to assume that he was a bit of both.

He got out of the car cautiously and, keeping his back protected by the wall of the building, looked around. He was relieved to see the two police cars parked outside a room toward the end of the block. There was a cordoned-off area and he estimated there were about half a dozen cops there, two in uniform, the remainder in plain clothes. A group of about eight people, probably guests, stood watching and chatting in the courtyard at a diskrete distance from the cordoned area. It was possible but unlikely that Keppler would be waiting for him in these circumstances. He took care in any case.

He cupped his hands and peered through the small glass window into the office. There was no-one at the counter and the office was empty. A door behind the counter led off into the building. There was a bell on the counter. He opened the screen door and entered. He found a position at the counter which was out of view of the interior door, and leaned on the counter with his left arm so that he could avoid having his back to the door he'd just entered. He rang the bell. There were sounds of some movement behind the other door and a woman emerged, peering over the top of her reading glasses. She caught sight of McAngel.

'Oh there you are,' she said. 'I can normally see guests from inside. Are you after a room, sir?'

'Yes ma'am,' answered McAngel. 'A single, for one night.'

She took the phony details he gave her and he paid in advance. He didn't want her to be coy when he asked her what had happened.

159

'You have some trouble here Madam?' he enquired of her, playing the Yank tourist.

She was disappointed he'd asked. He could tell. But she was an honest woman. She removed her spectacles with an air of resignation.

'An accident sir. The police are investigating it at the moment. I'm afraid it may not be to everyone's liking to stay in a motel in these circumstances. It's not too late to change your mind sir.'

She indicated the till.

'Oh no. I like interesting things happening around me. An accident you say?'

'Well perhaps it wasn't an accident, sir. If you know what I mean?'

'Suicide?' ventured McAngel.

She looked around her and then leant toward him confidentially.

'Murder,' she whispered.

'How interesting,' McAngel encouraged her.

That was as much as she needed.

'He only booked in yesterday morning. Called himself Phillip Ryan. Wasn't his real name. Big chap. Well dressed. But sour. Hardly said two words here at reception. He went out from here late in the afternoon, just after I put a call through to his room. Then I saw him come back. He drove through the reception driveway here very quickly. I looked out and saw him get out of his car and he was holding his head with one hand and opening his door with the other. Then later that night, about ten, the police arrived. Two young constables. They said they would like to look at room eighteen. So I let them in and there he was on the tiles in the bathroom, naked as a baby except for this singlet tied around a wound on his hand. It was terrible. Broken neck the police said.'

'Wow. And do the police know who killed him?' asked McAngel.

'Well no,' she said slowly, proceeding more cautiously on this point. 'The killing had nothing to do with the motel you understand. This young man was really not Ryan but someone else. Someone with a bad criminal record the police have told me. He mixed with some bad types. You know, in and out of gaol types. One of these probably killed him for some reason. Revenge, drugs maybe, that sort of thing. That's what I think anyway.'

'This guy who did the killing. Are you saying no-one saw him?' asked McAngel. *Too blunt* he thought, after asking her.

'Well ...' replied the woman after giving him a searching look. 'Are you a journalist or something?'

'Hell no,' protested McAngel. 'Just interested is all ma'am. If you can't say, well you can't say ...'

This mollified her. She went on, 'I mean no-one has reported noticing anyone unusual. In a motel like this anyone you see is going to be new to you. The police have interviewed all the guests who were here last night and asked them about who they saw around the place. They proceeded to describe one another.'

She thought this was funny, giggled conspiratorially, and handed McAngel his key. McAngel made as if to go and then turned back as if something had just occurred to him.

'Say, I bet that call you put through to him had something to do with all this.'

She smiled smugly.

'Well that occurred to me as well you know, and I told the police exactly what I'd heard.'

'Oh?' prompted McAngel.

'It was a call from a woman. A local call. But it wasn't her wanted to speak to him. She was somebody's secretary because she said, when she asked for Mr Ryan, she said, *Please tell him Mr Appleyard would like to speak to him.'*

'And Mr Appleyard is ... ?' said McAngel encouraging her onward.

'Well, this is it you see. I asked the police not long ago and they can't find who it is. Even though there was something else I heard, distinctly.'

She paused so that McAngel could ask her what it was she heard. He obliged.

'Well, when I first picked up the phone the secretary had obviously just been interrupted and I heard a male voice in the background say, *If he's not there leave a message* ... And then the same voice said, *and then ring White about the rigs.* Then the secretary apologised for keeping me waiting and asked for Mr Ryan.'

'Have the police made anything of that?' asked McAngel.

'Oh nothing yet. It's much too early,' she scolded. 'But it could be very important. That's what they said.'

When he left the office McAngel went to the bother of actually going to the room and messing up his bed and running the shower. He took a piss and flushed some toilet paper down. Then he left the keys on the table. Back out in the sun he saw that the activity around Olafson's room continued. But it was all fairly casual. There was no-one breaking their balls to get this one solved. He could see that.

As he was driving away from the Constitution Motel he suddenly made the connection. *Appleyard, Applecart, Applecart and Gregory!* The two men Tub and Gunner had spoken about back in the Pilbara! The lackeys to the man Arkett. And *White?* Throw in a rig and a mining town called Mount White and it started to make a glimmer of sense. Keppler was suddenly half a step closer.

Back at the motel, Stratton wondered who the bloke

with the Yank accent was who he'd heard in the office talking to Dulcie. The Yank had gone into a room then left the motel like a bloke who wasn't coming back. There was probably nothing in it but in this game you checked out everything. Even if it meant having to talk to that fucking Dulcie woman again.

15

Nick Milano emerged from the offices of the
Australian Securities Commission in London
Circuit burdened by the diskovery he'd made. He
wanted to mull it over uninterrupted but there was no
time. He had his six o'clock lecture to give at the
university.

When he arrived, only minutes late, and began the
lecture, his mind wasn't on the job and only his familiarity
with the course and the subject matter allowed him to get
through it. All the time the company search he had just
completed intruded on his concentration.

Wessex Holdings was the holding company. The rest,
including Abacus Australia, were its subsidiaries.
Unremarkable stuff, until you considered the directors and
major shareholders. And then one name popped up
everywhere. *Urquhart.* Until eight years ago it was all Sir
Samuel Urquhart. But then Sir Samuel disappears off the
books and is replaced by one Scott Campbell Urquhart,
Sir Samuel's son and heir and the man who, according to
Johnny Bora, crippled Ernie Barnes one night twenty
years previously.

164

Nick finished his lecture and did his best to deal politely with a couple of students wanting to know more about involuntary confessions. In the end he made an excuse and bolted for the staff common room. In the common room were two other members of the staff. One was Professor H.G. Carpenter, renowned company law expert, slight, balding, dressed impeccably in coat and tie and engaged in pulling books down from the staff library collection. The other was Ernest Mills, the *Mills* half of the standard text, *Grimm and Mills on Tort* who sat in a large armchair with a volume of the Commonwealth Law Reports in one hand and a curdling pipe in the other.

Nick had always found Mills a crusty old bastard and Carpenter was invariably aloof. Now they barely acknowledged Nick. He had been teaching at the university long enough to know the way they thought. He was a part-timer and a member of the practising profession and consequently someone with only the most dubious of motives for wanting to come to the university to teach twice a week. This suited Nick who, on this occasion, wanted to avoid talk at all costs. He grabbed a book at random from the shelf and pretended to read. In fact he began to toss over in his mind what he'd learned at the Securities Commission offices.

Crowbar! It had been there in black and white. One of the mines run by Abacus Australia in the late Sixties and early Seventies. Ceased production in 1976. Its product? Asbestos. Where situated? Inevitably—the Pilbara.

Why was Johnny interested in Urquharts again? What had he been up to? According to Johnny, Urquhart had walked away a free man when he should have gone to gaol for running down Ernie Barnes in Bondi Junction. Johnny's response to this injustice had subsequently shaped his life. His decision to become a lawyer had been part of a quest for justice for his people. Nick had thought that in embracing this larger ambition Johnny had displaced his more specific resentment of the outcome of the Ernie Barnes incident. He'd told Nick nothing of any recent reawakening of interest in Urquhart. Was it a secret obsession? If so, what was it he had on Urquhart?

Crowbar Mine? Asbestos? Dangerous stuff. Did Johnny's interest relate to the asbestos. A negligence action? Was Johnny looking to hurt Urquhart by championing an action for damages?

Then Nick remembered the other occupants of the common room, in particular Ernest Mills—expert in Torts and the law of negligence. He looked in Mills' direction. He was a scruffy old bloke with thick glasses and unruly dark hair finally going to grey, wearing no tie, an open collar and, most incongruously, a pair of tartan bedroom slippers.

'Professor Mills?' Nick interrupted him.

Mills looked up and Nick introduced himself as he had done on at least half a dozen other occasions over the years he'd worked at the university. As always Mills behaved as though it was the first time he'd ever laid eyes on him, regarding him suspiciously from head to foot before extending his hand off-handedly.

'Asbestos, Professor Mills,' said Nick immediately. There was no point wasting his own time and he could see that Mills was unlikely to bother with small talk. 'Has there been much in the way of negligence actions in the courts?'

'Not much,' said Mills curtly and returned his attention to the law report.

'Why not?' persevered Nick. 'I mean, it's dangerous stuff. It must have attracted litigation.'

Mills looked up.

'Why are you interested in this? You're a criminal law man aren't you?'

166

Carpenter joined in somewhat mischievously.

'You won't get much out of him I'm afraid. Mills thinks that explaining anything gratis is an act of naivety. You'll have to brief him or pay him a consultancy fee.'

Mills took the bait, but imperiously.

'I fail to see why these days I shouldn't expect something in return for my expertise, Carpenter. This fellow practices out there in the big world. He doesn't do it for nothing does he? He has a whole library to consult if he needs to know anything. Let him find out for himself.'

Carpenter raised his eyes to the ceiling. He and Mills had been cantankerous academic rivals for long enough to have developed a peculiar familiarity which some may have mistaken for a reluctant friendship.

'He's a prosecutor Mills. Paid, or rather, underpaid, as you and I are, by the government. We're on the same side you see. So there's no need to be such a mean old goat.'

Mills appeared to reappraise Nick for a moment.

'I thought you were a private practitioner,' he grumbled eventually. 'One of the mercenary ones. Why do you want to know about asbestos litigation? Tell me. If I find the reason interesting then I'll consider myself paid for my advice. If not at all interesting then I'll consider that I've given my advice *pro bono publico* and have to be satisfied with that.'

Nick smiled.

'An asbestos mine in the Pilbara which operated during the Sixties and Seventies was run by a company called Abacus Australia. It ceased production in 1976. I recently learned that a friend of mine had an interest in its activities. He's now deceased. I never found out why he had such an interest. He was a barrister. I thought that perhaps he was involved in litigation arising out of the asbestos production at the site.'

Mills was unimpressed.

'Looks like *pro bono* stuff as usual,' he sniffed. 'Nevertheless, I know the mine to which you refer. The Crowbar Mine was it not?'

'Yes it was,' said Nick taken aback.

Mills was renowned for an extraordinary memory. He went on without faltering.

'There was never any litigation with the Crowbar Mine. Abacus Australia was effectively run by the late Sir Samuel Urquhart. His policy was to settle out of court. The labour force for the mine was drawn from an Aboriginal community in Crowbar. Town in the Pilbara in Western Australia. Although there were never any identifiable asbestos-related diseases complained of or litigated on prior to the mine closing in 1976, shortly thereafter, with greater publicity given to the issue, it became apparent that many former workers were starting to show signs of such disease—pleural and peritoneal mesothelioma, asbestosis, lung, stomach and colon-rectum cancers. These workers had been employed in the mine in the late Fifties and early Sixties and it became apparent that there was a latent period for the diseases of some twenty years. And of course, the incidence of these diseases in the Aboriginal community was way above the incidence recorded in the general community.'

'Samuel Urquhart? Settling out of court? Sounds very uncharacteristic for *that* man,' chipped in Carpenter.

'Oh, he had it all worked out. I was labouring on a new edition of *Grimm and Mills* at the time so I followed the events closely. Like a lot of academics, I was waiting for asbestos-related litigation to hit the courts. It contained all types of potentially interesting legal issues. You know, questions of foreseeability in view of existing medical knowledge, the application of limitation periods in view of the considerable latency periods involved in the onset of the diseases. That sort of thing.'

168

Mills re-settled himself in his chair and began gesturing as Nick had seen him do in the lecture theatre when considering a question from a student.

'You see, a member of the Aboriginal community would no sooner show signs of developing something related to asbestos disease and the company immediately stepped in and made them an offer—usually a very cheap offer, but one nonetheless very attractive to anyone accustomed to a life circumscribed by modest material means, as were these people of the Crowbar community—and the victim would accept and waive any rights to further damages.'

Mills paused to tap out his pipe into an ashtray and then dipped into a pouch of aromatic tobacco as he continued.

'Ended up costing the company a couple of million but this was absolute peanuts, of course, when you consider the alternatives. Litigation costs would have been astronomical. The chances of losing were high given that medical knowledge of the harm inherent in exposure to asbestos was considerable by the Sixties and Seventies. And of course, there was the cost to the reputation of the company.'

'In what sense?' asked Nick.

'Oh, these people worked in appalling conditions. In the early years there are stories of employees working in thick clouds of asbestos dust; so much so that a worker shovelling asbestos dust into a sack could not see the man who was holding the sack. Things improved a little in later years when dust control measures were introduced but apparently these were still far from satisfactory and an inadequate response in view of the picture emerging of the hazards involved in mining asbestos. If the question had gone to court there would have been not only compensation damages but also punitive damages and the accompanying embarrassment. Urquhart saved himself and his shareholders millions by acting the way he did. It was damage control.'

'Are they still paying out?' asked Nick.

Mills shrugged.

'I imagine they would be following the same policy. Other asbestos producers did much the same thing for the same reasons. In the case of Abacus, an interesting sidelight was that the company's public liability insurer was Wessex, the parent company of Urquhart's group. Urquhart's influence on the group was such that Abacus never pursued any claims on behalf of Abacus or Wessex, even though they would have had a good argument that their policies covered asbestos. Mind you, it's the son in charge at Abacus now I believe.'

'Yes, and an objectionable lad indeed, I can tell you,' said Carpenter.

'You know something about him then?' pressed Nick.

'I certainly do. He was a student here for about nine months many years ago now. He failed all his exams. I was the Dean of the faculty. At that time we had a diskretion as to whether or not to allow students with poor academic records to re-sit exams. His record was abysmal and I can assure you, having put up with him in class, that he had little to recommend him by way of charm either. He sought an interview to diskuss a re-sit. It was usual for someone in his position to be sensible enough to be polite, contrite, conciliatory, to seek to create the best impression possible. Not young Scott Urquhart. The toad immediately started bullying tactics. Said the reason he failed so badly was because the teaching was poor and because there was little assistance from staff. This was something he said he hadn't brought to the attention of his father but which he felt he would be compelled to do if not given a post. Urquhart senior was responsible for some very large donations and sponsorships from which the university benefited. It was an outrageous attempt at blackmail. I immediately asked him to leave my office and advised the Chancellor of the University. The following year all contributions from his father's companies to the university ceased. As for young Scott, he left the university law school. I believe he married and his father found a position for him somewhere within the company's operations. Good riddance I thought to myself at the time.'

'Do you recall the year he left?' asked Nick.

Carpenter pursed his lips as he thought.

'Seventy-three, seventy-four.'

Nick thanked them both and left in a hurry. The *U* in the computer message had to be for Urquhart. Was it Scott? Did the message confirm that the young Urquhart had been made mine manger in 1973? It fitted with what Carpenter had just told him. But who was *S* and who was *L*? It seemed that something had happened when Scott Urquhart was mine manager and Johnny knew about it. Something someone else didn't want Johnny or anyone to find out. What was it?

They were both back at the hotel. Maggie sat at the table. She was tired, diskonsolate, distracted. There'd been a Mass, given by a Spanish priest, and then a procession to the cemetery where Maggie had sought to try to console Stella's distraught mother. It added wretchedness to Maggie's grief. She couldn't help but feel responsible for the woman's misery. It was Maggie who had brought McAngel, and the evil which trailed him, into the lives of Stella and Alfie. Yet what could she tell Stella's mother? McAngel's weird story? Hardly.

McAngel. He was in the bedroom with that gun he'd told her about. Taking it apart, cleaning it. Again she considered her relationship with him. What did she feel

171

about him? Shouldn't she be resenting him for the part
he'd played in bringing violence and death into her life?
She was no longer sure, and this of itself troubled her.
She should be rueing the decision to spend Christmas Eve
with him. Maybe she should be rueing the decision she'd
made to leave Washington.

'Like I said, I didn't think Keppler knew I was here,
Maggie,' she heard McAngel say, as if he had guessed her
thoughts. He stood at the door of the bedroom looking at
her.

She shrugged. She remembered a mildly crude
Americanism she heard somewhere.

'Shit happens, eh McAngel?'

'Unfair Maggie,' McAngel replied, simply.

'How'd he know you were here?' she asked. 'I suppose
he knows everything too, does he? This Keppler.
This ... what did you call him? Beowulf? Sorry. Taboo.
Word not to be mentioned. Like the Salzburg Club.'

McAngel moved over to sit with her.

'Keppler would have found out where I was eventually.
It was earlier than I expected that's all. I don't know how.
But they know. They all do ... '

He trailed off. Private grounds, private memories.
Maggie didn't pursue it. She'd given up trying to get out
of him what he didn't want to tell her.

'You know, I would never have met you had I stayed
in Washington,' she said eventually. It was reflective
rather than bitter. 'Stella and Alfie would still be alive
and I wouldn't be here sitting in the path of some
psychopath I may not even see coming.'

'Doesn't work that way,' McAngel said. 'There are no
choices Maggie. It's called destiny. Nothing you or I can
do about it.' And as if selecting an example to support
his point McAngel asked, 'Why did you leave Washington
rather than spend Christmas with your folks?'

It was strange. For Maggie, Washington seemed so reduced in importance. At the time it had mattered. Now it was like remembering something she'd seen only through the eyes of a child.

'My father was having an affair,' she told McAngel. It came out easily. '*Another* affair I should say. This time with an American woman. She was a librarian at the embassy. The first affair—the first we knew about—was with a woman who wrote cookbooks for a living. I was still in high school, comparing pimple creams. I weathered the dramas at home but I took it hard. The next one? Well she was a journalist. A New Zealander who thought my father was going to leave everything and marry her. It caused a huge scandal in family circles. I was called home from university to help look after my distraught mother, attend family powwows, offer advice. I advised her to leave him. She was too frightened of being alone. Eventually my father decided to stay with us. This resulted in great relief all round the family. As if my father had forgiven *us*. There was a touchy reconciliation at first and then things improved. The New Zealand journalist was placed in the *topics never to be mentioned* category and life seemed to be going on as before. The posting to Washington came along and my mother suggested that we all spend Christmas there together. Two days before Christmas, my mother and I decide to go to the theatre. To see, of all things, a production of *Who's Afraid of Virginia Woolf?* Mum forgets her spectacles and returns home. And there's dear dad, bonking the librarian on the living room lounge. I returned from the theatre during the interval and ran into an even better show. There was fighting, recriminations, threats and tears. I'd heard it all before. I couldn't stomach it. So I left on the first available flight.'

'Destiny Maggie,' McAngel repeated, seemingly

unmoved. But not indifferent. Maggie realised she no longer cared either. It had been a long day.

'In any case,' she went on, 'It wasn't just your irresistible charm that got me into bed on Christmas Eve. I wanted a diversion, some fun, some light after all the gloom. Look at me now.'

They sat in silence for a while then McAngel said, 'If something happens to me, I want you to leave a message with someone. Man called Byron Williams. You don't have to know anything about him. Although I can tell you that he was on Leonard Jackson's staff at the time Jackson was killed. He knows about Keppler.'

McAngel scribbled Maggie a New York number.

'Best if you memorise it,' he said. 'For Byron's sake.'

Maggie was going to say something. In the end she didn't bother. She looked at the number, memorised it and then crumpled the paper.

Within minutes Nick knew Rafferty was lying.

Nick was at his office. He'd slept badly, waking frequently to find himself sticky with perspiration and struggling to find the real world amidst a confused tangle of dreams and fantastic images. It was a night in which painted Aborigines with clubs searched for wigged and gowned barristers in clouds of asbestos dust while brutal men in convict garb waved computer printouts with impenetrable messages on them. He was awake when the light came at dawn and decided to go to the office. The night's phantoms could remove themselves from his house at their leisure.

When it was an appropriate hour he called the Perth based solicitor and apologised for the abrupt termination of their last conversation, putting it down to a work emergency. He then re-opened the conversation about Johnny's fee. Rafferty, as before, was chatty and familiar but with enough nervous edge to his voice to make Nick doubt just about everything he said.

In his mind's eye, Nick imagined a small man in a loud tie, wet at the armpits, pulling on a cigarette. Someone who was heading for the far side of middle age with a dark drawer in his office filled with arrangements he hoped would never see the light of a bright Perth day.

When he asked Rafferty if he knew anything about the Crowbar Mine there was a brief pause. For Nick, who had spent years listening to people giving evidence in the witness box, it was enough. It was what he recognised as a bullshit alert. What Rafferty would say next would be a lie.

'Crowbar Mine you say? Don't think I've heard of that particular operation actually Nick. Should I have?'

Nick was intrigued. Rafferty? He'd picked him as someone who was probably dishonest but why was he lying on this one? Nick baited a line. You never knew what you might catch.

'The Crowbar Mine is within the boundaries of the Wonyulgunna land claim, isn't it Rafferty? I would have thought you may have come across it in preparing the brief for Johnny.'

It worked. Rafferty scrambled for a plausible reply.

'Oh, the *Crowbar* Mine you say. You could be right there Nick. Just a minute while I check.'

Nick heard some opening of drawers and paper scuffling as Rafferty searched for sound effects.

'Oh look, here it is. Marked out on the surveyor's map. I thought I may have come across it. I remember now. The Crowbar Mine. Yeah. Old asbestos operation Nick. Years since it operated though. What's your interest in it Nick?'

Nick suddenly remembered the red utility in Johnny's street. He sweetened the lure.

'It's just that I found this large sealed envelope

yesterday afternoon at Johnny's house—in a cupboard. I haven't opened it but it has the words *Crowbar Mine* scribbled roughly on the front and what feels like some paperwork inside. I asked around and found it was an asbestos mine in the Pilbara. Thought you might be able to shed some light on it. I haven't opened the envelope of course. But I've kept it and next time I see Ruth Bora I'll ask her permission to examine its contents.'

Nick heard the click of a lighter again and the hasty pull on a cigarette. Steady now. Soon he'd be reeling him in.

'This is an envelope you have with you now Nick, is it?'

Affected casualness. Really he's panicking guessed Nick. Give him some slack.

'Actually it's still at Ruth's. Why do you ask?'

'Oh, I thought you could describe it to me. You know, it might ring a bell.'

Some relief for Rafferty there. Nick speculated on what was going through Rafferty's mind. Places like the DPP are secure areas. Prospects of breaking in are slim and in any case it was a dangerous move. If the envelope was at Ruth's he could get it.

'Just an envelope Rafferty—big white one with Crowbar written on it. Sounds like you can't help me.'

'No, I'm sorry, wait ... ' Rafferty got out.

He's sweaty now, Nick thought. He sensed Rafferty's relief as the right question to ask dawned on him and came in a rush.

'And when do you hope to see Mrs Bora again, about the envelope I mean? It's just that I thought you might tell her from me that her husband's fee will be in the mail shortly. You'll tell her that when you see her, won't you? Do you think you'll see her soon, I mean?'

Nick told him he'd be seeing her the next day and when

he put down the phone and realised the full implications of what he had done he felt a sense of exhiliration, a quickening in the rhythm of his life. He didn't know what animal his bait would attract, if any at all. But he couldn't help thinking of the villagers in India who try to capture man-eating tigers by tethering a goat overnight to a tree.

Of course he'd have to carry it through himself. No point pulling in Stratton. Even in the unlikely event that Stratton had an inclination to help there'd be no justification for police to commit resources to Nick's speculations.

Again Nick remembered the guy in the red utility. He took out the note on which he'd written the registration and called Liam Davies from Traffic Patrol. Liam told him to wait and was back within minutes. The ute belonged to a Gordon Harrison, a garage owner. He hired the ute out from the garage. It was out for a week, hired by a guy named Milan Dragos. Nick thanked Liam and quickly tapped out the number for Criminal Records. He got Jack Fowler. Good. Jack knew his voice and wouldn't stand on the security rules and make him send a DPP fax to get the priors.

Jack did a search and told Nick that Dragos had priors in Victoria. Burglaries, a couple of assaults and armed robbery. Thirty-four-years-old. Two lots of time behind him. Pentridge on both occasions. Last permanent address in Geelong, Victoria. No known criminal activity in Canberra.

Was this the guy who killed Olafson? More to the point, was this the guy they'd get to come and collect the non-existent Crowbar envelope? Maybe he was neither. Maybe he was just a guy visiting from Victoria who happened to have a criminal record and who happened to be in Johnny's street with a ute looking to earn an honest living. Whatever. Nick shrugged off speculation. What was important now was to watch Ruth's house. He grabbed his coat and hurried out.

It turned out Appleyard was employed by an outfit called Abacus Mines. Finding him was simple. Once McAngel had explained what they were looking for, Maggie went through the Yellow Pages and looked up the entries under 'mining engineers'. There were a couple. She rang one and got the receptionist. She told her she was looking for an employee of this mining company which had an office in Canberra. Couldn't recall its name. There were quite a few, the receptionist told her. Name of the person she was looking for? A Mr Appleyard? *Gotcha!* she said. *Knew him well*, she told Maggie. Originally from Perth. She could find him at the offices of Abacus Mines in Newcastle Street in Fyshwick. Abacus was a big operation, she said, with its main offices in Perth, but it had opened a small office in Canberra apparently to handle its government contracts. Been there since about November of last year. Maggie heard the receptionist ask her for a name as she hung up.

McAngel parked the car in Newcastle Street and watched as Maggie entered the office. Fyshwick. New territory for McAngel. Canberra's dumping ground for trade industries, light manufacturing and a colourful muddle of all types of wholesalers and retailers. Lively and busy by Canberra standards, he thought. Even a different class of human being out here, he noticed. No fluorescent pansies on bike paths. Not many suits. This must be where you get to see all the guys in overalls and singlets. Still, there was no dirt and no smells here either. No dirt, no smells, no character.

Maggie was soon back with a collection of maps and pamphlets about Abacus' mining ventures, which she chucked into the back seat.

'No worries?' he asked.

'No worries,' she confirmed. 'I met him. And Gregory. They've both got an office there. No receptionist in sight. I told Appleyard I was a schoolteacher and asked him if he could talk to my class some time. *Not in the near future*, he said but he would call me when he was available. In other words, *piss off*. Gave me the pamphlets and hurried me out. There he is now.'

She pointed to a guy, young face but probably about thirty, medium height and build, neatly styled hair, patterned home-knitted pullover. Looked like his mum still dressed him in the morning. Standing outside the premises, he lit a smoke, looked at his watch. He was edgy.

A red Toyota utility pulled up at the kerb near where Appleyard was standing. The driver was wearing white overalls. Appleyard jumped in and appeared to speak to him for a while before getting out again.

The Toyota took off.

McAngel started his car and followed.

'I thought we were going to watch Appleyard,' said Maggie.

'Appleyard hurried you out. He was nervous while waiting. Just a hunch, but this guy's worth following.'

The red ute turned into Canberra Avenue. They followed him for a couple of minutes until the ute turned off Canberra Avenue, around Dominion Circuit. He went past the Italian Embassy and continued south.

'Where are we?' McAngel asked her.

'Deakin,' she replied. 'Johnny's suburb.'

16

Nick had found the perfect place to watch. He had taken an office car. He didn't want his own recognised. Johnny's house was at the crest of the cul-de-sac. Where the cul-de-sac intersected with the main road there was a small park with some off-road parking sheltered by trees. By pulling beneath the trees he could survey the house but not be obvious.

Some time after midday the red ute came. He saw it pull into the street and stop outside Johnny's house. The guy in white overalls hopped out. He was squat and broad and seemed from that distance to be dark in appearance. He wore shades. Nick watched him walk up the path and go to the front door and wait. He then saw him go the neighbour's house. A woman came to the door and he appeared to talk with her for a time.

Smart move thought Nick. He's letting everyone know he's there. Playing the tradesman come to fix something. Nothing to hide. Nothing suspicious about his presence. He saw him go to the ute and pull out a ladder and place it on Johnny's front lawn. He returned and this time pulled from the ute some buckets and tins. A painter! He was going to paint something in the yard. And when it suited him he'd get himself in somehow. Probably through the side door.

The guy climbed the ladder and started scraping flaky paint from the guttering. Nick watched him for about fifteeen minutes. He moved from the front yard and disappeared around the back. Now he's getting in, thought Nick. He'd wait until Dragos came out empty handed and follow him. Chances were he would lead him somewhere that smelled of Urquhart. That was all he wanted at this stage. Confirmation that Urquhart was involved, then he'd sort out what to do next.

More time passed. The guy hadn't reappeared. Nick waited and watched. As long as the red ute remained where it was he didn't care how long he took. Suddenly there was the noise of his passenger door opening and even as he started in surprise the fist detonated into his face. He was still stunned as he felt himself being dragged violently by the head. Then came the frightening pounding of the car door against his neck and shoulders, which were wedged between the passenger door and the seat—two, three, four, five times. The release and the kick to his chin which lifted his whole torso along with his head. He fought to maintain consciousness, to focus on what was happening. He managed to register the white overalls and the sight of the shades before another massive blow to the side of his head. Then blackness.

There was a woman on her knees looking down at him. A beautiful blonde woman asking him something. Beside her somewhere a male voice. He tried to focus, had to focus if he was going to avoid the next blow. The woman began to recede from him and Nick reached for her and found instead another dark void into which he vaulted.

'I still think we should have taken him to the hospital

McAngel. This is not right.' Maggie said.

They both stood looking at the big man they'd managed to get back to their hotel room. It hadn't been easy. Nick was heavy cartage. Luckily no-one appeared to have seen them as they helped him, half conscious, onto the bed.

'Trust me,' said McAngel. 'He'll be okay. He won't want to go to hospital and he'll be grateful he's here with us in this hotel. No-one will know and I bet that's what he'll want when he's capable of applying his mind to it all.'

Nick groaned and began to regain full consciousness. When able to focus he recognised the woman he'd seen bending over him earlier. The guy next to her he'd never seen. His head pounded. He'd received his second beating in two days and his nervous system was taking an inventory of all the bruises. He struggled to understand where he was. He was on a bed. A small bedroom. A hotel? Too bad if they were going to beat him again he thought. There was nothing he could do about it. He was just too tired. He tried to set aside the pain and study their faces. They weren't looking as if they were going to beat him. Who were they?

'It's okay,' said Maggie, addressing the bewilderment in Nick's eyes. 'We picked you up in the park. The man who attacked you ran away when we came. Jumped in his car and took off.'

'The red ute,' recalled Nick.

His jaw ached too much for him to open his mouth. He began to feel the pain in his neck and shoulders.

'We saw him from a distance and came as quickly as we could.'

'You scared him off?' asked Nick weakly. He had some doubts.

McAngel gave a friendly laugh.

'Hey, that guy didn't run because he was frightened. He was a strong guy. You can tell. No, he wasn't scared.

182

He just didn't want us to get a good look at him. He obviously knew that you were watching him and didn't like it.'

Through the pain Nick experienced astonishment.

'You knew he was in Johnny's house? That I was ...'

'That you were watching him?' McAngel flicked the DPP identification card onto the bed. 'I figured it was you even before I looked in your wallet.'

Nick managed to raise himself to a sitting position.

'Who are you?' he asked of McAngel.

McAngel didn't answer but Maggie introduced herself. Nick recognised the name.

'Maggie Spires. You shared the house with Stella Sanchez,' he said.

Maggie nodded. Nick then indicated McAngel.

'Your accent. You're the American boyfriend. What the hell is going on?'

He tried to stand. The rush of pain to his head toppled him.

McAngel looked at the big man sitting on the bed with the battered face, then nodded to Maggie. He could trust this man. He didn't want to, but he knew he could trust him.

Nick slumped back. He felt overcome by tiredness again. But his fear was gone. These two were okay. He felt that. For now he needed some more sleep. He closed his eyes.

Dragos had just gone, slamming the door after him so hard that the office shook. Appleyard was sweating. It had all gone wrong again and he would have to break the news to Urquhart, something he'd hoped to avoid. Dragos had turned up nothing at Johnny Bora's house and he'd come back to the Abacus offices agitated. Appleyard, irritated, had called Dragos a stupid bastard. There had been no need to beat up the prosecutor he told him.

'Hey, don't call me stupid,' Dragos had threatened. 'You said do what it takes pal, to get the envelope. Well there was no fucking envelope, okay? And this prick's down there waiting for me to come out. Watching me. I could see him from the ladder. Then I watched from inside the house. So when I don't find anything I goes out the back of the house over the fence and double back down the street. I'm going to ask the prosecutor where the envelope is. But he's not going to give it to me is he? Not without some encouragement. And maybe there is no envelope and maybe he can tell me why there isn't if I ask him nicely. But I'm interrupted. Okay? So I was doing what it takes. Just like you said to do, you fucking fairy.'

Dragos had wrenched open Appleyard's coat and taken his wallet from the coat pocket. He helped himself to the five hundred he'd been promised and jammed the wallet back in.

'Next time I don't deal with you, right. I deal with the man himself or nobody.'

And he'd left.

Gregory appeared from a second office. He opened a pack of cigarettes, lit one and gave it to Appleyard and then lit another for himself.

'Lovely man,' he said. 'I told you we shouldn't have handled this ourselves Phillip. We need *real* professionals. Not thugs like him. We should have told Urquhart that the prosecutor had this damn envelope.'

'Sure, sure. Twenty-twenty vision in hindsight, eh Colin,' objected Appleyard. 'I was told Dragos was good. That he was the type we wanted to keep this bloody Crowbar business under control.'

He paced. He shook his head worriedly.

'My God. Telling Urquhart we didn't get the Crowbar envelope isn't going to be easy.'

Gregory was a small man, short cropped hair, high forehead, feminine in manner and in speech. He maintained a sanctimonious silence while Appleyard paced. Then he went into a small annexe where he helped himself to some hot water from a cistern and proceeded to dip a tea bag in his cup. Appleyard followed him and stood at the doorway.

'I mean, really, the man who should be doing all this heavy work is Keppler,' complained Appleyard.

Gregory stopped sipping his tea and looked alarmed.

'Urquhart doesn't want him to know anything at all about Crowbar, you know that. Anyway, can you imagine asking Keppler to do a petty burglary? No thanks.'

Appleyard looked unconvinced.

'He'd have his price I'd imagine. They all have their price.'

The sudden look of surprise and fear which appeared on Gregory's face made Appleyard turn around.

The man's presence always had a chilling effect on Appleyard. Now, as he turned his eyes to find Keppler's glacial stare half a metre from his face, he was forced to control the acute and silent panic that welled in his chest. And then, just as Applyard found enough composure to speak, Keppler interrupted what he was going to say.

'Gentleman, I believe you were discussing this matter of . . . *Crowbar?* Please continue.'

Fyshwick was fifteeen minutes from the hotel. McAngel drove. Maggie was next to him and Nick sat in the back seat nursing a sore head and trying to process what he'd just learned. So much had happened so soon. When he awoke in the early hours of that morning he felt better. Far more rested than he'd felt for many days even though his body ached. Then McAngel and Maggie had sat with him and told him the extraordinary story of this man

185

Keppler. How it was Keppler who had arranged for Stella and Alfie to be killed and had then killed Olafson. How in McAngel's opinion, it was Keppler behind the tribal killing of Johnny Bora.

Nick had never been convinced that the full story behind Johnny's death began and ended with Billy Jangala's people. Could this McAngel be right? That this Keppler was some sort of international gun for hire to eliminate people who were considered a threat to the establishment? And that Johnny was on the hit list? The American still refused to explain his interest in Keppler. From what he'd told Nick it was clear he'd pursued this Keppler here to Australia. But why? Was McAngel from the CIA? FBI? Maybe. McAngel hadn't denied that when Nick put it to him but he didn't confirm it either.

He liked the woman, Maggie. 'Now you know as much as I do,' she'd said with an ironic smile and an accusing glance at McAngel.

The whole story was crazy and improbable yet here he was, swollen face and aching body, in the company of two people whom he'd just met, heading to Fyshwick and the offices of Abacus Mines. Perhaps he should have simply walked out of the hotel, contacted Stratton, told him everything he'd learned and left it to the AFP to sort out. But he didn't. He knew that questions of legality should have been troubling him. Jesus Christ, he was a Crown Prosecutor after all! And here he was not reporting assaults on himself and travelling around Canberra with an American who in all likelihood would break a few laws himself before the day was out.

And what if they did find Keppler? Without admissions was Nick going to be in a position to prove anything against him? The answer was no. There was not a shred of evidence that he'd done anything wrong. So if and when they found him, what could they do? And what of

Urquhart? What could be proved against him at this stage? He didn't even know for sure how Urquhart entered the picture.

So what exactly was Nick doing here? He'd already confronted the possibility that he was intoxicated with the irresponsible thrill of it all. That his life had been too tame for a long time. Of course he wanted to find the truth behind Johnny's death. It was an important end. Something he owed his friend. But he also had to admit he was looking forward to the ride necessary to get him there, law or no law.

'Find Urquhart, you find Keppler,' had reasoned McAngel after they'd exchanged what they knew.

Nick agreed. And now here he was.

But Urquhart still worried him. What exactly was his role in all of this? For McAngel the connection was clear. Urquhart ran a mining corporation. Johnny was a land rights advocate and a powerful voice in Aboriginal politics. Mining interests were threatened. The solution? Have Johnny attended to. Nick could accept this. But the computer message continued to nag at him. Why bother to delete such a small message? In fact, without the knowledge of its deletion it would have gone unnoticed. In this sense its deletion was more significant than its contents. Was asbestos behind it all, as Nick suspected? McAngel had no explanation for Johnny's interest in the Crowbar Mine. Really, McAngel didn't seem to care much at all about Urquhart's activities. He was obsessed with Keppler, and if anything else mattered it was only to the extent that it had any bearing on finding Keppler.

They had a plan of sorts for when they arrived at the Abacus offices. Maggie would go to the office as the pesky schoolteacher once again, interested in more information on mining. She could then report on who was in the office. If Appleyard and Gregory were on their own, Nick and

McAngel could enter and try to coax them into doing some explaining. Nick had deliberately not asked McAngel what he meant by the word *coax*. But now as they turned into Newcastle Street he felt the pain in his jaw and decided that he was happy with as liberal an interpretation of the word as it would take.

They parked and Maggie crossed the road. They saw her push open the glass door and enter. Thirty seconds later she was out again and walking quickly and urgently back across the road. She pulled open the door of the Magna and got in. Something was wrong.

'Dead. They are both dead,' she said between her teeth, containing herself, resisting the welling hysteria, determined to stay strong.

Nick went to jump out. McAngel reached into the back and restrained him.

'Not yet,' he said. 'Maggie. Are you sure?'

'Yes,' Maggie got out between clenched teeth. 'They are dead. Two corpses. Appleyard and Gregory.'

'Is it possible that there is anyone else in there now?' he asked, looking over the road intently.

Maggie fought to regain her composure enough to speak sensibly. She knew what McAngel was asking her.

'Keppler isn't there,' she said. 'There's no-one there. Alive.'

'I'm going,' said Nick, pushing open the car door and crossing the road toward the Abacus shop front.

McAngel pulled the Taurus from under the seat and dropped it into his coat pocket.

'You okay?' he asked Maggie.

She nodded. She was concentrating on willing away the panic, settling the turmoil, recovering her wits. And it was working. Maggie could see Nick heading for the Abacus doorway.

'You better go after him,' she said.

McAngel followed Nick. It was barely past nine on a sunny morning, traffic was light, and he could see clearly all about him as he crossed the road. But it was still a dangerous moment. Much more dangerous, he knew, than Nick, who had disappeared into the offices, realised. When McAngel entered he locked the door behind him before finding Nick crouched over two bodies in a small annex off the main office.

McAngel did a quick search. There was a reception area and two small offices. The reception area contained a desk and a computer. Around the walls were some old photographs variously depicting big holes in the ground, huge trucks and men in safety helmets. The offices were small and sparsely furnished. It was okay.

Back in the annex McAngel recognised the body of Appleyard, the one he'd seen talking to the guy in the red ute. It had been dumped on top of the other guy's and he was on his back. There was a dribble of blood at the base of a strangely distorted nose. McAngel knew the technique. An open palm had been driven into the nose so that the shattered bone penetrated the brain. Appleyard's eyes, which remained open, contained all the astonishment he must have felt in his final moments as his young life expired at the end of that blow. McAngel assumed that the body underneath Appleyard was that of Gregory. The protruding tongue told him that Keppler had probably choked this one.

'Dragos could have done this,' said Nick who didn't know any better.

McAngel had gone back into the reception area. He checked the office space again, thoroughly, answering Nick as he did so.

'What you have there is Keppler. Believe me. It's Keppler.'

Nick emerged.

189

'These two were supposed to be on the same side as Keppler weren't they? Why would he kill them?'

'I don't know,' replied McAngel, his attention suddenly attracted by Nick going for the phone.

'What are you doing?'

'I'm ringing the police.'

McAngel pressed the receiver button down before Nick could dial.

'Think about it.'

The recommendation was firm.

'You're not suggesting ...'

'You ring the cops and we waste more time. Keppler did this and the cops won't find him even if we could convince them to look. You know that don't you?'

Nick paused. Interviews, statements, explanations, red tape ... It would go on and on. And what did he have to give the police? Speculations. Nothing more. It was best to keep moving. Slowly he returned the phone to the receiver. McAngel continued to look around oblivious to the effort it took for someone with twenty years as a Crown Prosecutor to make that decision.

There was an answering machine next to the phone. It occurred to McAngel to listen to the messages. There was one message. Nick recognised the voice instantly as that of Rafferty.

'Hello boys. Hear the one about the two Irish homos who ... Just joking fellas, just joking. Listen, Mr Urquhart's at Pitt Street. He wants to see me about the land claims. I'm at Perth airport now. I'll be staying at the Marlborough in Sydney. What's the situation with the Crowbar envelope? You better let me know. I'm seeing your boss tomorrow after lunch.'

A click and the message was over. McAngel looked questioningly at Nick.

'It's Rafferty, the Perth solicitor I told you about.'

'Pitt Street?' queried McAngel.

'Pitt Street is in Sydney,' said Nick, the company search still fresh in his mind. 'Urquhart's company, the big one, Wessex Holdings, has its head office in Pitt Street.'

'Urquhart. Urquhart,' McAngel repeated the name.

Then he found the connection he'd been looking for. Tub and Gunner's account of the men they'd taken to the Wonyulgunna settlement! 'Urquhart ... Arkett. It was Urquhart who was in Mt White with Appleyard and Gregory. Tub and Gunner had the name wrong!'

Nick saw the open phone book. It was a Sydney directory.

'Look at this,' he said to McAngel, showing him the page on which it was open.

McAngel ran his finger down the page and stopped.

'Marlborough Hotel, with address. Keppler heard the same message. He'll be wanting to talk to this Rafferty.'

McAngel turned to go. Nick didn't follow.

'I told you. We can't report this,' said McAngel, thinking Nick was having second thoughts. But Nick was looking at the wall, at one of the photographs. It was in colour. There was some sort of rig in the background, then some trucks and graders and other heavy machinery and in the foreground a group of four men.

McAngel joined Nick in looking at the photo. There was a legend beneath and he read it out aloud.

'Sixteenth of January 1975, the Crowbar Mine, left to right, Mr Scott Urquhart, Mine Manager, Sir Samuel Urquhart, Director Abacus Mines, Mr Geoffrey Rafferty, Solicitor and *Mr Christian Pearl, Senior Partner, Griffin and Power Solicitors.*

'Pearl,' repeated McAngel.

Nick didn't reply. Outside the bright day suddenly darkened as the sun disappeared behind a cloud.

17

'**D**on't get it like that every day do you sweetheart?' said Rafferty, pulling on his trousers.

The girl was young, seventeen maybe. She was relieved it hadn't taken him long. She'd been working all night and it was now well into the morning. She suppressed a yawn, grateful that he wasn't looking when she did and grateful that he didn't really expect an answer to his question. Soon he'd pay her and she could go.

She watched him as he reached for his shirt, this little guy with hairy shoulders and a flap of greasy red hair folded over against his bald freckled scalp. He reminded her of a yappy kelpie they had back home in Cowra on her grandparents' farm. He was a dog who made a lot of noise and always looked pleased with himself after working the cattle even though he wasn't much good. Her grandfather eventually shot him. The sad part was that no-one missed him much.

The farm. Nostalgia touched her lightly on the breast as she remembered the steamy warmth of the milk cow's flank on her cheek but disappeared immediately as

Rafferty leant over her and tickled her nipple with his tongue.

'Great tits,' he said approvingly as he straightened up and then he repeated it with a suggestion of self-congratulation as he reached for his shirt. 'Great tits. You been at the game long girlie?'

She shook her head. Bernice had told him the guy was a regular when he visited Sydney from Perth. Solicitor, but down to earth type. Tipped well. He usually asked for Lois or Gwenda but they were both unavailable. He liked them young. So Bernice sent her along. Now she was tired and just wanted to get out of there. She slipped on her camisole.

'Thought so,' said Rafferty knowingly when he saw her shake her head. 'I'll give you some advice. When you go down on a man sweetheart, he likes a bit of action with the tongue as well. Not just this in and out business. You with me? That's what the customer pays for. Remember that.'

She tried to look grateful for the advice. *Be nice to him, Bernice had said. He'll pay you well.* She continued to dress in silence. Rafferty went to the bedroom mirror and put his tie on. Meanwhile the girl reached into her bag for a cigarette. Her lighter wouldn't work.

'There's one out there,' said Rafferty, indicating the lounge and dining area of the hotel room.

She padded barefoot out of the bedroom over the thick carpet and spotted Rafferty's lighter on the coffee table. She lit her cigarette and when she turned she saw him. A man. Blond, blue eyes, expressionless mouth. Suit and tie. Sitting in the deep red leather armchair. He made reassuring gestures with an open palm and then by putting his index finger to his lips indicated that he wanted her to keep quiet.

She nodded. The guy must know Rafferty. Wants to

surprise him. She relaxed and puffed on her cigarette and waited. He was wearing leather gloves. In *this* heat? Kinky maybe. Well the two of them can be kinky with each other, she thought.

'You know, I always use cash with you girls,' called out Rafferty from the bedroom. 'I use cash. You know why? Because that way I'm safe. No-one can blackmail me by tracing cheques and credit cards. There's a few who'd do that. Try to blackmail me. Ruin my good name. So I use cash. And you know what that means, sweetheart. It means you can keep as much of my tip as you like. Don't have to go halves with old Bernice. And I want you to know that I thought you did okay, I want you to know that. And I like your tits. But I'm not gonna tip you as much as I tipped Gwenda last time 'cause I want you to try harder when we get together next time. When you go down on me I mean. I'm one of those guys who believes in performance pay. You know what I mean sweetheart?'

The guy in the chair shook his head from side to side and put his finger to his lips again. She shrugged. Weird guy. Had he been there long? While they were doing it? Maybe he was watching. She regarded him suspiciously. Maybe you get to charge more if someone watches. She'll ask Bernice tonight. She drew on her cigarette.

'I said, *you know what I mean sweetheart*,' Rafferty poked his head out of the bedroom door. Was this little whore ignoring him?

Keppler stood up so that Rafferty could see him and the girl knew immediately from Rafferty's reaction that she'd guessed wrongly about the relationship. Rafferty's mouth opened involuntarily.

'You,' he said.

'Me,' agreed Keppler.

'I don't ... I don't understand. I mean what can I do for you?'

194

Rafferty was shit scared of this guy, she thought. She cleared her throat. She wanted to go.

Rafferty continued to stammer and stumble for something to say.

'Look, perhaps later when this young lady leaves ... we can talk. Is that what you want to do? I mean ...'

'Pay her,' Keppler said abruptly.

'Sure, sure. Here sweetheart.'

Rafferty took his wallet from his back pocket and began fumbling for some notes. Keppler took the wallet from his hands. Calmly he reached inside and took out all the notes. They made a large wad. Without looking at the girl he held out the money.

'Here, take it.'

The girl hesitated. It was a lot of money. A hell of a lot.

'Take it. He wants you to have it. Don't you?'

She reached out and took the money. It was a big tip.

Rafferty perspired.

'There's a lot of money there Mr Keppler. Over a thousand dollars. You're not serious.'

'You don't want her to have it then?' asked Keppler, affecting some surprise.

'Well, like I said, there's a lot of money there. I ...'

He stopped, astonished as Keppler produced a small hand gun.

'Yours?' asked Keppler politely.

Rafferty looked over at his luggage in alarm. It was his. A .22 calibre Ruger pistol. He carried it with him on trips. Not that he ever dreamed of using it. He'd take it out and show it to people. When relaxing after conferences. It was a good talking point. Made him feel important, attracted attention. He told Keppler none of this except with his eyes.

'Ah,' said Keppler. 'You are not really a gun man.'

Keppler sighed as if disappointed.

'So you do not want this girl to have your money. Am I correct?'

Rafferty was confused. The girl looked on, summoning the courage to ask if she could go. This may get nasty, although she found the blond man strangely reassuring. As if he was not at all interested in her. But then she froze as Keppler said, 'And you would not of course, shoot this girl simply because she had all your money?'

'Of course not,' said Rafferty shaking his head, baffled.

'Then I will,' said Keppler, matter-of-factly.

And in one sudden, smooth movement he turned, aimed the barrel of the gun to the girl's head, paused briefly to look at Rafferty's appalled expression and then fired.

She fell to the carpet, still barefooted, her left hand clutching the notes from Rafferty's wallet.

'There,' said Keppler, 'Now if anyone asks we can both say that you shot this girl while she was stealing your money. That you lacked the courage to really do so will be our little secret. Okay?'

Rafferty stood there, horrified and nauseated as Keppler placed something in his hand. When he looked down, he saw he was holding his gun.

'And we can now chat,' said Keppler and he resumed his seat on the leather chair.

In the drab and musty confines of the old elevator to the twelfth floor of the AMP Building, Nick sought to collect himself. Pearl had answered the phone and told him to come right up when Nick said he wanted to discuss an ethics question. Pearl! The club had been found in his room and now it turns out that he was Urquhart's solicitor all those years ago.

Pearl met him at the elevator and was all hail-fellow-well-met. Their paths had rarely crossed over the years.

Pearl was a commercial lawyer. The odd encounter at Bar Association meetings or functions which Nick infrequently attended had been the extent of their knowledge of one another's existence. Now Nick found Pearl's bonhomie cloying. He didn't like the man. He was soft and pink, something of a dandy and full of phony solicitude. Nick declined the port. He opened in a forthright manner.

'Before Johnny was killed, the practitioner in question was briefing him on a land claim by Pilbara Aborigines. You know him I think. Name of Rafferty, from Perth.'

'Oh yes,' answered Pearl. 'Geoffrey Rafferty. Old employee of my former firm in Perth. Now there is a man I have not seen in a long time. On the phone you indicated an ethics problem?'

Nick nodded.

'Dear me,' said Pearl. 'Although I can hardly say I'm surprised from what I remember of Geoff.'

Nice move thought Nick. Pearl had just put Rafferty at arms length from himself. Maybe it was genuine. Up the ante, he thought.

'It's just that I've found out that your old firm once acted for Abacus Mines. You recall that?'

'Most certainly,' answered Pearl. 'I am hardly likely to forget it. The Abacus account was acquired by Griffin and Power largely because of my own efforts. As you know Nick, accounts of that size usually end up with the mega firms. But, I had a contact or two you see.'

Pearl had paused expectantly. He was ready to play.

Nick trod carefully. He had nearly asked if Urquhart himself was one of those contacts. It occurred to him that Pearl might be conducting his own fishing expedition to see how much he knew. He stuck to the Rafferty problem.

'Well, Rafferty's land claim matter involves land which is the subject of one of Abacus' mining leases. Abacus is a former client of yours and of Rafferty's. Back in the time

197

when you were a senior partner of the firm I mean. It's clearly a conflict of interest for Rafferty to now act on behalf of the Aborigines who are the claimants.'

Nick dropped each sentence carefully, waiting for a reaction. Pearl suddenly looked as if the same horrendous thought had just occurred to him.

You oily bastard, thought Nick.

'I see what you mean,' said Pearl as if he was turning over the proposition in his mind for the first time. 'From memory I'm almost certain that Geoff Rafferty *was* involved in work for Abacus. Well that just won't do will it? Neither side would be happy with that situation, would they?'

Nick pushed on.

'Particularly the Aborigines. Johnny was the top practitioner in the field. His approach to the preparation of his land claims would have been valuable knowledge to the mining companies. Not just Abacus but also any of the others who were expecting claims. You'd agree with that wouldn't you?'

Pearl was aghast. Bluffing. He raised.

'Of course I would. You are not suggesting that Geoff has deliberately betrayed his clients in this way? Why that would be outrageously improper,' he said pompously. 'Do you have evidence that this has occurred?'

No he didn't. And Pearl knew it. His cards were good. But he was worried about Nick and Nick could sense it. Why? Was he part of all of this? The club that murdered Johnny was found in Pearl's room. How much did he know? Olafson, the computer disk, Dragos, Crowbar?

Crowbar! Pearl didn't know that Nick's suspicions had been aroused by the Crowbar photo. Apart from that there was nothing connecting Pearl to Crowbar. Unless Rafferty had told him about the mythical envelope. It was worth keeping the game alive. He bet on.

'What do you know about Crowbar, Mr Pearl?'

Pearl showed no reaction. He replied casually.

'Very minor operation by Abacus standards, from what I recall. Asbestos mine wasn't it? Why do you ask?'

No bite, thought Nick. He was sure Rafferty had told Pearl about the envelope. Pearl wanted to find out what Nick knew or was pretending to know. Nick was too far into the game now to pull out. He'd bet the lot.

'Negligence,' he said. 'By the mine. Asbestosis. Cancers. Potential damages claims against Abacus worth millions. Johnny had been working on them.'

It was a dud bet. He could tell straightaway. Nick the experienced cross-examiner saw immediately the signs of Pearl's relief. The way he shifted his position in the chair as if to better seize the opportunity to be patronising. A new attitude of smugness replaced composed caution. Pearl knew he had the winning hand. He could call Nick's bluff.

'Really. How very surprising Nick. When I acted for the company we settled what claims there were for asbestos-related injury out of court. As far as I knew most of the potential claimants were compensated. Any further claims were also happily settled out of court. It made no sense to do anything else at the time. Of course, Mr Bora may have had the advantage of me and known of something that had transpired since I left the firm.'

Exactly what Mills had said. Nick now knew that asbestosis or negligence claims didn't figure in all of this. Pearl sat looking at him. Nick knew he had just told Pearl what he wanted to know. That Nick knew bugger all about the real reason for Johnny's concern with Crowbar. Nick had nothing left to play with. He folded.

'What exactly is it you would like me to do about Mr Rafferty, Nick?' Pearl asked. He was raking in the chips.

Nick stood up.

'I'll leave that up to you. I'm sure you'll do what's best.'

As he left he pretended not to see Pearl's outstretched hand. It was not an overt gesture of rudeness. Had he taken it he would have broken it.

It was all freeway to Sydney. Three and a half hours to get into town he'd been told. A flight would not have got him there any quicker. Besides, he had the Taurus on him. You didn't need to pass through a metal detector to ride in a motor vehicle.

He thought of Maggie. She was back in Canberra. He'd been honest. They'd get together again if they could. And if they couldn't ...? Tell Byron, he had reminded her. McAngel forced himself to think of something else. He settled on Keppler. He was close. He knew that. As close as he'd been to him since Rome. He smiled wryly. Of course Keppler could say the same thing about him.

Miles of road stretched in front of him. He was alone which meant he had time to do what he dreaded doing most. To think. To remember. To re-live the pain and the guilt that even the passage of fifteen years had not erased. McAngel turned on the radio. He searched the stations—pop, classical, current affairs, talk-back—nothing satisfied him, nothing kept his attention. He gave up.

Herat, Aghanistan in 1977. Twilight approaching. A hot trip through the desert behind them. Sitting on the steps at the back entrance of an old hotel temporarily without running water because the pipes had burst. A turbaned plumber and a couple of tall, bearded assistants with dark, proud eyes, digging a deep trench in the overgrown yard and releasing a not unpleasant mix of dank and aromatic odours from freshly turned earth.

With him some travellers he and Maria first met in

Kandahar. Aldo, the Italian journalist, dressed in white Indian calico and hippy beads had a small water pipe and was passing it around, the thin, keen smell of top grade hash cutting through the lingering evening heat. Simone, the lesbian from Marseilles, alternating between English and French, talked on about the hassles she'd had with the border officials in India and the hassles she'd had with her booking agent in Marseilles. Only Lefevre who was from Quebec, understood her when she lapsed into French and he'd reluctantly translate when she prodded him to do so. Lefevre had been grateful to leave for a time with a cooler box and he returned with some ice-cold bottles of Coke to distribute.

'He has found a fucking fridge. The only fridge in all of Afghanistan,' Vander had declared.

Vander maintained he was Dutch. McAngel didn't believe him. He'd done hard manual labour for some South African engineers during his last university vacations. *He'd get lost quicker in Amsterdam than in Johannesburg*, McAngel had observed to Maria. She shrugged. What did it matter? They were all travellers who met and parted easily. Trust wasn't important in those circumstances. Therefore neither was truth.

On the steps McAngel had mellowed out, letting the effects of the hash work on him in silence. He wasn't always a great talker particularly when he was stoned. Over the back of the mosque the sky was winding down through the afternoon colour display as the sun set—rich reds and yellows into deeper hues of crimson and purple. From a distance he could hear some dirgelike Afghani music, the long doleful strains of the instruments hanging in the thick evening air.

Maria appeared from inside the hotel. Her hair was wrapped in a towel. She had changed into some cut-away jeans and the cotton top with the embroidered edges he'd bought for her in Agra. The top was pure white and accentuated her dark slender arms, the tan in her face and her large brown eyes.

'Hey, you got water?' objected Lefevre.

'One tankful. All they had left,' she teased as she sat down on the step below McAngel. 'All gone now.'

Aldo passed her the pipe. She declined and passed it on. McAngel gave her the last Coke from the cooler box and she took a drink.

'Mmm ... cold!' she purred.

She paused and looked up and smiled at him— nineteen years old, dark and very beautiful. Two months only since they'd learned she was pregnant with his child. Not long after, on a fine morning in Srinigar, a dealer came paddling across the lake in his *shikkhara* to their houseboat and once inside had opened before them a velvet cloth in which were wrapped all manner of rings and jewels. She selected from them a thin gold band which she knew he could afford and which he later placed on her finger before the old Catholic priest back in Delhi, with Barillo, the Spanish photographer they'd met in Calcutta, standing in as best man.

McAngel was happy. He loved the feel of the changes in her body when they made love. Her breasts and hips were fuller, rounder, and there was about her a serene good health that he imagined was a response to the richness of the life force in a body holding within it not one life but two. He leant forward and kissed her on the lips, once, twice and then again for a long time as she pulled him toward her.

When they parted Aldo was looking at them, pleased.

'You two. You are very much in love, no? Is good, this love, no?' Aldo was giving his approval. And then to Maria, whom he knew understood, he spoke Italian. '*Anche io mi piacerebbe una ragazza,*' and he looked

202

around him pausing to wink at Simone before shrugging and adding, '*Ma qui? E molto triste.*'

'What did he say?' McAngel asked Maria.

'He says he'd like a girl too. But there's none here in Herat for him. It's very sad, he says.'

McAngel had laughed.

'Mmm ... the drink was delicious,' Maria said.

Simone said that Lefevre should go and and get some more drinks. McAngel felt some sympathy for the little Canadian. God knows why he had teamed up to travel with Simone. It obviously wasn't sex. McAngel volunteered to go instead and took some directions from Lefevre.

He went off with the cooler box in one hand, taking his time and enjoying the sensation of time warp as he strolled through the streets of Herat with its markets and carts and ancient motor vehicles. At one point, mixed into the aromas of tobacco and horse shit there came from a butcher shop the unpleasant stench of unrefrigerated meat carcasses. It made him shudder and he diverted his eyes from the skinned goat's head that sat eyelessly despondent on a table display.

He returned with the drinks some twenty minutes later. It was dark. The steps where they had been sitting were deserted except for one of the Afghanis who had been digging the hole. He was throwing a bucket of water over the steps. He saw McAngel and hurried back inside the hotel.

McAngel went up the stairs to their rooms. There was a gloomy corridor, dimly lit with a sickly yellow glow from incandescent light bulbs. He looked into his and Maria's room. A large bed, an old wardrobe, a small sink, threadbare carpet. It was empty. Aldo's room—some clothes on the bed, a long bag half open. Otherwise, empty. Simone and Lefevre's—likewise empty apart from some belongings dumped when they first arrived. Vander had a room to himself. McAngel was surprised to see that the door was open and that there was no sign of Vander or his belongings.

Had they gone out? Maria would have waited for him. He returned to the desk in the foyer downstairs where Ali, who had booked them in, sat idly behind the reception desk. McAngel asked him if he'd seen them. He shrugged.

There was a laundry area. From there he heard a tap running into a sink. He looked in and it was empty. The plumbing was fixed. Then an unaccountable dread. Inexplicable at the time. He ran back outside remembering something—the ditch. It had been filled when he returned. Done so quickly?

Dark now outside in the hotel yard and deserted. Some women, veiled, appeared briefly as they filed silently past the large gate which was the entrance to the hotel. McAngel felt tight in the chest. Again the dread with no explanation. He walked over to where the ditch had been. In the weak light coming from inside the hotel he could see the fresh earth that filled the hole. And in the light he caught sight of a reflection from some glass. He bent over. It was the top of a pop bottle. Tentatively, reluctantly, he began to brush away the earth surrounding the bottle. And then he saw the fingers and the gold ring from Srinigar.

On his right now was a large lake—Lake George. It distracted McAngel and he was relieved to be able to surface from the worst of the memories. They were gone, all of them, including his Maria. Gone along with his young heart and his innocence, buried years ago in the overgrown yard of a cheap Afghani hotel.

18

A s they'd agreed, Maggie was already at Johnny's house when Nick arrived. She had investigated the side door where Dragos had gained entry and she showed Nick how the lock had been forced. They went inside and there was plenty of evidence of a quick search. Books pulled from shelves, drawers and cupboard doors left open. In Johnny's study more of the same, only more intense. There was a mess of books on the floor and the contents of the drawers from his desk had been tipped out. A filing cabinet containing a collection of Johnny's past matters had also been pulled apart.

They began sorting through the mess. There had to be something among Johnny's belongings to explain his interest in Crowbar. Nick realised he had gone down the wrong track in assuming Johnny had been working on a compensation matter related the operation of the Crowbar asbestos mine. He had lost ground and he wanted to recover it as quickly as possible. Also, Pearl's look of smug self-assuredness lingered pungently in his immediate memory.

Together they began sifting through Johnny's papers.

Deeds, briefs of evidence, rolled up maps of desolate regions, affidavits, witness statements, cases, statutes. Dusty words and old paper. The world of the law. Nick paused. How long had all this been his own world. He looked at Maggie, who was caught in the light entering from a window, and he saw the youth still in her face. Something goes from the face, he thought, when you get older. What was it? He continued to look at her. For several seconds she hadn't moved. Her head was bowed and she was gazing into a book, the light behind her. Vermeer-like, he thought. She suddenly snapped the book shut and caught him staring at her. She gave him a curious but friendly look in reply and then picked up another bundle of papers.

Inexplicably he recalled how fresh rain on hot earth had smelt to him as a child, and the delicious sensation of the air cooling as he breathed it in. And now he longed to experience that sensation again. But he had not felt it for so long. And it wasn't for want of heat and rain. So why not? It wasn't just a question of blunted senses. There was something missing, something lost that he wished he could regain. It was still there in Maggie's face. And it occurred to Nick that Johnny had never lost it. It was something to do with innocence, with the capacity to enjoy sensation without the filter of logic or bitterness. Perhaps it was something a poet or a painter or a saint never lost and in its possession lay their genius. Strange thoughts. The sense of loss again embraced him. Johnny had been Nick's window into a world that was larger and more attractive than the narrow and grim world of the law. In that sense Nick had participated in that larger world by proxy. It also occurred to him that since the incident with Olafson, as macabre and as violent as it was, Nick himself had sensed, along with the danger and the tension, a reawakening of the imagination and the spirit. The normal and the humdrum along with the dangerous took on a vibrancy and immediacy that he had not experienced for a long time.

Maggie suddenly looked at him apparently puzzled. Why the hell was he just standing there looking at her? Nick smiled and continued to sort through Johnny's things.

Then Maggie found it. It was a photocopy from an index to some law reports. Such an item was hardly remarkable in a barrister's possession. Maggie asked Nick what it was. He recognised the index immediately. He worked with it daily. It was the index to the *Australian Criminal Law Reports*. The page photocopied was one which gave references to cases on sexual offences and there was a small neat circle around the words *child, upon*. It was strange. Johnny had done plenty of criminal work in the distant past but the major part his practice of late had been Aboriginal land claims.

Maggie asked him what it meant. He showed her the entries.

'This entry circled contains references to cases dealing with sexual assaults on children. If this has been circled by Johnny then it suggests it was something he was interested in at the time of his death, which is odd.'

'Why is it odd?'

'Johnny hadn't defended any criminal cases for years. He was specialising in land claims. If he was involved in a criminal matter I'm sure he would have discussed it with me. I saw him almost every day when he was in town.'

'Maybe it's something he was dealing with years ago,' she ventured.

Nick shook his head and showed her the circled entry.

'See the volume numbers indicated here? They are volumes of law reports. There are references here to volume 53. This volume was published in December of last year. The index is the most recent index to those law reports. So he was looking at this stuff just before he died. In any case, I can't see Johnny taking on this sort of defence work. He was so much in demand it was impossible to get him to appear in his areas of specialty, let alone something like this. Let's keep looking.'

Soon they turned up something else. It was a library notice advising of overdue books. Among the entries there was Ogilvie on *Sexual Offences* and Tanner on *Criminal Law and the Child*.

The date of the notice was 22 December, the day before Johnny was killed. Nick knew his friend well. He was always late—for appointments, for bills, for dinner, and in returning library books. They did a quick search of the room. It became more puzzling. Other books on the list were still there—Ford's *Cases on Trusts*, Sackville and Neave's *Property Cases and Materials* and other property and equity texts. But no Ogilvie and no Tanner.

Nick had an idea. He called the Supreme Court Library. Emma Martin answered. He'd known her for years. She checked on the computer for him. The Tanner text and the Ogilvie hadn't been returned. It was puzzling. Was this like the message on the computer? Something someone wanted to hide? What else had gone missing? What was Johnny up to?

For some reason Nick began to picture Johnny in the last few months of his life. Something had preoccupied him. Nick had attributed it to the problems in his relationship with Ruth. But now that he thought about it, he remembered a Sunday afternoon picnic on the river with both their families and his two girls had been playing with a ball. Nick and Johnny were sitting on a log drinking beer, watching them and occasionally retrieving a stray pass. Emily was twelve, almost thirteen, and little Faith was nine.

Johnny said, 'Sweet girls, your two.'

'Just like their mother,' Nick had replied, loudly, so Louisa could hear.

Louisa had poked out her tongue at him.

'They're lucky,' Johnny went on. 'They have parents who love them, look after them, protect them.'

Nick knew his friend well. He realised Johnny had something else on his mind.

'I agree,' Nick had said, thinking Johnny may have been comparing the girls' childhood to his own. 'It must have been hard growing up as an adopted kid no matter how much you were cared for. Materially I mean.'

Immediately it was clear he had misread Johnny.

'No, I don't mean it in that sense. I mean there's something very delicate, vulnerable about girls that age. So much can go wrong can't it?'

Nick was surprised and he laughed it off.

'Well, thank you very much for that little bit of anxiety inducing information my friend. Anything else you want to spoil my day with?'

Johnny seemed to snap out of it.

'Yeah, you're right. I'm sorry. I was really thinking about some other girls that age that's all.'

'Oh?' Nick had enquired. Maybe he wanted to talk about it.

'Don't worry about it,' Johnny had said, bright eyed and mischievous again, and with that he had dived athletically off the log and to his left to catch the girls' ball an instant before it hit the ground.

Nick looked at Maggie who had resumed sorting through more paperwork. He told her not to bother.

'We need to get back to the DPP.'

McAngel tried the radio again. The Canberra stations were growing faint. Yet he could hear well enough to pick up the news bulletin that reported the finding of Appleyard and Gregory at the Abacus offices. A guy delivering a parcel found them. Police were investigating.

He wondered what Keppler was up to. After the chief kill it wasn't unusual for him to hang around mopping up, making sure that blame was distributed as intended. Salzburg Club policy. Address local legal standards of proof. Ensure that the means adopted allows for doubt. Make it as difficult as possible to find a connection between the killing and the Club.

That was what they liked about Keppler. His methods were more sophisticated than those of his predecessors. He put in more time, researched more heavily, made use of his intellect, planned meticulously, arranged for back-up plans. His work had the sort of style about it that appealed to the type of people in the Club. Most of them were professionals in their own field. They recognised and appreciated the end product of the application of exceptional skill. McAngel wasn't sure how Keppler had managed to get a tribal Aborigine to execute the barrister but it was clear that no-one but the best informed, like himself, could ever conclude that there was any connection between the killing and the Club.

In this respect Keppler was streets ahead of Vander. Vander had been cunning. His hits were sudden, unexpected, and timed perfectly. But in the end there was always a residual suspicion that the apparent circumstance of the kill was not the full story. And he was messy and wasteful as well as ruthless.

As he thought of Vander, McAngel again felt the unhealthy mix of nausea and pain in his chest and he began to sweat. This time it was too acute and he pulled over to the side of the road. He sat upright in the driver's seat and closed his eyes. He needed to find sweet nothingness. *Maranatha*. He breathed deeply and then

210

sought regular inhalation and exhalation. *Maranatha*. His chest was tight. He had to be patient. *Maranatha*. Breathe deeply, regularly. *Maranatha*. Let the bad thoughts rise like bubbles from the deep and then disappear. *Maranatha*.

Initially the Afghani authorities could provide no explanation for the sudden and brutal slaughter of the four young westerners found buried in the grounds of the hotel. It became an international incident which kept busy for weeks the communication channels in embassies in Paris, Quebec, Washington and Kabul. McAngel, who'd been taken back to Kabul in a Volkswagen van by a kind English archaeologist and his wife, was for a while hounded by locally-based western journalists. Soon they realised that all they had to interview was a young man rendered rambling and incoherent by the incident. Without any other handle but his name and a sketch of the facts, most were content to further describe him as the young American law student who found the bodies. The one who had been travelling overland through Asia with one of the victims, his nineteen-year-old pregnant wife.

Soon after came the statement from the Afghani Islamic fundamentalist group no-one had ever heard of claiming responsibility for the deaths—a blow struck against the infidel westerners, a sign to the world that western corruption and decadence was not wanted in Afghanistan. Meanwhile, among international outrage at the fact that the killers were never identified let alone captured, McAngel's world left its customary orbit. All he could recall of that time was the agony of the loss of Maria and boarding an aeroplane. Otherwise, there was a blurred impression of time spent somewhere that he knew wasn't his home where he walked on neatly cut green lawns on sunny afternoons or stood half sheltering in the rain under

211

dripping awnings. Occasionally there was an argument with nurses who wanted to pull him away when he knelt sobbing and clawing at the rich dark earth of a flower bed looking for a ring.

And then one day there was a man and a woman who visited him at his mother's house in San Francisco, when he was getting a little better, and who took him out in the sun to sit together at the old pine benches and table under the vine.

The man was about forty, dark, short, slight, with watery brown eyes and thinning dark curly hair. He said his name was Achille Falcone and that he was from Milano. He wore a well-cut navy blue business suit, a spotless white shirt, an elegant red tie. He could have been an executive from Fiat. He carried a packet of Gaulois. McAngel remembered how Achille had tapped the bottom of the packet so that a couple of the unfiltered cigarettes protruded and then offered him one. He declined.

The woman was an Australian journalist, Gloria Glenning. She was a handsome woman, tall and thin, early thirties, granny glasses, minimum make-up, long dark hair prematurely streaked with grey, sandals, nicely tanned arms and legs, rolling her own from a pouch of Drum tobacco and exuding the scent of patchouli oil. She'd given McAngel a reassuring smile and he liked her.

It was Achille who first made a demand on McAngel's weakened capacity to concentrate. At that stage it was still difficult for McAngel to remain attentive for long periods. His rational self had, since the hotel in Afghanistan, taken refuge somewhere deep inside him. His senses on the other hand, unbridled by reason, were acute and receptive. In rich sensory environments he spent his time intoxicated by his surroundings. Achille Falcone had smoked Gaulois, one cigarette after the other and McAngel recalled how, in the sunbathed little garden, already fragrant with flowering jasmine, his light headedness and euphoria had been enhanced by the rich redolence of the cigarette smoke. During his illness he'd become accustomed to such sweet languor and wished not to be disturbed.

Achille said, *We have come to tell you why Maria was killed*, and McAngel felt the welling of sorrow and almost despite himself he said, as if he'd been expecting such a visit all along, 'Yes. Please tell me.'

Achille started at the beginning. His English was careful and meticulous as though he feared that it was so laden with his heavy Italian accent that any slip or error might irredeemably derail his conversation.

'There is a club—the Salzburg Club. It is called the Salzburg Club because it meets in Salzburg, in Austria. This makes sense, no?'

Here he'd paused and smiled at McAngel, making eye contact. He knew McAngel was still like a disoriented swimmer making his way to shore and that he needed to be given a reference point occasionally. When he saw McAngel was listening he went on.

'This Salzburg Club. It is a philanthropic organisation. The members of this Club are all very, very rich men. This Club, these rich men, meet in Salzburg and there they decide to give money to poor countries. Countries in Africa, Asia, the South Pacific, anywhere. The Club give these countries money when, for example, there is a flood or there is drought or there is fire or famine and so on. You understand, no? Yes. And this Club is known as an altruistic organisation. Its members are men of distinction. In matters to do with business, big business, they are men of international reputation. There are also other members. Men who are doctors, lawyers, engineers, you understand? They all have in common that they are rich, important men.'

213

McAngel remembered how tired he had felt at this point. Maybe it had been his medication. He liked Achille already and didn't want to be impolite but so far he had no interest in what he was telling him.

'I'm sorry. I am very tired. I don't understand what you are doing here. You said you could tell me something about Maria.'

Achille remained composed.

'Mr McAngel,' he said, 'We have an explanation why your beautiful wife was killed. But to understand you must be patient. If you are tired, we will come back after you have your sleep. Is no problem.'

McAngel had shaken his head and indicated to Achille to proceed. Achille looked pleased.

'*Va bene*. As I tell you, these men have in common that they are rich. But also in common they have something else. They are racist. You understand when I use this term—"racist"? Yes?'

Achille was probing to see how much was sinking in but McAngel had been miffed. He was sick, not stupid.

'Of course I do,' he'd answered.

'*Bene*,' said Achille satisfied. 'I will tell you more about the Club. In 1952 in London, there is a meeting. Present are some Englishmen, a number of Frenchmen, a Dutchman and a Belgian. They meet in London. The meeting is organised by an Englishman. His name is Sir George Brigganson. This was a man who was a *fascista*. Before the war he knew the top *fascisti* in Germany.'

Achille paused at this point. McAngel had been following with difficulty and now he must have shown signs of wandering. He was pleased for the break because he wanted to listen. But it was difficult. McAngel recalled how the two of them appeared to instantly understand. It was if they had been anticipating that this would take some time. Achille stood, removed his coat and then, smiling affably at McAngel, sat on the pine bench seat and smoked his Gaulois. Gloria examined a yellow flower in the shrubbery beside the vine. They could have been strangers together waiting for a bus.

Eventually, when Achille nodded to her, it was Gloria who took over. Where Achille had been dilatory and conversational Gloria was crisp and didactic.

'After the war it wasn't fashionable to go around announcing your support for the Nazis. But Brigganson knew there were plenty of like-minded European businessmen who wished the Nazis had never been defeated. He organised a meeting of a number of other European businessmen who had Nazi sympathies and held it in Salzburg in 1952. He had extensive business interests overseas—Indonesia, China, South East Asia, Africa. The others at the meeting had similar interests. It was a changing world. Independence movements, emerging nations throwing off colonial shackles. Brigganson and his pals were nervous about the prospect of nationalisation of their factories. There were also fears of new tariffs and discriminatory taxes on foreign owned manufactures and so on.

'The group originally called itself the EIAS, which was an English acronym for the European Investors Abroad Society, and resolved to meet regularly. It was too cumbersome a name and they eventually just called themselves the Salzburg Club.'

She paused to monitor how McAngel was doing. McAngel recalled that the fuzziness in his head was dissipating for the first time in many months. Concentration was becoming easier but he still had to work at it. Achille had nodded to Gloria and she went on.

'The Club's ostensible purpose was to promote the interests of European investors abroad. The Club's philanthropy assisted that end. It would throw a few dollars or deutschmarks at these countries when they needed them and then call in the favours later. Nothing wrong with that of course. Governments do it all the time. Trouble was that Brigganson had always intended to create an organisation with a clandestine agenda. That agenda took into account the use of any method, legal or illegal, to promote the interests of Club members. There was also a sort of loose and undefined mutual acceptance of a philosophy of white Christian supremacy. That non-white races and Jews were inferior. Really, for the members it was a case of the whole Nazi philosophy continuing.'

She rolled a Drum cigarette, used a match head to tuck in the ends and lit it. Her fingers were long and elegant.

'In the early years, the Club was fond of generous bribes. It targeted politicians mainly, sometimes public servants, often judges and police. It created a whole network of obliging people with influence in these countries so that when economic interests were threatened they could call in the favours. Occasionally they'd find an honest man and so they had to resort to other methods and there was some intimidatory stuff going on. A beating, a bomb planted and timed to go off when the target wouldn't be hurt, telephone threats. That sort of stuff.'

McAngel had shifted in his seat, perhaps looked away. Gloria instantly paused again. This time McAngel himself motioned her on. He wanted to hear this. Again Gloria appeared to exchange glances with Achille, then resumed.

'The organisation grew. Not only Europeans but now Americans, South Africans, Argentines, Australians—rich men from all over the world end up as members. Men who are rich and white and non-Jewish. The *raison d'être* of the Club ceased to be solely the protection of the interests of overseas investors. It soon became the protection of the interests of any member with big bucks whose economic interests were threatened by political or other developments in any country.

'For example, in some of the developing countries you have politicians trying to get inventive taxes and tariffs into place. Club members who export to these countries don't like this. Or you might have consumer rights people who want all sorts of expensive safety features on certain products. Anathema to Club members who make the products. Or anti-pollution activists who don't want factories pouring their poison into rivers. Nuisances to rich men of the Club. Men with large media interests are alert to any moves to restrict their media ownership in some countries. Uppity union leaders are a problem. And communists? Well communist are the worst of the lot. They talk nationalisation talk and this gives Club members heartburn. You understand?'

McAngel nodded. Achille lit a Gaulois with a gold cigarette lighter. Gloria waited. McAngel found nothing peculiar about the pause now. It seemed natural and expected. As if they were proceeding on the basis of some common expectation. Eventually Achille nodded and Gloria went on.

'The bribes and influence peddling remained a part of Club activities of course. And the philanthropist's mantle provided plenty of shade for cosy deals. But sometimes the deals and the bribes couldn't achieve everything. Sometimes Club members ran across someone who couldn't be bought off, someone who was a threat to business in a big way. Enter Beowulf.'

'Beowulf?' McAngel had queried.

'Yes,' said Gloria. 'After the mythical hero of the great Anglo-Saxon epic poem. Not surprising, I suppose, that the Club sought a name for its champion in Teutonic mythology. The quick story?'

She'd looked at Achille, not at McAngel. Achille had nodded.

'Back in the Dark Ages. Viking times. Hrothgar, King of the Danes, had built a magnificent great hall for feasting and drinking. However, a man-eating monster called Grendel has gotten into the habit of arriving in the night to carry away and devour drunken warriors sleeping in Hrothgar's great hall. It becomes a matter of some concern for Hrothgar. But help is at hand. Beowulf arrives and with his great strength kills first Grendel then the even more fearsome sea hag, Grendel's mother. The mother, by the way, is killed in her sea hall after Beowulf seeks her out by swimming into the depths of the ocean. The symbolism was irresistible to the Club I suppose. They arranged for their own Beowulf to be on call to deal with any fiends intent on spoiling their party.'

'Beowulf is an assassin?' McAngel had asked.

'Essentially yes. But the Club demands more from its Beowulf than simple assassination. You see, it just wouldn't do to have a clear trail from a victim to the Club. There'd be criminal charges of conspiracy to murder and attending embarrassment for a lot of very important people. No. Beowulf has to arrange for the death of the target so that there is as much distance as possible between the victim and the Club. That has become Beowulf's great skill. Beowulf himself will personally carry out a hit but ensures that it looks like something else happened. Suicide, an accident. Alternatively, he might arrange for someone else to do the killing. It doesn't matter as long as there is no trail back to Salzburg.'

'And who is Beowulf?' asked McAngel cautiously.

Thoughts were forming in his head which were making him feel uneasy.

Achille moved into a position where he could look directly into McAngel's eyes. McAngel recalled the intensity of his gaze. It was as if he wanted to see what was going on inside McAngel's head when he told him.

'Beowulf, Mr McAngel, is the person responsible for the death of Maria.'

McAngel had stood up, weakly angry.

'Maria. Tell me about Maria.'

Achille stood up with him and, taking him by the arm, sat him down again.

'Come my friend, you sit again, please.'

When he resumed his seat Achille lit another Gaulois.

'We have some coffee maybe. Yes?' said Achille.

'Yes, I'm sorry,' apologised McAngel. 'I should have offered.'

But Achille was referring to the white haired-woman in an apron with the sad, kind eyes who had come out with a pot of coffee and some madeira cake on a tray. McAngel's mother placed it down before them.

'It's not espresso, but it's good coffee. And my cake is pretty good as well. It's Wade's favourite.'

She had run her fingers through her son's hair, something she hadn't done since he was a boy, and had begun doing again after he'd come home.

'You join us *signora*,' Achille had urged. But she declined and returned inside. Achille patted McAngel's hand.

'You know Mr McAngel, someone said once, *What does not kill me makes me stronger*. Drink your coffee, eat your mother's delicious cake. We will talk on after you have finished.'

19

*H*arvey Brown looked after the Supreme Court matters. He was in his early forties but looked older mainly due to the streaks of grey in his dark hair and his diet of sixty cigarettes a day washed down with coffee. He had stomach ulcers and a cadaverous face. Despite an alleged sense of humour, he rarely smiled and appeared permanently tired. He was a workaholic who spent most of his time at the grindstone. Unkind rumour was that when he finally agreed to his wife's demands that he pack and leave the family home, his kids never noticed he was gone.

Nick entered Harvey's office. Harvey had his head over a police brief.

'You still work here Milano?' Harvey said flatly to Nick on looking up and noting the condition of his face. 'Or have you joined a travelling boxing troup?'

Nick ignored him. Some people liked Harvey's laconically delivered dry sense of humour. Described it as *real Australian*. Nick didn't care for it. Too often Harvey's humour reeked of stale resentments and jealousies. *A bean who wants to be an oak tree*, Johnny had once said of him.

'Another couple of murders, eh Milano?' drawled Harvey going back to scribbling something on the brief.

Harvey came from good working-class stock. He was proud of the fact that he'd never changed the way he spoke just because he was a lawyer. He now went on about the murders, assuming correctly, if for the wrong reasons, that Nick knew about them.

'Fyshwick this time,' he went on. 'Fucking silly season in Canberra by the looks of things. Never known it to be like this. What's that now? Johnny Bora's gone then there's five more in two weeks. And none of them related.' Harvey looked up. 'Lucky we've got great prosecutors like you around Milano,' he added without a trace of a smile.

So they'd found the bodies. Nick had expected it. He was in a hurry. 'Harvey, what's doing with the Billy Jangala matter?'

'What's doing with the Billy Jangala matter?' Harvey repeated. 'Hollywood's going to use it to show everybody what a great humanitarian he is. That's what's doing.' He returned to his paperwork without elaborating. Nick didn't follow. Hollywood was Alex Hurtleman, the Director of Public Prosecutions. He had that nickname even before he was made a silk. He was a certain type. Personable, photogenic, well dressed. He had a reputation for being good with the press. Nick liked him. Harvey didn't. Harvey was given to using Hurtleman's nickname disparagingly, as if it was a measure of the man's narcissism. Harvey kept on with the paperwork as if Nick wasn't there.

'What do you mean?' Nick was forced to ask.

Harvey seemed to like doing this sort of thing. Some assertion of self importance, a demonstration he wasn't about to be hurried by anyone. Nick didn't know why. But it was irritating. Harvey answered eventually, but without looking up from his brief.

'Defence are happy to plead guilty as long as we

221

support their submission that Jangala not go to gaol. Hollywood's making noises of approval.'

Here Harvey pulled a piece of paper from a pile on his desk and read, apparently trying to imitate Hurtleman's smooth delivery, 'There is in Australia a body of customary law, the dictates of which may from time to time conflict with Australian common law and statute law, and obedience to which may leave its adherents subject to the sanctions of the criminal law. In such circumstances this office should not argue against submissions from defence counsel that obedience to customary law be regarded as a strong mitigating factor in the sentencing process'.

Harvey threw the paper back on the pile. 'Sounds like bullshit to me. But it'll keep the trendies in the media smiling.'

The news that Billy may not go to gaol didn't make Nick unhappy. But it was still all too unsatisfactory. It just wasn't as simple as that. The responsibility for Johnny's death lay elsewhere. There were others who should be paying for Johnny's murder. He noticed Harvey had gone back to ignoring him and was suddenly tired of his small-minded affectations.

'Sally, the Aboriginal woman—does Hurtleman intend talking to her at any time?' he asked, brusquely. Harvey gave Nick a peculiar look. Milano wasn't normally pushy. Harvey adopted a tone of weary cynicism.

'Yes, as a matter of fact. He wants her here. So he can interview her in person and assess the situation. Mind you, the press will love her, and they'll love Hollywood because he's got her here from Western Australia just for them. And what's a couple of grand of an adoring public's hard earned tax money when you can buy the press's devotion just like that?' He snapped his fingers. 'Anything *else* Milano?'

'So she's coming?' persevered Nick.

222

'Mount White police rang me this morning. She's on the plane. She knows someone who lives in Canberra. She'll be staying with her.'

'Her? You've got the name of the friend? Address?'

'Why?' asked Harvey, turning away to fiddle with something in his filing cabinet, clearly aware now that this would annoy Nick.

'Because I want to tell her what a prick you are Harvey,' Nick said, abruptly. 'Just give me the name and address, will you.'

Nick's agitation surprised even Harvey. He gave Nick a curious look and then scribbled something on a Post-it tab.

'Take some more time off, Milano,' he said as Nick walked out of the door. 'You need it.'

It was only when he was at the elevator that Nick looked at the name Harvey had scribbled down.

Lindy Mays—54 Gresham, Curtin.

Mays? Meant nothing. But he remembered the computer message. *S and L will talk but not in court.* Nick took the lift to the ground floor.

McAngel pulled the Magna back out onto the highway. He was now feeling relaxed and breathing easily; meditation had soothed him. First the thinking had ceased and the worst of the panic had subsided. He had found his calm centre and, for thirty minutes or so, profound peace. He could recall the conversation without the pain.

'Why did Beowulf want Maria dead?' McAngel had asked Achille.

He recalled feeling conscious of how weak his body felt. Of how his physical strength may just be inadequate to manage the emotional concussion he knew the answer to his question would bring.

'You remember Aldo?' Achille had asked McAngel.

McAngel did of course.

'He told you he was a journalist?'

McAngel nodded.

'Unfortunately for Aldo that was true,' said Achille. 'He was a true journalist. Here.' Achille tapped at his heart. 'For Aldo, this was not a description of his occupation. It was a description of himself.'

'You knew Aldo well?' McAngel had asked.

'I knew Aldo. As for well? Who knows anybody well, Mr McAngel?'

It had been peculiar. McAngel recalled feeling less tired. Curiosity had focused his mind. Achille had obviously sensed the change. He was now less solicitous, more intense.

'Aldo was a reporter for *Il Messagero Milanese*,' he said, pausing, to light a Gaulois, and sending a long plume of smoke into the air. 'He was a man of leftist convictions. *Il Messagero*, of course, was not a radical paper. Politically it was conservative. When there were elections it supported the Christian Democrats. It criticised the Red Brigade. It supported conscription for our young men, and so on. Aldo, on the other hand, liked to be modern. You saw him. He was a *tipo* hippy, long hair, beads, wore jeans to work. He liked to smoke the marijuana. He was employed to cover issues of interest to young people. Pop concerts, the student demonstrations, drug reform, conscription, popular artists. But Aldo found this restrictive, trivial, unchallenging. He was impatient for the big assignments. I was his editor. He always asked me, *Can I cover this? Can I cover that?* Usually it was something of political significance. I tell him, *No Aldo, this is not your area. We have other journalists covering that story. I am sorry.* The truth was that the political stories were written by journalists who wrote the things they were expected to write. Like all papers, *Il Messagero* had the convictions of its owners to consider. You understand, no? Aldo would have given us something different. Aldo felt the newspaper only gave him opportunities to cover stories which were ultimately frivolous. He wanted a serious assignment.

'One day he come to me. He said he had a good idea. Aldo had heard that neo-Nazis, who in Germany had organised again, were now also forming in Milano, in Roma, in Torino. Aldo said to me, *Achille, I can infiltrate the group in Roma. It would be a storia fantastica.* I say to him, *This is very dangerous Aldo.* But he insisted. He said it was his opportunity to do the journalism he wanted to do. To be taken seriously. I see my Editor-in-Chief. He agreed to let Aldo do it.'

Achille turned to Gloria.

'Please, Gloria,' he said cordially.

She obliged.

'Aldo and I knew each other. We went right back. We actually met at college in the States. We were both doing Masters degrees in English Literature at UCLA. I was on an Australian post-graduate scholarship and Aldo, who had done very well in English studies at Perugia, had picked up a scholarship awarded to non-native speakers of English. I was writing a thesis on Nathaniel Hawthorne. Aldo's thesis was called "The Politics of Poetry". We liked each other but eventually I returned to Australia and he to Italy.'

She rolled another cigarette quickly, pausing to lick the gummed edge before resuming.

'Years later when I'd chucked in my job with the *Sun* back in Sydney I went to live in Italy. I wanted to write a novel. The great Australian novel. I wrote chapter one the first week I got there. Twelve months later I still hadn't started chapter two. I was doing a bit of freelancing. Travel pieces, bits on Italian politics, the odd short story. I ran into Aldo again. We took up where we'd left off as students.

A bit of romance but mainly we were good friends.

'The idea for Aldo's story on the Nazis came to him during a meal we were having at a *trattoria*. The very next day Aldo rang me very excited. He said he'd got the assignment. I told him to be careful.

'Aldo went to Rome on the day of a big anti-government student demonstration. At that time Italy had compulsory military service for twenty-year-olds. The students were marching in protest at the laws.

'Aldo knew from his contacts that the organisers were expecting trouble from the neo-Nazi group. He went along and joined the thugs who waded into the marchers and started beating and kicking them, Aldo made some pretence of doing the same thing. He and some of the neo-Nazis were arrested. But they were never charged. The police let them all go. One of them actually told Aldo he was doing a good job, and to keep it up. That they'd let him go the next time as well.

'Back outside some of the Nazis asked Aldo who he was. He told them he was unemployed and that he hated the Jew communists who organised these student demonstrations and that he thought that what had happened was a spontaneous act of outrage on the part of the thugs and that he couldn't resist joining in. The Nazis promptly invited him to join the Roman cell of the neo-Nazi movement. The group called itself *Italia Potente*.

'Aldo spent about two months with the group. He took part in their activities. There was some paramilitary-type training, ideology classes, some minor violence against left-wing groups, some destruction of property belonging to Jews. The usual thing. But in the end Aldo concluded that the people who joined the Nazis were usually men of low to middle intelligence, with a smattering of education, who were easily led by just about any garrulous bigot or racist who spouted anti-communist or anti-Jewish slogans.

'He recognised that they were ultimately capable of being violent but were, for the present, of no long-term threat to any existing institutions. He told me he himself ceased to have any personal fear of them within weeks of joining. They might beat him up but they would never kill him. He could handle that. Some he quite liked and pitied. Their membership of the group, he said, was no more than attention seeking. The only people they had the courage to hate were those they perceived to be even more powerless than themselves. Poor coloureds, Asians, some Jews, the gypsies, students. His report for the paper was going to be one which dismissed the group as a bunch of incompetent idiots who should be laughed at instead of feared or taken seriously.

'One night all that changed. There is a small restaurant in Via Republica called La Scena. I was there dining with Aldo. It was intended to be his last week posing as a member of the group. Late into the night, into the restaurant came Guido Marcosini. He was the head of *Italia Potente* in Rome. He was alone. He saw Aldo and he joined us. He was pissed. Very pissed. He was one of those loud braggadocio types. He demanded to know if I was *on side*.

'Aldo introduced me to Marcosini and told him my name was Eva Strasser and that I was from Munich, and a fellow Nazi. We'd both been drinking and Aldo was being mischievous. He regarded Marcosini as a buffoon. Of course, Aldo knew from the newsletters that circulated within the movement that there was in fact an Eva Strasser from the Munich branch who held some type of minor office. I was merry with the alcohol and feeling mischievous as well and so I played along.

'Marcosini believed that I was Eva. It was a name he was familiar with and there was some prestige in coming from the Munich branch, given its historical significance,

227

and so he was impressed. He set about letting me know that he too was an important person. He seemed concerned to make it clear that it was he who was the leader in Rome, not Aldo. That Aldo was only a recent member. That if there was anything I wanted to know I should talk to him, not Aldo. He had respect for Aldo. He had promise. But Aldo didn't know much. Mind you, he seemed to think that all this would sound even more impressive if he groped away at my thigh while he was telling me.

'He motioned to me to lean close to him so that he could whisper in my ear. He whispered a name— *Koningsberg*—and he tapped his nose. As I said, I was playing along with Aldo's deception and I nodded wisely and tapped my own nose. This made him very happy. He said, *And Aldo knows nothing of this, eh?* I said no, he knows nothing of this. This satisfied him greatly at first. But I said that because Aldo was a good friend I proposed to tell him about Koningsberg later. It was a tease. Marcosini became indignant. He said hardly anyone knew about Koningsberg outside of Munich. He himself only knew because of a friendship he had with Emil from the Munich branch. None of the other cell leaders knew. He was getting excited and angry.

'Aldo was delighted. He knew Marcosini pretty well by now and could see that his main concern was that in talking to me Aldo might learn something that Marcosini himself didn't know. This would diminish Marcosini's prestige as cell leader. Aldo, still enjoying himself, suggested a compromise that he knew Marcosini would go for. He said, *Look Marcosini. Eva could tell me all about Koningsberg and you wouldn't even know what she told me. Let us here at this table solemnly swear that what passes between us will never be told to anyone else unless there is permission from the other two. I suggest that you first tell me all you know about Koningsberg and that Eva promises to tell you anything that you don't know. That way we will all be privy to the same knowledge. I, of course, will swear that I will never suggest to anyone that I know what you know about Koningsberg.*

'When he said this I thought the game was up. Marcosini couldn't be that stupid. But he was. Marcosini was at bottom a silly gossip. He couldn't resist the temptation of learning what I supposedly knew. He agreed and began talking. But what until then had been comedy and high farce suddenly turned very serious.

'Koningsberg, it transpired, was a Munich factory owner who'd helped revive the Nazi movement in that city. He had made a lot of money very quickly and he had made some influential friends in the business world, in Germany and elsewhere. So influential in fact, that he'd been invited to join the Salzburg Club. Aldo knew it was a club for rich philanthropists. There was nothing remarkable about Koningsberg becoming a member. Except that Marcosini started raving about how, now that they had somebody inside the Club, the movement would soon be able to dispose of their enemies in a professional and efficient manner. At first I thought it was all a part of Marcosini big-noting himself. But soon there was something about what he was saying that began to ring true. Our journalistic instincts told both of us that something worth knowing might emerge here. So we played the game in tandem. Aldo would ask a question and I would say to Marcosini as if I knew the answer, *You tell him Guido.* Marcosini was only too pleased to have such an attentive audience. Remember he was very drunk. He told Aldo about the real activities of the Club. He didn't know much about the details. We found that out later. But he knew the names of former victims of the Club's hit list. There had been half a dozen deaths of politically significant people in the previous four years.

Not names that would have been well-known to the international public but names that were significant to journalists. For example, one was Klaus Rudiger an anti-pollution activist who appeared to have committed suicide by poisoning himself. Another was an American advocate of consumer rights called Henry Mowbray who had died in a hit and run accident. And others. All of the deaths so far as we knew had been explained as either accidents or misadventures of one type or another. None of the deaths were linked to the victim's political activities. Certainly to our knowledge, none had been linked to the Salzburg Club.

'At this stage I suppose both Aldo and I had realised that what he was telling us was plausible but we weren't totally convinced. After all, why would someone with the apparent clout of Koningsberg tell the Munich Nazis about the activities of the Club? It turned out that Koningsberg and Emil were homosexual lovers. Had been for years. And Emil was one of Marcosini's old sexual partners and so he told him.

'In any case, whatever doubts I had about Marcosini's ramblings evaporated when Marcosini suddenly started telling me about Harry Gilbert, the boss of an Australian waterfront union. You see, I'd done an interview with Harry for the *Sun* newspaper before I left Australia. And that very afternoon, before I'd even met Marcosini, I'd been talking by phone to a journalist friend of mine back in Sydney. He mentioned that the police had pulled Harry's body out of Sydney Harbour. Pathology tests showed Harry had been inebriated and police concluded he had fallen out of his boat and drowned. A lot of people, my friend said, were dubious about that conclusion and were awaiting the inquest.

'You see there'd been a long strike and international ships had been waiting for over a week outside the harbour for the opportunity to unload their cargoes. It was Harry amongst the union executive who was intransigent on the issue. The others on the executive were starting to waver but Harry had insisted that the ships could stay out there until union demands were met.

'It was big news in Australia but of little significance in Europe, except to those exporters who happened to have their stuff on the ships and to those ship owners whose investments were out there bobbing up and down idly off Sydney Heads.

'Yet here was Marcosini at a restaurant in Rome, who, by way of boasting about the reach of the Salzburg Club, begins telling me that he learned that day that the Club had successfully arranged the assassination of an Australian trade unionist. It frightened the hell out of me. I knew that what Marcosini had heard must have been the truth.

'Eventually Marcosini passed out at the table. We left him there and on the way home I told Aldo about Harry Gilbert. We were very excited. For two journalists Marcosini's story was irresistible. We decided that we'd work on a story about the Salzburg Club together.'

Gloria took a final drag of the rolled cigarette and stubbed it out, looking expectantly at McAngel.

'Maria?' he reminded her. 'We seem still to be a long way from Maria.'

Maggie was waiting downstairs in the car.

'Qantas booking office please driver,' Nick said to her.

Maggie pulled away into the traffic before asking him why.

'I just talked to Peter Oliver. Asked him if he knew exactly when it was that Pearl left for his overseas conference. Peter checked with the law clerk. Pearl was in his office working the day before Johnny was killed. He was booked to fly out at noon on 23 December. Johnny

231

was killed that night. Pearl had been booked on a Qantas flight to London.'

'So?' said Maggie.

'I want to see if Pearl took that flight.'

They pulled up in front of the Qantas office. Standing outside it, hitching up his trousers over his belly with the inside of his forearms, was Fred Arthurton.

'Thanks for coming Fred,' said Nick after introducing Maggie.

Fred shook his head in mock despair. To Maggie he said, 'Why is it that this bloke always manages to catch me either after hours or when I'm on leave? It's bloody uncanny.'

Nick gave him a *never mind* pat on the shoulder.

'You're getting obsessed with this murder Nick,' he continued as they went inside. 'You know it's all sown up. This is a waste of time. You realise that, don't you? Besides, it's Stratton's case. He or Lardner should be doing this for you.'

'Neither of them is as sweet as you Fred. Like I told you on the phone, it'll only take a minute. Besides, they'd be out at the murder wouldn't they?'

Fred nodded.

'Yeah. Unbelievable eh? More murders.'

He patted the pager on his belt.

'They'll be calling soon.'

He changed his voice, mimicking the detective in charge of the crime scene.

'*Hello Fred. Sorry to disturb you while you're on leave. We've got a small problem with the blood samples here. You better come over.*'

Nick smiled. Good old Fred. Nick felt some guilt at his deceitfulness. He was tempted to tell him that he'd been out at the scene earlier. But it was all too complicated. In any case, Fred would probably prefer not to know.

232

They went inside the office. Fred showed the Barbie doll behind the counter his ID and asked her to check the bookings for 23 December. She asked them to wait and went and talked to a pimply faced kid behind another computer terminal. He promptly came over, all service and efficiency.

Nick asked him to check the flights for 23 December to see if Pearl was on the plane. He was astonished when the kid didn't bother.

'Mr Pearl was booked on the 23 December flight, sir, but he cancelled and actually rebooked for the next day. He flew out on the twenty-fourth.'

Fred and Nick looked at one another.

'You've got a good memory, son. You don't need a bloody computer terminal,' remarked Fred.

The kid looked puzzled then understood what he was on about.

'Oh I'm sorry, I assumed you'd forgotten what I told the police yesterday. I thought that you'd come back to check again.'

'Yesterday?' said Nick.

'Yes. Detective Sergeant Stratton was in here. Wanted to know the same thing you've just asked me.'

After they'd hurried outside Nick turned to Fred.

'All sown up is it Fred? Stratton obviously doesn't think so.'

He and Maggie got into the car.

'Why did Pearl lie?' he asked Fred, through the window.

Fred shrugged, pulling up his trousers as he did so. Not his field. He was a lab man. It wasn't a guessing game in the lab. That was the way he liked it.

'Some little more patience Mr McAngel,' Achille had said to him before going on. 'Aldo called me in Milano the day

233

after he'd talked to Marcosini. He told me he wanted to postpone publication of his story. He assured me it was no more than an introduction to a much bigger story. I agreed to let him do as he wanted.'

Then it was back to Gloria Glenning.

'Aldo and I worked our bums off. We asked around and learned that for many years, rumours circulated about the Salzburg Club and its real activities. But nothing definite. Then we managed to get hold of what amounted to a membership list of the Club. You see, we'd gone to Salzburg on a day when the Club was meeting. Aldo chatted up one of the waitresses from the restaurant where the members were to dine that evening. She got a list of the place names from the tables and passed it on to us.

'It was astonishing just how many of the names were familiar to us. It was a who's who of international business. Or at least *white* international business. The bulk were European names but there were Americans, South Africans, Argentinians, even a couple of Australian names I recognised.

'Aldo and I put weeks of research into matching names to business interests. It turned out that each of the assassinations Marcosini had boasted about was of great convenience to someone in the Club.

'But then there was something else came out of the list. On the list of names was also that of Leonardo Garini, the man who in effect owned *Il Messagero*. Very awkward for Aldo.'

Achille patted Gloria on the arm and took over.

'Aldo learns that our proprietor is a member of the Club. *Bene*. Aldo, being Aldo, wanted to judge how far he would be permitted to go. He writes some of the story, enough to reveal the flavour of his ultimate intentions. He sends it to me asking that our lawyers give an opinion on whether or not it is defamatory. To me it appeared an exciting story.

Aldo did not tell me that Garini was a member of the Club that was the subject of the story. I give the story to our lawyers. The very next day I am summonsed to see the Editor-in-Chief of the paper, Cesare Frumentone. He tells me shortly and emphatically that Aldo is wasting everyone's time and the resources of the newspaper in pursuing the Salzburg Club story. It is a ridiculous story, a fantasy, he says. No-one is interested anymore in conspiracy theories. Aldo is to return to Milano immediately. Aldo could, if he wanted, publish his story about the neo-Nazis, but the rest is too implausible to publish. His words were accompanied by a warning to myself. *Off the record.*'

Aldo put his index finger to his lips to indicate secrecy as Gloria cut in again.

'When Aldo got this message it only confirmed his suspicions. He never returned to Milano. He resigned from the paper and together we continued the research.

'Then I returned to Sydney for a couple of weeks. Family wedding of all things. But it gave me the opportunity to ask a few questions about Harry Gilbert. I learned that the inquest on Gilbert showed up something interesting. Witnesses turned up to say that while Gilbert had in the past been a heavy drinker, he hadn't touched a drink for twelve months. His wife said that he'd left home on the night of his death to put out some of his crab nets—he had a favourite spot in Middle Harbour—with the intention of returning in the morning and pulling them in. As far as she was concerned it was inconceivable that he would have a drink before or while doing that. But on the boat there were three empty large bottles of Glenfiddich—prime stuff. Certainly too good to spill all over the floor of the cabin but there was plenty there. Almost as if it had been forced down Gilbert's throat. Nevertheless, the coroner returned an open verdict. Death by drowning when intoxicated. Beyond that no-one could say.

'As you'd expect, the cops put it all away after the inquest. Except for Gilbert's nephew, a young cop, pretty keen on his job and pretty upset about his uncle's death. He told me he was very close to Gilbert and didn't believe that Gilbert had got back onto the grog. So he went around asking at pubs and bottle shops whether someone meeting Gilbert's description had bought three bottles of Glenfiddich on the night he died. Spent weeks doing it apparently. Eventually he found a bottle shop manager who, while he couldn't identify Harry Gilbert from the photo he was shown, said he did sell three bottles to a guy with a South African accent. He was able to pinpoint the night because the order cleaned him out of the last of his Glenfiddich stock and he wrote out an order for some more. He had the carbon. Gilbert's nephew tried to get the detectives interested again but it wasn't much to go on. All they had was a purchase of some scotch by someone with a South African accent. So the matter stayed buried.

'I remembered this when I got back to Europe and I had an idea. There was an old contact from Australia who'd been posted to Rome with the Australian Federal Police. I gave him a call. I wanted to know of anyone travelling on a South African passport who'd left Austria on, or soon after, the date given us by Marcosini as being the day the execution was ordered and who arrived in Australia in time to kill Gilbert. If the same person had left Australia immediately after the kill, we were in luck. It worked. My friend had a bit of pull at Interpol and they searched the records. There was one guy. A South African who'd connected up from Salzberg with a Lufthansa flight to Australia and who had spent less than forty-eight hours in the country before flying out again. We got his name. We were certain we had our Beowulf. And it turned out we were right.

236

'We had enough to float the story. Aldo and I cobbled it together. The lot. From Aldo's infiltration of the Roman Nazis, Koningsberg, Marcosini, Harry Gilbert's death and finally Beowulf. Then we looked for publishers. We sent the story off everywhere—Italy, England, Germany, France, Spain—you name it. No-one would touch it. Neither print media not television. And it was no surprise. Through its business contacts the Salzburg Club had a long reach. Eventually we just gave up. Or at least I did. It had been very stressful. Aldo and I had seen enough of each other for the time being. I returned to Australia to find work. The last I heard from him was that he was hitting the old overland hippy trail in Asia. That he wanted to go to an ashram in India and find himself.'

'Maria,' said McAngel, calmly and simply now. 'Tell me about Maria.'

He remembered that by this stage he could probably have finished the story off himself. But Gloria went on.

'Aldo became the target of the Club. I didn't know then that Aldo had put into place some plans for when he returned from India. He wanted to go to America and get into pirate radio broadcasting with some American friends he had known during his student days. They had the boat and the equipment already organised off the coast of Miami. It was no secret that he intended to use the pirate broadcast for political purposes. Part of his plan was to begin to expose the Salzburg Club. Somehow Aldo told the wrong people. It was inevitable that the Club would go after him.

'Beowulf planned the killing meticulously. He had to. Quite apart from Club policy that there be as much distance between the victim and the Club, there was the added concern that Aldo had contacted a lot of people in order to try to get his story published. Not all of these had direct contacts with the Club. If the reason for Aldo's death were too transparent then some people may have felt a sense of guilt or responsibility and been obliged to pass on what they knew.

'Beowulf found out about Aldo's travel plans. He arranged it so that he met up with Aldo in Turkey, posing as a fellow traveller going to India overland. Aldo must have told him of his intended route and Beowulf left him in Ankara, saying that they would probably meet up again in Afghanistan. It's all in Aldo's travel diary. When he wrote about Turkey he included a piece about this South African who was pretending to be a Dutchman for some reason, who was particularly friendly and who wanted to meet up again in Afghanistan.'

'Vander,' said McAngel.

'Right,' said Gloria. 'Vander. Vander then went on ahead to Herat and there arranged for the death of Aldo.'

She paused longer than she intended. Knowing that McAngel had by now guessed the plot wasn't going to help her get through the next bit. She told it as dispassionately as possible.

'The other travellers, including your wife, had to be killed to make plausible the planned official explanation for the deaths. An anti-European, fundamentalist Islamic group which no-one had ever heard of, killing European tourists. Vander knew that had Aldo been killed and none of the others, someone may have asked why. The men were murderers who did the job for money—Salzburg Club money given to them by Vander. You were lucky that you left the hotel. You would have been slaughtered, like the rest. The bodies were buried to give the murderers time to escape back to the hills. You found the bodies but the murderers were never apprehended in any event.'

McAngel's visit to the hazy dreamworld on the other side of sanity had ended there and then.

238

20

Scott Urquhart shook the tumbler, playing the ice in his scotch against the glass sides as he paced the perimeters of his office. He paused by the big window that looked out over Sydney Harbour. A couple of the bigger ferries were ploughing away from the quay. Unhappy clouds menaced away above the Harbour Bridge and he could see the foam trailing behind the ferries was being lashed by the wind. The gulls were taking wider arcs to wheel their way back into the coming squall. Despite the air-conditioning, Urquhart shuddered involuntarily.

He returned to his desk. All jarrah and polish. He looked at the phone. It remained silent. That little shit Rafferty should have been here by now. Where was he?

He paced again, this time pausing when he caught sight of himself in a long wall mirror. He stopped for a while. His hair was going grey at the sides. He liked it. Made him look more like his father. He patted his small paunch. That needed working on. He looked at the scotch in his hand and put it down. He shouldn't be having those.

Fucking doctors. His heart was a bit of a problem they'd told him. With his temper anything could happen. Watch it, they'd said. What he ate, drank, stress levels. What a joke! Stress levels. How could he not be stressed with all this going on about him? He looked at the mirror again. His new fitness conditioner didn't understand his body like the old one. He'd have to get rid of him.

He remembered Rafferty again. Where was that little cocksucker? He was supposed to be here to fill him in on those bloody land claims around Mount White. And what about Appleyard and Gregory? He hadn't heard from them all day either.

His mind switched to Johnny Bora. That black bastard! He'd still be alive if he hadn't started nosing around his past. Silly prick. All because he wanted to chase him down after so many years. Over that footballer friend of his. What was his name? Ernie something or other. Ugly bastard deserved what he got, pushing him around like that. They both deserved what they got. Black bastards.

The intercom interrupted his thoughts. Pearl was on the phone. He told his secretary to put him through.

Maggie and Nick pulled up outside the address in Gresham Street. Nick knocked on the door. A woman, early thirties, glasses, dressed older than she looked, answered the door. She surveyed them warily.

'Are you from the police?' she asked. 'I was told someone from the police would be here. For a statement. For the sentence.'

Nick introduced himself and Maggie. Told her he was from the DPP. The woman nodded tiredly.

'We would like to ask Sally some questions,' said Nick. The woman took them inside.

Seated at the table was a beautiful woman dressed in

240

a simple white frock and next to her an old man, very black, with a crop of white hair. Nick recognised him as the man who'd appeared with Billy at the magistrate's court.

'This is Sally and her uncle, Monyu. I'm Lindy Mays,' said the woman who opened the door.

Sally and the old man nodded.

The five of them sat around a large table in a spacious, well-lit kitchen. Nick didn't know where to start. Maggie helped him out by being direct.

'Sally, we know you're going to give some evidence about Johnny Bora's killing. But we're not really here about that. We're interested in what you know about a man called Scott Urquhart.'

'What?' said Lindy Mays.

She seemed surprised. She and Sally looked at one another as if in mutual recognition of some irony.

'Scott Urquhart,' Nick repeated. 'You know him?' he asked of Lindy.

'My step-father,' she replied, matter-of-factly. 'Many years ago. Why are you here? What does he have to do with all this?'

Her step-father? Urquhart was this woman's step-father! Nick thought fast. Tried to weigh up the implications for what he wanted to ask Sally. Should he go ahead?

Lindy noticed his hesitation. She pulled a bottle of brandy down from a cabinet and asked if anyone else wanted a drink. No-one did. She poured about three fingers into a brandy balloon and took a large swallow before going on.

'I have no affection for my step-father. I have had no contact with him for many years.'

Good, Nick thought. He didn't know why but for some reason Lindy was going to make it easier for him.

'I'm interested in your step-father's time as the manager

241

of the Crowbar Mine. Must be near twenty years ago now.' said Nick.

He had the computer memo well and truly in his head—*Called S 9.25 pm—L will talk but not in court—Confirmed U made manager 1973.*

'I was twelve years old. Same age as Sally. We were friends then. We've kept in touch over the years.'

The two women smiled fondly at one another.

'Your mother ... she and Scott Urquhart are still married?' Maggie asked.

Lindy took another drink. The expression on her face was a mix of pain and distaste.

'Why are you asking these questions?' she tried again.

Nick sensed that she'd already guessed why. He felt the pain in his face where Olafson had punched him and the bruises on his neck and shoulders where Dragos had slammed the car door on him. He had in his mind a picture of Johnny's body lying on the floor of his room in chambers. This was no time to be delicate. He'd already sensed the subject was in the air before they'd arrived. The woman was ready to talk. She just needed some prompting.

'Your step-father could be in trouble. You don't have to tell us anything about him if you don't want. Sometimes it's better to get things off your chest. That's all.'

Maggie gave him a look that said *slow down.* Maybe she was right.

Lindy looked over at Sally. Sally looked down at her feet. This was a decision Lindy had to make on her own. She poured another drink with some resolve. She was going to talk. Her mouth curled up at the edges. Far too bitter an expression to be described as any sort of a smile. She now addressed Maggie's previous question.

'My mother married Scott Urquhart when they were both living in Canberra. He was a university student. She

242

was eight years older than him. She and my natural father had divorced some years earlier. He was a doctor, a surgeon, Richard Mays, and we lived very well. After he left, my mother didn't like the prospect of living a less affluent lifestyle. She went out of her way to catch Scott Urquhart. She knew all about his father's millions. She was an attractive woman in those days. He was twenty-two years old. My mother had just turned thirty. She was doing a part-time arts degree at the ANU. Scott was a law student doing some arts subjects. They met in tutorials. She turned his head with the attention she gave him. I remember her bringing him home in the evening. He'd stay after I went to bed. Often he was there when I woke in the morning. My mother would make out he'd just dropped in early.'

She paused. The resentment was obvious. The first feeling of betrayal?

'They were married eventually,' she went on. 'The father, old Sir Samuel, could see right through my mother. He wasn't happy about the marriage. When Scott failed his law exams it was Sir Samuel's idea that Scott be sent out to manage the Crowbar Mine. Scott took us to Crowbar with him.'

She gave a short and joyless laugh.

'Not exactly on a par with Toorak where my mother had expected to live. The marriage lasted eight years although it should have been pronounced dead after about one. I think Scott Urquhart hung on because he didn't want his father to say *I told you so*. And because ... '

Rancid memories showed in her face.

'It wasn't a happy relationship,' she tailed off.

She looked at her glass then held it up so that they could appreciate the irony.

'My mother drinks you see. And he ... '

She stopped for a long time, lost somewhere in the past.

243

Then, 'Well he is Scott Urquhart. Probably enough said.'

No way, thought Nick. There was *plenty* more to be said.

'You and Sally were close in Crowbar?' he asked. *Gently* he warned himself.

'We were very close. Originally Scott Urquhart, or at least his father, arranged for a private tutor for me. But I got very lonely. They let me go to the town school eventually. There was a mix of black and white kids. Sally and I played together. I would bring her home to my house ...'

She hesitated, looked at Sally, then turned her head away so she didn't have to look at her before going on, ' ... and we would play there. It went on for some time.'

'What was your father's attitude to your relationship with Sally?' Nick persevered.

She wanted to tell them all about it. Nick knew that now. Getting her to dredge up the pain was going to be the hard bit.

Sally stirred in her seat attracting his attention.

'You're Nick. Johnny's friend?' she asked.

Her manner remained soft, tentative. Despite her age, she had retained a schoolgirlish diffidence. It was very appealing thought Nick. No wonder Johnny spent time with this woman.

'Yes.'

Sally turned to Lindy.

'Johnny told me I could talk to this man.'

'Then you tell him,' said Lindy, with some vigour. She wanted it off her plate. For good. 'You tell him the lot.'

And she drained her glass of brandy.

There was a sign that pointed the way to somewhere called Liverpool and McAngel realised for the first time that he was now in heavy city traffic. At the lights he checked

244

his road map and memorised his route—South Western Motorway, King Georges Road, Canterbury Road and on into town.

It was hot. His air-conditioning had stopped working. He opened a window briefly and closed it again. Petrol fumes. The lights changed and the traffic crawled away. On one side of him growled a large coal truck, on the other a city bus carrying a row of people perched above him at their window seats, some of whom looked down on him. It was claustrophobic.

McAngel turned his mind to Keppler again. Keppler would go to the Marlborough to see Rafferty. Why? He didn't know. But he was sure something in Keppler's careful planning was unravelling. And if he was wrong? Didn't matter, he reminded himself. You had to follow hunches in this game. Stay the cat. Avoid being the mouse as much as possible. Basics. If Keppler's mind was on other things it was a good time for pursuit. A bead of perspiration broke away from his hairline and ran down into an eyebrow. Nausea again. Not as bad as before but lingering. Istanbul. It had been hot there as well. Traffic lurched and jolted about him. The heat clothed him. He gave up resisting and remembered Vander again.

McAngel remembered how in Istanbul he'd watched Vander as he came out of the airport and followed him as he picked up the hired campervan. It didn't cost him much to find out from the hiring clerk that the van was going overland to Tehran. What was in Tehran? A Club victim? McAngel didn't care. He had Vander. He remembered the care with which he followed Vander as he visited ruins from the ancient world at Troy, Pergamon and Ephesus. In Turkey the Mediterranean coast is very beautiful.

The pace was leisurely. Vander was in no hurry. A working holiday? After Ephesus he detoured from the

245

coast to visit the old Roman hot springs at Pammukali. Then on to Antalya where McAngel saw him at the waterfront buying fish freshly cooked in a moored rowing boat and slapped into a bread roll. Then, as usual, Vander booked into a camping area.

The next day Vander took the road inland. To Termessus. Hardly anyone went there. It was accessible only after a long steep climb. And McAngel decided he would kill him there. At Termessus. For Maria. No other reason. He didn't care about the others innocently slaughtered in Herat. It was Maria's death he was out to avenge. It was Maria's death which tormented both his dreams and his waking hours. He was sure that killing Vander would finalise it. Would close the chapter on Herat so that he could get on with his life.

And what if Vander killed him instead? Again he didn't care.

McAngel followed the Volkswagen as it began to climb into an area of coniferous forest where massive pines threw the cool shelter of their shadows over the road. He pulled up short of the ruins site and found a spot where he could watch with binoculars. Vander had stopped at the base of a steep hill. The location was otherwise deserted. A narrow dirt track snaked its way up the hill. Vander took it and was soon out of sight.

McAngel followed on foot. He had with him a .38 Smith and Wesson special he had selected from a collection of hand guns offered him by a gun dealer in Izmir. He was confident of his aim. If he needed more than one round to dispose of Vander then it was likely he wouldn't get to use it. This seemed as good a place as any to finish off Vander. So quiet. So deserted.

He avoided the dirt track; there was some cover on either side. He could move as silently as he had to.

Soon, up ahead, were the remains of the town's ancient

fortifications. Hellenistic originally and then improved on by the Romans. Looking on them from below, McAngel suddenly had an appreciation of the same problem which would have faced the town's enemies more than two thousand years earlier. From those walls it would have been possible to see the enemy as he approached up the hillside in any direction. Was Vander capable of recognising him after a couple of years? They'd spent two days, no more, in each other's company.

He had collected his thoughts. Look like a tourist, he thought to himself. He abandoned cover and climbed in the open. No sign of anyone. Once past the fortifications McAngel came across massive stone boxes littering the area. Sarcophagi, dug up God knows when. Further on and the city took shape. Remains of ancient buildings. Roman at some stage. Latin inscriptions on their exteriors. Large deep holes scattered about the remains. Grain silos? Then there were the other buildings. The melancholy of disuse had disappeared centuries ago. They were now dignified in their decrepitude. Gymnasium, stadium, necropolis.

Where was Vander? Nowhere to be seen or heard.

Up another steep series of steps and then McAngel almost fell into it. A small ampitheatre, left to the weeds but otherwise well preserved. Deserted. McAngel made his way round the upper rim of the ampitheatre. At the southern extremity of the rim was a precipice where McAngel paused. He looked out on some craggy mountains, an endless sky and not that far away the wrinkled blue of the Mediterranean. Immediately below him was a deep drop to some big boulders.

Then from behind him he heard a voice.

'Perhaps you and I can experience the acoustics together.'

Startled, McAngel spun around. Vander stood no more

than a metre from him. In his hand was a gun. McAngel searched Vander's eyes. Nothing in them suggested that he'd recognised him from Herat.

'Down you go,' said Vander indicating with the muzzle that McAngel descend the old stone steps.

As McAngel turned to do so he felt the .38 being whipped from his back pocket.

Vander followed then remained about halfway down the steps while directing McAngel to the stage area. When he got there he'd stopped and looked up. No chance of running. Vander had a clean shot at him.

'Now tell me, sir, why have you been following me? Please use your normal speaking voice. I think we will both be pleasantly surprised by the acoustics of this little theatre.'

'What do you mean?'

'Ah. Just as I thought. I can hear you perfectly. Remarkable. Please try again. Why were you following me? From Istanbul. You've been tailing me.'

'Hey come on now, man.' McAngel protested, trying on the American tourist bit. 'What are you talking about? I've been following the ruins. Troy, Ephesus, here. Just like everyone else. Hey, you got it all wrong, man. If it's that gun of mine you're worried about. That ain't nothing but a little bit of self-protection for these parts here. You got one yourself.'

Vander aimed quickly and put a bullet a matter of inches from McAngel's feet. The echo from the gunshot was startlingly clear but became progressively more forlorn as it gradually lost its bounce off the hills.

'Who are you?' Vander demanded when the echoing ceased.

McAngel hadn't replied. He'd tried not to, but he began thinking of Maria once again. Of the ring on her finger he saw protruding from the dark earth in the hotel yard. Of the clods of earth that fell out of her soft hair when he frantically pulled her limp body from her makeshift grave, of the blood on his hands and arms. Standing helplessly in the ancient Greek ampitheatre he felt once again the full force of the horror, the sense of desolation. Fear and anger welled. He wheeled toward Vander's spot on the stone steps and pointed at him.

'You killed Maria.'

The denunciation caused Vander's self-complacency to dissolve. He was now looking closely at McAngel trying to make the connection. And he did.

'Herat,' he said. 'The American.'

Vander raised the gun again.

McAngel charged the stairs with a thrust and speed powered by rage. He felt the hit of the bullet just below his left collarbone, a bullet intended for his heart but defeated in its search for that target by the angle of his charge up the steps.

Perhaps it was the surprise that McAngel hadn't dropped with the shot, or perhaps it was the alarm of the speed with which McAngel covered the ground toward him, but Vander did not get off another shot.

Instead McAngel reached him and with a flying tackle unbalanced him on the steps such that he fell with his right arm momentarily levered at the elbow against the corner of a step. Instantly McAngel had seized the arm and wrenched downward feeling something in it give. Vander screamed with pain and released the gun. Then he scrambled for his footing. McAngel recovered his feet first. His instep kick caught Vander in the throat in exactly the place the textbooks talked about.

It was enough.

Vander, suddenly crumpled and disabled, ceased trying to get to his feet. McAngel stood momentarily and watched the desperation in Vander's face as he gasped to get air past his crippled windpipe. Then powered by a second wave of rage, McAngel had seized Vander by the ankles and hauled his convulsing body bumpily up the stone steps and once at the top dragged it, still by the ankles, to the edge of the precipice.

There he had allowed Vander a last bug-eyed look at eternity before using his foot to push him into it.

21

'Scott Urquhart came to Crowbar as the mine
manager. Lindy and her mother came with him.'
Sally spoke quietly, gently, caught in the
restful light of the late afternoon sun which entered
through the large kitchen windows. It was a time for
memory, for pain, for cleansing.

'I met Lindy at the school. Small school. Miners' kids
and Aborigines mainly. We became friends. She invited
me to play at her house. I was young. To me it was a big
white man's house. Exciting place. No other black people
allowed except me and some of the older men.'

At the recollection of the privilege, a light touch of
pleasure showed in her face but disappeared quickly and
was replaced with disappointment at the indelibility of
human experience.

'Lindy's mum was always drinking,' she went on, as if
apologising on the woman's behalf. 'We used to talk about
it. Often when we got there, if she wasn't wandering
around the house just dressed in a petticoat, she'd be
asleep in her bed. She had her own big bed in her own
bedroom. She'd go in with a bottle of gin and she'd stay

251

there. Lindy and I played around the house.'

She paused for a while, brows compressed as if coping with a spasm of pain. Then she took a breath and resumed.

'One day we were both there at lunchtime. It was during school holidays in July. We were in year six, both twelve years old. We were due to go into high school the next year. There was a woman who cleaned up around the house in the mornings and who made lunch for Lindy, and this day, because I was there, for me too. It was a tomato sandwich and some milk. Then she went home. On her way out I heard her say goodbye to Scott Urquhart who had just come in.

'He was in a good mood that day. He said hello to us. Talked a little while in the kitchen then asked Lindy to go with him. I remember how she looked when he asked her to do this. She'd been happy before. Then she got worried, nervous and she looked back at me when she went off with him. I already knew that she didn't like her step-father much. She never wanted to talk about him. She'd change the subject if you mentioned him. This day Lindy came out after about five minutes and said that her dad wanted us both to go to his room. He was lying on this big bed. Bigger than any bed I'd ever slept in. He had his shirt off and the belt on his trousers was undone.

'*Come here Lindy*, he said to her, *Come on. Let's show your friend how you and Scotty like to play our game. Come on.*

'Lindy went over. She wasn't happy about it, I could tell. He pulled her onto the bed and rolled over on her and then rolled her back a couple of times. She was trying to look as if she was enjoying herself but I could tell she wasn't. He said to me, *Come on over. Come on over and play on this bed. It's good fun. Great big bed like this. Soft.*

'I remember I liked the look of the bed. What he was

doing did look like fun. Rolling around on the bed. Wrestling. Fooling around. So I went.

'Lindy seemed a little happier, relieved sort of, when I was on the bed and she and I fooled around and wrestled for a bit and he would occasionally grab us. But when he grabbed me he seemed to manage to touch me a lot. On the breasts, thighs, between the legs. It was play, I was thinking. It didn't worry me. But I noticed.

'Then he got me underneath him. He was moving all over the top of me. I remember not liking that. I couldn't move much. I felt like I was about to be hurt and I didn't know how or why.

'And then he told Lindy to take her clothes off. As if it was part of the game. He kept holding me down. She didn't do it straightaway. He repeated it, a bit firmer this time. I was thinking this must be a thing white people do in their homes. She still didn't do it. Started pleading with him and crying and snivelling. *No Scotty please don't. Scotty please don't.* But he yelled at her, *Do it!* And she did. She took all of her clothes off. *What about you young girl?* he said to me. *You want to take off yours too?*

'Taking off my clothes wasn't something that worried me that much. I hardly wore any anyway. Just a skirt and a pair of panties when I had to go to school. I was a bit scared and Lindy was standing there naked and so I took off what I had on.

'Then he stripped. He was ... you know ... aroused. We stood looking at one another. I was confused. Lindy was sobbing. I felt like running away. But I was worried about Lindy. And he was a very important white person. I was young.

'Then he lay back on the bed and pulled me down by the arm. Now I was frightened. His grip was strong. *Do it*, he said to Lindy. And she started to cry and blubber

and said, *Not in front of Sally*. But again he said, *Do it!*
Lindy came over crying and leant over and he made her
touch him. And then he began touching me. And then he
pulled away from Lindy and he pushed me down onto my
back and . . . and that's when he did it.'

Sally stopped. There were no tears. Maybe there were
none left. Lindy had her back to where they were sitting.
There was a very long silence.

'He did what?' said Nick tersely.

It wasn't a courtroom and he knew very well what
Urquhart had done. But he wanted it clear. Somehow, he
knew, Johnny had paid for the answer to that question
with his life. This was no time for euphemisms.

Sally knew what he wanted. Johnny had told her what
they needed to hear in court. But as she told Nick there
was enough discomfort and reproach and ironic rehearsal
in her voice to make him regret his bluntness.

'He inserted his penis in my vagina against my wishes.
I said, *No don't do it*, before he penetrated me. I struggled
and tried to get away while he moved his penis in a
backwards and forwards motion inside of my vagina. He
then ejaculated and got off me.'

'I'm sorry,' apologised Nick. 'In a court . . . '

'I understand,' she cut him off. 'Johnny told me.'

'You didn't report it?' asked Maggie.

'No,' said Sally looking at her feet. 'Not at first. After
he told me not to. He said that if I did he would go away.
There would be no more mine in Crowbar, no more school,
no more jobs, no more Lindy. He said that if I told he
would hurt me. He said that if I told he would deny it.
He said a lot of things. Then he said to Lindy, *It's our
secret this isn't it? This little bit of fun we have*. He said
to me, *Lindy doesn't tell either. It's okay*. He said the same
sort of things to the others.'

'Others?' asked Nick.

Old man Monyu intervened. His voice was deep, and he spoke like someone accustomed to respect. For the first time Nick noticed Monyu's eyes. How they shone. How they caught his own eyes and held them and then appeared to be penetrating his mind. It was disconcerting. Nick had to look away momentarily. When he returned to the old man's gaze, Monyu was talking and the sensation of penetration had abated. But the shine from those eyes remained.

'There was others went to the big house. Other young girls. The boss, Urquhart, he would ask them to come to the house for parties. One, two, three at a time. Young girls from the town. Girls nine, ten years old even. He'd give them sweets, ice-cream, toys. After, he'd tell them not to tell. Urquhart was a big man in Crowbar. The mine owned everything. Shop, pub, petrol. People worked for the mine. Got money. No-one wanted to upset the big boss. But soon it started to get around among the people about what went on at the big house.'

'Did anyone do anything about it?'

'The women and then the elders said *No more big house* to the young girls. Then Sally came to me and told me what had happened to her.'

'And?' asked Nick after the old man paused.

'I complained. To the police, in town. Nothing happened. I complained again. Nothing happened. I was younger then. Some elders eventually came with me a third time. Nothing happened. Police said it was lies.'

'Did you tell anyone else?' asked Nick.

'White people you mean?' said Monyu.

'Yes.'

'I told the priest. I told the schoolteacher. I told the doctor. They did nothing.'

This was a statement of fact. The old man was beyond showing disapproval.

'Then there was Sister Katherine,' said Sally. 'Monyu told her.'

Monyu continued.

'Sister Katherine came to us every couple of weeks. Mainly to talk about God, help out with things. I told her what was happening. How I went to see people about it and how nothing had been done. She listened. She talked to Sally and to other girls. She was very angry after listening. She cried a bit then was very angry. She left and then two days after she was back with police. Different police to the ones I spoke to. Not police from Mt White. They spoke to a lot of us. To the girls mainly.'

Sally sighed.

'We gave statements to the police about what had happened at the house. Then they went away. Then the lawyers came.'

'Yes,' said Monyu. 'After a couple of weeks two lawyers come to town. To talk to one of the elders they said. And they did. Went off up the road to Jackie Marikit's house. Then they left. I asked Jackie what happened. He told me it was for elders only. Then nothing else happened. Asbestos mine went on like before. Girls were told to stay away from the house, although some would still go in secret. Urquhart never went near no police station as far as I knew. Whole thing went under the carpet.'

'Sister Katherine?' asked Maggie.

Monyu smiled.

'Transferred,' he said.

Lindy had kept her back to everyone. She was still drinking.

'Lindy,' said Maggie wanting her to say something. Anything.

Lindy turned around.

She'd lived with it a long time. Nick had seen it all before. In the faces of the victims he interviewed before the trials. Pain, humiliation, the sense of loss. He saw something else in Lindy. Something he realised Johnny must have been waiting for. He saw the anger. When the anger came it took the place of fear. The anger was needed in court. Until it came you had no chance.

'I told,' she said. 'I told before I even met Sally. I told before we even went to Crowbar.'

She was vehement, bitter.

'You too. You told . . . ?' said Maggie, outrage bubbling. 'And nothing happened to this man?'

Nick knew who she had told. Happened all the time. He let Maggie ask the question.

'You told who?'

'I told my mother,' she replied with clenched teeth as if that was where the tears would come from. 'I told my mother . . . and she, and she . . .'

She tightened further. Her body, her face. Every part of her. Words wouldn't come.

'Did nothing,' Nick said for her.

'Did nothing,' echoed Lindy, released. 'She did nothing. She said it wasn't true and she had another drink. And she said not to come to her again with such lies. And she had another drink . . . And she said, *Don't tell your stepfather you've been saying such things or we'll both be thrown out of here. Do you hear me?* And she shook me by the shoulders and she said again, *Do you hear me?* She had another drink.'

The grief was too much and her body folded into itself as she wept wretchedly. Sally went to her and held her and wept softly with her. Monyu sat by quietly.

In the lobby of the Marlborough there was a fat guy in a grey suit and a blue shirt with overworked buttons who looked like a cop. He was questioning people and taking notes. Unlike the people he was questioning, who were still wide eyed and alert, he seemed bored and tired. There were more guys in suits who looked like cops waiting at the elevators. McAngel noticed that usually invisible hotel managerial types were fluttering around, apparently preoccupied.

Elsewhere in the lobby, puddles of guests had formed. Periodically an emissary from one or other of these groups would break off like an errant tadpole and set off for another puddle. Occasionally someone from outside the hotel would pick up the scent of drama and come inside and stand about looking marginally more curious than uncertain before being asked to leave by polite hotel staff.

McAngel watched all this for a while then sauntered over to one of the small groups and stood behind it. Soon a young woman in a yellow dress hurried into the hotel and headed straight for the group. An elderly couple, seemingly her parents, greeted her.

'There's been a murder and a suicide. Here in the hotel. On the eighth floor,' said the older woman.

'Gladys, give her a chance to say hello at least,' protested the father. Mum ignored him.

'I spoke to the porter. He told me there were two bodies. A girl, a prostitute, and an older man. He shot her, then he shot himself.'

'You don't know that that's true Gladys,' protested the father again.

Again she ignored him.

'The porter knew the man. Said he came here regularly. Said he was a solicitor from Perth.'

The father noticed McAngel listening. He was embarrassed and smiled apologetically.

'Just rumours,' he said to McAngel. 'We're just passing on rumours.'

McAngel smiled back at him before turning and heading for his car. Keppler wasn't far away.

When he put the phone down Urquhart felt a peculiar immobility in his limbs. He was conscious of his breathing. It was difficult to get the air in. He had to concentrate.

He felt no remorse for the death of Appleyard and Gregory. Didn't expect to. Instead there was this inexplicable dread, heavy and paralysing. Rafferty! He needed to talk to Rafferty. Where did the little shit normally stay? He buzzed his secretary. Get him, wherever he is?

With some effort he returned to the window. It had started to rain. You couldn't tell inside these bloody buildings unless you looked out the window. You couldn't hear the rain on the roof, couldn't feel the changes in temperature. It was like being in a mausoleum. Down below on Pitt Street the umbrellas were up. It had darkened since the last time he looked out. No more carnival of colours over the harbour. The greyness of the bridge now blended with the colour of the sky and the water. The dread numbed him again. He poured another drink, bigger, no ice. Maybe he should go out. Get some exercise, get rid of this feeling.

'Mr Urquhart.'

It was his secretary on the intercom. She was hesitant.

'I have Mr Sordini, the manager of the Marlborough Hotel on the phone. It's Mr Rafferty's usual hotel, sir. I made enquiries about Mr Rafferty and I've been put through to the manager, sir. He asked if he could speak to you about your interest in Mr Rafferty.'

Urquhart asked to be put through. He could barely pick up the phone the dread was so bad.

Eventually Nick had another question for Sally.

'You and Johnny,' he said, 'Was it true? I mean about ...'

Sally intercepted the question. She'd been expecting it.

'About being lovers?'

There was some small defiance showing through the gentleness.

Nick nodded.

'Yes, it was true.'

She didn't offer to elaborate but held her eyes on Nick's for some time. He saw the pain and he realised that she'd loved Johnny.

'And the order by Jackie Marikit to Billy Jangala that he kill Johnny. That was true?'

Her sadness deepened perceptibly. She'd been through this before.

'Yes. It was true. They both kept it secret until after it was over. The other elders didn't know.'

'Was it because of your relationship with Johnny?' Maggie asked.

'That's what Billy Jangala thought. But it wasn't the case. Jackie was an old man. He didn't care about those sorts of things. Not any more. Ours was a traditional marriage. It's not always the same as with white people. Jackie did it for other reasons. I don't know why.'

Monyu interrupted.

'I reckon he did it for money. Jackie had plenty of money. They gave Jackie money years ago. Them lawyer fellas that came to Crowbar before we went back to the bush. Jackie never said anything but everyone reckoned they gave Jackie money not to go on with any court action about the girls and the boss man Urquhart. Then there were other white men came to the settlement last year. While Sally was living in Mt White in the motel with Johnny Bora. They came and it was Jackie they talked to.'

'What did Jackie do with the money?' asked Nick.

Monyu shrugged.

'Jackie went away a lot. Into town, away to Perth. No-one knew what he did when he went away. Some said when he was younger he liked to spend it on white women. You know. Pay for it. I don't know. But he always had money. Maybe he just liked money.'

'You found him dead?' asked Nick.

'Yeah. He was dead. Near the creek. Some of the young fellas found his body. I went and had a look at him. He had a mark on his head, here.'

Monyu pointed to his temple.

'You don't know who killed him?'

'I didn't see no-one do it. But I reckon it was the big fella.'

'Big fella?'

'Yeah. Big fella came by one day not long after Johnny Bora was killed. Big fella with blondy hair. Him and Jackie went away and talked and had an argument. Couple days later we found Jackie dead, in the bush.'

Nick figured he knew who the big blond fella was. Had to be Olafson. He was in the area at the time. Why'd he kill Jackie? To shut him up, probably. Kill Jackie, a tribal Aborigine, out there in the bush miles from anywhere and who cared?

Nick called on Sally again.

'When did Johnny find out about Urquhart and his activities in Crowbar?'

She looked at her feet, reluctant to tell him. The realisation that she'd told Johnny about it as an intimacy deepened Nick's shame at his blunt questioning. But he had to push on.

'It was you who told him?'

'Yes,' she said. 'It came up ... one time. And I told him.'

'And you told him about the cover-up?'

'Yes.'

'And that would have made him very angry?'

'Very.'

'Did you know that he'd had dealings with Urquhart before?'

'Yes. He found out it was the same Scott Urquhart that had run over his friend with the car.'

'What did he intend doing about it?'

Monyu spoke up again.

'He came to see me. He didn't trust Jackie. Never did. Johnny and me talked a lot. About our land claim. I knew all about it. The people's history and traditions. Our traditional lands. So he came to see me. Not Jackie. Jackie only thought of himself. No-one else. After Sally told Johnny what happened to her, I told him what I knew as well. Johnny Bora said he was going to get it all together. The case for court. He said that with Urquhart you couldn't let him know too early what was going on or he'd get it stopped. When he had it all together he was going to make sure it got to court and was prosecuted properly. That's what he said. When he came up here to do land talk he also talked to the women. Those who'd gone to the big house and been interfered with. He'd write it all down in detail. Lots of detail.'

Nick wondered why Keppler had been brought in. Because of the land claims or because of Johnny's investigations into Crowbar? A thought occurred to him.

'Whose idea was it to employ Rafferty to run your land claims?'

Monyu knew what Nick was getting at.

'Jackie's idea. Rafferty was one of the lawyers who came out to Crowbar to talk to Jackie. About the girls who'd gone to the big house with the boss Urquhart. Him and another lawyer feller. Then it was Jackie who got Rafferty involved in our land claim. Me, I wanted to go through the Aboriginal legal people but Jackie said he trusted Rafferty.'

'And Rafferty briefed Johnny,' said Nick. 'All the time knowing his firm had acted for Abacus in the past. And who was the other lawyer who came to Crowbar?'

Monyu shook his head. He didn't know.

'Never mind. I think I know,' said Nick.

It was enough for one day. Enough for one lifetime. Sally saw them to the door. Lindy Mays stayed in the kitchen where she was pouring another drink.

22

*T*he Mercedes squealed its way around the downhill bend and Urquhart could then see the beach curving away to the headland at North Bondi. There were some late afternoon swimmers and board riders in the surf attracted by the swell created by the coming storm. The squeal of his tyres reminded Urquhart how fast he was going and he braked roughly. Some rain drops plopped onto his windscreen.

He'd needed to get away. That stupid bastard Rafferty. Sordini, the manager of the hotel, said it looked like he shot himself in the hotel room. A dead prostitute beside him. Shot by the same gun. Sordini told it to him in confidence. He had known his father, Sir Samuel, the manager said. That was why he was telling him. Otherwise it was still confidential. There were police all over the place.

'Stupid prick!' thought Urquhart, not sure if he was thinking of the manager or of Rafferty.

Urquhart pulled the vehicle into the concrete parking area not far from the Bondi Pavilion. The dread possessed him still. He had the air-conditioning going but his hands and brow continued to sweat. He shivered. His chest was still tight and breathing was difficult. Was he having a fucking heart attack?

He pulled off his tie and shoes and socks and got out of the car. Maybe a walk along the beach to think. The sand was warm and he was vaguely aware of it between his toes. It had been a long time since he'd done this. A couple of large drops of rain burst on his head and dropped about him, leaving little pillowed dents in the sand. The wind freshened further. As he walked he was barely conscious of the surfers in the water and the occasional jogger who panted by him. A flock of gulls passed over, filling the sky with their shrill abuse. Urquhart didn't notice. They couldn't penetrate the dread he felt.

Everything was unravelling.

Appleyard and Gregory gone and now Rafferty as well. It had all been so sweet, until that prosecutor started getting close to Crowbar. Even that may have been manageable. But now there was Beowulf.

He reached the southern end of the beach and took the path up the steps and around the Bondi Icebergs club and then down more stone steps. He kept walking. The surf was swelling, crashing angrily against the rocks and throwing spray over the path. He went on. The path took him among the rocks and then up and around the headland. From there he could see McKenzies Beach and he could keep going right around to Tamarama and then Bronte. He stopped. Momentarily he sensed some faint reassurance from familiar surroundings. He tried to hold it. But it was weak, elusive. Reassurance disappeared. He experienced a peculiar feeling of being physically lost.

The heavy drops had petered out and were replaced by a thin rain driven inland by strong gusts coming in from the sea. He felt enclosed, claustrophobic, trapped. As if he needed air. He walked toward the edge of the headland and tried to take the wet salty air into his lungs. But the tightness remained.

There was a bench nearby facing out to sea. He sat on it feeling the dampness of the wood seeping through his trousers. Again he was conscious of the tenseness in his body. He could barely lean his back against the seat.

Some people walked by quickly. A man and a woman with some young kids. Two of them were girls, ten or eleven years old, walking ahead of their parents. Their little skirts blew up and around their legs in the wind. Urquhart turned to look at them and caught the eye of the mother. She stared at him strangely before hurrying to catch up with her daughters and to take their hands.

The dread, the fear. Keppler. Beowulf. He'd been to the Club meetings in Salzburg. Heard the stories *soto voce* late at night over drinks and cigars. Beowulf. A killer. He'd killed Olafson then Appleyard and Gregory and then Rafferty. Just like that. And he was next.

He heard some voices behind him as other people hurried past. Then someone sat next to him on the bench. He didn't look. He didn't care. He could barely move. The dread was so bad.

Nick rang the chambers. Pearl had gone home he was told. He wasn't expected to return for the day. Good.

When Nick and Maggie got to the chambers the twelfth floor was quiet. The receptionist knew Nick well. She looked up briefly from her typing to give him a smile as they went past. He could have been going to see any of the barristers on that floor about a criminal matter. Outside Pearl's room Nick pulled out a bunch of keys. Another source of mild shame, another necessity. He'd got them from Peter Oliver, who kept all the spares, on the pretext that he wanted to look at Johnny's room.

266

They entered Pearl's room without being seen and closed the door. Nick sat himself at Pearl's computer and turned it on. He was in luck. It wasn't password protected. He clicked onto the file manager and a long list of directories and sub-directories appeared.

'A lot there,' said Maggie.

'What I'm looking for won't be among those,' said Nick.

He opened up a drop menu and clicked on the *show hidden files* command. Two new directories popped onto the screen. One was named Black the other White. Named that way by Pearl no doubt. Nick clicked open Black. Just as he thought. Johnny's Claims directory with its three sub-directories—Gove, Cape York and Pilbara appeared. He clicked open Pilbara and went to the end of the document. There it was.

Called S 9.25 pm—L will talk but not in court—Confirmed U made manager 1973.

Johnny's memo. Proof that it had been Pearl who deleted the memo from Johnny's hard disc. But not before he'd copied the whole file from Johnny's computer and then onto his own.

He went back to the file manager and clicked open White.

Another list of directories appeared. The Crowbar directories. Urquhart's dirty secret contained in a list of computer directories compiled by Johnny and pilfered by Pearl after he'd been killed. Nick went through some quickly. Statements from Sally and at least ten other women all recounting their experiences at the Urquhart house. And a directory labelled Lindy was there. Unlike the others it was empty except for one line presumably written by Johnny.

She can put the last nail in the coffin—get her to talk!

There were other statements. From bit players. And there was a long chronology with a statement of facts. He clicked into this and followed through the dates. He found the entry he was interested in—

26 January 1974—2 lawyers visit Jackie Marakit. Monyu remembers one. Griffin and Power acted for Abacus at the time. Check with the firm and trace the other lawyer—care needed.

So Johnny had known that Rafferty was one of the lawyers who bribed Jackie Marikit in the Crowbar days. He was keeping Rafferty in the dark until he had the prosecution brief together. No point spooking him too early. The other lawyer? Nick had no doubt. Had to be Pearl. Johnny hadn't considered it a priority to find out who it was. It made sense. If Johnny had started asking questions of the firm too soon it would have got back to Urquhart.

He scrolled through the directories. Indexes to taped interviews with the women. Lists of relevant case law. Names, addresses, memos.

It was a prosecutor's brief. A good one. Prepared and, except for a statement from Lindy Mays, ready to go. Handed to the police on a platter. Johnny wasn't going to take any chances with this prosecution. No-one was going to fix the result. Or at least that was the intention. In the end he fell victim to the ultimate fix. They killed him.

'Bastards,' said Nick.

Once again he was feeling the closeness of his friendship with Johnny and the grief pressed on him. And the anger. He felt Maggie's hand on his shoulder.

'We better hurry,' she said.

Nick pulled open the floppies he'd brought with him and put one in the A drive and began to copy the Crowbar files from the hard disc.

'Bastards,' he repeated.

At his home, in the kitchen, Nick was confident they now

had all the pieces. He sat himself at the table, putting a short black coffee Maggie hadn't asked for in front of her and then one in front of himself. He began talking, laying out an inventory of facts linked by logic.

'Monyu told us how Rafferty was briefed by Jackie Marikit to run the Wonyulgunna land claim. Wonyulgunna land contains Abacus mining leases. If the Wonyulgunna are successful then in the future the miners have to negotiate their leases with the Aborigines. Sacred sites become significant, price of the lease goes up, no more moves without negotiation with Aborigines.'

'Good opportunity for a crooked lawyer to sell out his clients,' said Maggie. She was beginning to see the shapes on the larger canvas.

'Yes,' agreed Nick. 'Rafferty, the slimy little bastard, is handed a fat brief by Jackie Marikit who knows, but doesn't care, that Rafferty has acted for Abacus in the past. Rafferty knows Urquhart from the old days at Crowbar. He sees the opportunity to ingratiate himself with Urquhart. As the Wonyulgunna solicitor he can keep Urquhart in touch with Johnny's litigation tactics. After all, Johnny's going to be a miner's opponent in the courts for years to come. If the miners know how he operates it gives them an advantage.'

'Enter Pearl?' queried Maggie.

'Yes,' answered Nick. 'Pearl and Rafferty are cronies from the Crowbar days. Pearl is sharing the same chambers as Johnny. President of the Bar Association no less. Johnny has no idea that Pearl is connected with Rafferty and with Abacus.'

'So Pearl is in a position to spy on him? On his computer work?' asked Maggie.

'That's right. Johnny works on a computer all the time. He keeps all his records there. He writes his opinions, stores his thoughts, memos, everything. Pearl knows this.

He is a computer man himself. Knowledge of Johnny's preparation for his cases would give his opponents an immense tactical and forensic advantage when the land claims go to court. This was Pearl's original role. Recruited by Abacus, through Rafferty, to get them this knowledge.'

Nick stood up now, energised, concentrating on the reconstruction. Maggie kept still, listening intently, merging what Nick was saying with what she knew herself, making the connections with Keppler, with McAngel. McAngel? He wasn't totally in the picture yet. Where did McAngel fit?

Nick had resumed.

'At first Pearl can't find any Pilbara stuff because Johnny's encrypted the files. It's a mild security measure. He doesn't expect to be spied on from inside his own chambers! Pearl eventually stumbles on to what Johnny is doing and clicks into Johnny's hidden file system with the intention of accessing his work on the land claims. But he finds more than he expected. What comes up are not only Johnny's land claim directories but other, hidden files. Johnny's Crowbar files. Files he is working on to nail Urquhart. This is dynamite. Not only for Urquhart but for Pearl as well, because it was Pearl who was with Rafferty when he bribed Jackie Marikit to hose down the Crowbar scandal.'

'Quite a skeleton to have in the cupboard of the head of the Bar Association,' Maggie ventured.

'In the cupboard of a *particularly ambitious* head of the Bar Association,' replied Nick. He went on. 'Pearl tells Urquhart about the files. There is panic. Somehow they decide on a solution. An unspeakable solution.' Nick became grim. 'Kill Johnny.'

The link to Keppler, to McAngel. Maggie took over.

'They get in a professional. McAngel's friend, Keppler.

270

He masterminds the plan to get rid of Johnny. By using Jackie Marikit. Jackie's a corrupt old man. And greedy. He is paid off to order Johnny's killing. Keppler's plan cloaks the real motive with a phony one. A traditional revenge killing—a *wanmala*.'

'Yes. And tracing the death back to Urquhart becomes almost impossible,' added Nick.

'But Jackie was prepared to take the risk?' queried Maggie.

Nick shook his head.

'Not much risk for him at all. We know he was a cunning old bugger. Had Jackie been alive he would have controlled the situation when Stratton and Lardner arrived out there in the Pilbara. There would have been no admissions by Billy, no assistance from Sally or the other elders. Jackie was too powerful. And you can bet that Billy would have been told to stay in the bush. No. I'd say old Jackie knew very well he didn't have anything to worry about from the legal system. Turns out he should have worried a bit more about Keppler though. And Olafson.'

'What about Beowulf? The Salzburg Club?' Maggie found herself saying out aloud.

'What?' queried Nick, puzzled. The words meant nothing to him.

'I'm sorry,' apologised Maggie. 'Something McAngel said to me. I don't know where it fits. One of McAngel's big secrets. Go on.'

Nick mentally brushed them aside. Things were complicated enough without starting to explore the dark side of McAngel's life and times. He slowed up now, putting the events into order.

'Johnny is clubbed to death by Billy Jangala. Billy takes off. Before he leaves the building he disposes of the club. In Pearl's log coffin.'

Maggie said, 'Pearl wasn't on the plane. He was still in the building, right?'

Nick nodded and went on.

'Pearl is concealed somewhere on the twelfth floor. He waits for a while to allow Billy to do the killing. Then he goes to Johnny's room and copies what was left of Johnny's land claim files onto his own discs. In the process he comes across the Crowbar memo. He congratulates himself on his good fortune in finding it and deletes it, not knowing that Johnny had downloaded those files and the memo onto a floppy. The Crowbar files had to come off altogether so Pearl deletes them holus bolus. Johnny wasn't going to notice was he?'

'No,' agreed Maggie. 'And while Pearl's doing this, Billy is well out of the building and heading for the bus stop. But not before he put the club into Pearl's coffin. Pearl's office is near the fire exit. After the murder, Billy is in a panic to get rid of the club. The only office open, other than Johnny's is Pearl's, because he is still in the building. Billy notices this when he's heading for the fire exit, rushes in, dumps the club in the log coffin and takes off out of the building. Meanwhile Pearl comes back. Copies Johnny's files from the floppies onto his own hard disc, then leaves, locking the door after him. I bet he was as surprised as anyone else when the club turned up in the coffin.'

Nick nodded. He'd arrived at the same conclusion himself once he'd confirmed that Pearl had not been on his scheduled flight to Paris. He remembered Peter Oliver telling him how upset Pearl had been when the club was found in his office. No wonder.

'What about the guys at the Abacus office at Fyshwick?' said Maggie. 'McAngel says they were killed by Keppler. Where do they fit in?'

'Rosencrantz and Guildenstern,' said Nick.

'What?' said Maggie.

'Bit players. Somehow they got in the way of Keppler.' He shrugged.

'Can we prove any of this? In a court I mean?' asked Maggie.

Nick looked despondent. The perennial problem. Proof beyond reasonable doubt. Onus on the prosecution. The golden thread of Woolmington's case. There was enough there to get Urquhart to court on the sexual assault charges. More than enough. Particularly when Lindy talked. But on a conspiracy to murder Johnny Bora?

He reviewed the evidence. Urquhart had a motive. Sure. But Jackie Marikit was dead. No Appleyard and Gregory. No Olafson. No-one to say that Johnny's killing was the product of a scheme worked out by this Keppler and paid for by Urquhart in collusion with his cronies. Nowhere to go without admissions. And who was going to admit anything among those who were alive. Pearl? An experienced barrister? No way. He'd know that the prosecution had a circumstantial case, but in the end a weak one. Too much speculation and hearsay. Experienced counsel would shoot the case down in no time. The changed travel date? Easily explainable by Pearl. The stuff on Pearl's computer? Anyone could have put it there. Nick could just see Pearl telling the court that he was keeping it there as a favour for Johnny. A sort of back-up in case his own computer went down. No. For the moment Pearl was immune. Rafferty? He'd do what he was told to do by Pearl. Keppler, a hired killer? No prospects there. Nick imagined with a shudder trying to prove to a jury that Keppler was an international hired killer who was the brains behind a conspiracy to have Johnny killed by traditional Aboriginal *wanmala*.

That left Urquhart. If everyone who'd given Johnny statements testified, Urquhart would be found guilty on the sexual offences. The evidence was overwhelming. But would he talk about his involvement in a conspiracy to murder Johnny Bora? Would he admit that he, in collusion with Pearl and Rafferty, paid Keppler to dream up and put into practice this scheme of a revenge killing? Hardly.

The prosecution must prove. The golden thread. Nick knew it was impossible and he felt dejected. There had been no justice for Ernie Barnes and now it looked like no justice for Johnny.

23

'S tand up,' Keppler said to him.

Urquhart didn't move. He couldn't. He looked out to sea rather than at Keppler. Out to somewhere near the horizon over which there was now an aching, beckoning clear sky.

'I see. You require some assistance,' said Keppler.

Urquhart felt the fingers close around his right arm and lift. He went with them.

'You stink,' said Keppler.

For a moment Urquhart thought Keppler was being metaphorical. He wasn't. Urquhart realised he'd shit himself. He felt the warm shit running down his legs, inside his trousers.

'What type of a man are you Mr Urquhart?' asked Keppler.

Philosophical rather than accusatory. They were now both looking out to sea. Keppler holding Urquhart's arm above the elbow. Urquhart rock hard with fear, shit cooling in his pants and on his legs.

'You don't answer, eh?'

Keppler moved toward the edge of the cliff. His grip

on Urquhart's arm remained strong. Urquhart moved with him, dragging his feet, bereft of any but the most minimal volition.

'Why am I here Mr Urquhart?'

Urquhart managed a stiff shrug. He heard the surf ripping away at the rocks below.

'You like to have sex with children, Mr Urquhart. Sometimes even black children. I am correct am I not? Please answer. Perhaps a nod.'

Urquhart nodded, once.

'Yes,' said Keppler and went silent as if considering the answer in a haze of distaste.

Then he moved Urquhart closer to the edge. For several long seconds Urquhart ceased to breathe altogether. Then he began again, with difficulty.

'And it is because you like to have sex with black children that I am here. Correct?'

Urquhart remembered his submission to the Salzburg Club. A submission that Beowulf intervene in the activities of a black barrister in Australia. A man who was a potential threat to mining interests and the political stability and economic prosperity of its predominantly white population. In his mind he recited once again the lie he told the committee: *No, I have no reasons of an exclusively personal nature motivating this request.* He didn't look at Keppler. Didn't dare. This was Beowulf. This was the killer.

Then the pain hit Urquhart. Down his left arm, excruciating in its intensity. The pain. Now in his chest muscles. He nearly dropped. Keppler held firm and shifted more weight underneath the arm. Urquhart gasped. For the first time he looked at Keppler squarely and met the contempt of the cold blue eyes with his own. And then for just a split second Urquhart thought he saw the contempt falter. Keppler looked back out to sea.

'Feel, feel the wind off the ocean Urquhart. Such a cool wind. Such a cool, cool wet wind. Take the memory of it with you Urquhart.'

Keppler manoeuvered him closer to the edge. Then Urquhart's body was beset by another paroxysm and he gave a stifled cry. Keppler let him fall to the ground. Urquhart lay there silent, his head resting on a rock, looking out at the ocean. A footstep away below him was a vast drop. His face was contorted with the pain of the seizure. His eyes closed. The big house at Crowbar appeared to him, in flames.

Keppler leant over and felt for a pulse in the neck. There was none.

Two shirtless joggers came running across to Keppler.

'Is that guy alright?' asked one of them.

'He looks bad,' said the other.

Keppler didn't answer. He walked away and left them to it.

Old man Monyu left the women. There was some bushland out the back of the house. Some type of nature reserve. He went through the gate and into it and walked for some time, away from the houses and the roads. It had been dry for a long time. The gum leaves on the ground cracked under his feet. There were big gums here. Big trees reaching to the sky. Not like home.

Monyu inhaled deeply. It was good, the smell of the gums. Away to the north a big, dark cloud bank was building and coming. He smelled and he listened. There was silence and stillness. The hard grey earth, the long dry-bladed grass, the tops of the trees were all waiting. For the rain. Then came a strong breeze and the trees appeared to breathe it in and then as the breeze grew into a wind, they began to sway like intoxicated dancers. A couple of bush birds began to sing. Singing the cloud to come.

And then he heard it. The screeching diatribe of the white cockatoo. Monyu looked up and picked out the noisy messenger alone in the northern sky, getting louder and louder as it approached. Soon it was high above him, where it continued to screech out its message as it circled in the darkening sky.

Monyu felt in his pocket and extracted a small cylindrical wooden object, incised and tapering at both ends. This, the *tulu* of the Aboriginal doctor of the great Western Desert. His *tulu*. The *tulu* of his initiation so many years ago. He held it skyward then returned it to his pocket. The big white cockatoo ceased circling and landed in the uppermost branches of the biggest of the surrounding gums.

Monyu walked into the bush. So much magic he had now, so much power now that Jackie Marikit was gone. He hoped he was using it wisely.

McAngel, back out on the street, used a pay phone to ring through to the Abacus offices in Pitt Street. He had some news about Mr Rafferty he told the receptionist. For Mr Urquhart. It was a polite way of asking if Urquhart was still alive.

'Mr Urquhart is out of the office at the moment, sir. Can I get him to call you?'

McAngel hung up. He'd go and watch Urquhart's office. See who came and went. Maybe he'd see Keppler. He felt for the Taurus in his coat pocket.

The car was parked at a meter down the road. As he made his way back, he felt faintly troubled. It was a sixth sense. It wasn't the first time he'd experienced it. It was the feeling of being on the end of a string held by someone who was watching or tailing you. The string stayed loose so you couldn't feel any sudden tugs but you felt the light drag of it. When you felt it you stayed careful.

McAngel looked around casually. It was a city, late afternoon. The end of the workday. The pavements were crowded with people. It had grown darker the way it does when it is about to rain. Still it was hot, close. He was conscious of the light film of city grime on his skin. Around him the human din—traffic, voices, strains of Muzac from nearby department stores. A bus spewing exhaust fumes pulled up at a stop next to him. He jumped on just to watch who followed. There were three people who followed him onto the bus. Two middle-aged women with shopping bags and a kid carrying a skateboard. He paid the driver and jumped off two stops later. Those who'd got on with him stayed on the bus.

There was a pub, tiled exterior in classic pub style. He entered and ordered a beer before sitting at a stool by the window and watching the people traffic pass by. When it suddenly started to rain he saw how it scattered those who were outside, standing at traffic lights, crossing roads, moving in uncanopied stretches. The sudden opening of the heavy glass doors gave him a start. It was okay. Some young men dressed in work clothes came in wet and laughing and ordered some beers. McAngel felt tense, alert. The uneasy feeling stayed with him. Maybe he was being over cautious. Was it getting too much for him?

He thought again of Vander. It had been different then. Vander he'd wanted to kill because of what he'd done to Maria. After Vander he was no longer sure of his motives. He was no idealist. He had no vision of a better world freed of all the bastards like Vander and Keppler and the members of the Salzburg Club.

He just knew he was involved in a struggle of some sort. Him and them. And that's all there was to it. Maybe. Thinking about it all was an effort. Just doing was enough.

He looked over at the men in work clothes. They settled in. Beers, cigarettes lit, one of them popped a coin in the jukebox and some rap number that annoyed McAngel came on. Ordinary guys. Went to work, went to the pub, made love to wives or girlfriends, lived in a house, slept in the same bed each night ... Was that what he wanted? Probably not. In fact he was certain he didn't want it. He thought of Nick Milano. Seemed like a good man. He had a wife, family, kids. But now he too knew the rush of death-laced adrenalin. Going back to a normal life wouldn't be easy for him.

And Maggie? Before she found Stella and Alfie she thought her worst problem was that her father was screwing around. Now ... ? Who knew what was in store? She blamed McAngel for the uncertainties ahead of her. Maybe one day she'd thank him. Maybe if she got through this she'd realise that he'd probably saved her from a destiny of middle class matronhood, living in Canberra married to some petty, deceitful, stiff-collared, loose-flied replica of her old man. Maybe.

Life was very complicated. He raised his beer in a salute to Mistress Fate, tossed it down and as he left he gave a thumbs-up gesture to the young men.

He joined the throng in the street. There was a smell of wet hair and clothing. Animal smells accentuated by the rain. At the meter where the Magna was parked he paused and had a look around. He quickly unlocked the car door and jumped in. It was then he heard the click of the lock on the passenger door and saw the figure get in next to him. The .38 was level with the man's waist and pointing up at McAngel's heart. Then the intruder reached over and tapped at McAngel's coat. He found the Taurus and slipped into his own coat pocket.

'Drive,' he said.

McAngel put the car into gear and pulled out. He was

calm. If he'd wanted him dead he'd be getting cold by now.

But the face. He'd seen him somewhere before. Where?

After a while he remembered. The TV coverage of the Stella Sanchez murder. This was the other cop he'd seen with Maggie.

'You're the cop. From Canberra,' McAngel said, not trying to conceal his surprise.

Stratton said nothing.

24

*F*rom a concealed position between the houses at the top of the hill overlooking the path, Lardner had seen the man with Keppler fall to the ground. Keppler had leaned over him briefly before walking away, back along the path toward Bondi. It was raining. One of the runners who had stopped near the fallen man was looking around anxiously. He pointed to the houses just behind where Lardner stood and in response his running partner sprinted up the hill spying Lardner as he got near the top.

'We need a doctor, we need a doctor!' he panted, and ran past Lardner and into one of the houses. Back at the path his friend was on his knees and leaning over the prone body.

Lardner looked to where Keppler was walking back along the path toward Bondi. Then back down at the guy who'd fallen and the runner trying to revive him. He was there to follow Keppler. That's what he'd do.

Lardner moved down the hill and onto the path, keeping Keppler in his vision as much as possible. When Keppler went down some steep stone steps he watched, as he gradually disappeared from view, then followed, expecting to see him again on the long stretch of path visible from the top of the steps. When he got there all he could see was the concrete path curving away toward Bondi for some two hundred metres before swinging sharply to the left, around a cliff face and out of view.

Keppler should have been visible but he had gone.

Lardner stopped uneasily. *This bloke could be dangerous*, Stratton had said. *Or he could be nothing*.

Lardner thought about it. Keppler couldn't have covered the distance in the time he'd been out of Lardner's sight. Not even if he ran. The rain was falling more heavily now. Lardner peered through it scanning the area ahead of him. There were large boulders on the left of the path and bushes and small trees. Keppler might be behind them. Or he could have simply dropped from the path on the ocean side and onto the platform of pool-pocked rocks, most of which now ran awash with each heave of the ocean.

Suddenly, a burst of much heavier rain. Lardner could see that the cliff face ahead had, at some stage, been hollowed out at the bottom by waves. It was shelter and he sprinted for it.

He stood there under the overhanging rock, panting a little and gazing once again back up the path, wondering where the hell Keppler had gone. In the shelter there was a faint whiff of urine. He looked around. A couple of empty beer cans littered the rock floor along with cigarette butts and something that looked depressingly like a used condom. He stood a moment or two watching the rain and the sea, and half expecting a drenched Keppler to appear from some hiding place along the path.

And he did.

He came from the sea rock platform, hoisting himself

up from a rock with a push of his arms. His shirt was soaked and clung to his body. His fair hair was plastered down to his forehead. Once on the path he walked toward Lardner's shelter. It was difficult to see in the rain but he appeared to be staring straight at Lardner. Straight at his eyes. The man's bearing, the way he held his head, the control in his walk, the unerring step toward where Lardner was standing, intensified the sensation of danger.

He tapped his coat pocket feeling for the gun on his waist. As he did so he saw Keppler pause very briefly before continuing determinedly toward him. Their eyes locked and it was Lardner who looked away returning to Keppler only when he had reached the shelter.

'Who are you?' said Keppler.

'What mate?' replied Lardner feigning surprise.

Keppler ignored the water which was dripping down his face.

'You were following me. Why?'

'Piss off mate,' Lardner said and looked away towards the ocean.

It was intended to convey indifference, bravado. But he was so glad to escape the intensity of Keppler's icy-blue stare that it came out weakly. As he looked out at the ocean he experienced a despairing feeling of inadequacy, like a brave child in a playground desperately trying not to display fear in the perilous presence of the school bully. He felt a surge of self-righteous anger. He was twenty-eight-years old, bigger than this guy. He was fit. He could fight. And he was a detective and he had a gun on his belt. What the hell was he scared of?

He looked back at this Keppler and met the eyes again. They stared back, unwavering.

'Look, what's your problem mate?' said Lardner aggressively. 'Why would I want to follow you?'

In an instant, before Lardner could react, Keppler flicked open Lardner's coat and was looking at the holster on his hip.

'Police?' said Keppler. There was genuine puzzlement in his voice.

Indignation welled in Lardner. He flicked away Keppler's hand.

'Don't you fucking well ever do that again,' he warned. Immediately he was overwhelmed by a feeling of impotence as Keppler continued to stare at him, assessing him, in silence.

Lardner began to sweat. He was conscious of being trapped in some impossible place between the extremities of fear and indignation. One demanded aggression, the other counselled caution. And this other guy remained so cold, so totally without demonstration of response or feeling.

The rain pelted down around them. Keppler continued to stare. Lardner now wanted to run. Only pride and a barely conscious feeling, that this wasn't the way it was meant to be when you were a detective of police, prevented him from doing so. Without conviction he resumed the posture of someone waiting for the rain to end.

Suddenly there was excruciating pain as Keppler's right thumb and forefinger squeezed the top of his throat at a point just below the ears. With his right hand Lardner went for the gun on his holster. Keppler's left fist drove sharply up and under Lardner's rib cage. All strength went out of Lardner's body. His legs dissolved from under him and he went down with Keppler's fingers still around his throat.

'Tell me why you are following me,' Keppler demanded increasing the pressure.

Lardner raised his right hand in frantic supplication.

Anything to stop the pain. Anything to stop from dying. He would tell him. He would tell him.

Stratton directed him to turn into George Street and to head for Broadway.

'Quite frankly, to me you don't look like someone who'd be called Martin Lloyd Grant,' drawled Stratton.

McAngel didn't answer. Instead he asked where they were going.

'Newtown,' said Stratton with affected pleasantry.

'Newtown?'

'Yeah Newtown. You don't know Newtown Mr . . . ?'

Stratton invited him to provide his name. McAngel had already considered his situation. He'd done nothing for which the police could hold him. He'd assessed Stratton. The guy was an experienced policeman. Grating in manner, with the sensitivity of a toilet seat and not too fussed about the rules. But he was a professional who was good at his job. That much McAngel could tell. And all Stratton was doing right now was trawling for answers to the murders in his bailiwick.

'You already know who I am, Stratton,' said McAngel.

'Well, I know your name I suppose. Doesn't mean I know who you are pal. It's wise not to jump to any quick conclusions in this game. *Wade*.'

He gave some emphasis to the name as if to taunt him with it.

'Alright if I call you *Wade* is it? Very American isn't it? *Wade*. Bit like *Chuck* and *Elmore*.'

And he gave a short laugh without too much humour, studying McAngel for a reaction. He got none. He went on.

'Your niggers over there have got funny names too, eh? *Leroy* and *Shaquile* and *Jamaal*.'

Again he gave a humourless laugh. McAngel drove on in silence.

286

Stratton seemed to have a need to talk.

'Yeah,' he said. 'We're going to Newtown, Wade. Used to work there myself once. When I was a young cop in uniform. Back in the Seventies. Joint was full of wogs then. Greeks mainly. Greek food shops everywhere those days. Didn't go for it much myself. Greasy shit. You like wog food, Wade?'

McAngel didn't answer. Stratton looked out of the window for a while before resuming.

'You know those days you could call a *wog* a *wog*. No-one cared. Except the wogs. Now we've got fucking multiculturalism and fucking ethnic diversity. Diverse alright. Look around you *Wade*.'

Stratton waved his hand generally around the streets. They were near Central Station.

'Power-point eyes everywhere you look. Gooks! Everywhere! Sydney eh! You poor old tart. Glad I'm out of the place.'

Stratton was now looking at McAngel.

'You like gooks, Wade?'

McAngel didn't answer. He'd met Stratton's type before. They were pig shit ignorant usually. There was something else about this guy. It was as if he wanted confirmation that his prejudices were okay. Like he wanted reassurance that he wasn't practising a faith for no better reason than he was brought up in it.

'So you *do* like gooks,' Stratton concluded from his silence. 'And I'm an ignorant racist as far you're concerned. That right Wade?'

Again McAngel didn't answer. It was peculiar. It was like Stratton wanted to bully him into disagreeing with him. He wanted an argument on the issue. He wanted someone to disagree with him, openly, aggressively.

They drove along Broadway for some time without speaking. Then Stratton spoke again.

'It's a free country here McAngel and I'm entitled to be a racist arsehole. That's my view. I don't like wogs and gooks and I think they've screwed up this country. That's what I think. Turn left here. You've got the lights. City Road.'

'What about your Aborigines, Stratton? Hate them as well?'

McAngel had now sensed the opportunity to get Johnny Bora into the conversation. What did Stratton know?

'Abos get too much for nothing in this country. They don't have to work. They get paid to sit in the sun and drink piss all day. That's a fact.'

'Johnny Bora didn't do that.'

Stratton regarded McAngel in silence for some long seconds before speaking.

'What do you know about Johnny Bora, McAngel?'

Different tone. He'd momentarily lost the initiative.

'What I read in the papers,' replied McAngel. 'I found it interesting. He was a man of some accomplishment wasn't he?'

'Don't bullshit me McAngel. It's all connected isn't it? Johnny Bora, you, that Olafson shit, the Stella and Alfie double, the Abacus boys, Mt White. Then there's that Rafferty back at the hotel. From Perth. What's the connection McAngel?'

McAngel didn't answer. This was going to be delicate. Let Stratton ask questions for a while. He could then pick and choose what he knew and didn't know.

Stratton persevered.

'You and this Keppler dude. You in all this together are you?'

Keppler! So he knew something about Keppler as well. McAngel spotted a loading zone outside a hotel. He braked and quickly pulled into it, turning off the ignition and turning toward Stratton who was leaning back against the door with some concern but with the gun pointing at McAngel's heart.

'Where are you taking me now?' McAngel demanded to know.

'You just start this car up and drive, mister,' Stratton ordered.

McAngel ignored him and continued to stare at him.

'Or what?' he said. 'You going to shoot me? You've nothing to even hold me on, Stratton. Who are you kidding?'

Stratton lowered the gun with a sigh. Sometimes you can get away with it. Other times you can't.

'Just tell me McAngel. Are you one of the good guys or the bad guys?'

McAngel relaxed.

'Depends who you talk to Stratton. Now where are we going?'

'You know a woman called Gloria Glenning?' Stratton asked him.

'Oh shit,' said McAngel throwing himself back into his seat. 'Why the hell didn't you just tell me that before, Stratton?'

'Because I didn't know if it was you or not McAngel. I was hoping she could tell me when I took you there.'

'Where's she living now?' McAngel asked. 'And how the hell does she know someone like you?'

There was a beeping sound. Stratton turned off the pager on his belt. He spotted a phone booth up ahead.

'I'll tell you when I get back,' he said and hopped out. Through the window he said, 'Don't go away now.'

Nick remained at his house with Maggie, wondering if Stratton had received his message. He'd expected Stratton and Lardner to be at the murder site at Fyshwick or at least somewhere in town working on it. They weren't. But

Fred Arthurton was. As Fred had predicted, he'd been pulled into work and was now at the lab.

'Stratton and Lardner flew to Sydney straightaway,' he told Nick. 'They heard from the Sydney homicide people that a guy and a prostitute were shot in the Marlborough Hotel there. Guy was called Rafferty. Seems he may have shot the girl and then himself. Apparently he's got something to do with Abacus. They found the Canberra Abacus number on him. Stratton's sure it's all related. Don't ask me how. He was out of here with Lardner as soon as they heard about this Rafferty. If you're desperate to hear from Stratton you can have him paged. Oh and by the way, word is that even before today Stratton had a lead on the Olafson murder. A car seen near the Constitution Motel. He got the same car description from someone who saw it near the Abacus offices yesterday afternoon as well. A crystal green Commodore. We've got cars on the lookout for it here and the New South Wales cops are keeping an eye out as well. Joint's really jumping Nick.'

Nick had asked for Stratton to be paged and to ring him at home. Urgently. He waited impatiently. Maggie waited with him, wondering where McAngel was.

The phone rang. It was Stratton. *What do you want, Milano? They said it was important.* Nick heard coins dropping. Public phone. Nick began to tell him about Pearl's computer. It was convoluted and complicated and he didn't get far because Stratton only listened for a few seconds before interrupting him with an address in Newtown.

'Get yourself there on the next flight.'

'But where are you now?'

Another coin dropped and then there was a long whining sound.

On the way back to the car Stratton thought of Lardner.

290

Last he'd seen or heard of him was at the Marlborough where the Sydney detectives had told him they had the green Commodore under surveillance. Lardner hadn't paged him yet. He looked down the road. McAngel was still there. He fished out some more coins returned to the phone box and rang the AFP in Canberra. It was Lucy on the other end.

'If Lardner wants me tell him I'm at Gloria's address. Oh, and tell him I'm with this McAngel guy.'

25

*L*ardner talked and Keppler listened. Keppler now had Lardner's gun in his left hand, so that it was concealed from passers-by whose presence occasionally interrupted the flow of Lardner's narrative. Keppler wanted to know how it was he was being followed. The rain had let up a little. Lardner was in no doubt that this man was capable of killing him. For now, as long as he talked, he knew he was alive and that was all that mattered.

'After we found out this McAngel guy had been to Mt White, Stratton rang the hotel where he'd stayed. He found out McAngel had been asking questions about a guy called Keppler. Stratton checked the name through immigration and visas and we found out you arrived from Austria late last year. We also found out you hired a car in Sydney. A crystal green Commodore. A car of that description was seen near the Constitution Motel on the night Olafson was killed. And again yesterday near the Abacus offices. We found the dead guys at Abacus this morning and we found out about a dead bloke called Rafferty at a Sydney hotel. There was a connection between him and Abacus. We asked the Sydney police to keep an eye out for your car and we flew up here straightaway. When we got to the hotel we were told that the New South Wales boys had you under surveillance. You were sitting in a car in Pitt Street down near the Quay. I came down and took over from the CIB bloke and followed you to Bondi. I followed you when you walked around the path and I saw the man you were talking to drop to the ground. I followed you here.'

Keppler stood.

'The other policeman. This Stratton. Where is he now?'

'Last I knew he was at the Marlborough Hotel. I have to make contact with him and let him know your movements.'

'How do you make contact with him?'

'Pager. Messages.'

'Take off your coat,' Keppler ordered. 'And that,' he added indicating the gun holster.

Keppler put on Lardner's coat and holster and inserted the gun.

'Move,' he said and together they walked in the rain along the path toward Bondi.

'Harry Gilbert's nephew. That was you?' said McAngel, surprised. He remembered well Gloria Glenning's account of how she'd traced Vander.

Stratton nodded. Some people you get to feel comfortable with immediately. It was like that with this McAngel. Stratton had dropped some of his cynical defences.

'As I said, that's how I met Gloria. It was me that found the bottle shop that sold the Glenfiddich to the South African. Didn't do us much good as it turned out. Gloria's told you about that, eh?'

McAngel nodded. Stratton seemed pleased.

The lights at the corner of Missenden Road and King Street changed to red and they stopped.

'King Street, eh. Still looks much the same. Except for the yuppies though. Look at them. Walking their poodles and alsatians. With their pooper scoopers of course. Once the streets here were a sea of black, you know, with all the Greek women. That's all they'd wear. Hey, there's old Con's shop on the corner. He used to make those sweet little cakes the Greeks are so fond of. And Sol the pawnbroker just across the road. Fat Sol. Thieves used to do it over occasionally. He'd collect on the insurance and by the end of the week he'd fence all the stuff back.'

'You're sounding nostalgic Stratton. Thought you didn't like the place,' commented McAngel.

'I didn't say that McAngel. I said I worked here in the days when you could call a wog a wog. It was okay working here.'

'So you kept in touch with Gloria,' asked McAngel.

'She wrote and told me all about this bloody Salzburg Club after she traced this Vander character. The one you eventually took care of.'

Stratton paused to take a look at McAngel who didn't move a muscle. There was a long pause. Traffic behind them started to pump their horns. The lights had changed to green. McAngel nodded. It was brief but it was the acknowledgment Stratton needed. They moved off from the lights.

Stratton went on.

'She included some articles that she and this Italian ex-boyfriend of hers had got together on the Club. I didn't know what to make of it. Then I asked my old man if he knew about it. He'd been into a lot of right-wing shit in his time. RSL was just the start of it. Australian Nationalists, White Australia. All those ratbag right groups as well. Though at the time Harry was killed my father was a sick man and wasn't active in anything anymore.'

Stratton momentarily dwelt on the memory and then gave a coarse laugh.

'You think *I'm* a racist? You should have met my old man. Compared to him I'm Albert Schweitzer. Anyway, my old man hadn't heard of the Club either but he was very interested in what Gloria had told me. He asked where he could join up or at least send a donation. Then got serious and advised me to keep my nose out of it. *What about poor old Uncle Harry?* I said. *Bugger Uncle Harry*, he said. He and old Harry never got on real well. He thought the unions were run by the commos. *You'll end up the same way if you follow up on this shit*, he said. Well, I wasn't happy about it but I had a young family myself in those days. So I stopped worrying. But I tell you what, after that I kept an eye on the newpapers and I didn't believe half the explanations they gave when politically embarrassing people were suddenly knocked off in funny circumstances. Turn here.'

'How did you come to pick me up today?' McAngel asked him as he swung the car to the left down a narrow one-way street.

'I saw you hanging round at the hotel back there. At the Marlborough. We'd just got into town. Heard about this Rafferty bloke. What do you reckon? Was it Keppler did it?'

He looked at McAngel shrewdly.

'How'd you know what I looked like?' said McAngel ignoring the question for the time being.

'Easy. I saw you at the Constitution Motel when you were sniffing around asking questions of Dulcie. You gave a phony name but we had a description of you we'd got from your girlfriend after the Alfie and Stella double. We heard you'd been staying at Stella's house with Maggie and we had to check you out. Learned you'd gone to Mt White, which put you in the clear as far as that murder went. I found the coincidence very interesting and checked out what you'd been doing there before you left. Found out you'd been asking after a guy called Keppler. You see, I'd already been a little suspicious about a number of things to with do the Johnny Bora investigation.'

'Like the message on the computer disc?' said McAngel.

It was Stratton's turn. He shook his head in amazement.

'How the fuck did you know? ... You been involved with Milano on this?'

McAngel nodded. Stratton didn't know the half of it yet.

'Go on,' said McAngel. 'I'll tell you about Nick Milano later.'

'Nothing's going to bloody well surprise me any more, I can tell you that much,' said Stratton. He went on. 'Even before Milano got that disc I was suspicious. I'm talking about murder weapons found in rooms supposedly locked on the night of the murder. Of a barrister lying that he was overseas on the night of the murder when he didn't have any reason at all to lie. About a shitbag called Olafson who I find on a slab at the morgue and who, among other things, also happened to have spent some time in Mt White ... and the list goes on. Turn right here.'

McAngel turned the Magna into another street. They were coming into residential Newtown. Rows of terrace houses and semis. Most with fresh paint jobs and new looking, sand-blasted brickwork and doors with shiny knobs and knockers. Lots of four-wheel drives parked outside them. The odd sports car.

'Fucking yuppies,' said Stratton. 'We're nearly there.'

There was a parking space outside a freshly painted

terrace with shining green wrought iron work top and
bottom. Its sister half looked dilapidated. In fact, it looked
like the impoverished cousin of the rest of the houses in
the street. Old bricks, city stained, rusting iron work top
and bottom, paint peeling from the window trimmings and
the doors.

'Which one's Gloria's?' challenged Stratton as they
hopped out.

McAngel smiled and pointed out the old one. No risk.
He was right. Stratton pushed open the rusty gate and
invited him through.

There was a phone booth back at the pavilion. It was
getting dark. Lardner felt cold and wet. He spied his
vehicle in the carpark and not far from it, the green
Commodore.

'Which is yours?' asked Keppler.

Lardner pointed it out.

'Keys,' said Keppler and held out his hand.

Lardner gave him the keys. He had long ago lost his
capacity to think totally rationally so that now he struggled
to understand his predicament. He'd told Keppler what
he wanted to know and now Keppler wanted him to find
Stratton. Why? No answer suggested itself.

Keppler pointed to the phone booth and they walked
over. Lardner was conscious of the sand between his shoes
and the paving stones. A couple of kids making the most
of the fading light played on skateboards, weaving in and
out of the covered section of the pavilion. The rain had
ceased almost completely. There were small groups of
people sitting about the promenade, on the wall at the
sand's edge, and on the grass hill behind the parking area,
taking in the evening sea air.

Lardner wondered if he should call out to someone.

What then? Would he be any safer? With this Keppler he didn't think so.

A group of seagulls landed near the phone booth and began squabbling over some scraps. They scurried way with comical alacrity, complaining as he and Keppler reached the booth.

'Ring,' Keppler ordered.

Lardner had some coins. He rang the AFP number. He heard Lucy on the other end.

'This is Lardner,' he said. 'Any messages for me?'

Keppler whipped the phone from Lardner's hand and put it to his own ear.

'Oh hi,' Keppler heard, from Lucy. 'Detective Sergeant Stratton left a message for you.'

A brief pause then, 'He said to tell you he was at Gloria's address and that he was with a person called McAngel.'

Keppler hung up. Lardner shuddered. There was something new in Keppler's eyes now. Something that told Lardner he had ceased to be of any major concern in Keppler's life.

'Take me to Gloria,' he said to Lardner, barely looking at him.

He gave him the keys to the Commodore. Lardner moved towards it looking longingly at his own car as he walked past it. What had initially been straight surface fear was now replaced by a profound misgiving. He'd take Keppler to Gloria's. Maybe Keppler would let him live.

26

Gloria opened the door for them and it was the scent of patchouli oil as they stepped inside the house that triggered McAngel's memory—of the time in his life when he emerged from the cloud of unknowing. Since then he'd often wondered whether he may not have been better off still enveloped in its downy protection.

Seventeen years or so had passed since the talk in the garden with Achille and Gloria. He'd seen Gloria from time to time. Occasionally she'd given McAngel something useful on Beowulf. But second- or third-hand stuff. Something she may have learned from others who were now working on the story, risking their lives. As she had grown older she hadn't wanted to push her luck, revive the Club's interest in her. She was, she'd said on the last occasion they'd spoken, increasingly conscious that there was such a thing as a sensible mix of discretion and valour.

They greeted each other warmly. There was another woman in the house. Introduced to him as Francesca. Tall, close cropped hair, younger than Gloria, wore lots of black

299

and heavy leather boots. She said she was going out for a while. McAngel wasn't surprised to find she was gay. He'd always thought it was probably that way with Gloria. It seemed she'd finally accepted it as well.

'I knew it had to be you,' she said. She was pleased to see him.

Meanwhile, Stratton asked if he could make some calls and went to a phone on a small table near the entry to the kitchen.

Gloria was one of those people middle age selects to treat generously. Her hair was still long and was now a uniform powdery grey. She wore a flower-embroidered, high-bodiced, long flowing dress, the type you could still find in shops selling oriental bric-a-brac, and the same style granny glasses and no make-up. She had filled out a little and had enough of a tan to suggest sturdy good health. The roll-your-owns were gone. She was the type the ads were starting to use when they wanted to attract the baby boomer market to health insurance.

She went and put on the kettle and when she returned McAngel asked her what she'd been doing.

She had now let go completely on the Salzburg Club, she said. No-one believed it when you told them or they were too frightened to let on that they did. And then there was the nerves. She'd needed treatment. It had got to her. The fear was cumulative. You get older and you start caring more about the people you know than the ones you don't.

McAngel thought about the woman Francesca.

'Some things aren't worth losing for a cause McAngel,' she said. She paused for a while and looked very sad. She went on. Different topic.

She had been active in the feminist movement for a while. The gay movement as well, she told him candidly. Now it was environmentalism. She was a greenie. She smiled. There were elections coming up. Senators to get elected. Pamphlets to publish. Politicians to lobby. Donations to be collected. *Whales, trees and the Antarctic to save*, she declared with an unabashed flourish of self-parody. And *what had he been doing?* she'd asked with mock innocence. Seriously, 'To tell you the truth I'm surprised to see you still alive. I'm sorry, that does sound callous. But you know better than anyone . . . '

'Yeah,' McAngel cut her off. 'That's the way it is.'

She saw the need to talk about it again.

'I stopped being involved after poor Achille.'

'Achille?' asked McAngel.

'I'm sorry. You don't know?'

'Tell me,' he said.

'Bomb. In Palermo,' she went on. 'In his car. It was put down to the Arabs. Achille had been writing pro-Israeli stuff. No-one was ever charged. But it sounded like the Club to me. I gave up then. It's like one of those terrible wars that goes on and on, with everyone watching and everyone reading about it over their cornflakes, and everyone just accepting the explanations because that's what newspapers and television say is the truth. In the end the perpetual existence of the lie and its acceptance becomes a truth in itself. An eternal paradox.'

McAngel sighed. He'd liked Achille. He would have liked to have talked to him again some time. It hadn't worked out that way. *Vale* Achille. Someday he knew it was going to be *vale* McAngel. He was getting tired of this shit. Maybe that's all he really wanted. He changed the subject.

'You and Stratton . . . ' he began.

'He told you he was Harry Gilbert's nephew?'

McAngel nodded.

'And that he knew all about the Club from what I told him?'

He nodded again.

'I know it seems like a strange combination, he and I. But we get on okay. I got to know him when I was looking into that Harry Gilbert stuff. Later, after I came back to Australia, I got a job with the *Herald* covering the law courts. He was often about the courts, as you might expect, so I saw a bit of him at the time. It became one of those love–hate things. He didn't like my hippy, liberal sanctimony and I didn't like his boofhead insensitivity and bigotry. We gave up on each other as a lost cause. But in the end there was a mutual regard of sorts, I suppose. Then he transferred interstate. Two days ago he calls me and tells me about this Johnny Bora murder and asks me what I think. On the face of it, it certainly sounded like Club business. I said I didn't know. I'd read the papers. I knew about the Aboriginal boy who killed him. It was always possible I said. He mentioned your name and told me that he'd heard you'd been in the never-never in WA somewhere asking about a guy called Keppler. Well, I surmised that it must have been you. I told him to be careful. Knowing the Club, someone may have been using your name.'

Stratton had finished his calls.

'This Keppler,' he asked. 'Who's going to kick his arse McAngel? Keeping in mind that I have a badge that says I can kick his arse and you don't.'

McAngel's expression changed.

'Don't take Keppler lightly,' he said sharply.

Stratton took it as a reprimand.

'No-one's taking him lightly mate. When you've been a cop as long as I have you don't take anyone lightly.'

'Tell me what you think you know about Keppler,' said McAngel.

He had realised that Stratton was seriously underestimating Keppler. He needed to know by how much. Stratton missed the point and was on the defensive again. He spoke like a man whose own capacities were being challenged.

'I'll tell you what I *think* I know. I think Keppler's one of the bad guys. I think he's behind the Johnny Bora murder and I think he's the one who's left the trail of dead bodies in Canberra and here at the Marlborough Hotel. What's more, I think you're out here to find him and kill him on behalf of those you would describe as the good guys. How am I doing McAngel?'

'Go on.'

'I know someone called Keppler came here direct from Austria late last year and hired a crystal green Commodore. I know that this particular car was seen here in Sydney in Pitt Street earlier today and was under surveillance by the New South Wales cops. And I know that from early this afternoon my young partner Lardner has been keeping an eye on the car and its occupant to see where he goes.'

'What!' exclaimed McAngel. He was now out of his chair.

'Settle down McAngel,' said Stratton, doing his best to look appalled at McAngel's agitation. He hadn't liked the earlier suggestion that this Keppler was someone he couldn't handle. And now McAngel was getting all excited because he had someone on Keppler's tail.

'Where is Lardner now? Do you know?'

Again Stratton took this as censure.

'He's a big boy, you know,' said Stratton. 'I don't have to know where he is every second of the day.'

'So you don't know?'

McAngel was insistent. He didn't have time for defensive jousting by Stratton.

'He may well be on his way here,' said Stratton, voice raised, getting ready for argument. 'I've left him a fucking

303

message if you really want to know. To tell him I'm here and what's more, that I've got you with me. And he was given the message less than half an hour ago. I *do* know what I'm doing McAngel.'

McAngel didn't speak. He immediately turned off the light in the lounge room and went to the windows. It was dark. He looked along the street. Fat lot of good that would do now. He went to Stratton and before Stratton could move a muscle McAngel pulled his Taurus from Stratton's coat pocket.

'Hey,' said Stratton.

'Shut the fuck up,' replied McAngel.

Stratton became angry. Who did this Yank think he was?

'Don't tell me to shut up ... ' he began and stopped as McAngel wheeled around and glared at him.

No-one had ever looked at Stratton like that. The extent of McAngel's alarm finally communicated itself to him.

'What are you worried about McAngel?'

McAngel didn't answer, moving rapidly and evasively into various viewing positions beside the windows. Stratton went on, wanting some reassurance that it wasn't as bad as McAngel was making out.

'I mean we're in a house with a bloody telephone. I can have half the New South Wales Police Force here in minutes if I want to. There's no need to be worried. Lardner's going to be here soon as well. Who do you think this Keppler is?'

Still McAngel didn't answer. He went to the phone. It was dead. He put it down quickly when he noticed that in picking up the phone he was in the light from the kitchen.

'Phone's gone. He's out there,' he said shortly.

'But I just bloody used it,' Stratton objected. 'They told me Lardner got my message.'

'Lardner's dead, Stratton,' said McAngel curtly.

'What are you talking about? Lardner dead?'

He scoffed uncertainly.

'And the phone couldn't be out.'

Stratton moved to the phone. Out of the dark and into the light.

'No,' cried McAngel. Too late.

There was the sound of a breaking window and with it Stratton unaccountably pushing with his chest against the wall. Just briefly he turned and stood staring at McAngel and Gloria with a sort of dumb bewilderment. And then he slid to the ground leaving behind him on the wall a long slick of blood.

Gloria screamed and moved towards him. McAngel put his hand over her mouth and pulled her down with a one handed, savage twist of the neck. She began to struggle and kick. She'd lost control and was now in full panic. McAngel hung on and tried to concentrate on sounds from outside. It was no good. Suddenly he felt her biting him, hard on the palm of his hand. He let her go. She got to her feet, screaming again.

'No, Gloria!' he yelled as he saw her heading through the kitchen and for the back door.

She reached it and frantically felt for the right combination of door knob and door latch to get out. She seemed to find it. McAngel saw her clearly as she opened the door and, in an instant, staggered back with a peculiar gait, before falling heavily onto the floor. And then the light from the kitchen was gone.

McAngel stared through the dark at the now open door, nerves electric. Where was he? Where was he? Keppler had just laid out Gloria. Where was he? Was he in or out? In the dark you couldn't see? Could he see him? Was he watching him right now? Where was he?

McAngel stayed on his stomach and kept the Taurus out in front of him. It was dark all around now. Maybe

Keppler was outside still. If he came at him he'd have to come at him front on. There was nothing behind McAngel except a wall.

He heard a sound to his left. The chill ran the length of his spine as he remembered where he was. A terrace house. He'd forgotten there was an upstairs in this place. There were steps leading to the top floor, to his left.

Without looking he knew that's where Keppler was and he felt sick.

He waited for the bullet and it didn't come. Was he wrong? There was another sound like a small grunt. With a quick movement he rolled to his right and onto his back so that the gun and his right arm pointed directly at the stairs. He saw a barely discernible shape at the lower end of the banister rail and he fired once. Accurately, he was sure.

All time ceased. He lay there holding the Taurus in front of him with both hands. Was it possible? Had he killed Keppler?

Eventually he got to his feet and painstakingly moved toward the stairs. There was no sound. No movement. It was still dark. He began to feel his hands ache from the strain of holding on tight to the gun. He relaxed them.

A sound, a type of scuffling up the step. But not from the shape at the banister rail. McAngel dropped again, rolled, stood and hit the light switch and in another movement rolled again toward the bottom of the stairs.

And instead of pulling the trigger, he lay transfixed.

At the top of the stairs, looking down, stood a muscular young Aborigine; painted face, naked except for a bundle of feathers attached to each foot, and carrying a handful of long light spears. Their eyes held each other for a moment and the man was gone. Only then McAngel looked back down to the body hanging over the banister rail. It was Keppler. In his right hand was a gun with a

306

silencer. All comprehensible. What wasn't comprehensible and what McAngel continued to stare at in mute astonishment was Keppler's neck. Piercing it through was a two-metre-long spear.

27

*T*here was no answer when Nick knocked at the
front door.

'No answer and no lights,' he complained.
'Come on Stratton. Where are you?'

'I'll try the back,' said Maggie.

As she disappeared down the side of the house Nick
saw it. A crystal green Commodore. Parked up the road a
bit and under a street light. The car Fred had told him
about?

'Maggie!' he cried as he realised what it meant, and at
the same time he heard her calling him from inside the
house.

Nick put his shoulder to the door and felt it give way.
He kicked the remaining obstruction in and heard her
more clearly.

'Oh God,' she was saying, 'Oh God.'

He ran down a short hallway and found himself in the
lounge room. Maggie was standing there with her hands
to her face. On the carpet was the body of a woman, her
eyes open but clearly lifeless, a small trickle of blood at
her nostrils. Like Appleyard back at the Abacus offices.

And the body on the banister rail. A spear? What the hell had happened here? He spun around nervously looking for movement, hoping the danger had gone.

'Nick,' called Maggie.

He saw her pointing toward the wall, near the phone, where there was another body. A man on his stomach. Something about the shape of the body became familiar to Nick as he got closer. He went to it and turned it over.

'Stratton?'

He was dead.

Nick grabbed for the phone. No dial tone.

He saw something else. Resting near the phone was another gun. A Taurus 9 mm semi-automatic, and underneath it a long feather.

Above them a jet roared over and some crockery in a cupboard shook with the vibrations it caused.

Nick looked up and across at Maggie.

'Yes, it's McAngel's,' she confirmed, indicating the gun, but appearing distracted, listening to the sound of the jet as it receded. She remembered for the hundredth time Byron Williams' number. Somewhere inside her, there was relief. No need for Byron's number now.

Nick came down from the top floor. There was no-one up there. With his hands he made a gesture of helplessness.

'How do we start explaining this mess?' he said.

Maggie didn't answer. The panic had all gone. She felt cool now, in control. She wondered how many violent deaths you had to see to reach this point. Not uncaring. Not traumatised into numbness. Just desensitised. Objective. Rational. This was McAngel's world, Keppler's world, the world of Beowulf and the Salzburg Club. Whatever part of her that had refused to acknowledge the raw truth of its existence now surrendered. It must be like this to be a soldier in war, she thought. The first battle over. The next one around the corner. In between, you were transformed, forever.

She looked around her, at the bodies of Keppler, of Stratton, of this woman she'd never seen before. At Nick, standing there. At McAngel's gun, now resting on the table again. Byron's number continued to play in her head like a bad spot in a recording. Maybe just one short call, she found herself thinking. Later. After this was all cleaned up. There would be no harm in asking after a friend.

EPILOGUE

*O*ld man Monyu stretched and got out from under the blanket beneath the big old gum.

Once the rain stopped he borrowed a groundsheet and a blanket from Lindy's house and went into the scrub behind the house. He slept there amongst the rain-beaded grass which glistened in the moonlight.

The morning came and the freshness of the evening's rain lingered. Monyu sat and watched and listened to the morning bird traffic. So different from the desert here. Occasionally he heard the discordant sound of a car starting up somewhere back amongst the houses and he tried to ignore it.

It came. From the north. The cockatoo screech tearing the virgin blue fabric of the morning sky. He saw the bird arrive. White, pure white. Screeching. It settled in the tree above him. Monyu looked up onto the gum's highest branches and spotted it. He heard a scratching sound as the bird bit away up there and a small branch came spinning down. Old man Monyu picked it up and twirled it in his fingers.

It was over.

Many days now he had presided over the events following the inquest on Johnny Bora. Not the white man's inquest. But his inquest. The inquest of the *mabanba*. He'd held the fire sticks up into the air and watched the sparks fall and he knew, he knew, that the murderer of Johnny Bora had come from a long way and had not been acting alone. And he remembered the visits from the white men who came with the kangaroo shooters and who'd been taken into private conference by Jackie Marikit. In Mt White he'd seen them again talking to Urquhart, the boss man from Crowbar, at the hotel. He knew that it was not Billy Jangala who was responsible for the death of Johnny Bora. Yes, he'd wielded the club, but the evil came from elsewhere. From the white men and from Jackie Marikit.

Monyu had gone into the desert and he'd taken out his *tulu* and the magic had been strong and one by one, beginning with Jackie Marikit, each was killed. Even the man from far away. By *wanmala*. Yes, even in the city the featherfoot can be found. Among the brothers of the city.

Monyu took out his *tulu* and held it to the sky. The white cockatoo screeched once and flew off, out of the tree and flying higher and higher and further and further finally disappeared from the old man's sight.

Not far away, in the Canberra suburb of Red Hill, Moira Pearl slept on into the morning, not even dreaming that beside her, her husband Christian lay with a spear in his heart and a feather on his pillow.